JOYCE CAROL OATES has been a recipient of the National Book Award and the PEN/Malamud Award for short fiction, and was an Oprah Book Club Selection for *We Were the Mulvaneys*. Her recent novels include *Middle Age: A Romance* and *I'll Take You There*. She is a member of the American Academy of Arts and Letters and is the Roger S. Berlind Distinguished Professor at Princeton University.

JOYCE CAROL OATES

The Tattooed Girl

A NOVEL

HARPER PERENNIAL

Harper Perennial
An imprint of HarperCollins*Publishers*
77-85 Fulham Palace Road
Hammersmith
London W6 8JB

www.harpercollins.co.uk/harperperennial

This edition published by Harper Perennial 2004
9 8 7 6 5 4 3 2 1

First published in Great Britain by Fourth Estate 2004

A catalogue record for this book is
available from the British Library

This novel is entirely a work of fiction. The names,
characters and incidents portrayed in it are the work of the
author's imagination. Any resemblance to actual persons,
living or dead, events or localities is entirely coincidental.

ISBN 0 00 717078 5

Set in Monotype Garamond by
Palimpsest Book Production Ltd, Polmont, Stirlingshire

Printed and bound in Great Britain by Clays Ltd, St Ives plc

For Philip Roth

ACKNOWLEDGEMENTS

In Chapter 4 of Part III, a passage from *Survival in Auschwitz* by Primo Levi, translated by Stuart Woolf (1960), p. 29.

Lines from Catullus's "Lesbia" poem (87), quoted in Chapter 11 of Part II, are taken from the translation by Horace Gregory.

Lines from Homer's *The Odyssey*, quoted in Chapter 16 of Part III, are taken from the translation by Robert Fagles.

Lines from Virgil's *The Aeneid*, scattered through the text, are taken from the translation by Robert Fitzgerald.

Chapter 6 of Part II appeared, in slightly different form, in *Blind Spot*, Spring 2002.

CONTENTS

I

The Tattooed Girl

I

HE HAD KNOWN it must happen soon. And yet he wasn't prepared for it happening so soon.

"I can't do it any longer. No more."

He meant, but could not bring himself to acknowledge, *I can't live alone any longer.*

2

Easy is the way down into the Underworld: by night and by day dark Hades' door stands open . . . He smiled at these lines of Virgil floating into consciousness like froth on a stream. He told himself he wasn't frightened: his soul was tough as the leather of his oldest boots.

He would hire someone to live with him. And really he did need an assistant for his translation project.

He was a discreet man, a private man. To friends who'd known him for more than twenty years, and even to most of his relatives, an enigmatic man.

And so his initial inquiries were discreet, made among acquaintances in the city rather than friends.

"I need an assistant . . ."

He disliked the sound of this. Need?

"I'd like to hire an assistant."

Or, "I'm thinking of hiring an assistant."

Better to make it more specific, defined.

"I'm thinking of hiring a research assistant for a few months beginning in November."

Adding, "Preferably a young man."

Women, even quite young women, had a disconcerting habit of falling in love with him. Or imagining love. He would not have minded so much if he himself were not susceptible to sexual longings as some individuals are susceptible to pollen even as others are immune.

Seigl was sexually susceptible: less so emotionally susceptible. He'd had a number of love affairs since late adolescence but had never wanted to marry nor had he been weakened, or flattered, by another's wish that he marry. "Intimacy, on a daily basis. Hourly! How is it accomplished?" He laughed, but it was a serious question. *How* is intimacy accomplished? Even while deeply involved with a woman with whom he'd shared a residence in Rochester, Seigl had kept his house in the hilly suburb of Carmel Heights and worked there much of the time.

The love affair had ended abruptly several years ago. Seigl had never understood why, exactly. "But if you love me? Why would you shut a door against me?" he'd asked in all sincerity. For finally a door had been shut against him, disturbing as a riddle in a code Seigl couldn't crack.

The tyranny of convention. Marriage, "family." Seigl hated it.

So, a female assistant was not a good idea. And there were practical reasons for preferring a young man to live with Seigl through the winter months in this glacier-gouged upstate New York terrain where the weather could be treacherous.

And so he began to make inquiries. Hesitantly at first, even shyly. Seigl was a large bewhiskered gregarious-seeming man who in fact prized his independence, even his aloneness. *Joshua Seigl? Hiring an assistant? To live in his house . . . ?* Word spread quickly in Carmel Heights, he knew. He hated to imagine himself talked-of, even without malice. Always he'd been self-sustaining, self-sufficient. As a writer he'd never applied for a grant. He had never accepted a permanent teaching position at a university because he'd felt, early on, the powerful attraction of teaching, as an emotional substitute for writing. (The curious mesmerizing intensity of teaching! A brightly lighted space to shield us from the darkness surrounding.) Seigl wasn't a vain man and yet: he'd long taken pride in resisting the efforts of well-intentioned others to make him less alone.

"Join you? Why?"

A question he'd kept to himself.

Yet now he was weakening, now a new alarming phase of his life had begun. Yes, he would hire an assistant: ideally, a graduate student in classics. Since Seigl's project was Virgil, someone who knew Latin. The assistant might also help with household accounts, pay bills. Do secretarial work, filing, computer processing. (The computer screen had begun to dazzle Seigl's eyes. The luminous afterimage quivered in his brain through nights of disturbed sleep.) If things worked out, the assistant might live in guest quarters on the ground floor of Seigl's house . . .

Seigl made discreet inquiries among his wide, casual acquaintance in the area: administrators and faculty at the University of Rochester, at the Jesuit-run College of Mount Carmel, at the Eastminister Music Conservatory where, since his father's death, he'd taken Karl Seigl's place as a trustee. He didn't wish to place a formal notice in any publication that would include his unlisted phone number or e-mail address, and he was even more reluctant to make inquiries through friends.

His parents had died several years ago. This house wasn't theirs, but Seigl's maternal grandfather's, which he'd inherited by default. Seigl and his older sister Jet were trust-fund beneficiaries of a family estate. The subject of finances embarrassed Seigl, and made him restless. His Marxist sympathies aroused him to a vague self-disapproval and yet: receiving an income freed him from any obsession with money-making. There was a purely romantic, unworldly quality to Seigl, his discomfort at being paid for his writing, for any expression of his "spirit." For wasn't writing a spiritual endeavor, in essence? It was conceived in the privacy of a man's heart, and therefore had to be pure, uncontaminated by greed.

Maybe, he'd lived too long alone.

He dreaded his sister Jet hearing of his plan to hire an assistant, knowing how possessive she was of him, her younger brother whom she'd ignored while they were growing up. *Joshua! Don't let a stranger into your life, you know I am here for you.*

Jet's language, which grated against Seigl's ear, was taken from pop-culture almost exclusively. Her values, her relentless "enthusiasm." Once Joshua Seigl had become well-known in intellectual circles, Jet had turned her basilisk-eyes upon him, greedy and yearning.

Jet was self-named: "Jet Steadman-Seigl." In fact, she'd been baptized in their mother's Presbyterian church as "Mary Beth Seigl." But this bland name lacked the manic glamor of "Jet Steadman-Seigl" and had to be cast off. (Steadman was their mother's surname, one that signaled inherited money and social position in the Rochester area since the 1880s.)

Their parents' marriage, intensely romantic at the start, had been what is quaintly called "mixed." That is, Protestant, Jew. Seigl's full name was Joshua Moses Seigl. There was a name with character! He'd been named for his father's father who had been a rich importer of leather goods in Munich, Germany, in the 1920s and 1930s; not many miles from the small rural town with the name, at that time innocuous, Dachau.

THE DOORBELL RANG, the first interviewee had arrived.

Seigl sighed. "Good luck!"

The young man was a twenty-six-year-old classics scholar who came highly, in fact lavishly recommended by the Jesuit president of the College of Mount Carmel. He was articulate and intelligent and knew Latin, Greek, German, French, and a "smattering" of Italian. Like one with exquisite taste in food forced to swallow something very coarse, he spoke with barely concealed disdain of doing "secretarial work" when required. A young man with brattish charm who reminded Seigl of himself at that age. Seigl admired the way he dared to court him with verbal thrusts and parries and disagreements on the relative merits of English translations of the *Iliad*, the *Odyssey*, the *Aeneid*. Finally Seigl said, rising, "Thank you! Your opinions are impressive. May I see you to the door?"

The second interviewee was more promising. Initially. A graduate student in twentieth-century European history at the University of Rochester who shook Seigl's proffered hand with just the right degree of force and modesty. As if he'd practiced for this interview he gave precise answers to Seigl's questions, while licking his lips nervously and staring at Seigl as if memorizing him. Seigl, annoyed, saw the young man's eyes drift to a nearby bookshelf into which Seigl's several books, in English and in foreign translations, in hardcover and paperback, had been crammed; there were copies of the recently re-issued *The Shadows* stacked horizontally on the topmost shelf. At last the young man said, with that simpering little smile that invariably accompanies the asinine remark, "I'm afraid I haven't read any of your books, Dr. Seigl. But—"

Seigl heard himself say briskly, as he rose from his chair, "And I'm afraid I haven't read any of your books either, Mr.—. May I see you to the door?"

The next interviewee, who came highly recommended by a dean at the Eastminister Conservatory, was a short, compact, smiling and capable-seeming young man in his mid-twenties, a musician and composer who shook hands forthrightly with Seigl and murmured, "I'm honored, sir!" but, to Seigl's relief, no more along those lines. Seigl quite liked him, and decided to hire him. Except within ten minutes he himself sabotaged the interview by provoking a quarrel on the merits of "traditional" and "postmodernist" music. Seigl said with curious zest, "Well! We have a clash of temperaments, I see. But thank you for dropping by."

There came then a perspiring fattish boy with acne and an attitude; an ash-blond Adonis with an insinuating, seductive manner who repeatedly called Seigl "doctor"; a young man with glittery greedy eyes and a wispy goatee who declared to Seigl almost immediately that he, too, was a novelist.

"But not in your style, Mr. Seigl. More, like, minimalist."

Seigl smiled. "I see."

Next morning there came an unremarkable but sensible-seeming young man whom Seigl made up his mind to hire, who, when Seigl excused himself to answer a ringing phone, was accidentally glimpsed by Seigl via reflecting surfaces in his study leaning over to peer at framed photographs on Seigl's desk; these were only photographs of Seigl's immediate family, yet Seigl reacted as if insulted. He strode to the desk and turned the photographs away from the young man's eyes, in a gesture so abrupt and clumsy it alarmed him and left him short of breath. "I'm sorry. The interview is over. Thank you for your time. I'll see you to the door."

When he returned, he put the photographs away in a desk drawer.

It pained Seigl to expose his house, his cluttered study, his intimate life to the roving eyes of strangers. Maybe it was a mistake to hire an assistant after all . . .

"But I must. I have no choice. It's time."

Seigl didn't want to concede, it was more than time.

For a flawed soul yearns to be healed: in secular times, we require the stranger to complete us, where we lack the strength to complete ourselves. And so each time the doorbell rang, Seigl's foolish heart leapt.

There came, on the third day of interviews, a young man with the surname Essler, which Seigl knew to be the same name as that of relatives of his father, in Europe. The Esslers had been a large Munich family of the "assimilated" bourgeoisie who had, like the Seigls, mostly died at Dachau. If the young man knew this, and knew of the possible connection to Joshua Seigl, he gave no sign.

Yet Essler introduced himself frankly as an admirer of Joshua Seigl. "I'm honored to meet you, sir, if—very nervous!" His handshake was both diffident and eager. His eyelids quivered over avid, staring eyes not unlike (Seigl supposed) his own. He was shorter than Seigl by several inches but strongly built; he looked like a hiker. He told Seigl that he was a third-year Ph.D. candidate at the University of Rochester, Religious Studies, writing a dissertation on post-Holocaust literature, and that of all the material he'd encountered, both European and American, *The Shadows* remained to him the most haunting because it was elliptical and poetic, rarely direct. He said, "In the world you've created we see the shadows of things, not the things themselves. We are forced to imagine what the writer doesn't reveal. We become collaborators in shadows . . ."

Seigl sat stony-faced. All this, so very close to what he'd intended in that novel.

Essler, mistaking Seigl's silence for complicity, continued eagerly. "It's almost as if, though we aren't present, we are remembering that we were, once. A long time ago and yet everything seems to be happening right now. As if—"

Seigl heard himself say, "Bullshit. Maybe the novel's 'poetic' language is a willful distortion of what wasn't poetic. Maybe the author didn't know enough actual history. Maybe the whole thing was a mistake."

Essler blinked at Seigl as if he'd kicked him.

The Shadows was Seigl's only work of fiction, and his only book to have found a substantial readership. Through the years it had sold beyond a million copies: impressive for a densely wrought literary novel, if not very impressive in the realm of mega best-sellers. Seigl had long been deeply ambivalent about it. If a stranger had written *The Shadows,* he would have found it fascinating, seductive; since his younger, callow self had written it, he could hardly be deceived. No artist can deceive himself! In the years of distancing himself from his early success Seigl had blurted out startling things but he'd never actually said the novel might be a mistake, and he was red-faced now, embarrassed and annoyed at himself. For here was the most unconscionable sort of vanity.

Somehow, Seigl was on his feet. Looming over the startled younger man who was still seated, awkwardly. Seigl was a tall bearish man with springy dark hair, untidy whiskers, and shiny slightly protuberant eyes so dark as to appear black. Friends spoke of him behind his back as Rasputin: an avalanche about to slide.

Yet the avalanche never slid. Not yet.

Essler got to his feet, confused. Still he smiled, like a son who has been ambiguously rebuked. Was the interview over? So suddenly? So *abruptly*? Had he offended the very man he so admired? *How* had he offended?

Seigl said grudgingly, as if relenting, "Hell. One never knows. 'Art' is the easy strategy, life and history are too hard. Even the repudiation of art can be an easy way out."

Whatever this meant, Essler didn't get it. He said, apologetically, "I—I didn't mean to be so personal, Dr. Seigl. It's just that I first read *The Shadows* when I was thirteen, I was extremely impressionable, and it made a powerful impression on me. I didn't read it, I memorized it, practically! You see, I was only just becoming aware of the Holocaust, about which my parents had never spoken, and my— heritage." (Heritage! Seigl grimaced.) "I asked my parents about relatives of my father's family, the Esslers, who'd died in Dachau. They were upset and, at first, didn't want to tell me much, but . . ." Seigl was staring at the floor. He said nothing to encourage more of this. Truly, he didn't want to hear! When Essler went on to speak of Seigl's play *Counter/Mime,* Seigl's translations from Greek and Latin poetry, Seigl's essays collected in *Visions of the Apocalypse,* Seigl stood frowning and somber, ominously silent. He was dismayed, liking this young man so much. *We may be distantly related. Cousins? Not impossible.*

Sure, he was falling for Essler. The kid was obviously superior morally and spiritually to the arrogant youth Joshua Seigl had been at that age. Seigl wanted badly to grip Essler's tremulous hands to still them and assure him, Fine! You're hired. I'm not a great man but it's fine, I will hire you.

Yet thinking, no. Impossible. He means to write about me. He'd devour me alive.

Mid-sentence, Essler fell silent. He saw that the interview was over. He wouldn't be offered the job. His boyish face stiffened, suffused with hurt.

Seigl led him back to the front door. He could think of no banal pleasantries. He could not meet the young man's eye. Yes, he knew he might have offered to give Essler a copy of one of his books, inscribed to him, but the possibility was repugnant, such vanity! His vision swam. On an edge of a carpet in the foyer Seigl tripped and lost his balance for a split second, and Essler caught immediately at his elbow.

"Dr. Seigl? Are you—?"

Seigl drew away. For certainly he was all right. He said curtly, "Will you latch the gate, Mr. Essler, on your way out?"

Seigl tossed away Essler's name, telephone number, address and a reprint of an essay by Essler on "post-Holocaust literature" that had appeared in an academic journal, so there would be no temptation to summon him back.

NEXT CAME AN adjunct instructor at Genesee County Community College whose specialty was computer technology. A burly young man whom Seigl was determined to hire and yet: the way in which he enunciated "Doctor Seigl"—sounding like "Doktor Seegull"—set Seigl's teeth on edge. You could wonder if this character was mocking him. Seigl brought the interview to an abrupt end by saying, "Excuse me. I'm afraid my 'doctorate' is only honorary. Especially, I am not Herr Doktor."

The burly young man went away rebuffed and sullen. Seigl had a sensation as of sand, sliding, beneath his feet.

When the next candidate arrived, Seigl thought, I'm becoming ridiculous even to myself.

Yet this young man's edgy manner, his evasive eyes and smudged skin and snuffly breath made the thought of hiring him impossible. Seigl shuddered at the prospect of hours spent in the young man's close proximity, let alone weeks, months. A sour smell emanated from him. In the itinerant years of Seigl's early twenties when he'd traveled frugally in Europe, he'd often stayed at student hostels and residences with youths like this one, and he'd vowed that when he was fully an adult and had the luxury of adult freedom, he would never subject himself to such encounters again. "Thank you. I have your number, I'll be sure to call if . . ." What a crude liar Seigl was. The young man snuffled in contempt.

Afterward the room smelled of oily hair, underarms, constipated melancholy; the sour breath of another's soul. A sound of faint snuffling, too, seemed to linger, like a jeering echo of Seigl's own increasingly anxious breathing.

"Imagination. Open a window!"

What a mistake he'd made, sending Essler away.

Next came a likely candidate: a paralegal named Boyd Bixler who had strong recommendations from the Seigl family lawyer. Seigl felt optimistic at once greeting this vigorous moustached thirty-one-year-old who made no pretense that he'd read Seigl's writing. No pose of reverence here, no toadying. No breathing down Seigl's neck. Bixler was a little older than Seigl had anticipated, but intelligent and capable and in need of a "good part-time job" in the Carmel Heights area. Seigl said, "The job might turn out to be more than part-time. And the salary would be proportionate." He made up his mind to hire Bixler, he'd had enough of interviews, but almost immediately, as in a script with a comic subtext, Seigl began to be distracted by the way in which hairs in the young man's bushy, moist-looking moustache stirred as he breathed, and their amiability hit a snag when Bixler asked, "Would you be wanting me to drive you places, Mr. Seigl? Like a chauffeur?" Seigl said, "Possibly, yes. When it isn't practical for me to fly. If I don't want to drive myself, but need to work in the back of the car." Bixler pressed for details: "How many miles, on the average?" Seigl said, annoyed, "It depends. I wouldn't expect to be driven to New York City, for instance. But to Buffalo or Albany, maybe." "How often do you go to those places, Mr. Seigl?" Bixler asked gloomily. Seigl said, "Not very often, if I can avoid it." Bixler said, stroking his moustache in a fretful manner, "And would your assistant be expected to help out with parties? Like, serve drinks? Food?" Seigl said stiffly, "I rarely give parties." Bixler said, "And housecleaning? Dishes, vacuuming, like that?" Seigl said, "I hire professionals for such tasks. My assistant would be working mostly in this room, my study."

At this point Seigl excused himself saying he had to make a phone call. He needed to get away from the younger man stroking and picking at that damned moustache.

No: he was determined to succeed with this candidate. A paralegal, who might be of help in legal matters. Seigl had an almost superstitious dislike and distrust of lawyers.

He stayed away for several minutes. He'd have liked to flee the house. *No you don't: finish this task. You need an assistant.* When he returned, before entering his study he paused in the corridor to peer into the room. There was Bixler on his feet and restless, swaggering about Seigl's study examining his bookshelves with a disdainful expression. Through the house Seigl had perhaps fifteen thousand books. Too many. Some were new but most were secondhand, ordered through the local bookstore or more recently the Internet, and a number had been inherited from his father who'd been obsessed with the history of Germany and Austria before the rise of the Third Reich. Seigl had shelved most of his books by subject and alphabetically but many of the more recent purchases were floaters. He was running out of bookshelves, his very brain was filling up.

In his study, Seigl kept his most cherished books: a bookcase of first editions and limited editions. Unlike certain of his friends he wasn't a collector. (He'd come to see something naive and futile in the very concept of "collecting" now that first-edition copies of *The Shadows* were priced as high as $5,000 in dealers' catalogues.) Still, over twenty years of collecting he'd acquired some valuable books.

Seigl watched alertly as Bixler, imagining himself alone and un-observed, took up a book and opened it, still with that disdainful ex-pression on his face. Seigl thought, alarmed, He's going to crack the spine, yet of course Bixler did nothing of the sort, merely opened the book and leafed through it. And his expression wasn't so much disdainful as skeptical. Why is this book so valued? Why is any book so valued? Seigl felt some sympathy with the position. In the new millennium, books had become the repository of the past; but the very past was being questioned.

Seigl entered the room to see that Boyd Bixler was holding a slen-der volume titled *Anna Livia Plurabelle,* a sixty-one-page excerpt from James Joyce's *Finnegans Wake* published in 1928 in an elegant hand-set edition of eight hundred copies signed by Joyce in his delicate fil-igree hand. Seigl said, exuberantly, " 'O tell me all about Anna Livia! I want to hear all about Anna Livia.' Does Joyce interest you, Boyd?" Bixler said, stroking his moustache, "Well, to be honest, Mr. Seigl, not to read. But to own, sure. Something like this must be worth a mint, eh?"

Seigl stopped dead in his tracks. Coldly he said, holding out his hand, "Give the book to me, please. I'll see you to the door."

Bixler departed stunned, chewing at his moustache.

Seigl's final candidate was a young man unnervingly like the first. Another brilliant scholar from the College of Mount Carmel who knew several languages including Latin, Greek, and German but was dubious about secretarial work and typing. He spoke in a voice heavy with irony as if he and Joshua Seigl were in league together across the generational divide against a tide of American "mass-cult" products and performers. Seigl countered his dislike of young Mr. Kempton by offering him coffee. He took him on an abbreviated tour of the house which he saw, through Kempton's narrowed eyes, as rundown and slatternly. "You always wonder what houses up here on the Hill look like inside," the young man said tactlessly, "now I know." Seigl had no idea how to interpret this enigmatic statement though it seemed to him impudent. He took Kempton out onto the stone terrace at the rear of the house where a canvas chair had been blown over in the previous night's wind and puddles from a recent rain glinted with an eerie savage sheen. Through young Kempton's eyes Seigl saw the view from the terrace as if it were new to him: the Tuscarora River two hundred feet below, a tangle of trees, vines, sumac on the riverbank; the hazy old industrial city on the far side of the river with its concentration of high-rise buildings at the city center, looking at this distance like a necropolis; beyond the city, a dozen miles to the north, the smudged pebbly-blue of Lake Ontario. Kempton leaned onto the wrought iron railing, gazing out. In the wind, his lank thinning hair blew fretfully. He wore a fresh-laundered white shirt for the interview, trousers with a conscientious crease, absurdly large jogging shoes. He intoned, " '*Apparent rari nantes in gurgite vaso.*' " (This was Virgil, book one of the *Aeneid:* "Odd figures were glimpsed in the waste of waters.") Seigl winced at the prospect of having to bear on a daily, intimate basis this priggish parody of his own long-vanished youth.

"That railing. Don't lean too hard on it."

The annoying Kempton seemed scarcely to hear. Or, playing the reckless son, chose to take no heed of his elder's caution. Seigl, who was outside on his terrace constantly, in all weathers, working at a table, pacing restlessly about, staring dreamily into space, rarely saw it. He wasn't a property owner who took the owning of property as a responsibility. This property in the city's most distinguished old residential neighborhood was one Seigl had inherited, not one he'd sought; coming into its possession, he'd simply moved into a few of the furnished rooms as a squatter might have done, and left the others unexplored. Prestige meant no more to him than it meant to the numerous birds (the messiest being mourning doves, pigeons, and seagulls) that dirtied the terrace. He had no pride of ownership, feeling so little ownership, but seeing now the condition of the terrace, the splatter of bird excrement across even windows, and the rust-flecked wrought iron railing that creaked when his young visitor leaned his elbows on it, Seigl felt a stab of dismay.

Thinking, If he falls through, if he's killed, I will be to blame.

Kempton said in a snide nasal voice, "Sir, you probably don't even see this view. I mean, people who live on the Hill take their views for granted."

"Do we?"

Seigl was preparing to grab hold of Kempton's arm if the railing broke. The two might fall together and their broken, bloody bodies would be discovered not in the river but in the tangle of trees and foliage and storm debris on the bank. What lurid headlines, what extravagant concocted tales would follow in the wake of such a denouement . . .

"Mr. Kempton? Come."

Seigl took the young man, now brooding and sulky, back into the house. There was a definite odor here, embarrassing to Seigl, of un-washed flesh, laundry, hair lotion as in a low-budget youth hostel in the Netherlands. Kempton slicked back his fine, thinning hair with a sniff of reproach. The matter of salary had yet to be negotiated: Seigl had made inquiries, knew what research assistants were gener-ally paid, and was prepared to nearly double the sum. For now he was feeling desperate, like one rapidly running out of oxygen.

"I'm not married, I don't have a family. Did I explain?"

"No. But I knew."

Seigl laughed. "And how did you know?"

Kempton shrugged. As if to say, It's obvious from this place. Or, Everyone knows of your sorry private life, Seigl.

Seigl led Kempton downstairs, a flight of narrow steps that left him oddly dizzy, to show the young man the room that would be his if he accepted the position Seigl had no choice but to offer him.

Seigl saw to his relief that this room was all right. He had not glanced into it for months. (Years?) It was a guest suite with an adjoining, smaller bedroom and bathroom; its tall narrow windows overlooked not the vertiginous river view but a foreshortened view of evergreen shrubs and flaming sumac and a fraction of the grandly ugly English Tudor mansion next door. The furnishings were covered in chintz, the carpet was of good quality, there was even a small-screen television that had not been used, Seigl supposed, in a decade. In the white-walled bedroom was a handsome old brass bed with a pale satin coverlet; an elegant brass chandelier hung pointlessly from the ceiling, gauzy with cobwebs. Seigl was mortified to see, crammed into a bookcase in a corner of the room, an overflow of paperback books from his library. Their presence here signaled their exile even as, in a patch of waning sunlight, their titles were enhanced. Erich Neumann's massive *The Origins and History of Consciousness,* Karl Jaspers's *Reason and Existenz,* Carl Jung's *The Archetypes and the Collective Unconscious* and *Symbols of Transformation,* Herbert Marcuse's *Eros and Civilization.* And a dozen paperback copies of Seigl's *Visions of the Apocalypse: Ancient and Modern,* a collection of far-flung essays that had originally appeared in small-circulation intellectual journals, which Seigl should have given away long ago except for shyness. Now, their very presence in such quantity exuded an air of desperate vanity.

Kempton, who'd been perusing these titles as if they possessed some significance, said, sniffing, "It must be a good feeling, to know, sir, that you've made it."

Seigl winced. The intercalation of the subtly damning "sir" stung like iodine on a fresh wound.

Seigl turned on his heel and careened into the other room.

(He would recall afterward: not a walk but a careen. A roaring in his ears and a bizarre pins-and-needles sensation in his right leg.)

Kempton followed. His schoolboy brashness had turned at once to repentance. "Mr. Seigl? Did I say something to offend you?"

"Offend? In what way?"

"If so, I'm sorry."

The interview was over. Seigl led the younger man back upstairs. In the front hall they stood awkward as a couple uncertain of their future. Kempton said, "I would like the job very much, sir. Except I'm not sure . . ."

Seigl said quickly, "Take your time. I haven't even told you the salary."

". . . that I need or want to live here. See, I can commute. I live just down the Hill, actually. On Huron." Kempton paused. He sounded both embarrassed and proud. "I'm living with my fiancée. She teaches English at Holy Redeemer."

Seigl said, "I see. Then the position isn't right for you, Mr. Kempton, after all."

"But—"

"Thank you for coming to see me, Mr. Kempton. Maybe I walk you to the door?"

Basta!

Seigl had several more "highly recommended" numbers to call, but tossed them away.

He thought about Essler. It would be no problem looking the young man up in the phone directory. But he was through with that, wasn't he? The dead hand of the dead dead past.

Disgusted with himself. These strange moods that were coming over him, short temper, willfulness, self-sabotaging. He wanted without knowing what he wanted. He'd never been like this, always he'd been rational and reasonable to a fault. The world's perfect victim, his sister chided. Now he'd wasted hours of his own and others. He'd exploited the good will and hope of young people who were in need of jobs, he'd wasted the time of the men and women who'd provided him so generously with recommendations. He was an utter fool. "What the hell is wrong with me? I'm hiring only an assistant, not an heir."

He realized then. That was exactly what he was hiring: someone to outlive him.

Joshua Seigl was thirty-eight years old.

3

THE TATTOOED GIRL, as she would be called by some observers, began to be noticed along Mount Carmel Avenue in the fall of the year. Her first name was known to be "Alma" and for some time she had no last name.

The Tattooed Girl shyly entering the vestibule of Trinity Church at midday, fumbling with the heavy front door as, from inside, the harsh chords of an organ sounded like muffled thunder: the organist was practicing, the interior of the church was darkened, a smell prevailed of chill incense, polished pews . . . A face and a voice accosted her *Sorry, miss. Church isn't open.*

At Calico Cupboard, at Bon Appetite, at The Grotto Tavern & Restaurant, at Premiere Hand Laundry and Renée's Fine Apparel faces and voices informing *Sorry, miss. No openings.*

The Tattooed Girl had the look of flotsam that had floated up from the city below to this hilly district of small expensive shops, bakeries, restaurants. An improvident tide would seem to have lifted her to Carmel Heights and deposited her here as a river, after a flood, retreating from its banks, deposits debris in its wake.

Amid such debris, it requires a sharp yet patient eye to discern treasure.

4

IMMEDIATELY, his keen predator's senses were aroused.

Though he didn't approach her immediately. He was a sidelong slantwise type. One of those silent—gliding—lethal—deep-sea predators with lateral vision, eyes on both sides of a flat blade of a face.

"Dmitri" as he was known at The Café. Possibly this was his real name, though probably, frequent patrons of The Café thought, not.

His last name was Meatte. There was no romance or mystery to Meatte.

He'd sighted the girl with the disfiguring facial tattoo or birth-mark the previous day, in fact. She'd appeared on Mount Carmel Avenue wearing a backpack and carrying an oversized shoulder bag and other bags with the dazed look of a Greyhound bus passenger who has gotten off, or been ejected, in a place utterly unknown to her. Dmitri watched to see if she intended to beg: Mount Carmel was not hospitable to beggars. She looked too earnest and pained to be a hooker, and not nearly glamorous enough, though her hair was ash-blond, tumbling past her shoulders, and her face was young, sensual, striking; round and boneless as pulpy bread dough. Her skin was very white except for a magenta, moth-shaped mark on her right cheek. Her eyes were bruised and droopy-lidded and her small glistening mouth was slack as if she were breathing rapidly through it, a breath that was shallow and quick. Her forehead was low. Her breasts swung inside her shirt heavy as the breasts of a nursing mother. She was a fleshy girl who might have been sixteen or thirty. Dmitri wondered how she'd gotten to Carmel Heights. And why. It was at least four miles, mostly uphill, and across a bridge, from the shabby bus station downtown.

Unless someone had given the girl a ride. A man, or men.

Her home was elsewhere. In the impoverished going-to-seed countryside of upstate New York or western Pennsylvania. If a girl, she was a runaway; if older, a woman who'd walked away from her life without a backward glance.

She'd been dropped off by unknown persons. They'd had their use of her, and abandoned her.

Almost, you could feel sorry for her.

Almost, a thrill of pity.

Dmitri wondered where she'd spent the previous night. If someone in this new place had taken her in, he too had abandoned her.

Now it was a wanly sepia late-October afternoon shifting to dusk, and autumn chill. The Café, a popular French-style bistro, still had sidewalk tables for patrons. Dmitri observed the girl with the blemished cheek making her way with seeming nonchalance yet unerring instinct to one of the outermost tables where she sat in a wire-backed chair, in a liquidy movement that suggested both relief and utter exhaustion. Dmitri Meatte, lover of strays and starvelings, felt a sexual charge. Almost he could hear *Oh! oh God!* in the girl's murmured voice though she hadn't said a word. *Oh God I am so tired.*

He busied himself clearing other tables, as if oblivious of her. He would not hurry to her as he'd have hurried to a legitimate customer. Nor would he ask her to leave as he'd have banished a male vagrant, or a less desirable female.

Fortunately, the proprietor of The Café wasn't on the premises.

Fortunately, no one was waiting for a table. Most of the tables were vacated.

Sharp-eyed Dmitri had noticed immediately that the girl was sitting not at one of the cleared tables but at a messy uncleared table. What would have repelled legitimate customers attracted her. Wineglasses with a little wine remaining, a single espresso cup, two plates containing crusts of sourdough bread and the remains of potato salad and dill pickles. Dmitri knew her strategy: like a feral cat that senses it must not arouse suspicion by betraying hunger and must make only slow, cautiously executed moves, she would sit casually for as long as she could bear it; she would glance neither to the left nor the right; she would appear to be watching, with a faint smile, mourning doves on the pavement near her feet waiting to be fed as they'd been fed sporadically through the afternoon by diners; at last, she would pick up a bread crust and break it into bits and toss them to the mourning doves even as, with a sleight of hand worthy of a magician, she would lift the other crust to her mouth and eat it. As the birds cooed and scolded and fluttered their wings to beat one another away from the meager bread-bits, the girl would scoop up the potato salad in her fingers and lick her fingers clean. Panting now, reckless, she would lift the wineglasses in rapid succession and drain them . . . Dmitri made it a point to turn away from the girl, hoisting a heavy tray to his shoulder. He wouldn't watch. Let her do what she would. He pushed his way through swinging doors into The Café.

Thinking, Poor cunt.

WHEN HE RETURNED to the sidewalk a few minutes later, it was to discover that the girl with the blemished cheek and snarled straw-hair had moved to another uncleared table. But there were only emptied beer glasses and a crumpled bag of potato chips here. She seemed to have given up foraging for food and sat slumped forward amid the dirtied plates, her head on her arms. Dmitri stood over her and saw with interest that the girl's forearms and the backs of her hands were finely marked as with calligraphy, or embroidery; where her hair parted to reveal a portion of the milky nape of her neck, there was a filigree of magenta and dull red. The marks on the girl's hands, across her knuckles, looked like wispy remnants of lace gloves. If these were tattoos, they weren't very vivid or emphatic; they looked more like a miniature language. The needle tracks of a junkie mainlining heroin, morphine, Demerol? Like a dog—yet an elegant breed, a borzoi—Dmitri stooped to sniff the girl's odor: female, fleshy, underarm hairs, a dense bush of pubic hair, fattish voluptuous young-girl breasts with nipples like soft blind eyes, moist creases in belly, thighs, buttocks ... A swoon of sexual need came over him, like a suddenly ringing phone.

"Excuse me? Miss?"

The girl lifted her head and stared at him. She had mineral eyes threaded with tiny broken capillaries. Junkie eyes, maybe. Or the eyes of one who is exhausted.

On her right cheek, hovering beneath the eye, was a moth-figure, or a faint iridescent gray-magenta smudge in the shape of a moth, about the size of Dmitri's big blunt thumbnail.

"Is that a tattoo, or a birthmark?"

It was Dmitri's style to speak forcibly with females who didn't reside in Carmel Heights. From experience he'd found it to be exactly the style such females responded to.

Stricken with embarrassment the girl touched her cheek. As if she'd imagined it might be hidden, private. And this stranger had seen.

She shook her head, mutely. She rose clumsily from the chair. She would shrink away like a kicked dog. She groped for her soiled denim backpack, her fake-leather bag that had overturned beneath the table. Dmitri glanced quickly about and saw that, except for two chess players deeply engrossed in their game, the outdoor café was empty. "Wait. I'm your friend." He touched the girl's shoulder, not lightly but firmly, reassuringly. He gathered in his hand a wad of her dried snarled hair as he would, later that night, grab a wad of her scratchy pubic hair. He saw with pitying tenderness that she was wearing a man's shirt she'd been given, obviously it didn't fit her, oversized at the shoulders and even at the breasts; and a pale-rose gauzy wraparound skirt that fell to her ankles, layers of fabric so diaphanous it seemed without texture or design. She was very attractive despite her slattern look. Perhaps because of her slattern look. The milky skin, the slack sensuous-red mouth, a soft baby's face beneath the strained and frightened face of a woman closer to thirty than sixteen. Dmitri smiled. Gently he said, "Don't know? If it's a tattoo, or if you were born with it?"

For he was one whose questions must be answered. You quickly learned: Dmitri's questions must be answered promptly and honestly.

Yet the girl mumbled inaudibly. She would have run from the café leaving behind some of her possessions if Dmitri hadn't blocked her way. He took her hand and gripped it tight. "Hey. I told you, I'm your friend. You're safe with me. I won't call the cops."

He liked it that, at once, the girl believed him. The wish to believe him was so strong. Not a panicked feral creature, this sad-eyed girl, but a domestic creature who has been beaten and traumatized but can be reclaimed.

ALMA, she was.

No last name?

Yes the mark on her cheek was a tattoo. Maybe it was meant to be a moth, how should she know.

The other marks, yes they were tattoos. Sure.

Crude tattoos, Dmitri observed. Wondering who'd done them.

(Prison tattoos? That was a possibility.)

He was feeding her now, watching her eat. Not leftovers from customers' plates but decent leftovers from the kitchen he'd heated up himself. Sometimes watching females gorge themselves disgusted him but Alma was different. A beautiful soft fleshy goose you wanted to fatten. Stuff her milky white face and throat with the richest foods till her liver swelled, ripened, burst.

It was Thursday, a chess night at The Café. He'd brought the girl inside and seated her at a booth near the kitchen door. Alma was more intelligent than he'd believed. Out on the street he'd thought she might be mentally retarded, schizzy, a junkie. Maybe she was a junkie, or a drinker, obviously there was something wrong with her but it might be, he was speculating, a wrongness that could be turned to advantage. "Poor girl. Poor beautiful girl. Eat all you want. Somebody has treated you very badly."

Tears of relief and gratitude glistened in her bloodshot eyes.

Her mouth was full, she couldn't yet thank him.

He loved it that she ate so hungrily. She even lowered her head toward the plate, strands of brittle ashy hair fell into her food, and he lifted them out, amused as an indulgent father. His girl was so clumsy! So sensual. He was becoming sexually aroused watching her. Her rapidly chewing mouth, heavy-lidded eyes, glimpses of her slightly stained, imperfect teeth and her moist pink tongue he imagined would be scratchy as a cat's tongue . . . Saliva glistened in the corners of her mouth, she wiped her mouth repeatedly on the back of her hand, scarcely pausing in her eating. Dmitri loomed over her, liking it that he was making her self-conscious: this meant she placed a value on his opinion of her. He had the power to make her uneasy, anxious. He would knead her soft white skin like bread dough. He would turn her inside out the way, tugging with a forefinger, you can gut a fish.

"More? I'll bring more."

Alma was embarrassed of eating so ravenously in his presence yet she ate ravenously for she needed to eat, and in that need she was unashamed. Dmitri saw in the girl a fleeting, socially-determined embarrassment masking a deeper absence of shame.

Very good. If you are the Tattooed Girl, you must be without shame.

He wanted to talk more about the tattoos. Who'd perpetrated them upon her?

Alma seemed not to hear his question. Her eyes were moist and heavy-lidded as if she were in the throes of lovemaking. She ate, lowering her head. Dmitri closed his fingers in her hair and gave her a small jolt.

She winced. She told him she didn't know, didn't know who had marked her up. She didn't know their names.

Their names?

Alma laughed. It was a hissing, explosive laugh. A laugh of no mirth. Her eyes squinted nearly shut, in this sudden convulsion of laughing. Unconsciously she was squeezing her upper arms against her rib cage. As if lifting her heavy breasts. She said she didn't know, maybe there was one and maybe there was more than one, it had happened a long time ago, she never thought about it.

Or maybe another woman marked you. In prison?

Dmitri was one to fasten onto theories. Could be a strength, could be a weakness. Obviously, his sign was Capricorn. *Brooding, egoistic, unforgiving, self-sufficient. Controlling.*

He wanted to know: where'd she come from?

Her eyes blinked slowly. Just now? Or—then?

Then.

Her forehead crinkled. As if she was trying to remember. She said, almost inaudibly, what sounded like "Akron"—"Acheron"? Dmitri asked her to say it again and again she said what might have been "Akron"—"Acheron." But this place wasn't in New York State, it was in Pennsylvania. In the mountains.

Where, Alma said giggling, there's been fires since 1962.

Dmitri doubted this. Fires since 1962?

Sure.

Dmitri squeezed Alma's chin between his thumb and forefinger. Obviously, you'd be a fool to believe everything this female says.

Alma caught that look. She wasn't so sleepy-eyed as she appeared. She protested yes there were fires where she came from. Down in the mines. Started before she was born. A long time before.

Yes? And when was she born?

Alma's expression turned crafty. She didn't want to answer this question. Dmitri guessed she was trying to calculate his age. He was older than he looked.

Dmitri glanced about The Café. No one was watching.

He took Alma's hands in his. They weren't very attractive hands for a woman so feminine. The fingers were stubby, with broken and dirt-edged nails. And the crude tattoos like cobwebs sticking to her skin. Like graffiti, or drunken speech. Dmitri moistened his thumb and forefinger and rubbed at the tattoo on the back of Alma's right hand, thinking it was nothing but filth and would come off.

It didn't. The tattoo was real enough, inked into Alma's skin.

Tiny grains of dirt did roll up beneath his fingertips, however.

Dmitri laughed. What a dirty, coarse child Alma was. "Haven't had a bath in a while, eh? I'll give you one tonight."

"GOOD EVENING, Mr. Seigl."

"Good evening, Dmitri."

"Espresso, Mr. Seigl?"

"Please."

Each exchange the waiter had with Joshua Seigl followed this pattern: Dmitri anticipated Seigl's request which was predictable as clockwork, and was met with a look of startled gratitude, as if a genie had materialized beside the older man.

Three nights a week after The Café closed as a bistro serving meals, chess players congregated at the rear of the restaurant in an area where tables were smaller, and inset with chessboards; floor-boards were unfinished; there were no potted ferns, cloth napkins, romantic candlelight. In an earlier incarnation dating back to the somber years 1968–69, The Café had been a coffee shop and gathering place for anti–Vietnam War poems to be chanted and amateur musicians to perform; its walls were raw, roughened brick, and its ceiling hammered tin. For some reason germane to the mutinous energies of the era, several windows in this space had been painted in black panels, and these panels remained like blinkered eyes. Atmosphere meant little to the dozen or so hardcore chess players who were oblivious to all except the boards before them and their opponents' poised hands.

The youngest was seventeen, a high school boy with sand-colored hair and a perpetual squint; the oldest was a professor emeritus of medieval philosophy at the College of Mount Carmel, in his early nineties. There was a stocky, attractively buff-faced woman of about thirty-five with hair trimmed short as a man's, a self-employed taxidermist from the small town of Niles, New York; there was A.G., a former Rochester elementary school principal of whom it was said he'd been urged into retirement for reasons never made public; there was a plumber-poet, or poet-plumber, a veteran of the 1960s who wore his straggly gray hair in a ponytail. There was a grimly convivial middle-aged man from St. Catherines, Ontario, who spoke of chess as his legalized habit. There was Fen, the player generally conceded to be the best of the lot, at least when he wasn't in a nervously manic state and likely to sweep chess pieces off the board in mid-game; Fen too was middle-aged, with a goatee and shaking hands; rumored to have been a chess prodigy who'd had a nervous breakdown at a world chess tournament in Paris in the early 1970s on the eve of what should have been his great triumph. There was the younger, aggressive Hector Rodriguez, who took up more space than his small burly frame would seem to require. There was Joshua Seigl.

"Is this table satisfactory, Mr. Seigl?"

"Perfect."

Big bewhiskered absentminded Seigl sank heavily into his usual place at his usual table, where, this evening, he would play his usual brooding chess game with the palsied, near-blind but cunning Professor Emeritus, which game would stretch on to midnight when The Café closed.

Seigl smiled, rubbing his hands together heartily. A shy man, yet determined to seem gregarious in such settings. He was much liked, perhaps even loved, among the chess addicts for his kindness, wit, and good humor even when he lost. "Chess," Seigl said, sighing, "like humankind, a useless passion. But here we are."

In the chess culture there are crucial caste distinctions, but the great distinction is between the chess addict and the mere chess player. No chess genius is not a chess addict though a chess addict may not be a genius. Seigl wasn't one of the addicted, and so not one of the best, though he took the game seriously, sighed and muttered to himself, struck his forehead with his fist, often stumbled away from the game board to pace outside The Café, waiting for his opponent's dreaded move. Dmitri with his shrewd predator's eye singled out Seigl among the motley chess players as the only individual of interest, or promise. It seemed to Dmitri (who occasionally played chess himself, but only with opponents he knew he could beat) that Seigl was different from the others: he freely chose to play chess five or six times a month at The Café as a respite from life, while the other players were driven to play of necessity: chess was their lives.

"Your espresso, sir."

"Why, thank you."

Absorbed in the crucial opening moves of the game, Seigl glanced up blinking at the graceful-gliding waiter who'd materialized out of nowhere. Had he ordered espresso? Evidently.

His elderly opponent, professor emeritus of medieval philosophy,

drank only ice water. He supported one finely trembling big
hand with the other and leaned over the chess table like a vult

"Will you have an espresso, too, John?"

But John grunted no, irritated with so much talk.

Dmitri backed off, but would keep an eye on Seigl through the
evening. (As he was keeping an eye on the tattooed girl now nodding
off in a corner booth.) When Seigl glanced up, unconsciously seeking him, Dmitri would glide forward anticipating his request: another espresso?

Of habitual customers of The Café, Seigl, who sometimes dined
in the bistro with friends, was known for his generous tips. Though
he drank sparingly, he often left tips with a drunkard's wayward
largess. Amid the chess players, who had little money, and were by
nature tightfisted, Seigl could be depended upon to leave behind not
coins but bills, and not one-dollar bills, either. Dmitri sensed that
Seigl was ashamed of having money, crumpling ten-dollar bills to
push beneath plates for a waiter to discover only after Seigl had
slipped away. (Sometimes, depending upon who Seigl's chess opponent of the evening was, Dmitri had to salvage his tip, which could
be as much as thirty dollars, before Seigl's chess opponent finessed a
bill or two into his own pocket. Fen, the ex-prodigy now eking out a
living in Mount Carmel by tutoring students in math, was the most
treacherous.) To be thanked by waiters was an embarrassment, too,
to Seigl; of The Café's staff, it was only Dmitri with whom Seigl felt
comfortable, for only Dmitri knew how to express gratitude in just
the right, understated tone. Thinking *I know, sir! How clumsy it is for
you, giving money to people like me whose rotten luck in life is that they must
serve you, and not you them. And maybe one day our situations will be reversed,
what then?*

It didn't help that Joshua Seigl was a Jew. Or maybe it did help,
Dmitri hated Jews.

Seigl was glancing up from the chessboard, crinkling his forehead
like an overgrown baby. That big-boned swarthy-Semitic face Dmitri

supposed some women would think was handsome, even sexy. Distinctive as something hacked out of stone. Yes, Dmitri hated this man: hated serving him, accepting his lavish tips, having to be grateful and having to like him.

Dmitri glided forward gravely smiling. "Cigarettes, sir?"

"Why, yes . . ."

"Your usual brand?"

"Please."

Unfiltered Marlboros. Crude, virile, cowboy-American.

And matches. Dmitri would bring a matchbook embossed with *The Café*. For Seigl never carried matches, as he never carried cigarettes.

Dmitri liked it that Seigl, who came so often to The Café and left such generous tips for waiters, was a minor celebrity locally. Among the general population no one would have heard of Joshua Seigl, of course, yet, in the affluent suburb of Carmel Heights, everyone who mattered knew him by sight. Seigl had published a much-admired novel as a young man. He'd lived in the area most of his life. He was from a well-to-do local family. (Dmitri wasn't one hundred percent bitter about rich Jews because there had to be a genuine money-making talent, possibly a gene, in the Jewish soul; their success couldn't be purely cunning and conniving.) Dmitri had never seen Seigl's house on the Hill but he supposed it must be one of those old stone mansions overlooking the Tuscarora River, protected from people like Dmitri Meatte by six-foot wrought iron fences, electronic burglar alarms, private security police cruising in unmarked cars.

"Cigarettes, sir. And matches."

"Thank you . . ."

Seigl glanced up smiling and grateful but vague-eyed: he wasn't remembering Dmitri's name. It was nearing 11 P.M. He and the elderly professor were in their second hour of chess. Seigl was hunched over the chess pieces, leaning on his elbows. Dmitri cast a veiled glance seeing that Seigl didn't appear to be winning.

Winning, losing: it never seemed to matter to Seigl. Maybe it was a Jewish thing, such equanimity. Seigl would leave as generous a tip in either case. *To show he's superior. Untouched like the rest of us.*

As a student at the city university a decade before, Dmitri had read *Shadows*. Or was it, *The Shadows*. Maybe he hadn't actually read the book but he'd skimmed it, he knew what it was about. The usual Jewish subject: the Holocaust. When certain kinds of things happen to a race you have to wonder why, don't you? Rotten things happened to everybody if you looked back far enough in history, you didn't see other people blaming who they were for what was done to them. And maybe, just maybe, they deserved it? Some of them, anyway. Not the Jewish type to which Joshua Seigl belonged (anyway, so far as Dmitri knew) but the other types, the moneymakers and connivers. Dmitri had heard that the Jews of Europe hadn't made much effort to escape or to fight the Nazis. They'd expected other people, American soldiers for instance, to do their fighting for them. It was like that in Israel now. The U.S. always bailing Israel out, billions and trillions of dollars down that rat hole, well how's about we don't bail them out for a change, give the Palestinians a break. At the time of Hitler, Dmitri read, there'd been plenty of Jews who "converted" to Christianity, guess why? To save their skins. Not out of any love of Jesus Christ. (Not that Dmitri was religious, he was not. He didn't give a shit for religion, God had never given a shit for him.) Whining, bellyaching, blaming people for whatever happened which some historians were doubting ever happened, in fact. *The Holocaust might be a hoax. Biggest hoax of the twentieth century.*

"Another espresso, sir?"

"Why, thank you."

Seigl smiled up at Dmitri from the quagmire of the chess game in which most of his pieces, the red, seemed to have disappeared from the board. His face gleamed with an interior heat. His lips were thin and strained inside the bristling black whiskers that seemed to fit him loosely.

Courteously Seigl asked the elderly professor if he would like a drink and the elderly professor said, as if doing Seigl a favor, yes all right: Johnnie Walker Black on the rocks. Seigl winked at the waiter signaling he'd be paying for both drinks, and Dmitri glided away smiling, but disgusted. *Of course you'll pay, that old fucker isn't going to pay a dime, none of the bastards do, Mr. Seigl, haven't you fucking noticed by now?*

It infuriated Dmitri sometimes, that Seigl, a Jew, was such a pushover in practice. Maybe he was too brainy for his own good and needed somebody to tell him the score.

For Dmitri did admire Joshua Seigl, in fact. You had to admire the man whatever you thought of the race. And maybe the race wasn't all bad; Jews were benefactors of charities and libraries and things like that. Dmitri knew from the newspaper that the Seigls were that kind of family: gave money for a new wing of the Mount Carmel Children's Hospital, for instance. Money for the art museum, the music school. There was Joshua Seigl's picture in the paper, a man trying to smile but looking trapped. Of course, people like the Seigls have money to give away, which not everybody has, and maybe if you had that much money you'd be a hot-shit benefactor too and get your picture in the paper. Dmitri's family on both sides—Meattes, Dillehoys—weren't exactly of that class, that was sure. If they ever got their hands on money, sure as hell they wouldn't be giving it away.

Dmitri felt a knife blade turn in his gut. Pain like sheer rage.

You had to be an asshole to give your money away, what if you need it sometime and it's gone? Down some fucking rat hole.

"Here you are, Mr. Seigl. And you, sir . . ."

In his large startled voice Seigl said cheerfully, "Thank you, Dmitri." The elderly professor, hunched over the chessboard touching his fingertips lightly across his pieces, didn't trouble to glance up. But he'd take a big swallow of the whiskey in a few seconds, Dmitri knew.

Old mick fucker, Dmitri should've spat into the Johnnie Walker.

Next time, for sure he would.

Seigl said, "Dmitri, here. I'd better pay now before . . ." Before he forgot, was probably what Seigl meant to say. Dmitri accepted the bills, which were far in excess of the tab. His heart soared: there were such good vibes between him and Seigl tonight.

Not like his ancestors, this Jew. Couldn't be. More like some holy fool. Turning the other cheek, giving away possessions.

"Sir, thank you."

In the Rochester *Sun-Times* the other day, Dmitri read that his customer Seigl had endowed a scholarship at the Eastminister Music Conservatory. "Endowed": that meant a lot of money. Dmitri hadn't read anything of Seigl's after that first book, but he had a dim awareness that Seigl had written others, and that he gave talks and lectures in the area, and he'd had a play produced somewhere. New York? Dmitri wasn't into reading much lately. His job wore him out, made him cynical and impatient with just words. When he'd been a student at the university he'd wanted to be a writer, composing his own performance pieces, monologues and lyrics like Bob Dylan (except Dmitri had a better voice than Dylan and was better looking, and sexier), also he'd wanted to make movies from his own screenplays. What came of his plans he didn't know, it was a combination of bad luck, bad timing, bad vibes, drugs messing up his head. But he did remember drifting into the rear of an auditorium and hearing a talk by Joshua Seigl titled "The Problem of Evil: Theirs, and Ours." The point of it was that there was no actual problem because there was no evil, and there was no devil, only a misuse of language, and people "demonizing" one another, Dmitri didn't remember what Seigl said too clearly but he remembered being impressed, the speaker had a forceful but warm way about him, and was obviously some kind of genius, the fact he was a Jew-genius didn't enter into the picture. *That's what I am meant to be, somebody like that,* Dmitri thought. Too fucking bad he'd been stoned for most of his year and a half of college.

It was 11:30 P.M. Half an hour until closing. Dmitri checked that Alma, his girl for the night, who knew for how many nights, was still slouched in the booth where he'd placed her, like a big boneless rag doll comatose with her head resting on her arms and her blemished face hidden.

"Alma." Dmitri mouthed the name aloud, tasting it. Probably that wasn't the poor cunt's name, she looked like a girl who's lost her name but still it tasted good. "Al-*ma*."

That stiff ash-blond hair did look like a doll's hair. Not a human-hair doll, but the cheap kind.

The other waiter spelled Dmitri for a few minutes: he used the toilet, had a quick joint out the back door with the kitchen boys. When he returned to The Café, there was somebody hanging over Seigl's table, clearly annoying him. Dmitri heard "Excuse me? Are you Joshua Seigl? I—" This happened sometimes, mostly when Seigl was having dinner, and Seigl usually responded with embarrassment, annoyed but too polite to send the stranger away, and if Dmitri was in a position to intervene he always did, deft as a bodyguard. Saying, as he did now, "Excuse me, the gentleman does not wish to be interrupted. This is a private game." The man, not a regular customer, began to argue with Dmitri, and Dmitri repeated, "This is a private game. The gentleman does not wish to be interrupted."

Seigl had risen awkwardly to his feet. He'd nearly upset the chess table. His face was flushed with annoyance, and a look like guilt; his hands were shaking. But he didn't intervene as Dmitri led the man away.

At the chess table, Seigl's opponent sat motionless, staring at the pieces as if catatonic. He hadn't heard the interruption, or was choosing to pay no heed. Very slowly, with claw-like fingers, he lifted a chess piece, deliberated for several seconds, then returned it to its square. By this time the board was nearly emptied of pieces. It was endgame, the time of crisis.

Seigl picked up his cigarettes and went outside, pacing on the sidewalk and smoking. When Dmitri came to join him, he appeared to be muttering to himself, exhaling smoke agitatedly. He stared out at Mount Carmel Avenue, where traffic was sparse at this hour. Across the street and at nearby Trinity Square the shops and boutiques were darkened; a Starbucks up the block was brightly lighted, and Mount Carmel's last remaining independent bookstore, the Book Seller. Dmitri said, in a voice keyed low to placate, to soothe and to assure, "Mr. Seigl? I'm sure sorry about that. But it won't happen again, I promise."

Seigl muttered, "It's nothing. I overreacted."

"In the middle of a chess game, anyone would be upset . . ."

"Not the middle. The end. I'm not upset. It was utterly trivial."

"But you never know, sir. That other time—"

Dmitri was recalling a ridiculous exchange of some months before. Two mildly inebriated women had approached Seigl as he was having dinner with friends in the bistro; they wanted autographs from him, but also attention from him. When Seigl tried to discourage them, one of the women became incensed. It had been a distressing incident at the time, like all such scenes in public places, but not without its comic elements.

Dmitri, not Seigl's waiter that evening, had had to watch from across the restaurant. He'd been disgusted that the maître d' hadn't intervened more readily. A good way to lose a celebrity customer.

Seigl wasn't listening. No doubt, Seigl had forgotten this incident.

Seigl took a final suck of his cigarette and snapped it into the gutter. "Utterly trivial. I should shake hands with anyone who wants to shake hands with me. Except," he said, with a harsh laugh, "I seem incapable of doing it."

Dmitri protested, "You don't have to shake hands with anybody you don't want to, Mr. Seigl. Who ever said that?"

Lost in thought Seigl stood plucking and scratching at his beard, staring at the street. Looking like a man, Dmitri thought pityingly, waiting for his pocket to be picked. He wore a sporty khaki vest with numerous pockets and zippers, over a rumpled white dress shirt with rolled-up sleeves exposing brawny, wiry-haired forearms. The shirt was untucked behind. The vest was unbuttoned, revealing the beltless waist of Seigl's trousers which were baggy yet of good quality lightweight wool. Seigl looked like a man who has dressed quickly in the dark, a man who avoided mirrors. On his feet were his usual jogging shoes, water-stained and gleaming dull white in the shadows, enormous as hooves. A big ungainly man with a curious kind of grace.

Seigl sighed. He'd been running his hands impatiently through his hair that stood up now spiky, disheveled with a lunatic energy. His wiry black beard glistened moistly around his mouth. He said, in a tone meant to be amusing:

"A mere trifle consoles us, Dmitri, for a mere trifle distresses us. Pascal knew."

"Pascal . . . ?"

"A luminous soul in a crippled body."

Dmitri pretended to understand. Waiters are primed to such duplicities. He'd been a waiter for more years than he cared to acknowledge. Waiter: waiting.

"Pascal" had a familiar ring. Didn't sound Jewish but maybe. Seigl was stuck on that Nazi-Jewish crap, poor bastard's brainy head must be stuffed with it.

Seigl returned to the café and went to use the men's room at the rear. You'd have thought the man was slightly drunk, the way he moved brooding and swaying like an accident about to happen. Dmitri watched as Seigl lurched by the booth in which Alma was sitting. Nearly colliding with a chair, shoving it out of his way with both hands. Dmitri woke Alma with a rough shake of her shoulder.

She groaned, confused. "Don't h-hit me . . ." Dmitri closed his fingers in her straw-hair and shook her until her bruised doll's eyes popped open. "Baby. It's all right. It's Dmitri, your friend. Nobody's going to hit you." Alma flinched at these words as if in fact they were blows. Her face was puffy and sallow-skinned, her mouth looked less sensual now than merely hurt, swollen. Dmitri asked how Alma felt and she shook her head dazed. She wasn't feeling too good. He hadn't medicated her—he had a half-dozen oxycodone tablets loose in his pocket—but she was behaving as if he had. "We'll be out of here pretty soon. Twenty minutes. Hang on, honey. Dmitri's gonna take care of you real well." When Seigl returned from the men's room he saw Alma, and paused. She was yawning, a wide humid yawn, unconscious as a cat. Stretching her supple arms. And the heavy breasts inside the man's shirt, suddenly straining at the cloth. On her boneless white baby face the mothstain quivered as if it were alive. Dmitri, hand on the girl's shoulder, stroking her, said in a low suggestive voice, "My friend Alma, Mr. Seigl. She's new to Carmel Heights." But Seigl was already backing off, as if he'd seen too much.

Dmitri smiled. Seigl the Jew bachelor. Sexy look but (probably) a momma's boy.

Or was Seigl gay? That would explain a lot.

Still, you could see that Seigl had been struck by the girl. Surprised. The Tattooed Girl had a look about her like she wasn't wearing any clothes but didn't know it. But you knew it. Seigl wasn't the type to betray curiosity, though. Too canny. His social class, living on the Hill. Jew snobs. Looking down their Jew noses at slut white trash.

Seigl returned to his chess game. Elderly professor emeritus smiled a small cruel smile moving a knight at last.

Seigl murmured, "Shit."

It wasn't like Joshua Seigl the classy Jew. He would pretend he hadn't said it, saying now, louder, laughing, "Touché, my friend. I knew it was coming but not so soon."

THE CAFÉ WAS CLOSING. Seigl had bought everybody drinks, and now the motley crew of chess players was departing. Seigl had disappeared in his usual abrupt way leaving behind a small wad of bills for Dmitri to count eagerly. "Alma baby, it's worth the wait sometimes." Though there was a turn in his heart as of a small tarnished key: he'd get his revenge on the Jew, someday.

The Tattooed Girl rose swaying on her feet. She looked like a girl with two flat feet and the kind of boobs, she'd waddle like a duck if she didn't watch it. In this state, she wasn't going to watch it. Cringing and making a soft cooing noise, guided by Dmitri's hand (gentle, not-so-gentle) at the nape of her neck. The best kind of female meat, that would move in the direction in which she was nudged, unresisting.

Not toward the front of the restaurant where it was darkened and locked up and the CLOSED sign in the door but toward the rear red-light exit, into the alley smelling of rancid greens and a short dreamy walk to Dmitri's car.

If drugs hadn't messed up his life, fuck it. He'd have graduated from college and maybe he'd be making films by now, he'd be making CDs and performing in places like Madison Square Garden. He had the talent, hadn't had the fucking breaks. Genius is ninety-nine percent breaks. The females he'd be screwing would be rich men's daughters or wives not slut white trash and he'd have married one of them by now. He was twenty-nine years old.

5

. . . friend Alma. New to Carmel Heights . . .

Sure he'd dreamt of the Tattooed Girl. Waking with an erection painful as toothache. But it faded, fled. Blood leaking out of it like a ticking clock. Already he'd ceased thinking of her. His brain churned with more pressing matters.

6

BUT IF IT'S A 'nerve disease,' what causes it? Diseases have causes, surely."

A pain in the ass. Seigl could hear himself. He'd become one of those distrustful patients who, intelligent and educated and accustomed to being deferred to, can't accept the passive role but must press their doctors for information, facts; interrogating instead of listening, like lawyers.

Of course, Seigl was uneasy, too. No matter his poise.

The neurologist told him that numerous causes have been suspected. But no single cause has yet been isolated.

In any case, Seigl's tests were "inconclusive." There was no reason to believe that he had the illness they were speaking of. There was no reason to believe that Seigl had any illness at all.

Seigl heard this. With a pounding heart he heard.

Nonetheless he asked, as if the pursuit of facts was the goal of this conversation and not the assuaging of an individual's private anxiety, "But this disease you call a 'congeries of symptoms.' Is it hereditary?"

Seigl was thinking of his father's melancholy, that deepened with the years. Faint tremors in his eyelids and hands. Karl Seigl had been a large, imposing, dignified man and yet: something had hollowed him out from within, you could see.

The slowness of his speech. As if sometimes he had to summon words from a distant place and time.

Munich, Germany, in the 1930s. And then Dachau in the 1940s.

No, the neurologist said firmly. It isn't believed to be inherited.

Seigl persisted. "Surely there must be a gene? There's a gene for everything now."

If so, this gene hasn't been isolated.

"Well, is it contagious? The illness."

No. It's certainly not contagious.

"Except in spirit, possibly?"

To this, the neurologist pondered a reply. He regarded his distinguished but irascible patient as if Joshua Seigl were speaking in code or alluding to some commonly shared joke which he, an educated and cultured man himself, ought to recognize.

But the neurologist could only repeat that no nerve disease or condition is "contagious." And that Seigl should recall that his test results were "inconclusive."

Seigl said, " 'Inconclusive.' I should be grateful, I suppose."

Yes, the neurologist said, you should.

Blood work. Electrocardiograph. Colonoscopy (in a blissful sedated state, he'd wanted this one repeated). Tests for collagen disorder (two Steadman relatives had died of quirky, deadly dermatomyositis) and for thyroid imbalance (in late middle age, Seigl's mother had had a thyroidectomy). "Magnetic resonance imaging" that left him exhausted and rueful.

Yet hopeful: for the tests showed nothing conclusive.

According to the neurologist, the "minute loss" of muscle tone in Seigl's face and neck suggested, but only suggested, the possibility of a condition called myasthenia gravis, which can be treated with medication if diagnosed early. And there was a barely discernible "trace sclerosis" of the myelin sheath, the insulating tissue that covers the nerve fibers. Seigl, listening to the neurologist's maddeningly matter-of-fact words through a heightened pounding of his heart, seized upon "sclerosis" and asked if this meant that he might have multiple sclerosis?—or, worse yet, for he'd been hastily reading about diseases of the nerves, Lou Gehrig's disease, amyotrophic lateral sclerosis? Again, the neurologist assured Seigl: no, this meant nothing of the kind. These were very remote possibilities. The results were, as he'd said, inconclusive. "Your symptoms, as you've reported them, might be the result of undetected allergies, minute disturbances of metabolism, fatigue, stress . . ."

Seigl was on his feet smiling. He reached over to shake the neurologist's hand.

"Doctor, thank you. I'm grateful for this consultation."

He left the neurologist's office on the crowded campus of the University of Rochester Medical School in very good spirits. He went away whistling. The battery of tests had been expensive, but illuminating. He felt a thrill of elation: like a gambler who has recklessly tossed dice, and has not lost, and has not exactly won. This was one of those situations where not-losing was infinitely more crucial than winning.

" 'Stress.' " Seigl laughed aloud.

He was striding to his car in a nearby parking garage. A damp wind off the river cooled his face which had become uncomfortably warm in the doctor's office. He drew a deep delicious breath. He was certainly having no trouble walking now. His legs felt strong, muscled, reliable as they'd been when he was in his early twenties, hiking in the Bavarian Alps. The piercing ache in his back after a hard game of tennis with a friend the previous week had long since vanished. The blurry double vision with which he'd been waking some mornings had vanished.

"Imagination! Exaggeration! I should be ashamed of myself."

He ran up the remaining flight of concrete steps to Level C where his car was parked.

7

T*he gods thought otherwise.*

Next morning, running in Mount Carmel Cemetery, Seigl fell.

His legs had buckled beneath him, suddenly. He lay stunned on a gravel path. Walloping heartbeat like a fist pounding him in the solar plexus. Yet his first reaction was embarrassment, that someone might have seen Joshua Seigl take a clumsy fall.

He tried to lift himself, and could not.

"God damn . . ."

Shameful to be lying in a public place, exposed to strangers' eyes, helpless as a broken-backed snake!

Seigl tried to think what might be wrong. (Seigl didn't want to think what might be wrong.) A man builds his body like armor, even a brainy guy like Joshua Seigl. Strong arms, muscled shoulders and biceps, and forearms, strong wrists, for just such emergencies. A man's disdain for the female body is: no armor, only just flesh.

It was 7:20 A.M. No one else was in the cemetery, that Seigl could see.

He'd fallen so suddenly, he had had no warning. One of his

ankles was throbbing with pain. But he didn't believe he was seriously hurt.

Inconclusive the neurologist had said.

No reason to think the worst, Joshua. You should be grateful, in your place I think I would be.

Seigl would think: strange that he should have fallen here, in this place that had become special to him.

Mount Carmel Hill above the river was a glacier hill, a drumlin, so steep that paths and roadways zigzagged from side to side like fran-tic snakes. The landscape was rock ledges, gulches, chasms and thin trickling streams that in flood time became raging creeks flowing into the Tuscarora River two hundred feet below. The old Catholic cemetery through which Seigl ran—or, in frigid weather, hiked—on an almost daily basis was a place of beauty and neglect; of wind-ravaged oaks and juniper pines amid a necropolis of grave markers, tombstones, rotted-looking crosses and shabby yet fierce-eyed an-gels, family vaults in neo-classic design with columns, fluted porti-cos, solemnly carved names, dates, exhortations from a simpler era. *I will lift up my eyes unto the hills, whence cometh my help. My help cometh from the Lord, who made heaven and earth.* Below was the river, and beyond the river was the aging industrial city in the anemic haze of dawn, with its concentration of high-rise buildings and spires amid squat rectangular shapes and old, abandoned flour mills on the river, like a mirror-replica of the cemetery above. Except for traffic moving on the elevated expressway, and plumes of pale smoke lifting skyward, the city looked uninhabited at this distance.

This was a tortured landscape, glacier-gouged many millions of years ago, and always there was something strange and haunting about it that stirred Seigl's imagination. Intellectually, it gave him nothing. He knew that. The history of the region—explorers, origi-nal settlers, battles and treaties with the Iroquois, Huron, Seneca Indians, the precarious establishment of a British-empowered civi-lization that threw off its links to England in a paroxysm of revolutionary fervor in 1776—meant little to him. He was European by temperament, not American. And, though he'd been a novelist once, and believed he would be again, by nature Seigl was a philosopher: philosophers hate history.

For to be a philosopher is to wish to believe that the human mind transcends the contingencies of time. To be a philosopher is to believe that the human mind is not yoked to time; philosophy is of the timeless spirit, while history is solidly of the earth.

Philosophy frees, history enslaves.

I am not my ancestors Seigl thought desperately. *I am not my father, I am scarcely myself.*

His eyes shone with tears. Everywhere he looked he saw eerily beautiful shimmering double images. A marbled sky above the river at dawn and, only a few yards above his head, patches of oak and sumac brilliant as neon.

You look as if you've had a good day, Joshua?

It was fine, Sondra. But now is better.

The evening before, he'd taken a friend to dinner. Like a fool he'd rushed to celebrate. The word *inconclusive* ringing in his ears like a deranged recess bell.

Seigl would order one of the most expensive wines on the menu. He would leave a twenty percent tip. He would laugh delightedly, a big bewhiskered untidy man drawing the attention of other patrons.

Is that Joshua Seigl? And who is with him?

Seigl's friend was Sondra Blumenthal, professor of Religious Studies at the university. An attractive woman of about Seigl's age with a fine chiseled face, intelligent eyes. Seigl had known her for years. Their friendship had begun when Seigl, in the first flush of literary success, asked to review a slew of theological-philosophical books for the prestigious *New York Review*, had passed judgment scathingly on all but Blumenthal's *From Genesis to Revelation: Ways of*

Re-Visioning the Bible, though he'd been critical in his praise. They'd met soon afterward. Seigl was grateful for Sondra's company, often at short notice. She had been married briefly, a long time ago; of that disastrous marriage, Sondra had never spoken, and Seigl had not inquired. He cherished the woman's good common sense, particularly when he endured periods of working intensely without feeling he accomplished anything of merit, or when he was in a despondent mood, which came to the same thing.

These weaknesses of character of which Seigl could never bring himself to speak to another person. Shame!

Seigl confided to Sondra, it was a day of gratitude.

Sondra asked why: had he hired his assistant?

No. He'd changed his mind.

But why? Sondra asked. It had sounded like a good idea.

Seigl sat silent, drumming his fingers on the tabletop. He didn't recall telling this friend that he was looking for an assistant. He was certain he hadn't.

He told her he didn't need an assistant really. He could hire a typist as he'd done last time, to type his manuscript drafts onto hard disks. *The prospect of having another person in the house, a stranger, at close quarters . . .* Seigl shrugged, indicating distaste.

Sondra asked *Why, then? Why gratitude?*

Seigl said enigmatically *Why not? Maybe because I didn't hire an assistant.*

He wasn't going to tell Sondra about the neurologist, the tests. The inconclusive results.

Nor about his reasons for having taken the tests.

Sondra offered to read Seigl's manuscript when it was in a state to be read, and Seigl thanked her. Often the two exchanged works-in-progress for mutual criticism. In recent years, Seigl hadn't had much to give to Sondra; he disliked most of what he wrote, though at the outset he was usually absurdly optimistic.

Sondra asked, was it his translation of *The Aeneid* he'd been working on, and Seigl said yes. He'd made a start a few years ago, re-examining the poem from the perspective of the contemporary world of divisiveness, nationalism, blood-consciousness and blood-feuds. He'd never been a great admirer of Virgil; he'd much pre-ferred Homer. But there was something now in *The Aeneid,* the shaping of an individual's destiny by historical, not personal forces, that excited him. The founding of a city, and of a civilization; the subordination of individual desire; the Trojan hero, so very unlike the Greek brute Achilles, carrying his elderly father on his back . . .

Seigl spoke with his usual enthusiasm. His friend seemed so very engrossed with his words. She'd read an uncompleted essay Seigl had written on *The Aeneid* a few years ago, and other, related work of his he had yet to shape into a coherent whole.

Remember, Joshua? I encouraged you not to quit.

Sondra's eyes brimmed with feeling. Seigl wanted to reach out impulsively to take her hand; Sondra Blumenthal's ringless hand, that rested uncertainly on the tabletop. But he hesitated. He knew that Sondra would misinterpret such a gesture, as other women had done. Seigl was often filled with feeling, a kind of generalized love, or excitement; a kind of Eros; yet not love as Sondra would wish to interpret it, nor even erotic desire which is impersonal, swift, and pitiless in its rapacity. Seigl fumbled to express himself. Fumbled somehow with the wine menu and there went the candlestick holder, the burning candle toppling onto the tabletop.

I've got it, Mr. Seigl. No problem!

A dark-clad waiter materialized to set things right.

And may I tell you our specials for this evening, sir? Madam?

It was the slim-hipped slick-haired young waiter who reminded Seigl of one of the minor gods. Mercury, maybe. Now you see him, now you don't.

Exotically named: Dmitri?

By all means, Dmitri. Do tell us.

A recitation. Appetizers, first courses, entrées. How, better yet why, could a waiter remember so many items of virtually no significance, night after night; how could a man so humble himself in the role of waiter, servant; the role of serving others, with a smile? Carrying in trays of food, hauling away dirtied plates and garbage. Seigl shuddered imagining himself in such a demeaning role.

Yes you'd do it. And worse. To live. If required.

Dachau. Bergen-Belsen. Buchenwald. Theresienstadt. Maybe you wouldn't have lived, but you would have tried.

Choucroute garnie . . . braised beef shanks with pine nuts and sultanas . . . risotto with smoked salmon. And for dessert . . .

Seigl made a show of listening with enthusiasm to the waiter but he never remembered such recitations. Invariably he ordered a meal he'd ordered many times before. Sondra was the one to incline her head to listen, even to ask questions. Taking the occasion seriously. And why not, occasions like these are to be taken seriously.

Seigl's gaze was drawn to the rear of the restaurant. The booth, now empty, beside the swinging doors to the kitchen.

Why?

IT WAS 7:20 A.M. Though ten or more minutes had passed. Seigl, perspiring inside his clothes, didn't want to think, yes time has stopped.

His watch, a thin gold disk of a face, grainy leather band, he'd had since 1986, in commemoration of an honorary doctorate of humane letters he'd received at a New England liberal arts college, was badly cracked across its front and obviously damaged within. In his fury and self-disgust Seigl wanted to rip it from his wrist and throw it down.

"God damn rotten luck. Fucking luck."

For it seemed to him luck, merely: losing his footing in the loose gravel, falling. Falling hard.

He was half-crawling, half-dragging himself to a grave marker about fifteen feet away. The marker was older and weatherworn and low enough so that he could hoist himself up onto it, stretch and massage his legs. The left leg was gradually regaining sensation: a bizarre feeling as of tiny roiling stinging ants. The right leg, which worried him more, was still strangely numb. This leg dragged at him like a false leg prankishly attached to his body.

At least he hadn't broken anything. Leg, arm. Hadn't sprained an ankle, dislocated a shoulder. Twenty years ago hiking in Arizona he'd broken his collarbone in a fall. Sixty miles from the nearest medical clinic in Flagstaff and a medic to give him a shot of painkiller.

Might've cracked his head. And then?

"Fuck this. Come *on*."

There was something ridiculous about a fallen man. A middle-aged ex-prodigy. Like one of those rotted stone angels blown from its haughty perch atop a family vault.

Seigl's great-grandfather had reputedly married into the Munich-Catholic *haute bourgeoisie* with the understanding that this act would make of him and his progeny non-Jews in perpetuity. Appropriate then that the great-grandson who could believe in no religion, who in fact disdained the very concept of religion as one of the evils of mankind, should be struck down in this place.

It was the fault of the sauvignon blanc of the previous night. Seigl had had too much of a good thing. Sondra had said several times she hadn't seen Joshua so lighthearted in some time and he'd allowed his dear friend to think that, yes she'd had much to do with his mood.

Thinking of Sondra. A pang of regret. Guilt. They'd said good-night at the restaurant, kissed cheeks and departed to their separate cars. Seigl had made a blunder in their conversation, seeming not to recall the name of Sondra's eleven-year-old son or even, in his vague affable way, that this son existed.

If he'd had a workable cell phone (which he didn't: the damned thing was always failing to function) and if he'd brought it with him (of course, he had not: why would he want to carry a cell phone while jogging?) he might have called Sondra Blumenthal and explained his predicament and Sondra would have come to get him, help him. She lived several miles away, on the other side of the river.

Though possibly she was at the university. Immediately Sondra would have come to him, ascending the long hill to Mount Carmel, making her way into Mount Carmel Cemetery and along the winding, zigzagging roadway. She would discover him sitting on the grave marker abashed and annoyed as hell . . .

The vision faded. Seigl would never have called Sondra, even if he'd had the damned cell phone. He could not. Simply could not.

Essler. The young man, a kinsman he'd seemed, whom Seigl should have hired as his assistant, but had not. He might have called Essler.

We see the shadows of things, not the things themselves . . . We are forced to imagine what the writer doesn't reveal.

Essler had spoken in praise, and warmly. Speaking as the reader of *The Shadows*. He had not intended criticism of course. Yet the words seemed to Seigl stinging, ironic. In the flush of youthful ambition Seigl had dared to appropriate, by way of his father's obsessive memories, the tragedy of his grandparents' lives and deaths, though he'd known nothing firsthand, and the details of the deaths were unclear. His very ignorance, he'd obscured in a gossamer-like prose. Of course, *The Shadows* was "fiction"—"a work of the imagination." It was not a family memoir, not the work of a Holocaust survivor and had not been presented as such. And yet: Seigl was wracked with an undefined shame when he thought of it. When he was introduced as *the author of.* His success of twelve years before seemed to him now a kind of card trick: somehow, he'd impressed his influential elders. *The Shadows* had been the lead review-essay in the most distinguished of American literary publications, and the identical thing happened in England, with a launching in the *Times Literary Supplement* comparing the young novelist to Elie Wiesel, Primo Levi, Aharon Appelfeld . . . He'd been the twenty-six-year-old "find" of the season. A very deft card trick, the kind you can execute only once.

And he'd been naive, then. In his young-man's arrogance. Seeing the world in fairy-tale terms. There is good, there is evil. Evil preys upon good. The tragedy of history.

His parents had been immensely proud of him. And yet.

His mother had wanted him so badly to marry, to marry. Marry!

In the last months of her life, fretting. *You never found the woman you liked, did you try? Did you try hard enough? And now it's too late.*

Mom, no. It isn't too late.

It is! Too late for me to have a grandchild.

In *The Shadows* he'd evoked elliptically the confused impressions of his Seigl and Schiff relatives transported to the Nazi death camp a quarter-century before he was born. Not invention but imagination. The stories haltingly told to him by his father who, aged seven, in 1939, had been sent to live with relatives on Eighty-ninth Street at Fifth Avenue in New York. And so Karl Seigl had had an American self: yet always, as he would one day confide to his son, he was a "posthumous" being, and moved like a ghost among living human beings, a wraith out of Hades. What was strange and magical to Seigl during the months of composing *The Shadows* was the fact that Karl Seigl himself hadn't been a firsthand witness to most of his family's experiences; he, too, had been told fragments of history, by the few relatives who'd survived and contacted him in the 1950s. Family history as a sort of immense spiderweb spanning part of two continents. If you know spiderwebs, you know that they are spun with infinite precision and patience; according to the spider's genus, they conform to a design; yet individual spiders spin variants of this design. If broken in one area, the web is constructed to hold in other areas. Nine-tenths of a cobweb might be broken yet the one-tenth would remain, holding fast, distinctive. Seigl had thought of himself as re-weaving a spiderweb, re-constructing and re-strengthening. A shimmer of fading impressions had been woven into a work of apparently durable prose, secreted by Joshua Seigl, born 1964.

One of the motifs of *The Shadows* had been the yearning of

displaced, homeless people for home. The physical dwellings, views from windows, trees, gardens, filigree of cracks in ceilings, random and unremarked sights of surpassing beauty and anguished worth, once they are lost. Joshua Seigl who'd never in his lifetime been lost, a cherished son, had played a ventriloquist's trick in reverse, taking as his own the voices of others who yearned for home.

Now he knew the feeling. Now, he was no trickster of words.

Hoisting himself up, grunting. Atop the grave marker of one Horace Joseph Renneker 1843–1871. He massaged his legs roughly. Sensation was returning in the left leg, which thrummed and throbbed like roiling ants, and more slowly returning to the right leg.

Now, he had something to report to the neurologist.

He was bareheaded, his tweed cap had fallen off and lay in the grass too far away for him to retrieve. Still it was 7:20 A.M. by his wrecked watch.

"Hello? Help . . ."

Seigl's voice was faint, blown by the wind. He cupped his hands to his mouth. Below the hill, perhaps a quarter-mile away, the cemetery groundskeeper lived in a small stone cottage. If the man happened to be outside . . .

"Hello? Hello!"

So Seigl called into the wind. Not panicking: he'd be able to drag himself, if all else failed. And sensation was returning to his legs, which maybe meant muscle-strength, too.

Easy is the way down into the Underworld: by night and by day dark Hades' door stands open; but to retrace one's steps and to make a way out to the upper air, that's the task, that's the labor.

8

Don't hit me.
  Don't hurt me.
  Don't send me away, please . . .

But why would he send her away when the Tattooed Girl was of use. So long as there was interest in the Tattooed Girl.

I can't go back.

I'm so tired . . .

I'm not pregnant I swear. I'm not sick like with any . . . disease.

A female mollusc she seemed to him. Boneless, white. As if somebody split open a giant shell, spilled out what was inside. Some guys are crazy for it. Female that's big soft floppy breasts all over.

The Easy Inn, the Bide-a-Wee. Where Dmitri had his reliable contacts.

This place I came from, they don't want me back.

My own family, see . . . They're kind of pissed.

Also in the county there's what they call bench warrants . . .

I don't know why. I don't!

I got mixed up with these people. These guys. They were trading in some stuff.

All some people want to do is fuck you up. If they can't fuck you, fuck you up.

Makes me so tired sometimes I want to die. But I won't.

Because I believe in God, yes. I believe in Jesus Christ as a hope someday, to come into my heart. Someday.

A mollusc is so soft you want to squeeze and squeeze until your fist shuts upon itself . . . But better not. Yet.

Hey listen: I'm not dumb! People misjudge me, see?

I can do lots of things not just . . .

Like wait tables, kitchen work. Been a nurse's aide, clerked in stores. I worked in a strip club in Pittsburgh, needed the money but I hated the work. Guys coming on to you all the time. Like you're raw meat and they're flies, or worse.

I graduated from high school. Akron Valley High. I did! I got my driver's license when I was sixteen. I was going to start classes at Akron Community College but . . . OK you're laughing at me, I guess. But I did these things.

DIDN'T LIKE TO kiss her or be kissed by her, her mouth was so wet and needy. And the tattoos.

They were mildly intriguing. Nothing to turn a guy seriously on. A guy who is into tattoos, body piercing, that kind of shit. To that kind of guy, Alma would be a disappointment.

In bright light the tattoo on her face looked like a faded blood-stain. Like a bruise from her eye that had slid down onto her cheek. Like her face which was this soft baby-girl face was marred, marked. Like a moth with frayed wings spread like it was trying to fly away except when you look closer the thing's dead, won't ever fly. And you want to swat it. Pow!

Oh! Oh why . . . Why'd you hit me, honey, I didn't do anything wrong did I?

Right away Alma's guilty. Takes the blame. Sleepy wide eyes and slutty hair like broom sage so dry somebody's going to light a match and toss it. The temptation is to swat the moth again, too. *Pow!*

Oh, honey! Don't, hey please don't hit me, I'm sorry, I'm sorry for whatever dumb thing I did, honey please?

AT THE EASY INN. He made the arrangements with the manager. They hadn't been in contact for six, eight months ... *Thought you were out of the business, Mikey. Welcome back.*

He'd taken her back to the house with him. Bathed her, disinfected/fumigated her. Shampooed the heavy tangled hair with his own bare hands fascinated if slightly revulsed. There was so much of this female, quivering in the soapy water. Practically kissing his hands she was so grateful. He'd fed her, he'd spoken kindly to her. He knew how to speak to strung-out females. Lost females. Females that other guys, including possibly their own fathers, have scraped off their shoes like dog shit.

I love you. Let me ... let me love you?

Wet, the Tattooed Girl smelled like a wet dog. Big beautiful white breasts like bags of warm milk. Nipples like big brown wide-open lidless eyes. And goose pimples in the flesh around the eyes. Just to touch her, stroke her head like a dog, Alma shuddered with being so happy, so grateful, grabbed his hands and kissed them so he laughed, embarrassed.

Shrewd-eyed seeing how fleshy this girl would get, one day. A female in her prime, already she's past her prime. Those boobs would droop to her waist by age forty-five. And at the waist she was soft, flabby. He pinched, his pinches were rough. And her belly, so round he thought for sure she was pregnant but she insisted no, she could not be pregnant, wasn't pregnant, a few days later she began to bleed which was disgusting but a relief.

Still, she looked pregnant. Fatty thighs, hips. That belly that was so tight and round like a drum. And the big milky breasts. Some guys are crazy for this, actually. They'd pay extra.

I told you: it wasn't done in any prison.

It wasn't done by any girl.

OK maybe I was inside a, what's it called, detention center for women, in Pittsburgh. Not a sentence, just booked. Forty-eight hours. Maybe some other place . . . But I was let go.

He didn't know how he felt about the tattoos. They made Alma a novelty, which is good, but they were amateurish, the ink was faded. Like scribblings, some asshole jabbing with a needle. On the back of the girl's neck, on her right shoulder, belly, buttocks, on the insides of her thighs. On the belly there were what looked like open gashes leaking blood. Or the raw female cunt leaking blood. Sick-o. But some guys would like it, Dmitri knew.

Honey, I told you: I didn't know their names. Whoever did this to me. But definitely it was men, or a man.

I don't remember too much what happened. It was a weird time for me. I know, I am lucky to be living. Not everybody is.

I run into those bastards again, I'm gonna kill them. I'll get a gun. Or a knife. Think I won't? I will!

I'm tougher than I look. Smarter, too.

FUCK AND FUCK and fuck and her wet screams in his ear. And her white mollusc-body heaving and bucking beneath him. And the scratchy-dry pubic hair, and the moist sucking-slapping noises between her legs. He sank himself into her up to the hilt. He pumped, spaded her like with a shovel. One of those sharp-curved pointed shovels. He had to press the palm of his hand over her mouth to quiet her. Subdue her. He was dripping sweat. Felt like blood drops oozing from his forehead like a fucking crown of thorns leaking blood down Christ's face. He was crazy for this female. He had a wish to finish himself off and her just closing his hands around her throat, and squeezing. And squeezing.

Eager as a puppy licking his hands. *Oh I love you! Love you so much. You saved my life . . .*

WHICH WAS TRUE. He did, and she owed him.

HE DOLED OUT meds to her. It was a ritual with all his girls: capsules on the palm of his hand lifted to the girl's mouth, and the quavering-grateful way she craned her neck for them, swallowed them down. He liked the sensation. He was a kind person, basically. The gene for being a doctor, a healer. The gene for leadership. Alma's wide wet fishy-gasping mouth aroused him. The way she breathed like her head was stuffed. He'd grip the nape of her soft neck, push the meds against her mouth and hold his hand against her mouth until she swallowed, swallowed again, began to whimper, choke. *Mollusc is so soft you want to squeeze squeeze squeeze.*

He wouldn't, though. She trusted him. He was a trustworthy guy. He had a soul, in his dreams he saw it bright and shining as a copper penny on the pavement.

Except: possibly when he was finished with her. When she went stale on him. That had to happen, that's life.

He'd have lots of takers. Customers. Sign her over to some guy who'd pay $$$ for the privilege of whatever he'd wish to do with the Tattooed Girl with no last name.

There was this in her favor: nobody was looking for the Tattooed Girl. Judging from what she'd said, nobody gave a shit about her.

Codeine. Oxycodone. Demerol. Anectine. Dmitri Meatte had his sources at the university hospital. Strung-out orderlies, nurses' aides. Himself, he had not dealt seriously in five years. He'd gotten out of the business in time. Just in time.

If he made it to thirty in another few months which it looked like he would, he wouldn't be dying young like he'd expected.

Hey no. Hey honey . . . no.

See, I love you. I love you.

I can do other things, let me? Please?

The Tattooed Girl wasn't cooperative always. There was this side to her, and it was a surprise, and he didn't like surprises. Like a big balloon you've blown up, a rubber balloon, suddenly it's resisting you.

No! I won't!

Her eyes rolled white in her head. She flailed, kicked. He had to take extreme measures. It began to be, after a week, ten days, twelve days of his investment, she'd wake up sometimes not the Tattooed Girl but Alma, and Alma had her own way of behaving. The Tattooed Girl was basically sweet female meat that could barely utter a coherent sentence and her eyes were out of focus and she breathed through her mouth like a dog and gave off a wet doggy heat but Alma was different, Alma could look straight at you and see you.

I said no I won't. Oh please, honey . . .

I'm not going out there again. I'm not.

He laughed, enjoying this. This cunt! This cunt was too much. Trying to fend him, Dmitri, off with her feeble outspread fingers like trying to fend off machine gun fire with your bare hands. Made him laugh aloud. Cunt, he called her, fat cunt, knocked her staggering backward with a clip to the jaw, so hard he hurt his knuckles, one-two slamming her in the fat boobs, he'd knock her fucking teeth out, she tried this shit again.

A human punching bag, the Tattooed Girl.

Every guy needs this, sometimes.

Her mouth was bleeding. Her nose. Handful of hair yanked out. A tear in one of the soft dopey-looking nipples. Toe of Dmitri's leather boot slammed between her legs, tearing. The Tattooed Girl screamed, fell to her knees clutching herself there between her legs like it was something precious she needed to save. Began to puke onto the rug which was more disgusting than funny.

SHE STOPPED TALKING. Hours, days. But she was unresisting now.

Those flat glassy eyes on him. Accusing him?

But no, she loved him. The Tattooed Girl loved who screwed her up the ass, kicked her in the cunt. Knew the names to call her.

He drove her to the Easy Inn Motel where he'd done business in the past. St. Paul Street South near the Greyhound station. There was a minimum of risk. Guys would pay $50. Some would pay $75. It added up. Except the Tattooed Girl was clumsy, dazed like a sleep-walker. Trying to smile, licking her lips like they hurt her. She wasn't a pro, didn't have the knack even when she tried. You'd be led to believe that any female looking like her would be a natural but not this one. Alma couldn't suck a guy off to save her life, not even Dmitri she was crazy for, said she owed her life to, not even him. Mellowed on enough oxycodone to put out a wild cat, still she couldn't. Strictly amateur. The poor bitch choked, gagged. Breathing loud like an asthma attack practically. Guys ended up disgusted, or feeling sorry for her. It wasn't exactly a turn-on.

He was thinking he'd have to dump her someday. Maybe soon. He knew just the place. Nowhere near the city. Thirty miles away at Point Huron on the lake. This empty stretch where you could walk out onto a spit of land, there was a drop-off and the water below was at least twenty feet deep. And an undertow would carry the body out farther. He'd weigh her down of course. No one would know. No one would trace her to him. He didn't even know her name. And she didn't know his.

Honey, why? I love you . . .

The tattoos were shit. If you had tattoos, you had gorgeous tattoos not shit like that. He thought of taking her to be tattooed across the river. The breasts, maybe the nipples. The big soft sweet white ass. He thought of dosing her with Anectine, the muscle relaxant, hauling her over to Rochester to this guy he knew, tattoo artist he called himself, it was a great idea except it could mean trouble, revealing Alma to somebody who knew him and what if something happened to her afterward, and the cops came looking for Dmitri Meatte . . .

In his new life waiting tables at The Café he was clean. He was believed to be one hundred percent clean even by people who sniffed around him pretty closely. All that could change.

It's OK, honey? Is it? I don't have to . . . ? I can work some other way?

SHE GOT THE wrong idea, and giving her the right idea took some time. Eventually it was the Bide-a-Wee in Waterloo. Onestorey cinder-block motel by the Thruway. Two of the crimson neon letters were burnt out so it was Bid-a-We. She'd begin to lose it half into the room. Like a big windup doll waking, blinking her eyes and seeing where she was and going crazy. *No please. Nooooo.*

Like a TV turned up loud. You wanted to kick in the screen to stop the noise.

GOD DAMN! He was disgusted with her lying on the floor twisted in the torn-out covers. A stink of vomit. Vomit in her hair. She was lying curled up, naked, knees to her breasts that looked rubbery, flattened out. Where the guy'd left her obviously disgusted. Her mouth was open and damp looking like a fish's where the hook has torn the flesh and she was whistling-breathing. He'd left her for two hours, that was the arrangement, drove to a tavern in town and returned and there she was alone, looking like she'd been kicked around pretty seriously and who the fuck could blame the guy. The TV was on loud, Dmitri turned it off. He'd thought she was unconscious but she was aware of him saying in this eager pleading voice like he'd plugged her in and immediately she was back to saying this. *I can work some other way, honey. Give me a chance?*

9

I N THE BOOK SELLER, negotiating the familiar creaking
spiral staircase to the third floor, where antiquarian and secondhand books in history, philosophy, classics and "the oc-
cult" were shelved, Seigl swore under his breath, hauling himself in
an upward direction by way of the railing. His cane, useful on reasonably level surfaces, was useless here.

Seigl's cane! Friends, acquaintances, shopkeepers and virtual
strangers in Carmel Heights expressed the most ridiculous surprise
and concern, seeing it for the first time. You'd think Jesus Christ was
hobbling about nailed to His cross. Seigl learned to steel himself for
the inevitable: "Joshua? Is something wrong?"

Tersely Seigl replied, "My knee." Or, "My back." Or, "Turned my
ankle, jogging." Sometimes he attributed the knee ailment to jogging, sometimes the back ailment. Sometimes he answered with an
unsociable grunt.

Strangely, the cane was often singled out for examination. As if it
were Seigl's surrogate limb, one that could be examined without
embarrassment. Seigl had intended to buy a cheap utilitarian cane at
the Carmel Heights drugstore where such items were sold along

with walkers, wheelchairs, bedpans and portable oxygen tanks, but rummaging through a closet in his house he'd found this specimen, very likely a cane used by his Steadman grandfather. It was sleek and polished as a mahogany carving, with a slightly discolored yet impressive ivory handle. It had, Seigl thought, a certain je ne sais quoi, which is more than one could expect of a prosthetic limb.

Often, in conversation, Seigl spoke of the cane dismissively as "temporary." Often in public he disdained to use it. (If he could walk reasonably well without it.) Yet, recalling the incident in Mount Carmel Cemetery, he carried it with him. It gave him an unexpectedly dandyish look. No doubt there was something primitive and appealing about a cane to which both men and women responded unconsciously. A talismanic scepter, a sword. A sleekly stylized phallus.

Seigl smiled. A mahogany phallus was a far better idea than a merely fleshly, mortal penis, you had to suppose.

Someone was speaking his name: "Joshua?"

"Yes? Hello."

At the top of the stairs there stood an attractive Carmel Heights matron, wife of a lawyer, a woman with literary pretensions, a social acquaintance rather than a friend, who had not seen Seigl before with his cane. She was asking him about it now: "Is something wrong? Did you—injure yourself?" Smiling uncertainly, and touching her perfectly coiffed streaked-blond hair.

Seigl hooked the cane over his arm. His face flushed with heat.

Politely Seigl greeted this woman (whose name he couldn't remember, though he'd been a guest in her home) and assured her he was fine, asked after her and her husband and, before she could exclaim anything further, or invite him to a dinner party, he eased into the next aisle of books.

Rude! Seigl was undeniably rude. His beard bristled with rudeness. Even his cane clattered.

Blame the medication, Seigl thought. Who knew what the side effects might be, with a steroid base.

Seigl lurched along the aisle of crammed floor-to-ceiling bookshelves, amid a smell of old books. The third, top floor of the converted Victorian house was stuffy and overheated; there were unexpected crannies and alcoves and narrow doorways through which you had to stoop, to enter; Seigl was too big and impatient for the place, yet invariably he returned. Out of revulsion at the contemporary world, Seigl had increasingly turned to the ancient world, drenched in its own species of blood, yet remote, sanctified by distance and the eloquence of its language. This was a kind of romanticism, Seigl knew. A privileged indulgence. Absurd for him to be translating the *Aeneid,* instead of confronting his own subjects, but what were his subjects? Many things engaged his interest but nothing sustained this interest for very long.

Seigl examined a leatherbound set of an 1882 Oxford edition of Seneca's *Epistles.* Formerly the property of a Carmel Heights physician who'd died a few months before. No doubt, these volumes hadn't been opened in decades. Seigl liked Seneca on the subject of suicide. *The wise man will live as long as he ought, not as long as he can.* You wanted to die before the matter of dying was taken from you; you wanted to depart before suffering a final, terrible illness.

Or worldly disgrace, failure. Kill yourself before losing your dignity.

Seneca, denounced by political enemies, was said to have comitted suicide "calmly."

Seneca, an older contemporary of Jesus who outlived Jesus by more than three decades.

Seigl had returned chastened and frightened to Morris Friedman, M.D., who was no longer "the" neurologist but "his" neurologist. Seigl had the cheerily grim idea that Friedman would be "his" neurologist for the remainder of Seigl's life.

How long do I have to live, Doctor? Seigl had wanted to ask. *As myself, I mean. Not crippled, incapacitated. Not in a wheelchair. Not in a bed.*

He hadn't asked. Friedman wouldn't have given him any kind of straight answer. Exactly what was wrong with Seigl hadn't yet been determined but it was now likely that he was suffering, at age thirty-eight, the onslaught of one of those mysterious "nerve diseases" after all.

Multiple sclerosis was only one of the possibilities. There were others, rarer and in some cases more deadly.

Yet: no diagnosis had been given him. Tests were still "inconclusive." Certain of Seigl's symptoms seemed to point to one disorder, others to other disorders. Conversely, there were symptoms common to these disorders which Seigl didn't (yet) have. And the symptoms from which he did suffer had so far been sporadic, unpredictable. He protested, "I can go for days without . . ."

Stumbling, falling. Mis-stepping.

On good days he walked, hiked, jogged (cautiously). A good day had come to be a kind of (secret) holiday.

(For Seigl, desperate not to be found out, just yet, by the community, still more by his relatives, had become inordinately secretive. He'd never shared secrets readily, kept his private life private, but now he was becoming parenthetical: he felt like an eclipsed moon. He was still there, but you couldn't see him.)

Every man ought to make his life acceptable to others, but his death to himself alone. Seigl leafed through volume four of the *Epistles*. His hands shook, but he could disguise it by resting the heavy book against a shelf.

He was breathing quickly. His face felt smudged, after the encounter with the woman. (But why so irritable with her, why so arrogant? She meant only well. She likes you. Why shouldn't she like you, why react as if she wanted to sink her talons into your flesh like a harpy? There are no harpies in Carmel Heights.)

Fifteen days since the humiliating incident in the cemetery. Since that time, Seigl's entire sense of himself had changed. He felt that every molecule had changed. There was matter and anti-matter in the universe, and he'd taken for granted that, being an American born in 1964 of well-to-do parents, he was *matter*, and he *mattered*. Now, he understood that he was becoming *anti-matter*. Death rising up his legs like the cold that rose in Socrates' legs as the old man lay dying in prison. In Mount Carmel Cemetery, Seigl had tasted that cold.

The proud young author of *The Shadows*. He who'd written so "poetically" about death, others' deaths. Somehow, even while transcribing the Holocaust, Seigl had seemed not to understand that all this applied to him, too.

Jet had called him the other evening. Her voice breathy and husky in his ear. "Joshua? Why haven't I heard from you in weeks? Months? Unless I call you? Why is it always up to me, to call you? It isn't as if you have family obligations. It isn't as if you have a demanding job." A pause. Jet, a rich woman, yet prided herself on having just such a job: demanding. "I've been having premonitions lately. About you, Joshua. You were in an emergency plane landing. You were carried out in some sort of wire contraption. When I saw you, your face was so changed, like melted wax, I hardly recognized you. I woke screaming, this was just last night, and too frightened to sleep, and all day today I've been exhausted, my assistant said to me, 'Jet'—I encourage Evie to call me 'Jet'—'are you having a migraine?' And I said—" Their parents had died within three years of each other, in the mid-1990s, and on nearly the same date in early December. That time was rapidly drawing near. Seigl shut his eyes, listening to his sister's monologue of accusation and angry affection, and when Jet worked herself up to her usual conclusion, that Joshua didn't love her, nor did he love himself, otherwise he'd have nourished his talent, not scattered it promiscuously, and the only solution was for Jet to come and visit with him for a while, Seigl said curtly, "Jet, I'm fine. Everything is fine. Your dreams are about you, not me. I'm too busy to have a house guest. I'm beginning a new project. Now I must hang up. Someone's at the door."

A homegrown Cassandra, Seigl's sister Jet. It mystified Seigl how this vain, narcissistic woman could have a premonition about him, his health, at such a time.

Seigl had told no one about his consultations with Friedman. If his condition progressed, to use the ironic medical term, his friends and relatives would find out soon enough. He'd begin by calling Sondra Blumenthal . . .

Thank God neither of his parents was living. He had no obligation to tell them.

Seigl's mother, Irene Steadman, had been a very attractive, seemingly weak woman who'd controlled others with the threat of her emotions: you never wanted to make Irene cry, for Irene in tears could make you feel sick with guilt. Seigl could imagine trying to console her. *Mother, I'm sorry I got sick! Hey, I didn't mean it.* A nerve disease was worse than the failure to marry, to give her a grandchild. (Years ago, Irene had given up on her daughter Mary Beth a.k.a. "Jet." Irene had sadly acknowledged that Jet wouldn't make a "fit mother" to any imaginable child.)

As for Karl Seigl, his son's illness wouldn't have seemed to him very surprising. Shouldn't a Jew expect the worst, for his children as for himself? Beneath the businessman's surface, American personality, there'd been this other. Seigl shuddered to envision his father's eyes. His look of resignation, guilt. As if he were a criminal discovered in his crime. Unstated the words would pass between them *Always I knew, Joshua. Something terrible would happen to my children.*

A comedy routine! A Kafka scenario turned upside down.

Maybe it was crude to think so, but yes, Seigl was relieved that his parents were dead.

Somehow, Seigl had managed to make his way home from Mount Carmel Cemetery that morning, after his fall. Using a broken tree branch as a kind of cane, he'd made it without requiring anyone's help. (And no one had seen him.) Almost, he could have told himself that his legs had merely cramped. Severe case of runner's cramp on a cold morning.

Now he was on steroids. Not a strong dose, Friedman said.

The immediate goal was remission. Blocking the "progress" of the deterioration. Beyond that, Seigl shouldn't think.

Fortunately, though he sometimes walked with a cane, and, on bad mornings, had trouble swinging his legs (heavy as sacks of wet cement!) out of bed, Seigl had no trouble driving his car. Once seated, his two-hundred-pound-plus weight solidly on his buttocks, he was fine. Exerting pressure on the gas pedal, the brake, fine. (He was in terror of his driver's license being taken from him. His father, in the last years of his life, had refused to stop driving though his vision had dimmed and his reflexes were slow as those of a man underwater.) Getting himself into the car, a not-new Volvo, was sometimes tricky, and hoisting himself out of it, that unthinking shift of balance you take for granted until you're losing it, was trickier.

Negotiating the nineteen stone steps to his house. Descending to the sidewalk, ascending to the front door. In wet weather it was becoming a challenge. In snow, ice, it was going to be treacherous.

Friedman had asked Seigl tactfully if he lived alone, if he had a family close by. Yes, said Seigl. And no.

"I thought I explained . . . I *told* you . . ."

Hidden from Seigl by rows of books, a man was speaking with exaggerated patience as if to someone very young or very stupid.

"Books in these boxes are on consignment, and should be shelved over here. See?"

A pause, and a timid murmur, and the man said in a voice heavy with sarcasm, " 'Consignment'? Don't know what 'consignment' means? There're dictionaries all over this place. English, French, German, Latin."

This was the Book Seller owner Lee Scanlon, chewing out one of the staff. Seigl had heard such scoldings in the past, and didn't approve. No doubt, Scanlon intended his remarks to be humorous; at times they were arias, made to be overheard. The Book Seller paid low wages, hired mostly college students who quit after a few weeks of humiliation. Often these were Asian, East Indian. This one was a girl, Seigl could hear her low, faltering, apologetic voice. Scanlon interrupted, "Never mind! Just do it."

When Scanlon saw Seigl, his demeanor immediately changed. He became jovial, flattering. "Dr. Seigl! Good to see you." Scanlon's shrewd eye took in the cane, which Seigl wasn't using at the moment, but Scanlon understood from the tension in Seigl's jaw that no commentary on this cane was wished. "Haven't seen you in a while, Doctor. I suppose you've been busy . . ." Seigl was impatient to move on, but had to be polite; he needed to feel welcome in the Book Seller, for which he felt an unreasonable sentimental attachment, as he often felt for lost causes. Each man was wary of the other: years ago, Scanlon had cornered Seigl in the store, pressing poems upon him, identifying himself as a poet in the surreal/Ashbery tradition. (Though John Ashbery had long ago departed upstate New York, he'd been born in Rochester and had grown up on a farm in Sodus, on Lake Ontario.) Scanlon featured the poet's books, new and old, prominently in the Book Seller, as he featured other "distinguished locals" like Joshua Seigl. Seigl had finally told Scanlon that he rarely read contemporary poetry if he could avoid it, especially poetry in the surreal/Ashbery tradition.

Scanlon had a way of standing near Seigl, breathing on him. As a dealer eyes a rare, valuable book whose owner is clueless of its worth, so Scanlon eyed his most celebrated customer. Today, as often in the past, Scanlon alluded to Seigl's "genius." He'd read a "brilliant" essay of Seigl's in, where was it, the *London Review of Books,* or was it *TLS* . . . It was a theme of Scanlon's that Joshua Seigl had a vast audience of both gentiles and Jews eagerly awaiting his next novel. Not wanting to reply ironically, still less turn and lurch away, Seigl stood silently. This is why, he thought, so-called artists become surly and reclusive; not out of a sense of their superiority, but of their failure to be sufficiently superior. Scanlon was speaking grandly of Seigl's "audience": you were meant to envision a gargantuan football stadium in the

American heartland crammed with these ghostly folks, all of them waiting impatiently for Joshua Seigl's second novel.

At last Scanlon backed off with a cheerful excuse of needing to return to work downstairs. He spoke of dropping by The Café to play chess with Seigl one of these evenings. Seigl said, "Good!"

Seigl walked on. He saw, in the next aisle, a girl crouched over a carton of secondhand, mostly coverless books, awkwardly stacking them on the floor. She was young, perhaps twenty years old, with a very pale face and synthetic-looking ash-blond hair spilling untidily over her shoulders. She was biting her lower lip, working her mouth as if trying not to cry. When Seigl approached she glanced up nervously. Seigl saw, on her right cheek, what looked like a birthmark.

This girl he'd seen somewhere before: where?

Wordless, Seigl stooped to lift several books out of the carton for her. As he bent over his face flushed with blood. *Man, God, and Religion in Late Medieval Europe. Science and Magic in 15th-Century France. The Origins of Demonology. "Thou Shalt Not Suffer a Witch to Live": A History of European Witchcraft. The Satanic Black Mass.* Any new delivery of secondhand books to the Book Seller was of interest to Seigl, at least in theory. These were weighty, decades old, smelling of mildew. A deceased professor's library, hastily dismantled and dispersed by his heirs. Seigl heard himself say, "Nothing so sad as unwanted books. Like spurned hearts."

The girl turned blank blinking eyes toward Seigl, wiping her nose with the edge of her hand. She wore a soiled lime green Book Seller smock over a cheap red turtleneck sweater, jeans that fit her fleshy hips snugly, and new-looking sneakers, without socks. Seigl set the heavy books on a nearby shelf as she rose to her feet, murmuring what sounded like "Thanks . . ." The girl was at least six inches shorter than Seigl with a childish face round as a full moon and strong-looking arms and shoulders. The mark on her cheek was unfortunate: it made her look smudged, despoiled. Your impulse was to reach out and brush the blemish away. Seigl said gently, "You're new here, I gather. Don't let Scanlon bully you."

He moved on. He didn't want to make the girl more self-conscious than she already was. And he was hardly a man to speak to strange women in public places; he wasn't a man who took much notice of other people, even sexually attractive young females.

Seigl thought of himself as a connoisseur of female beauty, but at a remove. Always, with Seigl, there was this remove. Like a pane of glass between himself and the Other. He admired the females of Botticelli, Titian, Ingres, Vermeer, Manet (*Olympia*), Degas . . . Less so the females of twentieth-century art, where, amid the fracturing of planes and surfaces, you could actually find a female shape. Living women Seigl tended to disregard as objects of contemplation. They were too human and immediate, too much like himself. Yet he'd never had a relationship with a woman very different from himself. He'd never had relations with prostitutes, for instance.

The fleshy young woman with her unnaturally white, soft skin and mica-glinting eyes reminded Seigl of prostitutes he'd seen in Prague a few years before. Very young, often slightly plump, glamorously made up, sulky, perhaps tired, yet childlike in a kind of stubborn innocence. He'd seen such girls off duty, so to speak, sitting in bistros with their lovers or pimps, and had wondered at their lives. He hadn't known whether to pity them, or feel outrage or even uneasiness on their account. Did they resent their lives? Were other lives available to them? What right has an American observer to feel pity, even sympathy, for them, if they don't feel this way about themselves?

Seigl spent some time browsing along the shelves. He'd nearly forgotten the girl. When he approached the staircase, he saw her kneeling now on the bare floorboards, lifting books from another carton. Seigl was touched by her awkwardness. She was working with methodical slowness. Clearly she was frightened of making a mistake. Seigl came by, and took a book from her hands. "This can go here, see? It's the third volume of the series." Seigl smiled down at the girl who was blinking up warily at him. The moth-shape on her cheek looked as if it were about to quiver into life and fly away.

The girl said, uncertainly, "You're a friend of his? Mr. Scanlon?"

"No."

"You like books, though?" Her voice was startling: flat, nasal, scratchy, as if it must hurt her to speak.

Seigl frowned. The girl's naivete was both charming and annoying. Yet he knew she was sincere. One must honor such sincerity.

"Not all books. Most books, no, I don't."

This answer seemed to baffle her. She rose tentatively from the floor, brushing hair out of her eyes. Seigl heard himself asking her name, and at once she said, with a girlish, obedient little tuck of her chin, "Alma."

As if she had no surname. Or her surname wasn't important, as Alma herself wasn't important.

Seigl now heard himself say, "My name is Seigl. Joshua."

"You're a . . . doctor, I guess?"

"No. Not a doctor."

"But he called you doctor."

"He's mistaken."

Alma smiled, taken slightly aback by Seigl's manner. She didn't know how to read him, Seigl supposed. He was nearly forty: in her eyes, old. His untrimmed whiskers, tweed cap, professional and aloof air, his way of speaking marked him as a certain type; yet he seemed almost to be conspiring with her. Speaking so bluntly of Scanlon, as if he and Alma were in league against the bookstore owner.

Seigl said, amending the harshness of his words, "Most people are mistaken about most things, Alma. Most adults."

Alma smiled doubtfully. As if thinking: but adults must be trusted, who else can I trust?

Seigl saw a wavering part in Alma's hair, a thin blue vein beating at her right temple. Her eyes were minutely bloodshot, yet beautiful thick-lashed eyes, moist and yearning. Her teeth were small and uneven and slightly stained. Seigl was touched by the blemish on her cheek, the disfigurement of what might have been Alma's beauty. He was disturbed to see further blemishes, ugly birthmarks or tattoos, or scars, perhaps burn scars, like webbing on the backs of both her hands, of the color of old, dried blood.

Seigl asked Alma how long she'd been working in the Book Seller, and Alma lifted a hand and moved the fingers in silent counting. What a literal mind! Clearly, Alma meant to be exact.

"Four days. It seems longer."

"Yes, I'm sure it does. And where do you live?"

The eyes went vague, evasive. "Different places . . ."

"But you're not from Carmel Heights, Alma."

It was a statement, not a question. The girl mumbled, as if embarrassed, "I guess not."

Ashamed of wherever she was from. Assuming that this big bewhiskered kindly man, overbearing as Scanlon in his own way, would pity her, or dislike her.

Seigl was consumed with curiosity. And wonder at himself. *This isn't like me* he wanted to protest. *This isn't me.* The gleaming ivory-handled cane hooked over his arm made him into a dandy. The Irish cap slanted on his stiff springy hair. His swarthy-Semitic good looks, something boyish and irreverent in his overlarge, glistening dark eyes. Seigl was hardly a dandy, and not a man who spoke to strangers in bookstores. Hardly a boy. Yet he smiled down at this awkward buxom girl standing so passively before him. Like a young farm creature, a sleek young calf for instance, waiting to be herded in one direction or another.

Seigl had seen Alma before, he was certain. The name "Alma" seemed distinctly familiar. He wasn't a man to remember names nor even faces but he'd seen this face before, and recently.

At The Café? The last time he'd played chess?

There was something disagreeable about the association. Later, he would try to recall why.

Though Alma seemed to be self-conscious in Seigl's gaze, she made no move to ease away from him. You could see her summoning her courage to ask this older man a question, as a nervous schoolgirl might ask her teacher a question; not the brightest student, but one who rarely spoke. She stammered slightly, mispronouncing words. Telling Seigl that she had been looking through some of these books—especially *"Thou Shalt Not Suffer a Witch to Live": A History of European Witchcraft*—and she wondered, were these things real? Had there been real witches? Or was it all made up, like in a movie? Eagerly she leafed through the book to point out to Seigl pages of illustrations, drawings and woodcuts of grotesque female witch-figures, ugly scenes of torture, sacrifice, immolation. In one illustration, captioned "The Divine Mother," the Hindu goddess Kali was represented with two faces, one benevolent and the other fierce and barbaric.

Seigl checked the front of the book: it had been printed in Great Britain in 1922 by the publisher Kegan Paul. It looked reputable, if lurid. "Witches aren't real, I guess?" Alma asked wistfully. Seigl said, "Witches were believed to be 'real' at one time in history, and they suffered for it." Alma said, "Because a witch can't win? God hates witches?" Seigl said, "No. God neither loves nor hates witches. God isn't a factor here. Only humankind. For the witch-hunters, 'witches' were heretics who had to be punished because they undermined the authority of the Roman Catholic Church; some of those persecuted as witches are believed to have been Cathars, a dissident Catholic sect. For those who imagined themselves witches, and there may have been significant numbers of these, 'witchcraft' was a collective delusion. A way of compensating economic, political, social powerlessness on the part of most women and some men." Seigl stopped short, embarrassed at seeming to lecture. Of all things, he didn't want to bore this girl who stood so ardently before him.

"But—were there witches? I don't understand."

"No, and yes. There were no witches. There is no Devil, and there is no empowerment from the Devil. But there were those who were perceived to be witches, and those who so perceived themselves."

"But they were killed anyway, I guess? The witches?"

"Yes. For centuries. 'Thou shalt not suffer a witch to live.' "

Seigl shut the book. Those ugly illustrations. He felt a wave of revulsion for the ignorance and cruelty of history; for the fact of his own involvement, as one who chose to know such things. By now he'd meant to leave the Book Seller. He'd been here far longer than he'd anticipated. Scanlon would be watching for Seigl to come downstairs: watching, and waiting. And the girl was far behind in her shelving. Seigl felt implicated, responsible. He said, "Alma? Quit this place. Come work for me."

II

The Assistant

I

M Y HEART IS filled with HOPE.
I seem to know: this is REBIRTH.
I seem to know: this is an act to SAVE MY LIFE.

RIDICULOUS! As he hadn't done for years, Seigl was scribbling notes to himself. It was a habit he'd first begun during his travels. Tearing off strips of paper, scribbling on them and stuffing them in his pockets. In later years, Seigl acquired a reputation for being endearingly eccentric, scribbling notes to himself in a fever of concentration even as he was being introduced to speak before large audiences, and glancing up startled by applause. These were not love notes. These were not notes in regard to love. They were to be seen by no one but Seigl. Discovered by others in Seigl's wake, on the floor for instance, such notes were rarely comprehensible. They were small, somehow shameful indulgences. Seigl laughed at himself, the fever had returned.

"INCONCLUSIVE": the heart's fate.

Out of the void, one to ASSIST.

(Not a nurse.) (Not yet!)

2

FROM A HIGH WINDOW he saw her climbing out of the taxi. He drew back not wanting to be seen if she glanced up.

The girl's legs appeared first, as she slid, pushed her way out of the taxi, clumsy, yet graceful in her way. Firm shapely legs, a sheen of stocking, a dark skirt. She was wearing a cloth coat and, around her straw-colored hair, a scarf of some cobwebby material that whipped in the wind. Seigl was struck by how unnaturally white her skin was. A milky skin, and very red lips. As before she reminded him of the young Prague prostitutes . . .

The taxi was pre-paid. Seigl had made arrangements. His assistant would arrive at 10 A.M. and depart at 6 P.M. At least initially, Alma would not be staying overnight at the house.

We will see, Seigl thought. See how it works out.

How it works out on both sides.

"Alma Busch" was the name she'd given him. Eventually, if Seigl decided to keep her on, he would have to formalize their arrangement, he supposed. Register as her employer. Pay into her Social Security pension. He wasn't thinking of that now. For now, there was an air of the clandestine about the arrangement.

Seigl watched closely to see that the taxi driver wasn't going to inveigle Alma into paying his fare. Or his tip. (Seigl had pre-paid the tip, too.) Alma was so naively sweet-natured, so credulous and simple seeming, anyone might take advantage of her.

She'd told him yes, she had graduated from high school. And she could type . . . *I can type, Mr. Seigl! I mean, I can type some.*

Seigl smiled. Alma, typing? Knowing how to spell the sorts of words Seigl would expect an assistant to use? Possibly.

Yet she was intelligent, in her way. Seigl believed she'd become more confident, and in that way more intelligent, under his tutelage.

Until the other day it hadn't occurred to Seigl that the chief impediment of his work-life had been for years this idiotic vision of him in others' eyes as a "genius." Or, cruelly, a "failed genius." Especially the women in his life, his mother, his sister, even so good a friend as Sondra Blumenthal, were like harpies picking at him, tearing at his flesh. No wonder he abandoned projects. It was like trying to work facing a funhouse mirror distorting your image, magnifying and mocking your every move, every twitch and grimace.

No wonder Joshua Seigl had been miserable. Impotent.

Now, he would make a fresh start. This very day.

The taxi was driving away. Yet there stood Alma Busch on the sidewalk, irresolute, clutching at an oversized shoulder bag and staring up at the house. What was wrong?

Seigl didn't want to rap on the window. Didn't want her to know he'd been watching for her.

The Hill was a neighborhood of old, distinguished houses, some of them small mansions. Sidewalks were made of paving stones, quaintly ill-fitting. At the cul-de-sac of Greaves Place there were three houses set back from the street, and high above the street, behind wrought iron fences and evergreen shrubs. Seigl saw that his assistant was looking intimidated by these surroundings. She'd taken out of her shoulder bag a piece of paper at which she frowned, moving her lips. All that could possibly be on this piece of paper, Seigl thought, was the address he'd given her, 8 Greaves Place, and the time. He'd been reluctant to give her his unlisted telephone number.

Seigl watched with dismay as Alma looked about helplessly. She couldn't seem to see the numeral 8 which was partly obscured by ivy growing on the iron fence. She was trying to peer through the gate at the facade of the house above, where there was no numeral. Before Seigl could rap on the window she backed away, stared at the piece of paper in her hand, and went hesitantly to check the number of the house next door, which was a small walk. "God damn. Stupid!"

Exasperated, Seigl went downstairs, gripping the railing. The last thing he wanted was to lose his balance and have an accident, at such a time.

Telling himself *She's shy. Not stupid. Of course she feels intimidated, put yourself in her place.*

Not very likely, though: that Joshua Seigl could put himself in Alma Busch's place.

It had never crossed Seigl's mind to tell Alma that he lived in such a neighborhood. He'd become hardly more aware of the nature of his surroundings than a mouse in its nest.

Still he was elated, excited. Where the prospect of working with, for instance, the young man Essler would have made him apprehensive, he was looking forward to working with Alma. Already this morning had been one of his good mornings. His best morning in fact, since beginning the steroid-based medication Friedman had prescribed.

When he'd first wakened at dawn he'd experienced some vertigo. This is to be expected, Friedman assured him. And getting out of bed, shifting from the horizontal to the vertical, was always tricky. You can expect blurred vision, a pumping heartbeat, that taste of panic that signals *Something isn't right.* But the interlude passed within minutes. Seigl had even gone outside for a brisk forty-minute walk into Mount Carmel Cemetery. He hadn't wanted to risk running, not today.

"Alma? This is the house."

Seigl called to her from the front stoop, waving. Damned if he was going to climb down those nineteen stone steps glistening with wet from an overnight shower.

Alma saw him, and waved. She hurried back to Seigl's gate and managed to open it, and fumbled to shut it behind her, and climbed the stone steps breathing through her mouth, agitated, deeply embarrassed. Seigl watched her in fascination though he supposed he was making her self-conscious.

"Mr. Seigl! Oh gosh I'm sorry I'm late . . ."

"You're not late, Alma. Don't be upset."

"I . . . I wasn't sure . . . I'm always afraid of going into the wrong house, see?"

Always? What did she mean?

Seigl said, amused, "What would happen then, Alma?"

"What? When?"

Seigl regretted speaking playfully. He had an impulse to take hold of the girl's shoulders and calm her. But any touch, any movement toward her, shaking her hand in greeting, for instance, would have alarmed her, he knew. Her silvery eyes were moist, glistening. She was short of breath from the climb. In the pale sunshine the moth-shaped mark on her cheek was a disfigurement, a cruel blemish. And the cobwebby marks on the backs of her hands, like frayed gloves. Seigl felt a stab of tenderness for the girl who seemed, this morning, rather slow-witted, plodding.

Seigl said, "If you went into the wrong house. What would happen then?"

Alma pondered the question, biting at her thumbnail. Her fingers were stubby, the nails bitten close. Seigl would have to remember that, if he asked Alma questions of a playful or ironic type, she would take these questions literally. Momentum bore her in a single direction forward, like a train on its tracks.

Not very bright, maybe. But steadfast, dependable. Likely to be loyal to her employer. And never critical.

Seigl invited her inside the house. Alma followed shyly, still pondering his question. Finally she said, breathless, urgent, as if the words had come to her from a long distance, and not easily, "It would be like a—a dream, I guess? A bad dream."

So THE FIRST MORNING began. The first day.

Wanting to make Alma feel at ease, Seigl showed her first to the downstairs room, the guest room where she could put her coat and bag, this room to which, as he said, she could "retreat" whenever she needed, to freshen up, even take a nap if she wanted. (Alma's mouth gaped at such a notion. Nap? During her workday?) Seigl saw that the very room intimidated her, and wondered if he was saying the right things. This young woman was accustomed to taking orders from her employers, not being made to feel at home.

Next, Seigl brought her to his study, the room in which she would be doing most of her work, initially helping him to sort, file, discard and/or reply to numerous letters he'd received in the past several years and hadn't gotten around to dealing with. (There were cartons of these letters! Seigl couldn't bear to look directly at them, their mere existence filled him with despair, but Alma considered the cartons without alarm, as she might consider baskets of laundry waiting to be ironed. This was a finite task, if laborious. A matter of doing.) Then there were files, desk drawers, and closet shelves crammed with drafts of manuscripts Seigl had worked on, these dating back— was it possible, fifteen or more years?—which Seigl was desperate to bring into some kind of order. Scattered among his things were several uncompleted novel manuscripts and countless essays, sketches for plays, isolated passages of translations from Greek and Latin texts. It had become Seigl's habit to write feverishly until his strength ebbed, to put away material and begin again, often without glancing at what he'd already written. (Why? He was fearful it was no good, of course.) Over the years he'd accumulated thousands of pages of manuscripts of which possibly some fraction was decent, valuable, he had to hope, and this, he told Alma who stood silent, arms folded tightly beneath her breasts as she looked about the room with moist, rapidly blinking eyes, he wanted to "bring out of oblivion" with her help.

Next, Seigl showed Alma the kitchen, where she'd be expected to prepare meals occasionally, lunch for instance, sometimes dinner, and he showed her where the vacuum cleaner and other cleaning items were kept, for she'd be expected to do light housekeeping as certainly something she could do. In the Book Seller Seigl had asked her bluntly what Scanlon was paying her hourly and he offered her twice that amount.

Seigl asked if Alma had any questions.

Alma mumbled no she guessed not.

"You said you could type? A little?"

Alma mumbled evasively yes. A little.

"Can you operate a computer? Use a word processor? Do e-mail?"

Alma folded her sturdy arms more tightly beneath her breasts, hugging herself, not breathing. Almost inaudibly she mumbled what sounded like *I can try*.

Seigl laughed. Just the answer he should have expected.

"Well. That's about my expertise, too. But we'll learn, Alma. The primary task is, to rescue my soul from oblivion."

To this playful remark, Alma wisely made no reply. She wouldn't latch onto Seigl's smile. He was in his Jewish mode, ironic and self-deprecatory, a mode which women invariably found sexually attractive, but Alma wasn't one of these women. She wouldn't even look at him, she was waiting for her instructions.

Alma had a natural instinct, you might call it a natural dignity, Seigl was beginning to see, that allowed her not to seem to hear what was fanciful or irrelevant. If Seigl spoke of something she didn't understand, something urgent she needed to know, she would inquire then. But only then.

Now Seigl spoke the words he'd prepared.

"Sometimes I might need help of another kind. Going down those stone steps outside, for instance. Or coming up. Getting into or out of my car. Sometimes I might need you to ride with me if I have to drive somewhere but this would be just within the city, not any distance. And you've said that you can drive, you have a license."

Alma nodded. Still she wasn't looking at him. But she was listening intently.

"As you might have noticed, sometimes I walk with a cane. I have a mild medical condition that isn't expected to worsen. And isn't contagious." Seigl smiled, wanting Alma to smile with him: this was a joke. Please laugh! But Alma listened gravely, lips pursed shut. Seigl continued, as if subtly rebuked, "Our understanding is this, Alma: you are not to ask me about my health. You are never to ask me about my health. It's a subject I don't care to discuss. If I tell you, it will be because I'm obliged to." Seigl paused, wondering if he'd said too much. Plunging head-on, beyond the words he'd carefully prepared to tell his assistant. Something in Alma's taut expression, a sympathy in her tremulous eyelids and mouth, encouraged him. *She is a born nurse. That's why I have hired her.* "But I don't think I will be obliged to. I mean, as I've said, it's a mild medical condition and it isn't expected to progress. That is, worsen."

Alma stood silent. Seigl imagined sorrow in her heart.

She'd made up her face for her first day working on the Hill. Her lips were vividly crimson, her pale eyebrows darkened with an eyebrow pencil, whether skillfully or clumsily Seigl was no one to judge. He was hardly a connoisseur of female cosmetics. He couldn't even tell if she'd powdered over the blemish to minimize its effect. Her eyelids had a bluish, bruised tinge, and there were bluish shadowy hollows beneath her eyes. No disguising the truth of the eyes.

"Alma? You understand?"

No. How could Alma understand.

"Y-yes, Mr. Seigl."

"But you can call me Joshua. As I've said, you're my assistant, not my servant."

SEIGL HAD INTENDED to begin with his manuscripts. Clearly, this was urgent. Yet, faced with the prospect of seeing what he'd accumulated over the past fifteen years, and of needing to reread so much, he felt weak, defeated beforehand. To be a writer was a moral commitment, maybe he hadn't the strength. The tragic grandeur of his subjects mocked his feeble talent. Even as Alma waited for him to instruct her, he lapsed into a sudden, stricken silence, reminded of that terrible hour a decade ago when, in New York City, at a black tie fund-raising gala at Lincoln Center, rising amid applause to accept yet another award for *The Shadows,* he'd stumbled on his way to the stage, lost his balance, regained his balance, and dared to say, at the microphone, that the award should have gone to another writer, Joshua Seigl had had his share, and more than he deserved. A visceral revulsion for the public nature of the private, spiritual enterprise of writing had swept over him. *The beginning of my illness, that night. My punishment.*

"We'll begin with the letters, Alma. These cartons. The Augean stables. And more coming in every day."

In Seigl's cluttered study Alma was warily brightening, wanting to begin work. She wasn't one who was comfortable with being talked-to by an employer, she wanted to be told what to do. Seigl saw that.

He would have to rein in his penchant for fanciful speech. Later, he would ask her to prepare lunch for them both. And a light dinner for him, he'd heat in the microwave in the evening. Maybe a little vacuuming, housecleaning.

They dragged cartons further into Seigl's study and opened them. Seigl was impressed with the strength of Alma's arms and shoulders. She worked with a clumsy sort of agility, doggedness. She should have worn more casual clothes, not her cheaply dressy pleated wool skirt and red nylon sweater with three-quarter sleeves, that looked like items purchased in a bargain bin at Kmart.

But Seigl wouldn't comment on her attire. He didn't want his assistant to feel self-conscious in his presence.

As a man, he had no authority to suggest to a young woman what to wear. Maybe later, when they knew each other better. But he was determined not to pry into Alma's personal life. He vowed.

Seigl said, "Letters in these cartons to which I've replied, I've marked with *R* in the upper right-hand corner. If the letters are professional, on letterheads, for instance publishers, magazines, universities, and they're marked *R,* they should be filed in this cabinet. Professional letters not marked *R* please place on this end of the table. Personal letters are another matter. Some of them are handwritten, you can see. Not many are marked *R* but if there are some, file them in this filing cabinet. Don't mix them with the other. Personal letters not marked *R* can be placed in a stack on this end of the table. Some of these I will want to reply to, but most of them probably not; probably they'll just be discarded. Still, I should look them over. My feeling is, if someone has taken the time to write to me, if my work has struck a chord with someone, I owe it to this individual to at least read his or her letter. In time, Alma, I will trust you to read these letters as they come in. Some you will pass on to me, some you won't. You'll learn to discriminate. In the basement are yet more cartons filled with more letters and manuscripts, galleys, books people have sent me. We won't even speak of these today. There were days, weeks, months when I couldn't deal with my mail, especially when I returned from trips and it was waiting for me. I don't have an answering service. I don't do e-mail. I haven't had a secretary. Until now I haven't wanted an assistant. I can't discard anything, I haven't the heart. Yet I can't seem to deal with these letters, either. It's like a nightmare, voices calling to me, strangers' voices, appealing to me and wanting something from me and a kind of paralysis comes over me . . ." Seigl heard the words he was uttering with horror.

Paralysis! He was revealing too much.

But Alma, with instinctive tact, chose to give the impression of hearing only what was instructive, practical. To spare Seigl embarrassment, she'd begun her task of sorting the letters.

She wants me to leave Seigl thought with relief.

Seigl went away to work on his Virgil translation in another part of the house. Already he was feeling calmer, optimistic.

He'd broken through the paralysis of months. Years!

It was something of a novelty to him, to be in the presence of a woman who seemed to want from him nothing more than he wanted to give. Long he'd been accustomed to women who wanted something from him even when they could not have defined what is was.

A piece of my heart. My soul.

Well, Alma Busch was not one of these. Clearly she'd never heard of Joshua Seigl, as she'd never heard of Virgil. What a relief!

How Seigle's friends and acquaintances would disapprove, he'd hired an assistant who barely knew English, let alone Latin. She couldn't operate a computer and was surely a mediocre typist. Her voice was rough, untrained: yet he would trust her to answer his phone.

This wasn't the first odd thing Seigl had done, he supposed. In the eyes of others.

Well, it was none of their damned business.

What Alma Busch lacked in intelligence and education, she compensated for in warmth, generosity. Seigl sensed this.

He took up his work sheets where he'd left off. It was his custom to write in longhand, crossing out most of his lines. After years of fevered work alternating with periods of inactivity, and numerous drafts, he was only in Book II of the *Aeneid*. The visit to Hades still lay ahead. Yet he felt optimistic now. Elated! As his assistant toiled in his study sorting through the detritus of his misspent life, he was beginning anew in a room with tall narrow windows opening upon a white sky blank as an unsullied canvas. He would immerse himself in the sacerdotal labor of translation. He would subordinate his doubtful genius to a poet of genius. For what sanity in Virgil's Latin. What precision. Even in the nightmare tale of the deaths of Laocoön and his hapless sons, what beauty of speech.

From Tenedos, on the placid sea, twin snakes endlessly coiling, uncoiling, swam abreast to shore.

AT 6 P.M. a taxi arrived to take Alma Busch away.

"Tomorrow at ten, Alma. I'll be expecting you. Goodnight!"

He'd switched on lights at the front of the house. From the front stoop he watched as his assistant, straw-hair blowing in the wind, descended the nineteen stone steps to the street. At the wrought iron gate, Alma fumbled the latch as she had that morning, but managed to open it, and to close it behind her. As she climbed into the rear of the idling taxi she glanced back up furtively at her tall bewhiskered employer who waved good-bye with such gusto, Alma was inspired to wave back.

Seigl went inside. He was one who never said good-bye to any guest without feeling a measure of relief. Alone! How good to be alone.

And yet. Already the house seemed empty, very quiet.

He'd hardly seen his assistant through the day. They had avoided each other. Only a few times Seigl heard Alma's footsteps, in the kitchen and on the stairs going down to the guest room, where she used the bathroom but otherwise didn't linger. Seigl ate the lunch Alma had prepared him in the dining room where he'd spread his translation work sheets, and Alma ate her lunch hurriedly in the kitchen, taking no more than ten minutes. There'd been no likelihood of Seigl asking her to join him in the dining room.

Never Seigl's mother would have cautioned. *If you do, you'll regret it.*

Well, he wouldn't. He knew better.

Alma had worked diligently for hours sorting, stacking, filing letters. Seigl was satisfied that his assistant had worked hard, if slowly. Around 4 P.M., restless, he went to stand outside his study door, which was partly ajar as he'd left it, where he observed Alma inside, so absorbed in her work she took no notice of him. It was wholly innocent, Seigl wasn't spying on her! If Alma had happened to glance up, Seigl would have continued into the room matter-of-factly as if this were his intention, but she didn't glance up. She'd removed her shoes and stood in her stocking feet, which were broad, squat, rather graceless feet, though her ankles were slender. Her hair was forever falling into her face and she brushed it repeatedly back. Seigl was touched by his assistant's devotion: you would think, from Alma's rapt, slightly pained expression, that she was doing calculus, not minimal office-work.

Or was she a temple virgin, in the service of a god.

Seigl decided to pay Alma in cash for this first full day. Eight hours of which she'd worked virtually every minute. Oh, he was tempted to overpay her! Out of guilt and anxiety, Karl Seigl had often overpaid certain of his employees. He'd lavishly overtipped. (Compulsively, Seigl's mother charged.) But it isn't a good idea, Seigl knew. Overpayment, like overtipping, sends a confused signal. Workers are most comfortable when they're well paid and receive the payment they expect; tips and bonuses make them anxious. For always then they will be expecting more.

After Alma departed, Seigl tried to return to translating Virgil but found himself too restless. He wandered into his study where there was a faint scent of Alma: yeasty, fleshy. And that acrid smell of (he surmised) her hair . . . He was stirred with belated curiosity about the marks on her face, hands, forearms.

Birthmarks? Burn scars?

Tattoos?

(But what crude, clumsy tattoos!)

Someday, maybe Seigl would inquire.

Out of curiosity, too, not suspicion, for Seigl wasn't a man to be suspicious, he went downstairs to the guest room. Alma's scent was here, too. Seigl had been struck with a kind of familial pride when he'd showed this room to Alma and she'd been impressed with it. In her awkward faltering way she'd mumbled what sounded like *Oh Mr. Seigl this room is so . . . nice.*

The guest suite, like the house Seigl had inherited from his Steadman relatives, with its expensive if faded furnishings, had long been of little interest to Seigl. Where he can work, there is a writer's home. Where not, not. Seigl had been far more productive as a writer in small, uncomfortable flats in Rome, Paris, London, as a younger man. Material things made little impression upon him except as responsibilities. He quite understood Ludwig Wittgenstein signing away his fortune, the equivalent of millions of dollars, to his siblings.

Seigl noted indentations on the satin bed coverlet. Alma must have sat down here, heavily. Perhaps she'd been tired after all. There was the distinct impress of her buttocks, and the palms of her outspread hands.

Almost, Seigl could hear her breathing.

Later that evening, in the upstairs hall, Seigl would discover Alma's scarf on the floor. It must have slipped from around her neck when she'd hurriedly left the house. The taxi had arrived early, at about 5:55 P.M., the driver had lightly tapped his horn. Alma had been anxious that the taxi might leave without her though Seigl assured her this was hardly likely. "The driver has come to pick you up, Alma. Why would he go away without you?" Seigl was bemused, but Alma continued to hurry, hastily buttoning her coat, descending the stone steps as if eager to escape.

Seigl lifted the long narrow gauzy scarf, made of layers of a cheap cobwebby rose fabric, to his nose, to smell. Whatever this scent was, it was Alma's.

3

S HE WAS IN LOVE, had to be. Christ she knew the symptoms.

Wanting to die. Like kicking a junkie habit clawing screaming puking your guts out. And they come in and hose you down, hose the puke and shit down a drain in the concrete floor, you're laying there sprawled naked like part-butchered meat.

He had that effect on her, he'd gotten under her skin. She knew the symptoms.

Wanting to say *Look I have a new life now, I have a job. I have a place to go. Where I am treated with respect. I am paid very well.*

Wanting to say *I don't need you. See?*

But she was in love, and wanting to die. Wanting to scream, claw, tear out his throat with her teeth. He hadn't touched her in how many days, she tried to count on her fingers and gave up. Seeing how she might set herself and him on fire dousing with gasoline and dropping a lighted match as she'd seen boys once setting fire to a limping muddied stray dog when she was a little girl and like the boys she would shriek with laughter at his antics in death. *How do you like it now! How do you like it!* She would wish to die herself, to see Dmitri Meatte burning alive.

For he'd sold her more than once and betrayed her.

For he'd kicked her out as of no use to him.

For he wasn't one to forgive.

She would have to beg. She would have to kiss his feet. Yet he would not allow it, he'd kick her away. (As he had done.)

Not allow her to suck his precious cock nor even to touch him as before. As before he'd liked, oh yes hadn't he! And saying she was his beautiful big Alma-doll.

Though she was no doll. She smiled to think!

She wished to tell him she had no further need of him, either. Yet the pleading came into her throat *Dmitri can we talk, don't send me away please, let me in, Dmitri please let me in, I love you, I love love love you Dmitri* and he'd slapped her forbidding her to say his name as if her very mouth defiled his name.

And now she was back, and he was disgusted saying who the fuck wants you, didn't I tell you cunt to get out of here but she had reason to believe he was liking it too that she'd come crawling back, the evidence of the Tattooed Girl's devotion to her lover in the eyes of his friends excited by her, and impressed. *That's Dmitri's girl Alma. The one with the tattoos.*

How many nights ago he'd kicked her out. She'd begun working at the Book Seller, he was furious, hateful. Shutting the door in her face. Opening it, and tossing her things down the stairs. She'd slept in his car in the backseat wrapped in a filthy blanket crying herself to sleep not minding the cold. Proving to him her devotion. Her brain jangled from the crystal meth. Might've been roach poison he gave her. *I love you Dmitri don't send me away, see?—I trust you.*

Men were impressed by devotion, loyalty. A man might be cruel but if you show your trust he will relent.

How many times she'd seen it. In her own family she had seen it. Crystal meth. Ice. Her brain never so alive and alert!

But at a distance she was watching herself curled up inside the blanket hunching her shoulders hugging herself and her face white as bread dough and her mouth slack and ugly, stupid cunt he'd called her, who wants you, who needs you, didn't I tell you stupid cunt this is a warning but he'd only raised his fist to strike, he hadn't hit her it was only words.

So she had reason to think there was hope. In Dmitri's eyes, in his fury that meant he cared for her, there was the connection between them.

What she'd done to provoke him: slipped from him to work at the bookstore for that man Scanlon and now she was working for the Jew Seigl with the whiskers and cane. And she would not make the money he wished her to make.

In Akron Valley there'd been no Jews, not a one.

No Jew would live in such a place only left-behind white trash was that it?

If you traced it back far enough, not whose names were on the mines but who actually owned the mines, these were banks, the international conspiracy of Jew-banks, you'd discover it's Jews. She had not needed Dmitri Meatte to tell her about Jews.

How do you know, well you know. She was twenty-seven years old and no child. Things you know like you know the earth is round, the sun is in the sky and going round and round in the darkness of space in a weird distended circle causing the seasons to occur, winter to last a long time at the poles of the earth, summer to last longer at the equator.

None of this you can observe with your eyes but you know. Even if they didn't tell you in school (and she couldn't remember if they'd told her in school, she'd missed so many days) you know. It's part of what you know. The air you breathe in like the poisoned air rising in white smoke-plumes out of the cracked earth and deep inside the earth the mines burning. There were jokes on the radio, wisecracks about Akron Valley: Hellfire PA. But people lived there because it was their home. *Akron is where I live* she'd say (though it wasn't true really, she hadn't been back in years and was not welcome there) causing people to smile. For men like to smile, and men like to laugh.

A Jew is a despised thing her grandfather had said screwing up his burnt-looking face to spit, and Alma said, Why? and he said, Because they are accursed of God and man, and Alma said, Why? for sincerely she wished to know, and her grandfather said, vague but angry, Jews killed Christ. Judas killed Christ, he was a Jew. And so she would set her heart against the Jew though he had been kind to her and had not touched her not even her hair that it was rare for men not to straggle their dirty fingers into, Mr. Seigl hadn't touched her though she had seen his strange black shiny eyes like marbles moving onto her. And the faint tremors he'd tried to hide in his hands.

And him standing outside the door watching her. For a long time it seemed but maybe no more than two or three minutes. Seeing if she was working hard? Or just seeing *her*?

Her grandfather said, It's in the Bible, all you need to know. About Jews and anything else.

Alma thought, A Jew is no different from anybody else except by accident maybe. Like being born in Akron Valley not twenty miles away in Erie, or Pittsburgh. Or Poland, or Saudi Arabia. It was a clear piercing thought but she had nowhere to take it, not to her scowling grandpa who was anyway near-blind, both his eyes milky.

Saying now, to make Dmitri who was sullen and sulky and disgusted with her love her again, as in high school she'd tried to make boys love her who'd gone out with her once, twice, three times then dropped her by saying weird wild things that flew into her head, anything to snag their straying attention, "Guess what? He said he had some sickness. 'Medical condition' he said. This cane he has . . ."

Dmitri laughed crudely. "Maybe AIDS. From sucking too many cocks."

Dmitri frowned at Alma's information, though. She knew, Mr. Seigl was a favorite customer of Dmitri's at The Café. Dmitri was mad as hell if another waiter waited on him. The Jew left big tips, he was a big friendly guy, it went against what you were led to believe of the race but maybe that was the point. Some kind of play-acting.

"See? He paid me for the day. Cash."

Her hand trembled held out for Dmitri to see. To take.

The bills she'd counted in the taxi. Fifty-dollar bills, twenty-dollar bills, she'd laughed in childish excitement. Seigl had given her money after just the first day's work. The first day of the week.

Dmitri shrugged. His eyes hooded like a snake's but he was looking, she had his attention now.

"Why tell me? What the fuck do I care?"

Alma said, hearing her voice beg, "But it's for you, honey, see? I want you to have it."

"Chump change."

Dmitri snatched the bills from her hand. His squeezed-together handsome face beat hot with resentful blood. The Tattooed Girl was his to sell across the river, and she'd eluded him.

Carelessly he counted the bills. Peeled off two twenties to toss at Alma and pocketed the rest. There was a certain swagger in his gesture for the benefit of his friends, one of them a gray-haired ponytailed ex–drug dealer now a parolee from Attica, mending his ways and hoping to "break into" the restaurant business like Dmitri.

Seeing this, sensing a shift in mood, Alma rejoiced that Dmitri loved her again or anyway would allow her to stay the night. And she would be friendly to his friends, that was understood.

Drawing near him now radiant-faced and sexy like a big slinky cat, where he lay sprawled on the sofa smoking a joint.

One of Dmitri's stinky Moroccan joints, he called them.

Alma said, in her scratchy pleading voice, "Know what I could do, honey?"

Dmitri shrugged, exhaling smoke.

"I could get him to like me. The Jew."

"Bullshit."

"I could! I know I could."

"Baby, you're not Seigl's type."

"What's his type?"

"He wouldn't even fuck you."

"Why not? What's his type?"

"A woman with class. Money."

"A Jewess? You think he'd only fuck a Jew-ess?"

Alma spat the word "Jew-ess." It was a word she'd never before uttered in her lifetime.

Dmitri and his friends laughed, the Tattooed Girl had become, so suddenly, so incensed.

"No," Dmitri said. "But she'd have to have class. He wouldn't screw around with anybody on a lower level."

"I could make him like me. I can make any man like me."

Wanting to say, He feels sorry for me. That's my way in.

The men were laughing at this. Not derisively but, Alma wished to think, appreciatively. Dmitri allowed her to tug at his hand, to bring the joint to her lips. She sucked deep, and held the smoke. Smiled to think of it seeping into her brain, her blood. The sweetest sensation, like love.

Alma said, "See, I could make him trust me. He trusts me now, he doesn't know me. He's smart, but stupid. I could steal things from that house of his, he'd never know."

Suddenly it was clear to her: all she might accomplish.

Dmitri said derisively, "Hell, you'd get caught. Seigl is a Jew, he's got eyes in the back of his head."

"Maybe for other people. But not 'Alma.'"

Alma fumbled through her shoulder bag for something she'd brought for Dmitri. Folded and slipped into her bag and how could Seigl know it was gone? Never.

Dmitri snatched it from her hand and opened it.

Dear Joshua Seigl,

Thank you.

The Shadows is a book of beauty and terror. My mother's people died in Treblinka. You have told their story though you never knew them. You touch our hearts. Such memories belong to us all.

Dmitri said, disgusted, "Jews! More Jews. Always the same Jew bullshit. It's *old*."

He crumpled the note-card and tossed it onto the floor.

Alma licked her lips that felt parched. Slyly she said, "It's just to show you. He has so much he doesn't know of."

4

IN EARLY DECEMBER the call came, that Seigl had been dreading for weeks. His sister's intimate, accusing, near-hysterical voice in his ear. "Joshua! Do you have—anything to tell me?"

These were Jet's first words. Not "hello"—not "how are you"—not "am I disturbing you?" Seigl cursed himself for answering the ringing phone; he'd been expecting a call from his neurologist's office.

"Is this Jet?"

"Who else! Who else but your sister! Your sister you have banished from your life out of—guilt? Shame?"

Seigl shut his eyes. Already he could feel his temples throb.

Steroid rage: now it would hit him.

Jet must have been calling from Palm Beach, Florida. More than a thousand miles away yet Seigl would swear, the woman was crouched beside him clawing at his arm.

As, as a girl, she'd tugged at him, whispered in his ear, dared to flaunt herself partly dressed (in panties and bra, an unbuttoned shirt flapping open) in the doorway of his room he'd hoped to block against her.

"Josh? Don't you dare hang up! I need to know: do you have anything to tell me?"

Seigl tried to speak calmly. Damned if he was going to be drawn into a quarrel with his sister, at such a time. (Midday. A chilly light flooding the dining room where Seigl was working with books and papers spread out luxuriantly before him. How good he'd been feeling, blissful in his slow dogged translating while in another part of the house his sweet girl-assistant Alma Busch labored to put his life in order.)

" 'Anything to t-tell you'—that's an unusually aggressive way of initiating a conversation even for you, Jet, isn't it?"

There. Seigl had managed to speak coolly, though under duress.

It was his public manner: taking questions from an audience after he'd given a reading or a lecture. Polite, but giving not an iota to any challenger.

But Jet fired back, immediately. Jet, too, was quick with one-liners, honed in a lifetime of zestful vengeful repartee and quarrel.

"Oh? 'Passive-aggressive' is more your mode, yes? That favored strategy of brilliant neurotic males."

Seigl sighed. Wouldn't defend himself. His mouth twisted softly in imitation of his dead father.

Jet spoke rapidly, passionately. Oh, she was angry with him: and she was right to be angry. Seigl could envision his sister's golden basilisk eyes. The madness shining like liquid flame in those eyes. Yet her primly sculpted mouth was controlled, even rigid. She would hold herself taut and erect as a cobra maneuvering to strike. "I can't sleep for worrying why you haven't called, Joshua. Why you've been so distant. A love affair maybe, I'd been thinking: 'Another of Josh's futile romances, with starry-eyed women he leaves broken by the wayside, like discarded bottles.' I've been dreaming about you, as I know you know. But now I've heard from"—Jet named an older female relative who lived in Rochester, hardly the informant Seigl might have guessed—"that you're in an 'emergency situation.' You need help. And I had better fly up there to be with you."

Seigl's heart clenched. God damn.

All he'd been dreading for weeks, Jet was pouring into his ear like molten lead.

" 'Emergency situation'? Jet, what the hell—?"

"I think you know."

"I—don't know."

Guiltily Seigl thought: my illness.

No: it must be Alma.

To Seigl's dismay, news of his unlikely young female assistant had spread through Carmel Heights. Seigl knew that Scanlon, infuriated that Seigl had stolen Alma from him, was telling customers at his store, with an air of incredulity and reproach, for some of these crude remarks had made their way back to Seigl. *Stupid but sexy. No brains but a great body. Frankly I'm disillusioned with Seigl. I expected better of that man.* Some of Seigl's male friends, calling him about other matters, had made allusions to his "new assistant" and asked after his "new project" with heavy-handed emphasis. There was an ongoing mythology of Seigl as a Don Juan, on a reduced scale, since it did seem to be the case that women fell in love with him, and now these remarks embarrassed and incensed him, and he could only stammer that there was nothing to such ridiculous rumors, and hang up the phone. Seigl hated it that people talked of him behind his back, and dealt with the predicament as he dealt with most predicaments: by banishing the thought from his mind.

Even Sondra Blumenthal had called. Innocently, inquiring after Seigl's "progress" with Virgil.

Seigl said, in his driest voice, "Jet, there's nothing remotely wrong here. It's been a quiet morning until now, I'm working on Book II of the *Aeneid*. I'm thirty-eight years old, not eighteen. My private life is my own business. I assure you that I'm not in the habit of leaving women by the wayside like broken bottles, any more than I'm in the habit of leaving broken bottles by the wayside. And it really isn't an ideal time for you to visit." Seeing with curiosity that his left hand was trembling as if minute electric currents were running through it.

Jet said, suddenly pleading, "But I could help you, Joshua. I could put myself in your service. For the sake of the family."

Seigl ground his teeth. The family! Here was the old blackmail tactic, old as Time. And how perverse that his sister who'd behaved selfishly through much of her life should make such claims now.

Seigl said, "It's very kind of you, Jet. You've made that offer in the past." *My brother the literary genius. When will the second great novel appear, all the world is awaiting!* "But you have your own life, too. Your own responsibilities."

Was this so? Seigl had long given up trying to calculate his sister's operatic personal life.

All he was reasonably certain of was that she hadn't married a multi-millionaire Cuban-American to whom she'd been engaged, or almost-engaged, for several years; and she was living in a "palatial" Palm Beach residence, with an older female relative, a rich widow for whom Jet was something of a companion.

Well, maybe Seigl wasn't certain even of this. With Jet, you never knew.

She said, "Joshua, *no*. Nothing in my life matters in the slightest compared to you. You're Joshua Moses Seigl. Mother made me promise . . . I mean, I promised Mother, voluntarily. We've had our disagreements, Josh, but you are my only brother, in fact you're the only person in the world I really care about. You've been critical of my life, I know, I too am critical of my life, but my therapies have taught me to confront the truth, however painful, and this is what I know, *I put my faith in you*. Especially since—"

Since their parents' deaths, Jet was going to say. Seigl knew.

It was the singular hold his sister had on him: his guilt.

For Seigl hadn't been able to grieve much for his parents. Not as you'd expect a normal son to grieve. Nor was he a hypocrite, to have pretended. While Jet, formerly Mary Beth, who'd caused both their parents heartbreak, was devastated by their father's death, and plunged into a serious, suicidal depression by their mother's death; a showy sort of grief that had involved a brief hospitalization and prolonged visits with relatives, yet, Seigl was inclined to think, sincere enough. For even narcissists grieve: perhaps narcissists grieve most profoundly, losing those who'd existed to love them and to mirror their exaggerated sense of self-worth.

Seigl missed his parents, often. Especially his father. He'd loved them both. Especially the reticent, mysterious Karl Seigl who'd been sent as a child to the New World, to escape the Old World, but in the journey seemed to have lost his childhood, as he'd lost his family for whom there could be no recompense. But Seigl, by temperament a Stoic, couldn't escape the conviction that when elderly parents die natural deaths after prolonged illnesses, no one has cause to feel that injustice has been done.

Karl Seigl had insisted as much, during the final weeks of his decline. Almost, he'd seemed happy. *To live to be eighty-one, a miracle. To be granted life at all.*

Still, Seigl felt guilty, often. He should have mourned more: he should have made his parents happier while they'd been alive.

Jet said, "You owe it to them, Joshua. To all of us. Your legacy. Our future. I'll come help you. You're too proud to admit how weak you are, how you need help."

The cobra in her unerring strike. Seigl cringed.

"Jet, please. This is very upsetting. This is emotional blackmail, I refuse to be blackmailed by you. I refuse—"

"What you can't accept, Joshua, is that your sister loves you. I'm the only living person now who loves you. Maybe you can delude yourself, women are attracted to you, very likely you have a woman now, or women, those pathetic Ph.D.s mooning after Joshua Seigl, their own husbands have long ago left them for younger women, but these affairs come to nothing, as I certainly know." Jet paused, draw-ing breath for the final line of her aria. "My plane, from Miami, ar-rives at the airport there tomorrow at 1:08 P.M."

Before Seigl could howl in protest, Jet hung up.

"MR. SEIGL?"

Hesitantly, Alma stood in the doorway.

Seigl was sitting with his head in his hands. His shoulders felt massive to him, muscle-locked with rage. How long he'd been here hunched forward at the dining room table since Jet had hung up the phone, trying to think what he would do, how he would deal with this invasion, Seigl couldn't have said.

Someone was speaking in a hushed scratchy voice. He looked up, frowning. There was his assistant Alma Busch informing him that she'd prepared lunch . . .

Thank God, Seigl hadn't yet asked Alma to answer his phone for him. The collision of Jet and Alma was too painful to contemplate.

"Not for me, Alma. Thank you. But please stop for lunch your-self, you've been working for hours." Seigl pushed himself to his feet. He wasn't feeling so blissful now. Some of his scrawled-upon work sheets had fallen to the floor, but it was too much effort to re-trieve them. Without explanation he lurched from the dining room leaving his assistant to stare after him, perplexed.

What he'd do: call Jet back, and order her to cancel her flight.

God damn if he'd allow her to interfere with his life when his life, at last, was going so well.

NEXT DAY, there was Seigl driving to the airport to meet his sis-ter's flight. Had she said 1:08 P.M.?

Somehow, during the night, in his exhausting parched-mouth

dreams of guilt, anxiety, and elation, Seigl must have had a change of heart.

This was like him: God damn!

Thinking it over he'd been touched by Jet's concern. True, his sister was morbidly possessive of him; as she'd been, intermittently through her life, of numerous other individuals, most of them men. Hadn't one of Jet's lovers, years ago, been so desperate to escape her he'd fled to—was it Tangier? (Where he'd died in mysterious circumstances, stabbed to death in a drug deal gone wrong.) But Jet was probably right. *I'm the only living person now who loves you.*

The remark was subtly insulting, but it was like Jet to insult even as she meant to flatter.

Seigl understood: life was careening past Jet, suddenly. She'd had love affairs but had never married, and had no child. Always she'd been young: now she was middle-aged. Always she'd been spoiled, vain, seductive, strikingly beautiful, charismatic. In adolescence, she'd been considered brighter than Joshua, only just too restless and "temperamental" to do well in school. And she'd gone to several schools, each of them an expensive private school where she'd gotten into trouble, and gotten others into trouble. More times than Seigl could recall, Jet had been deeply—tragically?—in love. Always there was something wrong with her lovers. They loved her too much, or not enough; they were as mercurial and unreliable as she was, or deadly dull, predictable. They were married, and refused to leave their families; they were married, and overly eager to leave their families. At least one had had a chronic illness. (Seigl wondered now if it had been, ominously, a nerve disease.) One had allegedly beaten and raped Jet when she'd tried to break up with him, causing Jet to fight him back in self-defense, stabbing him eleven times and inflicting "shallow, non-life-threatening" wounds; eventually, charges against both parties were dropped. (This alarming incident had occurred when Jet was in her mid-twenties, living in a loft on Varick

Street, Manhattan, with the lover, a cabaret performer; Seigl had been traveling in Europe.) Apart from the lover whom Jet had stalked and caused to flee to Tangier to die, there'd been at least one suicide.

Seigl smiled uneasily, thinking of these matters. He wasn't one to think about family problems, he wasn't one to have felt himself much involved. A bachelor, by temperament. Yet there was the bond between himself and Jet. They were soul mates, Jet had claimed. Some observers had believed them twins, in childhood; by the age of ten, Joshua was the size of his sister, who was two years older; certain of their facial features were similar, their mannerisms and dark springy hair. But Jet had grown into a willowy, sulkily beautiful girl while Joshua had become a plumpish, good-natured and affable boy, easily dominated by his sister. As a young adolescent, Joshua had seemed middle-aged; now in middle age, he seemed boyish, naive. Ridiculous to think that he and Jet were soul mates, still more that they'd ever been mistaken for twins.

. . . *the only living person now who loves you.*

Seigl thought, in protest: but there is Alma.

That is, there is the possibility of Alma.

The last time he'd picked Jet up at the Rochester airport had been nearly six years ago, when their mother was hospitalized and dying. Jet had made up her quarrel with their mother but after the funeral she'd quarreled with Seigl, bitterly. She had wanted to remain in Carmel Heights with him, living in his house on the Hill and acting as his caretaker, hostess, literary assistant, muse. *Joshua, you can't live alone. No more than Daddy could have: You have a tragic soul.*

At the airport, Seigl parked his car in a high-rise garage and made his way across a pedestrian bridge into the terminal. With new security regulations, he couldn't wait for Jet at the gate but at baggage claim; she wouldn't know Seigl had come for her, and would have some minutes to regret her outburst on the telephone. Damned if he would be blackmailed by his sister's emotions, Seigl thought.

In the terminal, amid so many fast-walking individuals, Seigl was conscious of walking with a slight limp, as if he'd strained a tendon. In his khaki jeans and corduroy jacket, his Irish tweed cap on his stiff springy hair, he resembled a fortyish ex-athlete, tall and broad-shouldered with a thick torso and thighs and a way of holding himself that was alert, vigilant. In the heedless past Seigl would have strode along the walkways brooding and indifferent to others; now he was cautious not to collide with anyone, for he couldn't risk being jarred or injured. He'd left his cane in the car. (In the trunk, not the backseat where Jet would see it.) In mirrors and reflecting surfaces along the concourse he had glimpses of his fleeting likeness, the bristling whiskers, flushed skin and deep-set searing eyes.

You wouldn't single out such an individual, Seigl thought, as suffering from a mysterious nerve disease.

The plane from Miami was delayed by forty minutes. Seigl waited apprehensively. He knew it was absurd but he'd begun to worry about the flight. If something should happen to Jet . . . Seigl knew he wouldn't feel relief. Nor would he have felt as he'd felt when his parents died, that nothing unnatural or unjust had occurred. Jet was young still, only just forty years old. Maybe she hoped to begin her life anew, as Seigl was hoping for himself.

At last the plane landed, without incident. Seigl realized he'd been clenching his fists, lightly sweating. What was happening to him? He'd become a mass, a mess of psychosomatic symptoms. He who was urged to think so highly of himself! He waited expectantly as passengers began to swarm into the baggage claim area. Jet would certainly have flown first-class and should have been among the first passengers to appear. Seigl was trying to prepare a plausible defense of his choice of an assistant: why he'd hired someone barely educated . . . He wondered if he could forestall Jet meeting Alma. Or explain Alma away as a cleaning woman . . .

"Joshua."

Seigl couldn't at first locate who had spoken his name. The

woman's voice was low, throaty, elated. Out of a crowd of strangers the figure rushed at him with her arms outspread, like an elegantly black-garbed bird of prey, claiming him, hugging him hard. His confused impression was of a glamorous woman with dark-tinted sunglasses and a cherry-red cloche hat pulled down onto her forehead. Was this Jet? But how could Jet, who was older than Seigl, look so much younger?

"Josh! Act like you hardly recognize me, your own *sister*." Jet laughed accusingly, kissing Seigl wetly at the edge of his startled mouth.

Like ashes, Jet tasted. A smell of cigarette smoke on her breath.

Seigl stammered, "Jet, hello. You're looking—wonderful."

Jet's arms around Seigl were unexpectedly strong. She pressed her warm cheek against his chest as if she'd stumbled into his arms out of a situation of grave danger. There was an explosive smell of expensive perfume. Jet drew back, and removed her dark glasses in a sweeping gesture. Her eyes were uncannily like Seigl's though not so dark, shiny as if laminated with a golden-tawny film, and thickly lashed; of course, Seigl realized she'd outlined her eyes in mascara, the lashes were separate and darkly bold as a spider's legs. Her lipstick was a dark purple-red suggestive of the retrograde 1940s, sexy and sullen, ironic. Her hair beneath the stylish cloche hat had been smartly scissor-cut and lightened, streaked with ash. Her appearance suggested a costume, selected with care: layers of fine dark wool cashmere, kidskin gloves and shoes with spike heels that looked, to Seigl's uneasy male eye, dangerous as hooves.

In her husky smoker's voice Jet was saying, marveling, "But— you look very well, Joshua. You drove to the airport—by youself?"

Jet stared at Seigl, perplexed. Afterward, recalling this awkward moment, Seigl would wonder if his sister hadn't felt cheated, just slightly.

It was then that Seigl realized: it hadn't been the issue of his assistant that so upset Jet, but the issue of his health after all.

His health! And he'd believed he had kept his secret so guarded.

Annoyed, Seigl said certainly he'd driven to the airport by himself, why not? He wasn't sick. He wasn't crippled. Hadn't he tried to explain on the phone, there was no "emergency" in his life?

Jet continued to stare at him searchingly. Half-consciously she fumbled in her handbag for a pack of cigarettes. She said, "Yes, but you so rarely tell the full truth, Josh. You're like an enigmatic character in a play. I have to read between your lines, and you're so sparing with your lines."

Seigl had to concede, this might be true. It never failed to surprise him, when they confronted each other, that his sister was so astute a judge of his character, while she seemed, in myriad other ways, so blind. Yet, he guessed it was with Jet as with many women of a contemporary type, who took their cues from stylized and exaggerated images of female behavior in the media: you never knew what was genuine, and what was invented. As a sexually precocious adolescent in the mid-1970s Jet had several times threatened to do violence to herself and others, and her parents had had to act upon the assumption that, yes Jet might be serious. (In boarding school she'd allegedly attempted suicide by swallowing two dozen barbiturates washed down with vodka, so many pills, so much vodka, she'd vomited everything back up within minutes.) Seigl had his doubts: he'd always believed that Jet was far too intelligent to mean much of what she said, but might be testing the limits of others' credulity.

Playacting at exaggeration', hysteria. But a face can take on the contours of the mask pressed against it.

Jet raked her eyes from Seigl's feet, in waterstained jogging shoes that contrasted pointedly with her own stylish shoes, to his face, which was flushed with annoyance. She said, bluntly, "I've been told that you walk with a cane now, like an old man."

Seigl said, furious, "Who told you that?"

Within seconds, a sister-brother squabble. For there is no one with whom we can squabble, bitterly, ignominiously, absurdly, like a sibling.

"I've been led to believe that you've had some sort of 'medical crisis,' Joshua. That's why I'm here. I need to see for myself what is going on. You have seen a neurologist for tests, haven't you?"

Seigl was still smarting from the remark about the cane. That fucking cane! He said belligerently, "That's my business."

"But—is it true?"

Jet clutched at his arm anxiously. She didn't seem to be play-acting but genuine. Her look of alarm unnerved Seigl: it was the alarm he hadn't wished to acknowledge in himself.

"I won't have you interfering in my life, Jet. I've warned you."

Baggage from the flight began to tumble onto the circular belt. Jet pointed out her several suitcases, and bulky suitcases they were, which Seigl retrieved for her. He smiled: how like his sister to allow another to perform a task for her, though that other was said to be unwell.

As they left the terminal Seigl remained silent, annoyed. He paid little attention as Jet spoke rapidly, animatedly of her life in Palm Beach, her dissatisfaction with her living arrangements. He would have liked to rudely interrupt to ask how long she planned on staying in Carmel Heights but knew he wouldn't get a direct answer. And very likely Jet didn't know, just yet. Her campaigns were mostly improvised.

Seigl had to grant, his sister was a vivid presence. That large medallion face, her taut smooth skin glowing with a fierce interior heat. Seigl, too, in positions of authority, on a stage for instance, commanded attention, but in this public place, on the walkway, it was Jet at whom strangers stared with interest. Who's that? A TV face? As if, carrying herself so extravagantly, Jet had to be a celebrity. There was something brutal and yet innocent about her, you were drawn to admire even as you disapproved. Jet had been the sort of child to squeeze a small pet to death, then weep inconsolably over the death.

Seigl wasn't sure if he loved Jet. He was more certain, he feared the woman.

"Jet" who'd emerged from "Mary Beth" when she was fifteen. Insisting upon the new name which was her true name, given to her centuries ago in another lifetime, as the Hebrew "Jetimah."

Of course this had to be magical thinking. Metaphorical thinking.

You did not, if you were the concerned parents of such a daughter, want to believe that it might be literal thinking for this was to admit that your daughter might be mad.

In the waning years of the twentieth century, when distinctions of *sanity* and *madness* were being recklessly, even gaily denied.

At twenty-one, Jet legally changed her name to "Jetimah Steadman-Seigl." There was a time when she spoke provocatively of herself as a "Jewess." It gave her power, she claimed: the power of inverted Jew-hatred.

Seigl had asked his sister what that was: the "power of inverted Jew-hatred." Jet said defensively that those who hate us hate us because they believe that we're dangerous in some way. That danger, or the possibility of it, gives us "power" over them. And so, to anti-Semites, Jews possess power.

Even if, as Jet conceded, with little-girl coquetry, she wasn't in fact a "Jewess."

(Both Joshua and Jet had been baptized by their mother in the Presbyterian church in Carmel Heights in which, many years before, she had herself been baptized. Their father had avoided the topic of religion as one who has nearly died of food poisoning might avoid eating the specific food that has nearly killed him; yet he'd believed, as Seigl did, that the warring distinctions between religions have their biological origins in the wish to survive and to conquer, and are at the heart of much of human tragedy.)

As Jet's younger brother, Joshua had been eclipsed by her through their childhood and adolescence. In that way, he'd been spared the over-zealous attention of their mother. He had made his own, somewhat idiosyncratic way, not neglected, only just not scrutinized by his parents. He'd never gotten into trouble at school, he'd been a friendly good-natured boy well-liked by his classmates and his teachers; he'd earned high grades without excessive work or worrying. By contrast, Jet had always merited concern. You could no more ignore Jet that you could ignore a screeching child.

Her first psychiatrist, to whom she'd been taken by her desperate parents when she was fourteen, had described her rather flatteringly as highly intelligent and imaginative but unstable: a "border-line" personality. Her second psychiatrist, to whom she was taken after the apparent suicide attempt, identified her problems as biochemical in origin, and diagnosed her, with gratifying trendiness, as "bipolar." In her early twenties when Jet had been lavishly involved with drugs and had precipitated several violent episodes in Manhattan, she'd been diagnosed as "latent paranoid schizophrenic." ("Schizophrenic"! That wasn't so flattering.) Each of these diagnoses had involved medications, of course. Pharmacological poisoning, Jet called it: "A kind of genocide afflicted upon free souls by the rest of shackled mankind."

It had long been Seigl's opinion that his sister behaved impulsively because it attracted attention of a kind Jet would not otherwise attract, and because, with her good looks and personality, she could get away with it. Even her stabbing of a lover had been explained away, and eventually dismissed with the excuse that she was "under psychiatric care." Jet was vain, self-centered, spoiled; skilled at manipulating others as a puppeteer. Yet, weirdly, you were drawn to her: you wanted Jet to like you.

After an episode at boarding school when Jet, then sixteen, had precipitated the dismissal of a thirty-year-old music instructor, and the breakup of his marriage, Seigl recalled her gloating over the sympathetic attention she was receiving. She'd told him, "I do what I want to do, Josh. What I want to do I do. Try it."

Seigl shuddered recalling these words. *What I want to do I do.*

Watching his sister now, as, making his way up escalators and across the pedestrian bridge to his car, Seigl was trying not to limp. Watching her covertly, yet with a kind of admiration. He knew how Jet would seize upon the smallest evidence of weakness in him. He had shrewdly worked out beforehand how he would spare Jet seeing his cane, by placing her suitcases in the backseat of the car. More effort, but worth it. He then lowered himself into the driver's seat carefully as one might lower a heavy, dead weight while, fortunately for him, Jet rummaged through her expensive handbag too preoccupied to take note.

As if she'd been overhearing Seigl's thoughts, Jet said suddenly, "You see, Josh, compared to your life, your accomplishments and talent, my life is trivial. I've long been deluded. Until Daddy died, and Mother, and the veil was ripped away from my eyes, and I saw. Never do we see so clearly as at the death of a parent."

Seigl mumbled something vaguely sympathetic. This was an extravagant claim, typical of his sister. But maybe she meant it.

As they drove from the airport, Jet lowered the window beside her and lit a cigarette. She hadn't thought of asking Seigl if he minded; or if he'd have liked to smoke with her. She said, "I want us to collaborate, Joshua. My destiny is a simple one: to aid you in fulfilling your destiny. We can collaborate. Of course, my name wouldn't appear on any book of yours. My dream is a sequel to *The Shadows* bringing the story of the survivors—and their children—into this new century. Looking forward as well as back. We owe it to the memory of our father and his people, and to ourselves. We are all Holocaust survivors."

Seigl gritted his teeth. What utter absolute bullshit.

"I know, you're offended with me. You're very sensitive about your work. But I've had such premonitions about you lately, Joshua. I've been in fear of . . ." Jet's voice trailed off ominously. "You seem to have lost faith in your talent. Or the courage of youth, which comes to the same thing."

"You know all about me, don't you? I'm a transparency held up to the light."

"Don't be sarcastic. That was your adolescent defense, as painful as acne."

Acne! Seigl was forced to recall his broken-out, boiled-looking face. Pimples the size of boils on his cheeks and neck. A few scars remained, hidden by his beard.

Adulthood was itself a kind of beard, a shield held up before him. And here was his sister plucking and pulling at it, threatening to expose him.

Seigl said, "Jet, *The Shadows* belongs to the past. The young man who wrote it is no more. I think now that we have no right to appropriate the Holocaust. We're two generations removed. We're Americans, for Christ's sake. It's sick."

There was another reason, too. But Seigl wasn't about to share this reason with his impassioned sister.

"Sick! You're the one who's sick, to say such things! This is our heritage, Joshua. Our duty. In America, we have every right to our own family history. Jewish and gentile combined. It's our way of honoring the—deceased."

Seigl was touched: his sister couldn't bear to utter the blunt word *dead*.

"Jet, you'll have to write your own morbid history. I'm trying to get out from under my own."

Jet said, hurt, "That's ridiculous. You're Karl Seigl's son. You know what his history was. His family. Hundreds of thousands of families! And Daddy adored you, he had such faith in you, Joshua. As he never had in me. You can't 'get out from under' your destiny."

"I've told you, I have my work. I care deeply about my work. I'm involved in translating—"

"Anyone can translate some old Greek—Latin?—poem! But not anyone can write a sequel to *The Shadows*."

Seigl thumped both hands against the steering wheel. He

laughed, incredulous. "Jet, that remark has got to be one of the most ignorant, uninformed—"

"—truth! It's the truth, and you know it."

Seigl drove in silence. Better not to reply.

Always it was like this: in Jet, you confronted not a storm of wayward emotions but a fierce and implacable will disguised as a moral principle, tightly wound as a cyclone at its base.

A little later, Jet tried another tack. Her voice was subdued, pleading. "Joshua? Don't be angry with me. I only want to know: *is* something wrong with you?"

Seigl refused to answer.

"You haven't seen a—neurologist? At the medical school?"

Seigl drove in silence. He'd swung along the lake shore, wanting to take a circuitous route to Carmel Heights. The winter sky was ridged with storm clouds like rippled, sullied cement. A north wind rocked the car. Jet blew her nose, as if she'd been weeping. She said, not as a question but as a statement, "The name 'Morris Friedman' means nothing to you."

Seigl gripped the steering wheel tighter. He drove on, unable to speak. His bones were dissolving to water with the shock of what he believed must be betrayal.

But who had told Jet? Surely not Friedman? Wasn't that a violation of medical protocol?

After a tense several minutes Seigl heard himself say, "Nerves quite literally fray in some people. No one knows why."

" 'Nerves'?"

" 'Sclerosis,' it's called. A scarring of the insulating tissue that covers the nerve fibers."

Seigl felt his sister stiffen. Sclerosis?

He waited for her to utter the dread term *multiple sclerosis.*

But Jet surprised him, only asking if his condition had yet been diagnosed.

"No. I'm 'inconclusive.' "

A coughing sound issued from Seigl's throat, which was feeling raw as sandpaper. Possibly the sound was laughter, or a muffled sob.

Abruptly, Seigl was telling Jet about his symptoms of the past several weeks. Falling in Mount Carmel Cemetery. Dizziness, weakness in his limbs. Double vision. The battery of tests, the steroid tablets. The possibility of "remission." All that he'd vowed he would not, he was telling the very person he vowed he would not tell, and Jet was listening with a bowed head, not interrupting for once. Serious illness, death, the exigencies of love: only for these would Jet remain silent, respectful.

What relief Seigl felt, telling Jet. What relief to confide in another person. He hadn't realized how lonely he'd been. And how frightened of what was to come.

Without speaking, Jet reached out to squeeze Seigl's hand on the steering wheel. She'd removed her kidskin gloves. Her fingers were reassuringly warm, and strong.

Seigl exited the expressway in a blur of emotion. For a confused moment he hardly knew where he was, and what time this was: he might have been driving his sister to the hospital to see their mother in intensive care. Or: was it their father who'd been hospitalized, and would never return home again.

In a fierce whisper Jet said, "Whatever it is that's happening to you, I love you, Joshua, and I'll take care of you."

Seigl thought, No you won't. I have other plans.

Jet said, fumbling to light another cigarette, " 'Nerves.' 'Sclerosis.' It would explain so much."

"In what way?"

"If you had a condition of the nervous system. Like MS."

"Explain what, to whom?"

"My own life, to me. How my life has unraveled."

Seigl laughed. "Unfortunately it won't explain anything, since you don't have my symptoms and are not me."

"But, Joshua, I have the seeds of—whatever it is. These things are inherited."

"In fact, no. They are not inherited."

"Yes, certainly they are. Everything pre-exists in our genes which we inherit at conception. All that we are destined."

"Like the fortunes in Chinese cookies, eh?"

"You joke out of anxiety. Freud said, 'The ego is the seat of anxiety.' Your egocentric soul won't allow you to imagine that another person, even your own sister, your soul mate, might share in your destiny."

Jet spoke with childlike solemnity, assurance. Seigl heard the gloating beneath. He saw that his mad sister wasn't to be dissuaded from sharing in his fate, in fantasy at least.

They began to laugh suddenly. Jet clutched at herself like a young adolescent girl being tickled. The giddy laughter of brother and sister rocked the car.

5

T HE VISIT BEGAN with promise. True, Seigl was fearful of his sister. Yet her company enlivened him, he had to admit. Made him laugh as rarely he laughed these days, even if his laughter was likely to be incredulous, disapproving. But now that Jet knew of his uncertain health, she would be gentler with him. He hoped.

On the way home, Seigl took Jet for lunch at a lakeside seafood restaurant with a dazzling view of leaden-blue choppy Lake Ontario. He listened to her words like surf breaking about him, hearing and not-hearing, thinking yes, of course he loved his sister, he was all that remained for her of their family and it had been selfish of him (if self-protective) to exclude her from his life for so long. Midway in the meal Jet abruptly excused herself to smoke a cigarette outside on the open, windy deck of the restaurant, within view of Seigl at their table inside who was testing the strength in his knees and thighs dreading the imminent climb of the nineteen stone steps to his front door. (In fact, there was another, easier but less attractive way into the house through a side door, but Seigl was reluctant to use this in Jet's presence.) After lunch, Seigl drove past the large white colonial that had been their family home in a hillside neighborhood close by his own; he parked in the roadway so that Jet could gaze at the house through a scrim of evergreens, wiping at her eyes. She appeared to be deeply moved. "Oh, Joshua, I was so happy here. If only I'd known . . ."

Seigl, to whom nostalgia meant little, like brilliant autumn foliage to the color-blind, tried to think of a consoling reply, but could not.

At his house, Seigl managed to ascend the nineteen stone steps carrying two of his sister's suitcases. By the time he reached the top his knees were trembling and there was a roaring in his ears as of a vast derisive crowd but no matter: he reached the top.

When he and Jet entered the house, it was to the reassuring sound of a vacuum cleaner in the living room. And there was Alma in shapeless work clothes, her straw-colored hair tied back in a kerchief and her expression startled. "Jet, this is Alma, who's helping me out these days. Alma, my sister Jet Steadman-Seigl, who's visiting me from Palm Beach." Alma scarcely raised her eyes to Jet's face. She stood mute and abashed, the nozzle of the vacuum cleaner gripped in her hand, as Jet said hello brightly.

They were hardly out of earshot when Jet exclaimed, "That ugly tattoo on her face! The poor thing."

Seigl objected, "But is it a tattoo? A birthmark, I thought."

"No. It's a tattoo. There's more of it on her hands, and at the back of her neck."

"Her *neck?* How do you know?"

"I saw."

Seigl was amazed that in those fleeting seconds his sister had absorbed so much that he, Seigl, hadn't noticed in weeks.

Jet continued to annoy him saying how relieved she was, that he had a cleaning woman to look after the house; she wasn't the only one among the relatives to worry that he might turn "quirky and reclusive" living alone, and let the house fill up with emptied tin cans and old newspapers stacked to the ceiling. Jet meant to be amusing,

Seigl supposed. He said drily, "In fact, there are cartons of papers in my study and in the basement. You won't be disappointed."

Ominously Jet said, "I won't! I want to see everything. I intend to be Joshua Seigl's literary executor, pre-posthumous."

Seigl had ordered a meal from one of the gourmet food stores in town, which Alma had placed in a warm oven before leaving at six o'clock. In the foyer she stood hastily buttoning her cloth coat, retying her kerchief around her head. Jet's presence seemed to have made her more than ordinarily self-conscious. Seigl now paid Alma weekly, though still in cash, but invariably asked if she needed money in the interim. Alma shook her head, no. Yet so insistently, Seigl guessed she didn't mean it. Perhaps she was sending money home: somewhere in rural Pennsylvania, he'd gathered. Much of rural Pennsylvania, like upstate New York, had been in a recession for years. It was clear that Alma was from a poor-white background. The taxi at her disposal took her to Mount Carmel Avenue, presumably to a bus stop; Seigl supposed she must live across the river in the city, where housing was less costly. He had not asked about her living arrangements, for this was none of his business as her employer. "Please. Take this." Seigl pressed two ten-dollar bills into Alma's moist hand. Alma crumpled the bills in her fist as if she were too embarrassed to acknowledge them. On her way out to the waiting taxi she mumbled what sounded like, "Goodnight, Mr. Seigl!"

That evening Jet observed of Seigl's cleaning woman that she was a "strong, solid, earthy type. Like a Ukrainian peasant."

Seigl laughed. "How many Ukrainian peasants do you know, Jet?"

But Jet was in a magnanimous mood. She was willing to laugh at herself, too. The visit to their former house, the news of her brother's medical condition, seemed to have both sobered and gratified her. She took time to set elaborate places for Seigl and herself at the dining room table and lit a half-dozen tall tapering candles; she insisted upon serving Seigl as if she'd prepared the meal herself, and was anxious that it met with his approval. Though Seigl told her he couldn't drink while taking his medication, Jet poured a half-glass of red wine for him anyway. "I can't drink alone. I can't even give the appearance of drinking alone." She spoke as one admitting to a charming eccentricity.

Out of politeness, Seigl lifted his glass and took a small ritual sip of wine. The taste seemed to spring into his mouth like a soft explosion.

Midway in the dinner Jet leaned her elbows on the table to gaze avidly at Seigl. She asked, did he have a woman friend?

Seigl shrugged evasively.

"What does that mean, Joshua?"

"It means that I don't 'have' any women. There are women friends whom I see quite often, but . . ."

"But no romance?"

Seigl was uncomfortable being interrogated. This was why he'd wanted to avoid any intimacy with his sister. Since their parents' deaths she seemed to have swallowed them both up in herself. She was greedy, insatiable. But Seigl's private life had always been private. His sexual life, certainly. Was Sondra Blumenthal a romance? The two had been friends for years. Well, perhaps more than friends. Seigl supposed that he had only to call Sondra. To speak frankly and intimately to her. To touch her hand, stroke her wrist. He had only to bring his mouth to hers . . . But the woman was too much like himself: he felt only affection for her. He dreaded misleading and hurting her. Sondra had the look of one already wounded in love.

And Seigl had to wonder if, these recent weeks, he'd have been sexually potent with a woman. Only in his sleep did he feel anything like sexual desire.

"It isn't good to live alone. How well I know."

Jet poured more wine into their glasses as if she'd forgotten that Seigl wasn't drinking with her. In the candlelight her darkly luminous eyes shone. Her ashy-streaked hair was buoyant. You would not have

guessed that Jet was forty years old for her manner was naively girlish. Before dinner, Seigl had heard his sister speaking on her cell
phone upstairs, animatedly, at times rather sharply. Speaking to a
lover in Palm Beach, perhaps. Seigl felt very little curiosity about his
sister's life. Twenty years ago when Jet began to behave willfully and
self-destructively, he'd learned that it was better not to know.

After dinner, at a time when Seigl would normally be reading and
taking notes in preparation for the next morning, Jet insisted upon
playing chess. Seigl was reluctant, recalling games from years ago
with his sister that had ended badly, in an upset game board and scattered chess pieces. Jet teased, "Not afraid I'll beat you, Josh, are you?
You're the prodigy."

It was true: between the ages of ten and fourteen, Seigl had been
something of a local prodigy. In Chess Club at his school he'd been
the star. At the College of Mount Carmel he'd played with Jesuits
and won. And there was the local coffeehouse where he'd played
with allegedly brilliant players, and won. Karl Seigl had been uneasily
proud of his son: a gift for chess must have been passed on to
Joshua from his grandfather Moses and his great-grandfather Jere-
miah whom he'd never known. As a thirteen-year-old, Joshua had
been entered in several state and national tournaments where he'd
played capably but not brilliantly, as if overwhelmed by the competition and by so much attention. A headline in the Rochester *Sun-
Times*—

13-YEAR-OLD CARMEL HGTS CHESS STAR BURNS OUT
IN NYC TOURNAMENT

had the power a quarter-century later to suffuse him with shame.

It was cruel of Jet to recall Seigl's "prodigy" years. But he supposed she meant no harm.

So they set up the chessboard. It had belonged to their mother's father: made of fitted squares of cherry wood, with exquisitely carved ivory pieces. Seigl had always felt more comfortable playing with cheap plastic pieces. Jet said casually that she'd been playing chess in Florida lately with "diverse Cuban-American friends." Always she'd been an impulsive player, one who trusts in luck. Which Seigl knew to be an illusory ally in chess.

Still, Jet made several inspired moves at the start of the game. He saw what she intended to do beforehand, but her decisions were good ones, and he allowed her to believe that he was taken by surprise, and that he was impressed. "You must be playing chess with some very good players," he said. Jet said, frowning, "Of course. That's how I learn." After a strong opening, however, the game began to move more predictably, and slowly. When Seigl checkmated Jet's king she appeared to be taken wholly by surprise as if both she and Seigl had stumbled into the situation. "It's over? Your side has *won*?" Jet couldn't bring herself to acknowledge that Seigl had won.

"Luck." Seigl spoke with gentle irony.

It would have been wise then to quit for the evening, as Seigl well knew, but Jet insisted upon another game—"To give me a chance to bounce back." The hope was comical and touching and yet Jet played with painstaking seriousness this time, inching a piece forward, moving it back, chewing at a strand of hair like an adolescent girl.

She was punishing him, Seigl sensed, for having won the first game. He had a choice of ending the game within a few moves, or allowing his sister to believe that her chess game was competitive with his; out of a possibly cowardly wish to keep things amiable between them Seigl chose the latter strategy. But he resented it, that his precious reading hours from 9 P.M. to midnight or 1 A.M. were so curtailed.

Jet said suddenly, "This game! I remember now, Joshua. *I dreamt this very game*. Two nights ago."

Seigl could only murmur, surprised, "Did you!"

Jet said, frowning, "You don't believe me? Think I'm 'confabulating'?" She groped for her wineglass without moving her eyes from his as if she dared him to look away in denial.

It must have been a psychiatric term: "confabulating." Not outlight lying, and not exactly fantasizing. But, yes. Seigl supposed that much of Jet's mental life was confabulation.

Jet persisted, in sisterly contentiousness, "Don't you? *Do* you?"

Seigl said, meaning to be conciliatory, "I neither believe nor disbelieve, Jet. I don't know enough." In fact, though the ancients whom Seigl revered took dreams seriously, as vessels of wisdom and warning from the gods, Seigl himself could credit dreams with no more significance than fleeting cloud formations, or the skeins of smoke rising from his sister's annoying cigarette.

Jet said, "It was this game. I remember. Exactly. Don't smirk like that. And don't try to tell me what my own psychic experience *is*. I've had enough of mind-manipulators in my life. And all of them *male*." The bitterness in her voice was unexpected, and revealing.

Seigl moved a chess piece. Three more moves and Jet's queen would be immobilized and her king checkmated and he could escape to the sanctuary of his bedroom to read.

He was midway in a scholarly study of Virgil's metrics. He was relearning much of what he'd once known. To be a translator is to be in perpetual training, for you can never know enough about your subject.

Jet was saying, with an air of pride, "It's *so uncanny*. I dreamt of this exact game. Wish I could see how it ended . . . The pieces are identical, the way they're on the board now. And you and I like this. And yet, we were mixed up with the actual game, somehow. As if we were chess pieces! And there was a female. The queen. There was only one queen in the game. Not Mother but a stranger, someone younger. Her crown was her hair all braided and twined. And her crown was on fire . . . somehow." Jet shuddered. The memory of her dream seemed suddenly to alarm her.

Seigl wasn't following much of this. He was waiting for Jet to make a move, any move. This slow dull game that meant little to him but an annoyance seemed to mean too much to Jet, a danger signal.

Jet persisted, "Your attitude toward dreams, and toward me, is insulting, Joshua. I sense your disdain. But dreams are *real*. They are hardly just smoke, or clouds floating in the sky. What you pretend to believe."

"I do?" Seigl was startled. When had he told Jet his feelings about dreams?

Jet laughed. "Your attitude! So *male!* Passive-aggressive fucking *male*. So superior, and so myopic. The myopia of rationalism."

Jet enunciated the word *rationalism* as if it were a comical obscenity.

Seigl was led into speaking defensively. A big clumsy dumb carp drawn to a baited hook. He said, stammering, "Rationalism is a—a frail vessel against the flood of superstition and barbarism in the world, I grant you. But it's all we have—it's civilization."

"Tell the Nazis about 'rationalism'—'civilization.' The Final Solution."

"Please, Jet, let's not get into this. The Nazis were mad. Europe was gripped in madness." He thought of the book on witchcraft Alma had been paging through in the Book Seller. Centuries before the inflamed collective soul of Europe in the twentieth century.

Seigl had purchased this book, in fact. For Alma. He'd thought that she might learn from it; she was intelligent, surely she had intellectual yearnings. He'd left it downstairs in her room, conspicuously on a table, but she had yet to mention it to him.

Jet said, "A dream *is* a rational event, in code. It's like the alphabet: you must know how to decode it, or you're illiterate."

Seigl said, annoyed, "How can anyone possibly know whether dreams 'mean' anything, let alone what they might mean?"

Jet stared at Seigl incredulously. "You don't believe in *Freud*? You don't believe in the *unconscious*?"

Seigl laughed. "Freud and the 'unconscious' are hardly identical."

Now Jet launched into a spirited defense of Freud. She spoke fiercely, if not altogether coherently. She groped for her nearly empty wineglass and would have overturned it if Seigl hadn't prevented her. She'd been drinking red wine more or less continuously since dinner and was obviously drunk and becoming dangerous. An addictive personality, one of Jet's doctors had labeled her.

And very likely, Seigl thought, Jet herself was taking medication. Tranquilizers, anti-depressants. Fashionable prescription drugs in place of the outlaw street drugs she'd experimented with years ago. She'd become addicted to therapies, psychoanalytic jargon and psychobabble, in place of religion perhaps. To Jet, this was a kind of religion. All this fed into her inflated sense of herself and her absurd mission to aid in her brother's thwarted destiny. Madness!

Jet was scolding Seigl: didn't he know that Freud was a "pioneer" of the "nocturnal landscape" within? He'd virtually discovered the unconscious! He'd formulated the distinction between "manifest" and "latent" which was a key to comprehending the collective unconscious.

" 'Collective unconscious'? Isn't that Jung?"

Jet frowned. "Jung. Yes. And Jung, too. They knew to respect dreams."

"Well, I question that respect. I'm skeptical. From a scientific perspective, no one can prove that there is any 'manifest' or 'latent' material in any dream. A dream is a mental state, a stream of impressions caused by the discharge of neurons in the brain. Why claim that it 'means' anything at all?"

"Joshua, I can't believe you're so—willfully—ignorant."

"Jet, I can't believe you're so superstitious."

Seigl's heart was beating absurdly. He knew better!

Jet turned back to their chess game. She fumbled with a chess piece, overturned several and righted them again. Seigl wondered if she was actually trying to recall her dream game. At last, half-shutting her eyes, she pushed a knight forward impulsively.

Seigl took the knight. And another of Jet's pawns. The game was narrowing. Jet's pieces were sadly depleted, while his army was mostly untouched.

Again it was Jet's move. While she fumed, murmured to herself, smoked and scattered ash on the chessboard, sipped wine, and chewed at a strand of her hair, Seigl mentally scrolled through the lines of Virgil he'd translated that day. What solace, in the dignity and sonorousness of Virgil's poetry.

Jet said, with maddening persistence, "*Why* do dreams threaten you, Joshua? Ask yourself."

Seigl said lightly, " 'Why do dreams threaten you, Joshua?' "

"Very funny. You've been hiding behind sarcasm and intellectual bullshit since childhood. The world rewards you for it. Sure."

Again Jet spoke with surprising bitterness, vehemence.

This woman hates me, Seigl thought.

"Jet, why don't we finish this game tomorrow? You're tired, you've flown up from Florida—"

Jet cried, "Noooo! You want to break the spell. Because I remember this game, and if I can remember the ending . . ." Jet hesitated, not wanting to claim *I can win.* For the possibility of Jet winning the game was obviously remote. Instead she reverted to her obsessive subject, dreams, saying that she'd had recurring dreams of Seigl for weeks, and of their parents, and that these dreams must mean something, for she had no reason otherwise to dream of them, she was certain.

Seigl said, "But family memories are literally encoded in your brain cells. Going back to infancy. It's natural to dream of them."

"But why *these*? And why *now*? And when I arrived here today, you revealed to me that, yes you are endangered. You appear to have a—" Jet hesitated. What was she about to say? *A nerve disease, an autoimmune disease, a fatal disease?* "—something wrong with you, and you don't know what. But I knew. I mean, I had a premonition. It's as if our brain cells are linked. Our souls are linked. Don't laugh at me, damn you: how did I know to call you? to come here? There must be millions of memories encoded in my brain cells, but I've dreamt of these. Why?"

Seigl stared at Jet. How like a harpy-Cassandra his sister was!

He was beginning to be frightened by her.

"Jet, I don't know. Truly."

"Yes. Because you don't want to know."

"Move, Jet. Let's wrap the game up."

"See, Josh, I *know*. I know what I *feel*."

I know what I feel. The boast of ignorance through the centuries.

After much deliberation, Jet finally moved her queen. As soon as she lifted her fingers from the piece she saw: Seigl would checkmate her king in the next move. She uttered a baffled, hurt cry, like a wounded bird, and before Seigl could prevent her she swept the pieces from the board into Seigl's lap and onto the floor, and in the process spilled what remained of her wine onto the carpet.

"You cheated! Damn you, Joshua! Distract me and confuse me and fucking *cheat me*! Just as you did when we were *children*."

Hardly children but teenagers. For Jet had behaved in this childish way well into adolescence. As she'd done then, she ran from the room incensed as if she'd been insulted, leaving her brother behind to crawl about on his hands and knees awkwardly gathering the scattered ivory chess pieces. And dabbing at the spilled wine with a wetted paper towel, without much success.

Seigl's joints ached. His temples ached. His eyes smarted from Jet's cigarette smoldering in an ashtray. Still the fact remained: "I won."

THE FEEBLEST OF BOASTS, as it would turn out.

Next day, Jet didn't appear downstairs through much of the morning. From time to time Seigl, working on his Virgil translation at the dining room table, could hear her on the telephone: she was contacting old friends in the area, making plans to meet them. (Former lovers included?) Her telephone voice was bright, vivacious. From a short distance it sounded like a parrot's cries. Each time Jet hung up the phone there was an abrupt, ominous silence overhead. Seigl thought uneasily, she will come for me now.

Seigl knew not to expect his sister to apologize for her rude behavior of the previous evening, nor to betray any sign of embarrassment or remorse. For Jet was one who, after she'd behaved badly, blamed the person to whom she'd behaved badly for causing such uncharacteristic behavior in her.

Unassailable logic! Seigl smiled.

He resolved to say nothing about the overturned chessboard, the spilled wine. He'd dragged a chair over the stain in the carpet and hoped that Alma wouldn't notice it next time she cleaned the living room.

And he hoped the house didn't stink this morning of Jet's damned cigarette smoke. He'd opened windows to freshen the air. But judging from a flicker of expression on his assistant's impassive face, when he let her into the foyer that morning, he guessed that Alma detected it.

He set Alma to work in his study. The massive task of sorting, stacking, disposing of and filing Seigl's correspondence was nearly completed; by next week, Seigl would be confronting the great challenge of his numerous manuscript drafts. Laboring over a few lines of Virgil—

> On the farther shore
> The great trunk headless lies unnamed

> On the distant shore
> The great/vast trunk lies headless and unnamed

—Seigl tried to banish personal anxieties from his mind.

"Joshua! Why is that cleaning woman working with your *papers?*"

Seigl looked up guiltily. There stood his astonished sister trembling before him, breathing in quick pants like a wounded creature. Presumably she'd gone into his study to discover Alma there. Seigl knew he should have prepared her, but he had not. Now he saw that Jet was terribly upset. This was not pretense or playacting but the real thing: hurt, incredulity. Like a betrayed woman she stared at her brother with damp blinking eyes.

In the light of late morning Jet's face looked hastily made up, her eyelids puffy and her hair far less buoyant than it had been the previous day. Still a striking woman but definitely middle-aged, and baffled.

Seigl heard himself try to explain that Alma Busch was not his cleaning woman primarily, but his assistant.

"Your *assistant? Her?*"

"Jet, not so loud."

Jet protested, "But—I'm your assistant, Joshua. I've always been your assistant."

"Jet, no. You've misunderstood."

"How have I 'misunderstood'? This is why I've come to Carmel Heights: to assist you."

This was exactly what Seigl had dreaded. Now that it was happening, he felt as helpless as he'd been in Mount Carmel Cemetery, his legs struck out beneath him. He said, "I never asked you to come and assist me, Jet. In fact, when we spoke on the phone I made it clear that—"

"You lied to me! You misled me!"

"Jet, how did I mislead you? I told you frankly—more than once—that I didn't need or want your help."

"But I've helped you in the past. I helped you with your play, remember? You always said you were grateful."

Eight years before, Seigl had accepted a commission from the prestigious Public Theater in Manhattan to write an original play derived from *The Shadows*. As it evolved over a period of arduous months, the play turned out to be very different from the novel; there were only two characters, both male, both Jews, one an agnostic and the other a rabid anti-Semite. *Counter/Mime* had received respectful if puzzled reviews from critics but Seigl withdrew it from further productions with the excuse that he wanted to revise it. Sitting through performances had been agony for him, the play had seemed so static, obscure. Jet's initial role had been to type Seigl's constant revisions of the script into a word processor during the pre-production period and, during rehearsals, to involve herself in the actual production. Seigl recalled the experience as one might recall a bout of malaria. Somehow, he'd gotten through it. But it wasn't an experience he cared to repeat.

Jet said, incensed, "And you misled me about that—creature! How can a cleaning woman be Joshua Seigl's *assistant*! You've done this deliberately to sabotage our heritage—and to spite me—haven't you?"

"Jet, don't be ridiculous. And don't speak so loudly, I don't want Alma to overhear."

The sound of Alma's name was a goad like a hot poker to Jet. Seigl realized his error as soon as he uttered it, provoking Jet to cry, " 'Alma'! What is this 'Alma' to you?"

Seigl pushed himself to his feet. He was trying to keep his voice lowered. "There's no need for you to be abusive, Jet. Alma is my assistant, I've hired her to help me with various projects. Not just my writing. She's very—"

" 'Capable'! I bet. She hardly appears to be literate, let alone literary. Just now I tried to engage her in conversation, I was scrupulously polite to her, and she blushed and gaped at me like an idiot. You're trusting your papers and manuscripts to an idiot. She speaks some sort of sub-English. She mumbles and wipes her nose on her hand. That tattoo on her face is grotesque. I wouldn't doubt she is a Ukrainian peasant, or she's been airlifted from Bosnia, Albania. I hope to God you're not having her answer your phone, Joshua. Everyone must be laughing at you."

"Jet, that's enough. You're becoming hysterical."

"*I'm* hysterical? What about *you*? Denial is a form of hysteria, like catatonia. You're deeply into denial, Joshua. Your career is in tatters and you don't seem to care. This 'autoimmune' condition: it's your own self turning against you. But in destroying yourself you're destroying others, too. The memory of our family. Our heritage."

Seigl couldn't believe what he'd heard: his sister was blaming him for his illness? *Your own self turning against you?*

Jet said, "I've been in denial, too. For much of my life. But I've never been so self-destructive as you, Joshua. Because I haven't your genius, for one thing. Why, this creature 'Alma' will be losing your manuscripts, if not stealing them. Can she get her hands on your checkbook? Your credit cards? And you, hiding in here, translating Virgil."

Virgil was pronounced like *Alma,* with infinite scorn.

Seigl said, incensed, "Jet, that's enough. You're a guest in my house, not a resident. You have no right to abuse my assistant, or me."

A new, lewd light came into Jet's eyes.

"That cow is your live-in whore, isn't she? That's it."

Jet was leaning onto the dining room table with both hands balled into fists, as if about to leap at him. Her bloodshot eyes glared, there was a glisten of madness in her face.

One of the Dirae his sister was. *Head entwined with coils of snakes and wings to race the wind.*

"Jet, come on."

"What explanation is there for this, otherwise? What would our parents say? An illiterate peasant, Joshua Seigl's assistant? About as blond-*shiksa* as you can get? What a joke."

Seigl knew better than to get into an escalating exchange with his sister who thrilled to such scenes and who navigated arguments like a bat flying and darting by radar. Yet he couldn't stop himself. He said, infuriated, "You're being ridiculous and vulgar. I'm not in the habit of bringing women into my house and paying them for sex."

"How would I know, Joshua? I don't know my brother any longer. I don't know your sick, sad heart."

Jet must have seen something in Seigl's face to deflect the course of her outrage. Abruptly she ceased her verbal attack, and backed off. She lifted her hands as if to shield her face.

Seigl said, disgusted, "Enough."

Jet fled upstairs. Seigl heard sobbing. Was it genuine, or simply part of the scene, he had no idea.

Guiltily he went to seek out Alma in his study. His heart was pounding dangerously fast, as it pounded at the onset of one of his attacks. But he couldn't succumb now. Even before the onset of his symptoms Seigl couldn't have borne so intense and so demeaning a scene with Jet, or with anyone, without a visceral reaction. He hated raw emotion, melodrama. He hated the willful sabotage of reason, the triumph of the blood.

The door to his study was partway closed but not shut. Had Alma heard? It didn't seem so. The young woman appeared to be oblivious of Seigl in the doorway, though he was breathing heavily. He was greatly relieved. He saw with what frowning earnestness Alma was inserting manila folders into the bottom drawer of his filing cabinet, awkwardly squatting on her haunches. In profile her face was childlike, rapt in concentration; the ugly birthmark, or tattoo as Jet insisted it must be, wasn't visible.

Seigl thought, She hasn't heard. She has been spared.

SEIGL WENT UPSTAIRS, and rapped on Jet's door. When she opened it he was surprised at how much calmer she appeared. She'd rinsed her face, she'd reapplied makeup and was dressing to go out. Seigl said, "Please promise me, Jet, you won't approach my assistant again? You won't speak with her?" and Jet said, annoyed, "Of course, Joshua. I promise. You've made a decision I can't understand, but I can respect it. Obviously, I shouldn't have come here."

Seigl let these words hover in the air for a beat or two before protesting politely, "Don't be absurd, Jet. Of course I want you here. It's just—I'd rather not quarrel."

Jet laughed lightly. "*I'd* rather not quarrel."

Shortly afterward, Jet left the house. She'd called for a taxi and was going to meet a friend in the city and she asked Seigl not to wait dinner for her, or wait up for her. "I have no idea when I'll be back." Seigl returned to his translating but was too restless to work. He, too, left the house on a pretext of needing to make purchases in the village. He stayed away for hours. When he returned it was late afternoon, well past dusk. Most of the first floor of his house was darkened, and all that he could see of the second floor. But someone, very likely Alma, had switched on the outside light for him.

Ascending the nineteen stone steps slowly, gripping the wrought iron railing as he climbed, Seigl allowed himself to think that perhaps his sister had departed the house. She might be staying with her mysterious friend. He would feel relief, though also guilt. And some regret.

Your sick, sad heart.

A curious remark for Jet to have made, after having boasted how well she knew him.

As soon as Seigl entered the house he heard voices. A single raised voice.

He listened in horror. He would afterward think of Nietzsche's aphorism *Around the hero, all things turn into tragedy; around the demigod, into a satyr-play.* Adding *Around Seigl, into farce.*

It was Jet, returned to the house, and to a confrontation with Alma. Exactly what she'd promised she would not do. God damn: Seigl was furious. He wanted to strangle the woman.

Seigl hurried to his study at the rear of the house. He heard Jet's peevish voice, "I'm not going to steal anything, for Christ's sake. I just want to look through these manuscripts. I have a right." There came Alma's faint protest, and Jet interrupted: "Get out of my way. You idiot." Seigl arrived just in time to see the women struggling. This was ridiculous! Appalled, he saw his sister slap Alma's face, he saw Alma crouch whimpering, pressing both hands over her nose; blood trickled through her fingers. Seigl would recall afterward how strangely passive Alma was: she hadn't shoved Jet away, hadn't done much more than try to protect herself against Jet's wild flailing blows. Yet Alma was clearly strong, and might have overpowered Jet if she'd tried.

When she saw Seigl rushing at her, Jet whirled upon him and began slapping. The color was up in her face, obviously she'd been drinking. "You! You're the cause of this! Traitor! I hate you, Joshua. I'm glad you're sick—I'll never forgive you."

Jet pushed past Seigl and out of the room. You could hear her on the stairs, heavy-footed as an enraged horse.

WITHIN AN HOUR Jet was gone from the house, with her suitcases. Wherever she went that night, to stay with her mysterious friend, or in a hotel, or to fly back to Florida, Seigl neither knew nor cared.

"Enough. No more."

6

WHERE WHITE SMOKE like steam rises through cracks in the earth.

Where the mines sunk deep inside the earth are burning.

Wind Ridge, Bobtown, McCracken, Cheet were the names of the mines when they had names. When the mines were still being worked, before the fires.

Where do you live, I live in Hell. I am a child of Hell. I am an American and a child of Hell. Ask me if I am happy, *I am*.

Mostly everybody has moved away. Grass grows wild where the pavement has cracked. Where people have abandoned their houses. The old grammer school. The asphalt playground. Berlin Street, Coalmont. Scottdale, Mount Union, Tire Hill. Where the smoldering is hottest, snow melts as soon as it touches the ground.

Lift up your eyes unto the hills where the vapor rises. Where help comes from the sky. Tall grasses, saplings. The jungle is returning. It's a gift for those who have refused to leave the Akron Valley, this peace. Old people mostly. Lead me to the still waters, restore my soul. The Anti-Christ is imminent. If the sky darkens, if there is thunder out of silence. A soul is like white smoke rising seeking the Lord. Out of the highway cracked everywhere like ice the smoke is rising like steam. Something breathing. They say that the fires in the mines could have been put out years ago but Akron County failed to act. The State of Pennsylvania failed to act. Why?

It's politicians. It's the Jew banker-owners, with mortgages on Wind Ridge, Bobtown, McCracken, Cheet. Let the mines burn, let the mines shut down, declare bankruptcy. Nobody gives a damn for the people who live here, that's how the Jew-bankers make billions of dollars and the U.S. government countenances like the U.S. government supports Israel.

Some places, the ground is hot to the touch. Sinkholes, poisonous gases. You couldn't play outside. After a snowstorm there's places like raw wounds, where the snow has melted. In 1983 it was declared a Hazardous Area. Residents of Akron Valley were evicted from their houses but there were those who refused to leave.

Yet the fires smoldering below are never seen. A visitor from the outside coughs and wipes at his eyes and complains of the stink but not people who live here. Why should we leave, this is our home.

The State of Pennsylvania has seized some properties within the Danger Zone but not others. There is less budget now for relocating. The ones who were relocated caused a stink of their own not liking the deals. Wait for people to move away on their own. Wait for people to die off.

Yet nobody will die. They are in their eighties, nineties. Some younger, like Delray Busch, not even sixty. Why should we leave, this is our fuckin' home. The county and the state pay welfare. We keep our lawns mowed. There are two churches: Methodist and Church of God. It's seventeen miles to Akron Center where the Consolidated School is. It's twenty-one miles to Frostburg where there's a discount mall and a Safeway. Eighty miles to Pittsburgh. This is not the edge of the world, there's TV.

You need a satellite dish, because of the hills. Once you have it there's how many stations? Maybe two hundred.

At first people thought the smoke would kill off the trees and grasses but it does not. Some houses, women grow roses. There was a warning about growing your own vegetables but not for years. A long time has gone by. Some days, the smoke is more like vapor than actual smoke. So maybe the fires are dying down.

Along Main Street there is the old Sunoco station, the shuttered Royal Theatre, Walgreens. Broken windows, rotting roofs. Strange to see grasses and saplings growing in the street, but beautiful, too. And at South Main there's people living in two or three of the old houses.

The bird population is up. Not just starlings and grackles but jays, cardinals, robins, songbirds. The temperature is higher on the average than anywhere in the state. Over their windows people tape polyethylene sheeting to save on fuel. It's too much trouble to take the sheeting down in the spring so the windows are permanently covered. Like glaucoma-clouded eyes.

Purest anthracite coal in the U.S. Can't trust the government but used to you could trust the Union but no more. My help cometh from the Lord who made heaven and earth.

Where do you live they asked the Tattooed Girl. I live in Hell she laughed. For always the Tattooed Girl was good for a laugh.

And yet. *If I forget thee, O Jerusalem, may my right hand forget her cunning.*

7

I N THE NEW YEAR, much would be changed.

Yet he lived as if in the historic present tense.

Lacking the shield of Aeneas. Lacking the personal/historic perspective.

"Alma? I've been thinking."

Rehearsing these words. So he might speak calmly, not betraying the excitement he'd been feeling all morning.

For it wasn't a comely thing, the quavering excitement of a man of young middle age in the presence of a girl of perhaps twenty who frowned like a schoolgirl uncertain of her lesson, not daring to meet her schoolteacher's eyes.

"I'll be needing you to assist me more hours of the day, starting next Monday. And so it might be more convenient for you to move into the guest room . . ."

Of course, Alma's salary would be raised.

In the New Year, much would be changed.

8

IN THE NEW YEAR.

"Fuck those steps. God *damn*."

Snow now came heavy and wet and the nineteen stone steps had to be negotiated with extreme caution. They had to be shoveled and kept clear of ice. Of course he'd hired a snow removal crew for that purpose and for shoveling the sidewalk in front of the house but still the steps were treacherous immediately after even the lightest of snowfalls, sleet, freezing rain. And could he ask his assistant to help him on these steps? Yes he could but could he ask her repeatedly? And was this fair, was helping a two-hundred-pound panting man up nineteen stone steps in a freezing wind a legitimate task for an assistant who wasn't an acknowledged attendant or a nurse?

"Alma. Thank you! This won't happen again, I promise."

Swallowing his pride then, not every time but sometimes he entered the house by way of the side, rear door, the old delivery entrance door leading to the shabby back stairs. At this door there were only three or four steps, and no one likely to observe if, on a bad day, Joshua Seigl leaned heavily on his cane and dragged himself up like a bundle of sodden laundry.

9

I N THE NEW YEAR.

She moved into the guest room on the ground floor of Seigl's house. For now she was a full-time assistant to the man. Her salary was raised. She was thrilled to tell Dmitri Meatte but did not tell him exactly how much higher her salary was now.

Seigl smiled the schoolteacher smile. Plucking at his whiskers that were shot with gray and needed trimming and sometimes she saw without wishing to see a gleam of saliva on his lips.

"Alma? If the room is too cold, or too warm, here's how the thermostat works . . ."

Yes, Mr. Seigl. Thank you.

10

S HE HAD NO clear idea why *I hate him. Hate his whiskers, his fat Jew lips.* On slow dull lonely days her heart would have stopped its beating except *I hate hate hate* made it kick and race. There was the swoon of anticipation of telling her lover such words to make her lover laugh and grunt with satisfaction and look to her listening for more. *See, he's having trouble walking some days? Climbing stairs. Doesn't want to say that's why he wants me around all the time now. It's like he's surprised every time he can't make it on his own. Bullshit. Like a little kid crapping his pants pretending he didn't know it was going to happen, it isn't his fault.*

Making Dmitri laugh.

The Tattooed Girl was funny as somebody on TV. Once she got going. Or once she was high.

Like liquid flame in her veins was the Tattooed Girl's hatred of her employer. The Tattooed Girl was one to hate her employers male or female but now the insult to the injury was, this fucker's a *Jew.*

I see him picking his nose. Noises he makes when he thinks he's alone. Pulling at his whiskers like there's ants in them. That drives me crazy. And all the papers and crap he has in that house. "Manuscripts"! Like it's something holy, he's the messiah and hot shit. Like the world should give a shit about him.

Sure she could concede, Seigl was kind. Sure Seigl was courteous. Sure Seigl was a gentleman not like every other asshole she'd worked for in the past ten years. Sure he paid her well and always on time. Never bossed her around mean and sarcastic like other men.

(Like Dmitri Meatte sometimes? But Alma was in love with Dmitri Meatte.)

The Jew never touched her, brushed against her. Anyway not yet.

She hardened her heart against him not wishing to feel sorry for him. Whatever was wrong with him. Seeing his shaky hands and the glisten of sweat on his face she turned away with a smile of childish cruelty. *Good! Now you know.*

Her father Delray Busch had had the shakes as long as she could remember. Raising his hand to his children in threat and the hand shook but you cringed just the same for that hand could strike, and strike hard. So too her uncle Mason, a tremor in both hands. And there was grandpa with something the doctor called Parkinson's. Half the men in the Busch family had emphysema. And Alma's mother was always coming down with bad colds, bronchitis. You couldn't blame just the mines the men worked or the smoky air, common sense told you it was cigarette smoking, too. Not that anybody gave a damn enough to stop.

There was asbestosis some people had, too. Like emphysema. You ended up hooked to an oxygen tank, sucking air twenty-four hours a day for the rest of your life. If you were lucky.

The Tattooed Girl was one of the lucky ones in fact. Why Alma was prone to be in a good mood. A single beer, a single joint, some guy feeling her up and saying kind words to her, Alma's in a party mood. What you'd call a party girl. Would've made a fantastic *Playboy* bunny! A guy she'd known in Pittsburgh took some photos like for a centerfold to send to *Playboy, Penthouse* . . . See, Alma left Akron Valley and never a backward glance.

Her father might be dead by now. Coughing out his lungs. For sure, her grandfather. Nobody'd sought the Tattooed Girl to invite back for any mourning or funeral not that they could've located her anyway. Nobody'd sent out Have You Seen Me? flyers seeking the Tattooed Girl.

Not that Alma cared. Fuck, no.

Not that she gave a thought to it. Back there. It was hard enough to remember last month, last week. Yesterday. And now there was this new thing in her life, this new job. In this new place.

Hate hate hate him: the Jew.

She could not have said if it was Mr. Seigl's Jew-ness she hated, or hating him, and knowing he was a Jew, that was why. Which came first. Maybe she'd never have guessed he was a Jew except Dmitri made so much of it. (She'd never have guessed the sister "Jet" was any Jew for sure.) Or was it maybe instinct? Something you could smell almost? But she'd hated that fucker Scanlon at the bookstore worse and Scanlon was purely white.

It was like trying to figure out why they'd tattooed her, the guys she'd trusted. Feeding her vodka and some kind of meth? crystal? she'd never know, and what the fuck difference did it make she was fucking grateful to wake up afterward, O Christ. Sweating so she'd dehydrated to the point, they would inform her at the ER, her kidneys and liver near about collapsed like sinkholes, leaving her to be found like trash behind a Big Boy Dumpster by the river. Pissburgh! She hated Pissburgh to her dying day. But trying to figure out why the tattoos, and why so ugly and scrawly, like the tattooist was nodding off, what the tattoos might mean . . . She couldn't.

It was like wrong-sized things had gotten inside her skull. Mismatched and broken boards.

Hate him! Panting and puffing like a hog. Red-faced hog. If he ever touches me . . . It infuriated her that other people seemed to like Seigl. So much! Now he was having her answer the phone for him and she took messages and these were invitations to dinners and to universities to give lectures and to teach and the callers spoke in respectful terms of Joshua Seigl and she was instructed to say yes she would give Mr. Seigl the message and yes he would return the call as soon as possible and hanging up the phone she was breathless with indignation and the urge to cry *Fuck him, and fuck you. Hot-shit you think you are don't you!*

And so many letters. To him: Joshua Seigl. Where she, Alma Busch, had never received any letters in her lifetime and would never. And no one of the Busches had ever or would ever.

To her lover Dmitri she'd brought some of these. A card she'd found inside a beautiful leather briefcase shoved away at the rear of a closet of manuscripts:

December 17, 1996

Dear Professor Seigl,

We want to thank you for this wonderful seminar.

Here is a small token of our gratitude. Please come back to Palo Alto soon!

Krista Jessica Eric Michael Kate Brian Scott Lyle

And Seigl hadn't ever used the briefcase, it was brand-new you could tell. Probably forgot he'd ever been given it.

(Dmitri frowned at the card and muttered *Bullshit!* and tossed it away. The briefcase he liked. Alma's heart swelled with pride, Dmitri liked the briefcase a lot. It was real classy made in Milan. He could sell it or pawn it. But maybe he'd keep it for himself.)

Gold cuff links she gave her lover, too. For he had a weakness for such things. As a waiter at The Café he oiled his hair and combed it straight back from his forehead Italian-style and made sure he looked good every night, sexy-smooth and cool. And he wore the gold cuff links engraved with initials *A.D.S.* Alma had found in a bureau drawer in the bedroom she slept in at her employer's house. He'd wished Seigl would turn up at The Café that night but Seigl had not. (In fact Seigl hadn't appeared at The Café for weeks. Not for dinner, and not to play chess.) Who was *A.D.S.*? Somebody dead probably. As near as Alma could figure out most people in the Jew's family were dead and he had no children and his crazy bitch of a sister had no children either. The cuff links weren't really Seigl's so it wasn't stealing to take them and he'd never know they were missing because he'd never known they were there.

Mostly that was why she hated him. Because he didn't know what he owned. Like a blind man his eyes were turned inward, like a deaf man he heard only the sound of his own voice inside his head. She hated him because he had money. Because he had money and didn't even spend it! Because there were checks inside some of the envelopes she'd opened, thousands of dollars in checks he'd never endorsed and never cashed because he'd never known about them. And he lived in that house. Alone in that house. How many rooms she'd never counted all the way and half of these rooms closed off because Seigl had no use for them. And people in Akron Valley with five or six kids living in some wood frame "bungalow" at the edge of a sinkhole or they lived in trailers.

Jew-money it must be Seigl had inherited. Because you never saw the man work. Never any actual work. Not even teaching you'd expect someone like him to do. (Some mail came to *Dr. Joshua Seigl* but he was no medical doctor. He'd told her why he was called *Dr.* but she couldn't remember.) Helpless as a baby he was. Could barely turn on the stove for himself. Couldn't find the vacuum cleaner. (Alma found it. In a closet.) His groceries were delivered. Other men came to shovel snow for him, trim trees after a windstorm. Not just whatever was wrong with him now, you could see he'd always been this way. Whoever had brought him up had spoiled him. Maybe it was a Jewish thing, spoiling the men, keeping them helpless. If Seigl rinsed plates to put in the dishwasher there'd be dried food on them. If he rinsed a cup he'd drop and break it. Two-thirds of his dishes were chipped and cracked and even Alma could see they were expensive china. Fancy heavy silverware, tarnished green. (Alma waited for Seigl to ask her to polish this silverware, anyway some of it, but he never did.) She'd smuggled out forks, knives, serving ladles to show to her lover but Dmitri said it was worthless to him, all ugly and tarnished and if he took any of it to a pawnshop he'd be finger-printed and under suspicion of theft so it wasn't worth it.) What re-ally pissed Alma, she had to laugh out loud, though Seigl had a washing machine and drier in the basement he sent out his laundry every week to Mount Carmel Laundry & Dry Cleaners and they sent back everything ironed, and charged Seigl about as much as Alma made in a week: not just white cotton dress shirts but his under-shirts, shorts, pajamas, towels and sheets!

(Why didn't Seigl ask her to do the laundry? Laundry was easy. Ironing was easy. Just one person, it would be so easy. But he never seemed to think of it, and Alma wasn't going to suggest it though she washed her own things now she was living in the house including her towels and sheets. She was starting to remember how she'd helped her mother with the laundry, hanging it outside on the line. Before the air in Akron Valley turned bad. How the fresh laundry smelled in the sun. Pressing her face against it, sniffing.)

Books by *Joshua Seigl* he had in his study. Some of them were in foreign languages. Dmitri said Seigl was famous but the Tattooed Girl had never heard of him so he couldn't be very famous! He pre-tended to be modest but Alma knew better. There was pride and vanity in those books. Just the fact they existed. Alone in Seigl's study one day she pulled one off the shelf and opened to a page of words solid as mud and gave up after a few seconds, it was such bull-shit. The way nobody ever talked, just meant to intimidate. Dmitri said the book to read was *The Shadows* and this looked more promis-ing, maybe she'd read it sometime. A story of some people in a fam-ily, Alma could follow. Though the story was set in Germany and in the "camps" as the back cover said and Dmitri said what the Jews claimed was done to them by Hitler was questionable, it depended on which side you wanted to believe.

Another thing that pissed her was: so many books.

It smelled in the house in damp weather, gave her a headache. Maybe there was mold or bacteria or something breeding in all those books. What's he trying to prove, Alma wondered. Some days, it was like a graveyard. And he'd left for her in the downstairs room the big heavy book from the Book Seller *"Thou Shalt Not Suffer a Witch to Live": A History of European Witchcraft*! Like she should want to know about centuries ago in Europe, or maybe he thought she was interested in witchcraft and the Devil and he was, too, and they could talk about it sometime, and he'd come on to her then, that was his plan. But he never asked her about it. Days went by, and weeks. And Alma never spoke of it of course. Actually she paged through the book sometimes sitting on the edge of the bed before turning out the light and she'd get kind of interested in it, and feeling almost scared like these things were real, they'd happened to real women like her, who'd been drowned by dunking, or burned alive, or "pressed" to death between boards while Catholic priests said prayers over them.

Some of the illustrations, Alma was fascinated by. Like nightmares. Like things that, if she'd had bad luck, could have happened to her.

Seigl's crazy bitch of a sister screaming in her face, slapping and clawing her. Almost, Alma had thought the woman would try to strangle her. "Jet"—a weird name. Didn't seem to be any kind of Jewish name. She'd seen something in the Tattooed Girl's face and it was like she knew Alma was the enemy.

Still, Alma hadn't been able to fight back. Sometimes, like that, taken by surprise, since she'd been a little girl she just panicked, froze. Could hardly lift her arms to shield her face from harm.

Couldn't scream for help. Couldn't scream at all like rags were stuffed down her throat.

Afterward, Seigl had tried to apologize. Stammering how ashamed and sorry he was. Like Alma wanted to hear this! He said his sister "had a history of" breakdowns. His sister was a "disturbed" personality. A "borderline" personality. And she had a "drinking problem," and she was on "anti-depressant medication."

Seigl said it would never, never happen again. Because his sister would never be allowed in this house again. And especially so long as Alma was there.

Alma didn't know what to say. Just stood there, frowning and staring at Seigl's whiskers, not meeting his eye but hugging her rib cage with her upper arms squeezing her breasts like she'd have liked to flatten them out not knowing what she was doing and feeling the ugly tattoo on her cheek pulse and throb until at last Seigl caught on, he was making her as miserable as his bitch of a sister had made her, and let her go.

Later that day it was. A slow dull lonely day after the sister left and the house was quiet again and Seigl mumbling to himself and pulling at his beard back at the dining room table with his books. And Alma made sure he wasn't creeping up on her like he did some-times (without him knowing she saw him in the corner of her eye) and she was prowling restless and hot *Hate hate hate both of you Jew kike bastards* and her heart pounding like she'd sniffed the purest coke straight up into her brain and she watched seeing her hand open a glass-front bookcase in Seigl's study and from a shelf she pulled a book that made her smile almost, small as a children's book which was what she thought it might be, the title sounded like a chil-dren's fairy tale, *Anna Livia Plurabelle,* but when she opened it and tried to read the tiny print swam in her eyes, fucking words made no sense like they were not English or any kind of English she'd been taught and her heart kicked in resentment and fury and her hands yanked the covers of the little book back until she heard the fragile spine crack and she smiled with childish satisfaction like a boy yank-ing a frog's legs apart tearing the frog into two pieces. *There! Fucker.*

Fat Jew lips like a baboon's asshole. Talking to himself and laughing and I think he's calling for me but he isn't. He's at the dining room table reciting poetry I guess it is "Vir-gil" rocking forward and back in his chair his eyes shut not knowing anybody else exists. I turn off the vacuum and listen. I watch him, I'm disgusted seeing a man like that unaware of another human being in his house like my drunk old blind grandpa Busch in his undershirt that showed every jutting bone and his boxer shorts laundered flimsy-thin so you could see everything that old man had dangling out of his belly like goiters it'd make you gag to see. The Tattooed Girl flailing her bare arms making lewd faces and a gagging noise like a late-night TV comic and they laughed at her marveling she could be so funny and she loved it basking in their attention though such attention was fleeting as lighted matches and always there was a letdown later. And there were other girls as frantic to be loved as the Tattooed Girl, one of them sexy and straw-blond like the Tattooed Girl but younger.

It might've been that night. Or the next. She couldn't stop sweating, and she was shivering, too. Which wasn't a good sign. A smelly sweat oozing out of her pores like crackling fat. Dmitri's friend Ermine (if that was his name, Alma wasn't sure) had crushed and mashed the painkillers into a grainy white powder and tamped it down in a ruby-red curve-handled pipe. Firing up the powder and sucking in the smoke be sure to keep the smoke sucked *in*.

Ermine grinned at her. Don't exhale, baby. You'll waste it.

She knew! She knew how to fucking smoke she'd been doing it since ninth grade for Christ sake. And I'm a long way from ninth grade now.

A jolt to the heart. That was what Seigl needed not boring old mildew books books fucking *books*.

So drunk she kept the smoke inside her lungs too long, swallowed and choked and couldn't breathe and began to convulse, thrashing on the filthy floor like a big hooked dying fish, in just her black lace bra and one of her breasts flopping out, Jesus did they laugh at her! One of the grinning guys prodded her ass with his booted foot saying in a singsong voice Al-ma Al-ma you dead or alive Al-ma?

It wasn't her lover. There was that solace, that sop to her pride, it wasn't Dmitri Meatte jeering.

Next time I won't. I will keep control of myself. I will make him love me like in the beginning.

AFTER THE WEEKEND, returning to the house on the Hill it seemed she hated her employer more than ever! Like vomit rising at the back of her mouth, her hatred tasted.

Ask why? For the Jew himself, and for his crazy bitch of a sister.

The sister! Who could figure such a glamorous woman, had to be thirty-five years old, or more, just the look of her enamel teeth and fingernails and her styled hair, such a woman turning crazy, going for Alma's throat? Slapping and clawing like a street whore and she'd have strangled Alma except Seigl was there to drag her off.

About the sister she'd told Dmitri Meatte not a word.

Why not?

Ashamed.

I can't. can't fight back. They'd see, then. How I want to kill them. Tear their throats with my teeth.

Hate hate hate him twice as much now for he reminded Alma of the sister and since the sister's departure there was beginning to be a weakness in the man like cracks so fine you can't see them yet but can sense they are there. Like Seigl was recalling the sister in certain rooms of the house. Like some days when he was trying to work (call what he did "work"!—a grown man sitting on his ass for hours scribbling on sheets of yellow paper) he could not concentrate but drifted into staring at the windows, and his mouth moved shaping words not meant to be heard. This behavior Alma observed in the corner of her eye. Since the sister, Seigl's hands shook more. His step was less steady. She'd see him leaning against a wall, panting. And he used the cane, because he needed it. Not every day, but some days. There was no joke about the cane now. (Alma would hand it to him, silently. And he would take it.) And now Alma accompanied him down the nineteen stone steps as well as up the nineteen stone steps and assisted him as he sank, half-falling, grunting and cursing into the driver's seat of his car and more and more frequently now in mid-winter Alma accompanied him in the car on errands in the village and across the river into the city and she was beginning to be seen, and known, by Joshua Seigl's acquaintances who spoke of her as Seigl's assistant and often smiled at her calling her "Alma" but Alma refused to respond, would not be suckered into smiling back or mistaking such gestures for kindness knowing that these people—especially the women!— didn't give a shit for Alma Busch, didn't care if she lived or died only that she was Joshua Seigl's assistant for as long as he wished to hire her.

And Alma knew to help Seigl with doors. Anticipating which door was going to give him trouble, and which would probably not. But always the car door which was heavy and inclined to swing back onto Seigl where the man was vulnerable hauling his bulk up and out of the car with brawny trembling arms.

Seigl's arms and shoulders were getting muscled, Alma could see.

Probably not his legs, though! He'd be looking like her wasted old grandpa Busch, in time.

◙

"THANK YOU, ALMA."

That quiet voice of his. She hated such weakness! You wanted to cry hearing such weakness in a man, fuck it.

"Alma, what would I do without . . ."

(WHAT HE'D DO: hire another assistant. It didn't take genius to figure that one out.)

SLOW DULL LONELY winter days and she was stone cold sober. And the delirium of the weekend was eclipsed behind her like soiled clothes she'd stumbled out of, kicked off her feet. And the weekend-to-come sickened her with its uncertainty for it hovered before her teasing as a slice of moon in the night sky you can't be sure if you are seeing but might be imagining. *For if he had another girl. If he had other women. Not ugly-tattooed and fat-assed.*

She believed she could make him love her, though. It would only just take time. He would see her devotion.

Like with the checks. He was interested in the checks, at first.

There were numerous checks Seigl had never gotten around to endorsing and cashing, that Alma had discovered in his mail. Some of these were months old and a few were years old. Seigl had asked Alma to make a stack of these checks on his desk and so she had but on the sly she'd selected a choice few (for sums beyond $1,000) to give to her lover. See? What I have for you?

It added up to $6,340. She'd counted.

But Dmitri disappointed her. Shaking his head. No good.

Like the tarnished pieces of silver, the checks were. In theory they were worth money but not in fact. You couldn't cash them, only an asshole would try forging Seigl's name. And so long after the checks had been issued.

Alma said, pouting, why couldn't she try? She wasn't afraid.

Dmitri pinched her breast. Just teasing.

I know you're not, baby. But we can make a lot better use of you if you're not in jail.

Hate hate hate the Jew because she caught him looking at her with pity. Her hand flew up to cover her cheek. Sometimes she felt a hot blush there, and at the nape of her neck. And across the backs of her hands. Her ugly hands! No fingernail polish could make those hands glamorous. For the fingers were stubby, and the nails were brittle. He wanted to ask (she could see he wanted to ask) was the thing on her cheek a birthmark or a tattoo? But he could not. He was shy of her at such times—this man who'd written *books!*

And the morning she overheard him on the phone. This impatient voice like he was trying to hide something beneath it: fearfulness. Talking to his doctor Alma gathered. He had warned her months ago not to ask about his health and for sure Alma would never yet she was curious, inclining her head to listen through the doorway where Seigl was leaning back in a chair scowling at the ceiling, and his eyeglasses (these were new, and made him look prissy) glinted with reflected light, and he was digging his fingers into his hair not knowing what he did. He was angry, anxious, saying, "This God-damned medication. The side effects are driving me crazy . . ."

Alma bit her lip. Wanting to smile.

Not that she cared if the Jew lived or died, for sure she did not.

(Wondering: what was wrong with him, exactly? And was it getting worse?)

Hating the man for his weakness. Any weakness.

But most of all she hated this employer for giving her orders in his prissy backward way. Like he needed to be polite to Alma Busch!

Almost, it was like a joke: "Alma, would you have time to—?" or "Alma, if it isn't too much trouble perhaps you could—?" or "When you have a chance, Alma, I wonder if—"

Alma mumbled some kind of reply. Why the fuck didn't he just tell her what to do!

And the things he came out with. Out of nowhere. Like they meant something she could comprehend like he'd taken for granted she knew the alphabet and could "alphabetize" his papers.

"You've heard of Primo Levi, Alma?"

Alma worked her mouth staring toward a corner of the dining room table. She'd polished it the day before, she liked how it shone. What was this guy saying? Who?

". . . in Auschwitz he never thought of suicide in two years. While always before, he had. And, after . . ."

Alma shifted her shoulders uncomfortably. Felt like her bra straps were cutting into her flesh. Why the fuck was Seigl telling her this?

"Levi did actually commit suicide, in 1987. He'd been freed from Auschwitz in 1945. That's quite a long time, I've always thought, for any suicidally inclined person to have endured . . ."

There was an awkward silence. Alma was fearful that her stomach would growl. Self-consciously she'd folded her arms tight and was squeezing her rib cage hard, lifting her breasts that felt heavy and raw, staring at the polished surface of the mahogany dining room table that was strewn with Seigl's papers in a way that suggested drowning. Alma could not have said which of them, Seigl or herself, was breathing so audibly and wetly.

Seigl removed his glasses and rubbed at his eyeballs. That habit of his! You could actually hear the eyeballs make a squishing sound.

Some bad habits, like Alma picking at her face, at her nose, biting her fingernails till they bled, her mother used to lunge out and slap away her hands. *Cut that out!*

When Seigl opened his eyes he seemed mildly surprised to see Alma standing there. Had he summoned her? Was it lunchtime?

"Alma! I don't mean to sound gloomy. I think I meant—it's a profound insight into human nature. In a camp surrounded by death you need not think of suicide. You never think of suicide when life is precarious and precious, when life is reduced to mystery. Only when it isn't."

He smiled at her. His fleshy lips inside the whiskers like wires. She found herself staring at him. She hadn't even heard what he was saying. The mark on her cheek burnt as if he'd touched her.

LATER THAT DAY, a Friday, the Mount Carmel Laundry & Dry Cleaners delivered. Alma took the items from the delivery man, not meeting his eye. Fuck these bastards coming on to her, and this one some kind of Hispanic not even white, like Alma Busch was somebody's live-in whore.

Straight-backed and trembling with indignation Alma tore off the cellophane wrappers from Seigl's laundry and dry cleaning. Put away his things in the bureau drawers in his bedroom, careful to keep them separate: pajamas, undershirts, shorts, socks. She hung his shirts, trousers, a tweed sport coat in his closet. Never in all these weeks of working for Seigl had she grown to tolerate the lavishness of his spending which she surmised to be out of ignorance.

Ironed pajamas! Fucking ironed underwear and *socks!*

I I

AND THEN SUDDENLY Seigl was well.

Overnight, it seemed. Amazing!

In the scintillant snowy light of early February as his thirty-ninth birthday veered toward him like a wayward comet Seigl wakened in his bed to find himself strong again in all his limbs. And clear-minded, and suffused with happiness.

"Can it be? My God . . ."

Trying to remain calm. Being the son of Karl Seigl he was no natural optimist. He would carry himself cautiously. He would test his legs and his strength through twenty-four hours, at least. For perhaps this was some mysterious spike of energy having to do with his new medication.

Friedman had said it was a less powerful medication than the previous. No steroids. Research into central nervous system disorders and diseases was continuous, always there were new theories, new medications and treatments. Yet Seigl seemed to know, his recovery had little to do with medication: no more than the sun easing out of a solar eclipse has anything to do with mere optics.

"It's over. I am *well*."

Wanting to sob with relief. Wanting to laugh aloud. Like a shy suitor he approached his bathroom mirror to examine his face for the first time in months without flinching.

Much of the color had returned to his skin. His cheeks were almost ruddy. His deep-set eyes seemed less blurry and bloodshot than they'd been in memory and he looked less fatigued, and depressed.

Daring to smile at himself: for he wasn't bad-looking, really.

Almost, you could see how a woman might be attracted to him.

A line of poetry came to him like a happy cry: *When at last after long despair our hopes ring true again and long-starved desire eats, O then the mind leaps in the sunlight—* Strange, for Catullus was hardly Seigl's favorite Latin poet.

"Sondra." He would call Sondra Blumenthal whom he'd been avoiding for weeks and whose feelings he knew he'd hurt. "Sondra. My dear." A wave of desire for the woman hit him. Or was it sheerly desire. He had not made love to a woman in a very long time and he was not going to allow himself to think (was he?) of the young woman dwelling now in his house for he understood that his assistant Alma Busch though hardly fragile-seeming was yet fragile in her emotions and so Seigl must not, must not . . . He would call Sondra Blumenthal. He owed this sweet kind patient woman several calls. He was eager to show her his Virgil translations. Oh, he wanted to take Sondra's hands in his, wanted to look into her eyes, kiss her . . .

"But don't mislead her, Seigl. That would be cruel."

Chastising his mirror-face. A lewd winking expression like a mask of Pan had slipped over it. He made a kissing-sucking noise with his lips. Hot with blood, rather full, fleshy, Seigl's lips reminded him of, of what, reminded him of genitalia, thin membranous skin rosily cast with blood . . . He laughed. He wiped at his mouth. Well, it was so. Why deny it!

Except: the whiskers.

God damn, Seigl was tired of those whiskers.

He'd let his beard grow out of negligence and despair. Like a wild ragged Hebrew prophet of old. And the beard was threaded with silver and gray wires.

Seigl laughed heartily. The idea came to him in an instant.

Myself again. But more than myself, a new man.

"Oh. Mr. S-Seigl . . ."

When Alma Busch saw her eccentric employer with his whiskers shaved away, his face naked and exposed, bleeding from a half-dozen small scratches, and his heavy cheeks, jowls, and chin red-smarting and swollen, she stood staring at him astonished. What a sweet comical simpleton the girl was, Seigl laughed in delight.

"Alma. I see now I should have warned you, dear. *This* is what the illustrious 'Dr. Seigl' looks like."

Alma stammered, "But—Mr. Seigl—your face is b-bleeding—"

It was true, Seigl had had to assault the thicket of whiskers. He'd needed a pruning shears! But he'd managed, with two pairs of scissors and more than one razor, trying to be patient initially but then with growing impatience until finally he was scraping away at his oddly tender skin not giving a damn how much it was hurting, or how he was lacerating the skin. Once he'd made up his mind to be clean-shaven again, that's to say to regain his old, youthful appearance, Seigl was ruthless.

"Blood is to coagulate. *That* has never been one of my so-called symptoms."

Alma continued to blink at him. How funny she was, his straw-headed big-breasted girl-assistant who read (he'd seen her!) by moving her lips and often drew her forefinger along a line of print, like a slow but diligent child. It wasn't just the glare of newfallen snow that dazzled her through the tall windows but Joshua Seigl himself exuding light like a two-hundred-watt bulb.

He was walking briskly as she'd never seen him walk. This was hardly a man who required a cane. Or an assistant to help him make his way in the world. The words flew out, "I won't be needing your services any longer, dear," without Seigl knowing what he was saying though seeing the shock in the girl's face he tactfully amended, "—I mean, assisting me as you were. It seems that I may not have been ill at all. It may have been some kind of misunderstanding, a misinterpretation of symptoms."

Seigl went away whistling, laughing to himself. You could see—certainly, gaping Alma Busch could see—how energy thrummed in this man's heavy thighs and strong muscled arms, and in the ebullient swing of his arms.

"DOCTOR? I'M CALLING to cancel our appointment this afternoon."

Seigl had insisted upon speaking with Morris Friedman in person. He'd had to be curt with Friedman's receptionist. For he wanted to be the one to inform the neurologist that his patient was cured, and unexpectedly. *And you had little to do with it, my friend.*

At the other end of the line Friedman was expressing some concern.

Seigl laughed, though he was beginning to be annoyed.

"Why? Why the hell do you think? Why would one of your 'nerve disease' cases cancel an appointment with you except there is no further need of you in his life?" Seigl felt blood pound dangerously in his temples. His heart was charged with adrenaline as if he'd initiated a sudden, good fight. He listened to Friedman for a few seconds before hanging up.

"Asshole."

WHAT A RUSE it had been, what a cheat. A hoax. Four months!

Seigl hadn't ever been truly unwell: he'd had a fall in the cemetery, injurious to his pride, and he'd overreacted. And Friedman had compounded the confusion with his costly "imaging" equipment that picked up every hairline imperfection in the brain and nervous system and so he'd misdiagnosed, innocently or otherwise.

Seigl's mother had been inclined to hysteria. In fact, other females in the Steadman family had been and were so afflicted. Seigl's sister was a prime example. (Seigl's sister! Since that ludicrous scene in his study, Seigl tried not to think the woman's name.) If there was a genetic weakness, Seigl would make every effort to avoid it from now on.

Soon after, as Seigl was rooting impatiently through one of his desk drawers, seeking a portion of a novel manuscript he'd begun and set aside years before, the telephone rang with annoying insistence. He heard Alma's flat-footed tread as she hurried to answer it in another room and as she lifted the receiver to murmur in her throaty nasal voice that always sounded breathless the rote words he'd taught her *Hello Mr. Seigl's residence who shall I say is calling please* he shouted at her, "No! Hang the fuck *up*." There was a shocked silence. Alma must have immediately replaced the receiver. Seigl called out to her, less stridently, "No need to answer the phone again until I tell you to, Alma. In fact, why don't you take the remainder of the day off. The night. Wherever you go at night. Visiting your friends, I won't be needing you."

Alma on her nights off. Weekends. Where?
    Can't ask. None of my business. She has a lover of course. Or lovers.

LOST TIME! He had to make up for four months lost time.

"Sondra? Hello! I—need to see you."

In his haste he failed to identify himself. But his friend recognized his voice, of course.

"Where have I been? I've been—nowhere. I mean, here. But I've been *no one* here. You know," Seigl said, laughing louder than he intended, "—in the One-Eyed Giant's Cave. Blind at work. I mean, hard at work." Seigl paused breathless. What was the One-Eyed Giant's name? Cyclops. The memory came to him unbidden of the blinding of the Cyclops and made him wince. Strange to have forgotten the name Cyclops which he knew as well as his own. "I've been missing you, Sondra, and I—hope you're well?"

Talking rapidly. As one might dance over hot coals in a simulation of exuberance. For Seigl recalled guiltily if dimly: listening to concerned messages from Sondra Blumenthal on his answering service which he'd erased in shame and despair of his medical condition and did his best to forget. And several times there had come his frowning assistant with the name SANDA BUMTHELL carefully written on a piece of paper in a large looping schoolgirl hand PLEASE CALL WHEN YOUR FREE.

Seigl was reluctant to pause to hear what Sondra was trying to tell him for he had the impression, exceedingly disappointing as a kick in the groin, that his friend he'd been counting on wasn't available to be taken to dinner that evening.

"But I must see you, dear! I miss you . . ."

His voice was young and aggrieved. Must see you. Miss you. Now.

A man is inclined to think, fairly or unfairly, that wanting to see a woman, wanting a woman, the scales of justice have been tipped against him, in the woman's favor.

"Sondra, are you sure we can't meet tonight? I really do need to see you. Why don't I drive over there and pick you up and we can go to La Maisonette. If—"

Still, Sondra was resistant.

How unlike her: this evident wish to make Seigl jealous. For there was a hint of another engagement with an individual or individuals whom Seigl apparently didn't know. For he surmised that, if he knew them, or was known to them, Sondra would readily invite him to join their party.

Always in the past this would have been the case.

"Sondra! Are you angry with me?"

A pause. A near-inaudible reply.

"I realize I've been remiss, dear, and I'm sorry. I've had a—complicated time. But now it's past . . ." Seigl removed his glasses, which were new prescriptions, with a bifocal lens, and tossed them exuberantly down. A halo of light shimmered in his eyes. Where was he? Sprawled in a chair before a tall radiant window. During this conversation he would lose his awareness of the person to whom he was speaking though if required to identify her he would have immediately responded: Sondra Blumenthal. My friend. What was urgent was that Seigl explain himself. His work that lay ahead: a mountain to be climbed. He was confident now as he had not been in years! Since his accidental fall in the cemetery he'd been experiencing an alarming double vision at times as if he were seeing what was truly in existence that had long been obscured from him previously. But now, the blurred double vision had vanished. Seigl was seeing *clearly*.

As it seemed, suddenly, Seigl could hear *clearly*.

For as Sondra was awkwardly explaining why she couldn't see him that evening—or any other evening?—Seigl heard the irresolution and hurt in her voice. It was the woman's wish not to experience again certain emotions which she associated with Joshua Seigl, but unfairly: for at the time of those emotions he'd been ill, or had been convinced by a neurologist at the medical school that he was ill, and only this morning he'd learned that he was *not ill*: he was *well*.

He interrupted, laughing: "But I need your help, dear. Darling! I think you promised? To look over my Virgil translations? Professor Blumen-thal: *blumen*. And even more I need your advice on something more imminent"—Seigl heard his voice with smiling astonishment, for this was a revelation to him "—planning my thirty-ninth birthday. I mean, planning a party to celebrate. Did you just mention La Maisonette?—we could have the party there, in that attractive back room. Or maybe here at the house? Catered, of course. My assistant Alma prepares simple meals for me but doesn't really cook, primarily she heats things in the oven I've ordered from the village, she's perfectly capable of serving but not serious cooking nor would I expect it of her. I was thinking—ten, twelve of our closest friends? Or a few more? Will you help me with the guest list, dear, and with the menu? I know, I haven't hosted a party here in so long, I'm ashamed. I am not a recluse! I've been lonely! Will you help me with the party, Sondra? I—care for you so much. I don't want to be alone on my birthday."

Seigl paused, struck by his own words. *Alone on my birthday* echoed in his head. Why hadn't he realized this before? Groping for his glasses which had fallen somehow beneath his foot, one of the lenses cracked. God *damn*.

By degrees now the woman's voice was softening. A contralto voice, a beautiful voice it was. Seigl felt a strong affection for that voice. (Yet: who was this woman, he kept forgetting! Had to laugh at himself. A middle-aged Don Juan he'd become, with the pummelled-looking face of an unlucky boxer.) The voice was speaking of someone named Ethan but who was Ethan, was Seigl expected to know Ethan, a male friend?—a university colleague of the woman's?—a *child?*

It came to Seigl then: "Ethan" was the name of the woman's son whom in fact Seigl had met, yet seemed always to be forgetting.

"Of course, Ethan is invited to dinner, too. Shall I pick you both up? Shall we say—seven? Or shall I come earlier, and teach Ethan to play chess?"

Seigl listened anxiously. He would not be rejected!

"Not tonight, well—tomorrow night? *Not* tomorrow night, then—the next night? You and 'Ethan' and me."

More than myself, a new man. So lucky!

IT WAS SO. Twenty-four hours passed, and forty-eight hours, and beyond. And Seigl persevered strong and luminous in his newly regained body. His energy rose steadily, a fever chart.

No longer did he require more than three hours of sleep each night. And these hours so sexually charged, his penis engorged with blood aching for release, he woke groaning, thrashing in his bed.

He'd set aside the Virgil translations. Temporarily. He was working on poetry of his own, and on a new novel set in the future where all times were contemporaneous, simultaneous. History was no longer linear but spatial, and human beings were no longer opaque but transparent as jellyfish. Their souls visible as quivering upright flames inside the skins and intricate skeletal structures of their bodies.

It would be a short lyric novel of less than two hundred pages. There was no model for it in any literature. Its structure was polyphonic and its language was dithyrambic. Its title was *Redemption*.

"In the future we will have evolved out of brute 'prejudice.' The opacity of our skins has been the issue."

Now ideas flew at Joshua Seigl like maddened hornets. Page after page he covered in a white heat of inspiration, until his writing hand cramped. Frequently his thoughts rushed at him too quickly for his brain to net them. Help, help! he laughed like one newly in love, for whom there is no help.

And sexual desire overcame him with the abruptness of a faucet turned heedlessly on. He was impaled upon his own sexuality.

A woman. Any woman.

No. Not *any woman*.

Prowling the house sleepless. Eyes burning in their sockets.

But only the second floor of his house, and the first floor, never the ground floor where his assistant, Alma Busch, slept in the corner guest room he'd provided for her. The door to which he had no reason to believe was locked against him, or unlocked. He never descended to that part of the house. *Nor ever thought of doing so.*

"She's safe under this roof. I am that girl's protector."

He'd spoken more than once of "enrolling" her at a local college where she might learn "computing skills." Or, should she wish to take any course of study, he would pay her tuition at some near-future time.

"I—want to help you, Alma. Improve your education. And in that way, dear, your life."

Dear. He'd begun using this term unconsciously. Or was it half-consciously.

(Was Alma becoming fearful these days of her fiery-eyed employer with the still reddened, swollen, now coarsely stubbled jaws? If so, the Tattooed Girl knew to chew her lower lip in silence.)

Ideas flew at him, he had only to glance up to catch one in the eye.

This: it was time to acquire a new car.

A Jeep? Always, disapproving of fellow citizens swerving the streets in SUVs and minivans like gaily-colored military vehicles, Joshua Seigl had coveted something massive for himself. Away with austerity, bookish modesty. "Why not? I'm a big man." Now that he was walking more confidently, and hadn't (much) difficulty climbing into (and out of) a car, it was time for Seigl to purchase a new vehicle, and more than time.

Disappearing into the city along the river and when at last he returned to the Hill he'd traded in his veteran Volvo for a new-model Volvo of essentially the same design, color. (Austere faded silvery-olive.) Nothing else he'd seen had been quite for him.

The new Volvo steered rather tightly. The leathery smells of newness were bracing, aphrodisiac. Distracted by crude sexual thoughts (and by very young hookers, black, light-skinned, and sickly white, in gaudy fake-fur jackets, tiny miniskirts and knee-high boots drifting in clusters along desolate Union Street near the city's waterfront, smiling and waving at passing cars in the twilight of a winter afternoon), Seigl turned a corner too sharply, jumped the curb and scraped the right front fender of the new Volvo against an already mangled stop sign. "God *damn*." He felt the pain in his groin. Like a wounded beast he made his limping way home.

Let the scraped and dented fender remain, Seigl thought. A judgment of the gods.

For what are the gods but our ancient passions. Where the Hebrew God and the Christian God have grown weary and faded, the ancient gods are ever young.

Instead: brooding upon good/healthy/bracing new deeds.

Through a very long windy sleepless night.

He would endow the Karl Seigl Memorial Fellowship in the Humanities at a major university. Two million dollars, or three, might be sufficient. No problem. He'd call what's-his-name, his Money Manager, in the morning.

He would marry. At last!

He would ask Sondra Blumenthal to marry him. He would adopt her son. His heart filled with dread/joy at the prospect. If only his mother hadn't died too soon . . .

Rarely did he sleep in bed for the three hours' sleep was a maddening waste of his time. "Sleep is what anyone can do. Sleep is what a sheep can do. A man with a brain and a mission does not need *sleep*." He hated to succumb to such weakness! When he did sleep, it was often in his clothes. At the dining room table where he slumped forward onto the strewn pages of *Redemption,* mouth agape and drooling. Also he slept in the new Volvo. He slept where he lost consciousness, like a beast. Otherwise the nights were long and arduous as a Yangtze River journey. It occurred to him to worry (but he dismissed such worries as hypochondriac, and certainly he wasn't going to creep back to Friedman) that more and more frequently he was lapsing into narcoleptic fugues at odd, unexpected times. These were bouts of intense brain-paralyzing sleep that lasted as briefly as two minutes and as long as an hour. He'd been overcome initially while rummaging through the morass of manuscripts in his study drawers, filing cabinets, and closets, undated and unidentified drafts of chapters of abandoned novels, detailed outlines of book-length projects, scenes of a second play titled *Why/Warum?* and countless hastily written pages of prose that gave evidence of having been written in a state of passion and yet ended abruptly, sometimes in mid-sentence. *Why/Warum?* was an apt title for the last several years of Seigl's life.

"Mr. S-Seigl?"

It was his assistant with the scratchy nasal grating voice. Asking was he all right, he'd fallen asleep amid his papers.

Yes he was fine! No obviously. Not.

Stroking his jaws which startled him for they were neither be-whiskered now nor clean-shaven, and he'd meant to remain clean-shaven, Seigl told his exasperating assistant that he'd simply been taking a nap. And that she could begin sorting his manuscripts that day. "And where you can, collating pages. Or arrange things in clusters, that seem to belong together."

Alma nodded vaguely. As always she nodded when her employer gave her instructions whether these instructions were comprehensible to her or not.

"You do understand, Alma, don't you?"

Possibly Seigl was sounding impatient. Possibly he was glaring at her. *A hooker in her former life. Peasant stock. But now I have saved her haven't I. Redeemed her. Yes, I take pride.* For Alma stammered yes she understood, she guessed.

"I should m-make sense of all this? Like it was meant to be?"

I 2

AND STILL SEIGL was well. Very well! A spiraling flame of *wellness*.

For he was working through much of the day/night. He was accomplishing more than ever he'd accomplished in his life. Working now on both *Redemption* and the dithyrambic play *Why/Warum?* which he'd abandoned in despair years before. And sometimes he returned to Virgil as a guilty son might return to his father.

"I will redeem myself. It's begun!"

The massive correspondence his assistant had so capably sorted for him, Seigl hadn't yet done much more than glance at. He was too restless for such a task. Replying to letters, explaining why he'd been so delayed, even the numerous checks for royalties, permissions fees, speaking engagements he needed to endorse and mail to his bank, how dreary, how dull, why waste precious energy? "Alma, I'll deal with this in a few weeks. For the time being, please put it away where I don't need to see it."

Alma asked where.

Seigl said, "I said: where I don't need to see it."

IT WAS EVENING, the phone rang. There came Alma breathless and apologetic saying there was "some woman wondering where you are." Seigl continued writing, refusing to hear. "Mr. S-Seigl?" Alma mumbled, "there's some woman—" Still Seigl continued writing, bent over the dining room table, his hand holding a cheap ballpoint pen moving furiously across a page. "She says she's waiting for you at her house? I guess?"

At last Seigl lifted his fierce mask of a face. Only then realizing who the woman must be.

He would blame the sleep-seizures. For his mind was so lucidly clear otherwise.

Annoying and embarrassing and (he had to concede) dangerous when he was driving his car especially. Overcome suddenly by a morbid fatigue, and then by sleep striking like a hammer blow. Hardly time to pull over to the side of the street before his heavy head fell forward like a guillotined head.

Dangerous, and mysterious. But unrelated (he was sure) to his (non-existent) illness.

At La Maisonette. With Sondra Blumenthal and her son, Ethan, who turned out to be a brightly quizzical eleven-year-old with an interest in solid geometry. Sondra in vivid red, the effort of a woman of conservative tastes in fashion to appear festive, sexy; Ethan with fawn-colored hair and delicate features who lapsed into shy/sullen silences, who knows why. And near the end of the lavish meal Seigl began to feel the encroaching drowsiness, his head begin to lurch as if about to topple into his lap. At the same time shoving his fingers into the romantic candle flame to *wake yourself up, Seigl* before either of his guests noticed.

He was sure, he'd prevented the narcoleptic attack in time.

Yet there was Sondra regarding her friend Joshua with tender worried eyes. For there'd been the misunderstanding that began the evening. (Seigl hadn't wanted to confess he'd totally forgotten the engagement that he himself had so insisted upon. Nor had he made reservations at the restaurant. All he could think to say was, he'd written the wrong date down on his calendar.)

"Please don't ask, Sondra. Whatever it is you're preparing to ask."

Seigl's private life had always been his private life. His health was his private life.

Sondra said hesitantly, "Joshua, I'd been hearing . . ."

"Really. Gossip is beneath you, Sondra, I'd thought."

But Seigl was smiling. Clean-shaven Seigl, in a parrot-bright necktie, smiling.

". . . you've had some tests? At the medical center . . . ?"

Seigl signaled for the waiter. As if not hearing. Through the meal he'd done most of the talking and the remainder of the time had listened attentively to Sondra and to Ethan but would recall little of what he'd heard so perhaps even then he'd been not-hearing.

Sondra fell silent, rebuffed. Ethan, a polite child through the ninety-minute dinner, began to squirm in his corner of the leather booth and noisily sucked up the remainder of his Coke through a straw.

Seigl said warmly, "Sondra: I am *well*."

Seigl reached over and between thumb and forefinger pinched the child's straw to cease the noisy sucking.

HE DROVE SONDRA and the boy home. He drove faster than Sondra considered safe. She invited him inside for coffee but he'd already had coffee at the restaurant. She sent Ethan inside and turned to speak to him, she took his hand in hers, twice the size of her hand nearly, she began to appeal to him *Joshua, this isn't fair. You draw me to you, then you push me away. For years this has happened. You know that I care for you. On the phone, you seemed to say you cared for me* . . . but Seigl cut her off before he could speak by framing her face in his hands and kissing her.

And kissing her.

○

"SEIGL! WHAT THE HELL'VE you done to your *face*?"

It was goateed Fen who addressed Seigl so bluntly. But Fen had had some beers by this hour of the evening, and was in a mood nearly as edgy and sparky as Seigl's own.

The chess players, by nature a subdued, withdrawn lot, appeared relieved to see their old companion Seigl of whom perhaps they'd heard dire rumors. They saw that he was walking without a cane and that his face was youthful and his manner was confident if not brash. They'd missed him, as the staff of The Café had missed him. Seigl's kindly eyes and sharp wit and intermittently inspired chess playing and his generosity in standing drinks for all.

The Café was unchanged since October. Christmas decorations had come and gone. Seigl was relieved. For he'd changed, and for the better; yet he liked it that the rear of The Café was as always, the rough exposed brick, black-painted windows, unadorned wooden tables. And chessboards inset in the tables. The thought came to him *In chess we are perpetually the age we were when we first began playing*. No wonder there was such comfort here.

And there was the booth near the kitchen door where he'd first seen Alma Busch.

"Joshua, hello! Welcome back."

His hand was energetically shaken. His shoulder was affectionately struck. The absence of his beard was jokily commented upon. The restaurant staff, maître d' and two waiters still on duty this late in the evening, smiled warmly at their very good customer Mr. Seigl and were greeted by him in turn.

It seemed that everyone wanted to play chess with Seigl. In his brash mood he decided to take on two opponents at once: the ex-prodigy Fen, and the ex-professor of medieval philosophy John.

Two opponents? *Those* two?

Seigl saw glances exchanged. He laughed, quickly setting up the boards. Though he hadn't played a game with a serious opponent since the last time he'd played and lost to John, yet he seemed to know he was at the peak of his chess-playing powers. Energy flowed through his fingers awaiting discharge.

Yet somehow it happened, both Fen (on Seigl's left) and John (on Seigl's right) wiped him off the boards.

"Again! Take me on again."

The men exchanged significant looks, and shrugged. Why not?

And so Seigl began another time. Buoyed by energy like a succession of white-capped waves of the Atlantic. He moved his first piece on Fen's board, and he moved his first piece on John's board, and they were different pieces, headed in different directions, yet both toward victory. *It has to be. I can't lose. I've dreamt this!*

Seigl had quite liked teaching Ethan to play. Of course, the boy already knew how to play, to a degree. After an intense hour with Seigl, he'd already improved his game. Seigl would make the boy into a champion, he'd promised, as he'd been at that age.

He would marry the woman, he would adopt the boy, he would make the boy into a chess champion . . . Swiftly it would happen, within the year.

"Seigl my man. Look sharp."

Were Seigl's eyelids closing? His brain shutting down like a faulty generator?

In *The Shadows* he'd dared to follow his grandparents Moses and Rachel Seigl into the gas chamber at Dachau, and by slow and then rapid degrees into death as their terrified brains, battling extinction, snatched at memories. A brash act for a young American writer in his twenties. For which he'd been almost universally praised.

Evoking death! The deaths of others, whom he'd never known!

Yet: it had been no more, and no less, impossible than evoking life. If you could do one, you could do the other.

Why not, when it's all words.

Only later had incredulity and self-disgust struck him. Too late, it had seemed.

"*Josh*ua?" This was John, nudging Seigl with fatherly solicitude.

His eyelids flew open. Immediately he wakened. He had not been asleep. He'd missed nothing.

"Is it my move? Both moves? It *is*?"

A number of spectators were gathered around. For this was something of a spectacle. Joshua Seigl taking on two seasoned opponents at once. Seigl without his beard, his shirt pulled open at the collar, sweating and breathing audibly. Even the waiters were watching with interest. Seigl's brain was deliciously blank: he was trusting to intuition, luck: saw his hand moving in one direction, and then in the other. He was thirsty. He'd already downed several beers. He needed a cigarette. (One of the waiters handed him a pack, and matches.) Where was his hand moving now? So many of his (plastic) pieces had been swept from the boards . . . He knew that neither Fen nor John was cheating and yet: he'd seen to the end of each game, and he knew the outcome. Why then wasn't he winning? Or winning more visibly?

Endgame was nearing to the left (where Fen was playing with the vicious efficiency of a master butcher wielding his knife) but it was yet mid-game to the right (where elderly Professor Emeritus was playing with a subdued, shaky hand).

Quickly the beer ran through Seigl's kidneys. He excused himself to lurch from the tables. In the men's room he leaned against a wall beside a urinal and fell asleep while urinating and wakened in nearly the same instant splattering urine onto the floor. Confused and ashamed of himself he wetted paper towels and stomped them onto the floor with his feet. Through that day he'd drunk Peking tea at home. Hot black Peking tea charged with caffeine like steroids. His assistant fetched the whistling teakettle to bring to him. Awash in liquids Peking-black and tawny-gold. But it was rare for him to drink so much beer in so brief a period of time. "Mr. S-Seigl?" He heard her meek query that both touched and exasperated him. For he feared that the young woman revered him. As many of his students and numerous others had revered Joshua Seigl, wrongly. He wanted to shout at her *For Christ's sake don't revere me, I'm not worthy of you. You have lived, and I have never lived.*

Seigl returned to the chess games. Within two moves, Fen checkmated his king. Within three moves, John checkmated his other king.

"Well."

His instinct was to strike the few remaining pieces off both the boards. His instinct was to pound with both fists. He'd been cheated of the victory that was his . . .

Instead, Seigl managed to laugh. Though shinily red-faced as a balloon close to bursting. "Well, you see . . . 'Hubris.' "

It was so. But *hubris* has its comical side.

Magisterial/magnanimous Seigl rose like a cresting dolphin out of the choppy sea to invite "my friends" to have drinks, sandwiches on him. And this extended to the staff of The Café too, of course. "A belated celebration of the New Year. I've missed you."

(Was this true? You'd certainly have thought so seeing Seigl tremulous with emotion, ruddy-faced, moisture shining in his eyes. One of the lenses of his new glasses appeared to be cracked.)

Beer, single-malt whiskeys, bourbon, straight gin. Vodka. And beer.

Roast beef sandwiches, ham and Swiss cheese, grilled chicken breast. Out of the kitchen's larders.

Toasts were made to Seigl. Seigl in turn made toasts. One by one the chess players departed. Not all were sociable, though all accepted drinks and several were observed cramming sandwiches into their coat pockets. "Another drink, Mr. Seigl?" The attentive young waiter with slicked-back Valentino hair, white dress shirt tapered to fit his slender torso, gold-glinting cuff links, was close at hand. (What was his name? Something exotic, unlikely: Dmitri? One of the Karamazov brothers?) Elderly professor emeritus of medieval philosophy observed his young friend Joshua with frowning eyes. Casting doubt on whether Seigl should "drive his own car" home that night which struck Seigl as nervy, for Seigl was hardly drunk, hardly was Seigl even mildly drunk, look at the steadiness of his hand holding a drink... "You might share my taxi with me. It should be out front right now." Seigl objected: how'd he get his own car home, then?

Dmitri the waiter stepped forward. "Sir? I could drive you."

For some confused moments it seemed that, yes Dmitri would drive "Mr. Seigl" home. (In Seigl's car? In his own?) Seigl was resistant, and resentful. And Seigl's chess friend John was forcibly arguing the good sense of sharing a taxi. And others voiced opinions. Seigl was incensed. He threw off hands meant to comfort/restrain him. "I've told you I can drive myself. It's deeply offensive to me to be discussed as if I'm not present. I'm fucking *well*." He swallowed down the last of his drink. Pushed from them to get to the men's room, and some quiet. God damn! His kidneys were bloated and floating and another time the sinister fatigue dragged at his eyelids but he was able to resist, didn't fall asleep on his feet, and splashing cold water on his face he saw an astonishing rubefacient face, *rubefacient* a word rarely employed for rarely is there a *rubefacient* object encountered in the world, still less one's own face. And Seigl noted with alarm how his clean-shaven jaws were in fact covered in an ominously glinting stubble, as if he'd neglected to shave for days, and there were his madly lucid Seigl eyes...

"It can't be. I must be some mistake."

He was fully wakeful now. He departed The Café by a rear door eluding his would-be protectors who'd gravely insulted him. Did the bastards think he was a drunk, just because he'd lost at chess? A cripple? He had MS, or worse?

WOULDN'T ARRIVE BACK at the house until nearly 3 A.M. For he'd made a stop elsewhere, across the river.

13

Joshua? This is Sondra. Please will you call me? I need to speak with you . . .

And,

Joshua? This is Sondra again. I hope nothing is wrong? I haven't heard from you, please will you call me? We need to talk.

"Need to fuck yourself."

Savagely the Tattooed Girl struck "3" to erase the urgent messages. Whoever this "Sondra" was, she guessed the Jew was fucking.

FOR OFTEN SEIGL was away in the evenings now. And into the night. Telling Alma to take the evening off, he wouldn't be "needing" her.

Like he was giving some great gift to her! Like there was a life of Alma Busch's, a place where people awaited her, she could so easily return to.

Telling him thank you but she guessed she might just stay in.

Mornings Seigl was always at work in the dining room before Alma came upstairs. Mornings were precious to him he said. Always now her employer was loud-talking, excitable, a glisten of saliva on his lips. A glisten of craziness in his face. Wearing one of his white dress shirts but it was rumpled and soiled and crookedly buttoned. And maybe a ratty vest sweater dragged down over it half in and half out of his beltless trousers. And his big white bare feet in slovenly bedroom slippers. Alma could smell (she could!) the woman on him from the previous night, the mucky smell of cunt. She was disgusted having to wonder where those fat Jew lips had been.

HE WAS IN some state! Her Jew employer. Think she couldn't see? He was coked to the gills. His eyes. You can tell by the eyes. Except he'd been in this weird state for weeks. By now a cokehead or crystal meth user would've crashed. Crashed bad. Not the Jew. His brain was frying. You could feel heat coming off him like a radiator at six feet.

In remission it was, maybe. Like her grandfather Busch, with his Parkinson's. *In remission* means you aren't sick right now. But it can return any time.

14

"D MITRI"—THE NAME was magic to her. Never in Akron Valley had there been a Dmitri, or anybody like him.

In the movies, maybe. Tom Cruise. Brad Pitt. Sexy guys who didn't mind you knowing how they loved themselves best. And, loving you, it's maybe themselves they are loving.

"Babe, see if the Jew owns a gun. Check it out."

"A gun? Like . . ."

"A gun for Christ's sake. *G-U-N.* He'd have it in his bedroom maybe. In a drawer by the bed. In some cupboard or closet. Maybe in a safe."

The Tattooed Girl asked what she should do, if she found the gun.

"Just leave it. If you find it. For now."

So the Tattooed Girl looked through her employer's house. She spent the most time looking through his bedroom. And his study. The basement and the attic, she hadn't bothered with. Figuring if the Jew owned a gun it wouldn't be in those places because how could you get to it in time? Her father, Delray Busch, had kept his rifles and shotgun close at hand, like all the men in Akron Valley.

There was no safe in the house, that she'd discovered.

(Was she worried that her employer would catch her or suspect her of searching his rooms? Hell, no. Seigl trusted his assistant so, she could be stealing him blind in front of his eyes and he'd only just smile at her saying, *Alma! Good morning.*)

The Tattooed Girl was reluctant to disappoint her lover. Telling him she guessed Seigl wasn't a man to own firearms. You could sort of figure that by looking at him.

Somehow, this remark pissed Dmitri off. He said, sneering at her logic, "Anybody's a man to own firearms, babe. Like anybody's a man to want to use them."

15

I *am a child of Hell, I am lonely.*

Listless at 2 A.M. turning the pages of a book. A book!

What the fuck did the Tattooed Girl care for a *book*.

The Jew's house was filled with books. He'd written some of them himself. So what?

The Tattooed Girl with greasy hair and hair itchy beneath her arms and between her legs. Belly and big breasts sprawling inside her ratty pink flannel nightie stained from menstrual blood that wouldn't launder out one hundred percent even when she scrubbed it between her hands.

What the hell, nobody saw. Like the shitty tattoos straggling across her breasts and back, ruining her face men were always saying was a doll-face, so pretty, pretending her face wasn't ruined so they could fuck her which they could do without looking at her face. The tattoos she'd given up trying to make sense of. Like stains that are faded but will never fade *out*. But what the hell.

So they'd fucked up her life, those guys she'd trusted, for fun. What the hell.

The witch-book she called it. Always she opened it with a sickish little thrill. Like a nasty comic book her brothers had showed her when she was five or six. Ugly pictures of cut-up female bodies you couldn't believe you were seeing but every time you looked there they were.

Seeing Alma's shocked little face her brothers howled with laughter like hounds.

Fuckers. She hadn't seen them for eight years. Since they'd "disowned" her like Daddy had done.

Alma was propped up against pillows in the creaky old bed in the room—"suite" he called it—the Jew let her sleep in. This room was OK. Fancy furniture she was fearful of soiling or breaking. Other employers, they took it out of your pay if you fucked up. So mostly she only just sat on the bed. Too restless to sleep tonight. The Jew was out. With some woman. Here she was hot-eyed and angry turning the pages of the witch-book.

The TV didn't work right, she'd tried it. But she couldn't bring herself to complain to Mr. Seigl.

(Why not? Just couldn't.)

Let me know if there's anything you need, Alma.

Shit. Just couldn't.

"Yeah, mister. I need some loving. But not *you*."

Oh Christ she was wanting it. Her lover. Or just held by him, touched. So she knew she was *here*. She dreamed of him kissing her.

A man like Dmitri wasn't one for kissing, much. He'd make a face if she tried. And now he seemed never to want her the way he'd used to. (She couldn't figure it: she was looking much better now, a hell of a lot better than she'd looked then.) She was ashamed, he mostly passed her along to his asshole friends.

Hey babe, sure I love you. Crazy about you. But I'm busy, see?

(Not too busy to take money from her. Not too busy to ask when there'd be more.)

"Thou Shalt Not Suffer a Witch to Live" fell open to pages of illustrations at the center. Immediately Alma's eye moved upon a crude

drawing of a girl with long tattered dark hair and a pure Madonna face, half-naked, bleeding, kneeling on the floor of a dungeon and praying with doomed eyes cast heavenward. This was Jehane de Brigue. She'd been accused of witchcraft in 1390, in Paris. She was locally known as a "healer" and jealous persons accused her of "having intercourse" with the Devil in exchange for her powers. Hers was the "first secular witchcraft trial" in France. Like all the others, through the centuries of witchcraft persecution, Jehane de Brigue had been tortured by the religious authorities, made to confess, and executed.

Once you were accused, there could be no escape. For you would be tortured until you confessed, and when you confessed you would be executed. And anyone could accuse you. And you could accuse anyone.

" 'Jehane de Brigue.' " The Tattooed Girl whispered the long-ago name. She had no idea how it was meant to be pronounced.

Reading the witch-book late at night made the Tattooed Girl's skin crawl. Especially the tattoos. A scared shivery sensation. But sometimes it made her feel sexy, too.

Kind of angry-sexy. Like she was being cheated of something she deserved. Between her legs the throbbing, and a swollen feeling. And she knew that even if she touched herself hard, and sweated to make herself come, the sensation wouldn't go away, really. It was like Dmitri was off somewhere jeering at her.

Quickly she turned the page. But all the illustrations were ugly, and familiar to her. As if it was a child's book she'd grown up with. Drawings of (male) witch-hunters torturing their (mostly female) victims: needles driven up beneath fingernails, crushing by weights, thumbscrews, cutting off hands, tearing off female breasts with red-hot pincers. There was the "rack." There was the "press." The "strappado." (The victim was hoisted high by a rope beneath the arms, then let to fall the length of the rope. Eventually, the arms were disjointed from the body. That was the strappado.)

"Why'd God let it be done? In His name?"

The Tattooed Girl really wanted to know. Except for shyness she'd have asked her employer.

Say what you would about him, the Jew knew everything.

Not that Alma Busch and God were on close terms exactly. She guessed that Jesus had given up on her, at least for now. She went to church, though. Sometimes. Seigl knew, he'd dropped her off in town. Maybe he was amused by her but he was respectful. (As a Jew, Seigl never went to church, that Alma knew. Unless he kept it secret from her.) She'd gone to Wednesday evening services at Trinity Church in the square because it was closest. And at the Presbyterian church a few blocks away, and the Lutheran church. Alma in her showy new clothes and her face glamorously made up would sit alone in a rear pew and try to keep her thoughts focused on what the minister was saying and not distracted thinking how the ceiling of the church might collapse or a bomb might explode and these rich people would be screaming in agony and terror, and it would serve them right . . . She never joined in the singing knowing herself not welcome. In Akron Valley she'd gone to the Church of God with her friend Emmeline and she'd liked that. People like herself, she'd felt OK. There, Alma hadn't been afraid to sing. Emmie wasn't much better than she was. *Make a joyful noise unto the Lord* the minister was always urging. *It's the spirit that counts with the Lord.*

Then one Sunday she'd gotten it into her head, the minister felt sorry for her. Her family. Her old man Delray Busch who had a certain local reputation. Wanting to tell him *Fuck you I don't need you. Don't need Jesus Fucking Christ either.*

In Carmel Heights where nobody knew her name the Tattooed Girl was made to feel unwanted and freaky. Nobody felt sorry for her here—that was for damned sure. If she went into a store, even the drugstore, sales clerks eyed her coolly like they were watching to see if she'd try to shoplift. In Banana Republic, Gap, Talbots she was approached and asked *Can I help you, miss?* in that tone of voice meaning *You are not wanted here.* They were reluctant to let her try on clothes as if fearing she would damage or contaminate anything that touched her skin and sometimes in her rage she made certain she smeared lipstick onto a collar, or jammed a zipper, or wiped a patch of material between her legs or in the crack of her ass, biting her lip to keep from laughing. And catching sight of her swollen-looking white face and defiant red mouth in the distending convex mirror above the cashier's counter she would think, trembling with indignation, *That isn't me, that's somebody they made me be.*

On the street it was worse. Right on Mount Carmel Avenue sometimes. At Trinity Square. Local high school kids stared at her and turned to watch her pass, grinned and laughed in her wake. The punk bastards! It was like these kids could discern she didn't belong here like their sisters and mothers and the girls they went to school with, they saw no need to respect her. Older guys whistled and made sucking noises at her when there was no one to overhear. They behaved this way to the younger Hispanic, Guatemalan, Filipino women who worked in Carmel Heights and waited at Trinity Square for the bus to take them across the river. But why Alma was singled out among the white women, she didn't know. She liked the attention (sort of) but not the rudeness of it, and the guys laughing among themselves like guys always do.

Look: I am not a hooker.

Know who I am? I am Joshua Seigl's assistant. I have a room in his house.

Alma's eyelids were drooping. The heavy old book smelling of mildew tumbled onto the floor. It was too much effort to switch off the light. She was sprawled on her side facing the wall breathing harshly and trying not to cry. Her thick knees were drawn to her chest. She was doubled up hugging herself like she'd done as a little girl trying not to cry. She hated to cry in bed, the tears run hot down your face in all directions and wet the pillow. Feeling sorry for herself: she was so lonely. She missed home. She missed Akron Valley. The smoke lifting like white vapor from cracks in the earth, the way tall grasses and saplings were growing out of the broken pavement, there was a strange beauty in these things. Even the smell of the air that made your eyes sting. She missed the old hymns. *Lift thine eyes. There is a better land awaiting. Help cometh from the Lord.* She missed her mother. Though she'd taken no snapshots with her and the faces of even Mom and Daddy had become corroded with time. In dreams she could see them clearly, but not in wakeful life. Knowing they'd quarrel if ever Alma returned which Alma could not for she'd stolen from them, and they would never forgive her. And they'd never seen her freaky face and body and for sure if they did they'd be disgusted knowing the tattoos were a judgment on her.

The first time she'd been with a boy. Eighth grade. The boy was older. Her mother sniffed her out. Her sweater her grandmother had knitted for her was torn and muddy, there were burdocks in her hair. She stank of sweat, beer, sex. She'd smoked what the guys called hemp till she was sick. Her mother screamed at her, slapped her and chased her from the house. It was like TV: you wanted to laugh but if it's you, you can't. Later she knew to steer clear of her mother even if it meant staying away overnight. There was a confused time of cutting classes. Drinking with the older guys in the high school parking lot. What the fuck let people talk about her. *Alma Busch is a slut.* There were plenty of sluts in Akron Valley. Mostly, the other girls were jealous of her. She was prettier, more mature for her age. At thirteen looking like sixteen, or older. She loved to dance. It wasn't hard to get Alma drunk, she was warm and wild and funny when she'd had a few beers. Some of the senior guys had whiskey in flasks. They called her Firecracker. They would drive to the river, there was an urgency in their voices she loved. Not joking now, they needed her. *Alma, OK? Alma? C'mon.* She had a way of teasing them but not for too long. It was a mistake to tease any guy for too long. Sometimes there was another girl with Alma, in the backseat of the car, or Alma was in the backseat and the other girl in the front, but mostly

Alma was the only girl, and there was more than one guy. *Alma babe c'mon cut the crap.*

Her body was quicksand sliding away beneath her.

Sometimes she woke as she began to gag, and puke. The hot acid vomit so strange, such a shock, the thought that vomit is inside you, only you can't taste it till you begin to gag.

Sometimes she woke and there was one of them straddling her.

It was like being spaded, she thought: like she was soft soil, collapsing in their hands.

There was a boy she was trying to remember his name she loved who'd been different from the others or she'd believed so, with him she had not thought *I shouldn't be here, they don't care which one I am.* This boy would kiss her while he was making love to her, as other guys never did. She knew they called her Pigface, sometimes Pig Tits. There was one who'd played at choking her. It was only play but she'd been scared as hell. The look in some boys' eyes of anguish and fury. Her breasts were reddened and smarting, bruised afterward. Between her legs stinging like fire. There was a time in high school when sometimes they left her at the side of the access road by the river three miles from home and she felt the hurt as a child might feel desperate to be forgiven for whatever she must have done, to provoke such hurt.

"Fuckers."

Lying on her side, she felt her heart beating uncomfortably but it was too much effort to move. And her bare feet were cold, where was the damned cover? She was laughing remembering how she'd brought a coil of wire one night. This was later, in high school. The boy had straddled her and pushed her thighs apart and pressed his eager penis against her and into her where she was dry as sand and hurting and when it was over he lifted himself from her and lay beside her panting. He had not told her he loved her. He had not told her even that she was pretty. She looped the wire around his penis and tightened it and when he began to scream and thrash and claw at her hands she tightened it more.

AT ABOUT 3 A.M. there was a sound that woke her. Not any of the guys from Akron Valley, not the wind, but somebody urgently calling her name—*Alma?* At first the sound was at a distance, then close outside the window. *Alma? Alma help me.* She'd drawn the blind carelessly earlier in the evening and went now to peer through the slats seeing a man's shadowy figure about ten feet away in the dense sinewy evergreen shrubs, too dark to make out the man's face but of course Alma knew who it was.

"Mr. Seigl . . ."

She was thrilled: he needed her help.

She called to him to tell him yes she was coming, she'd be right there. In a rush now, terribly excited.

Something must have happened to him. More than just losing his house key. He'd sounded stricken, desperate. Maybe he couldn't get up the steps. (Not even the back steps? That would be serious.) Alma guessed it was his legs again. He'd lost his energy, his strange strength she'd known would not last. Outside he would lean heavily upon her. He would be panting, his hot breath in her face. Very likely he'd been drinking. He'd been with a woman. Now he needed help from Alma Busch. Just getting back into his house, he needed help from Alma Busch. In fact, Alma would bring his cane for him: she knew exactly where it was, tossed onto the floor of a closet as if Seigl had believed he would never need it again.

He would say something like *There's nothing wrong with me, it's just my legs.*

The Tattooed Girl hurried to put on her coat, her boots. She laughed to herself. She was excited, nervous. She guessed the *remission* had ended.

III

Nemesis

I

THAT WAS IT: "remission."

Somber and chastised, Seigl listened. The neurologist was explaining in detail what was known of the phenomenon as it occurred in nerve diseases. He learned that it wasn't uncommon that feelings of "euphoria"—"hypomania"—accompanied such interludes which could last as briefly as a few hours or as long as several weeks. As in bipolar disorder—formerly known as manic-depression—interludes of remission sometimes alternate with disease symptoms. The disease itself might show signs of "progressing" when remission ends.

Feeling the need to say something witty, for otherwise he couldn't speak at all, Seigl murmured, "I feel like the prodigal son, Doctor. Limping back home."

He'd limped into the neurologist's office. He was serious, clean-shaven. He comported himself with the dignity of the mildly depressed. His exuberant high spirits and energy had been exposed as mere mania, gone now like air escaped from a helium balloon.

His sexual energy, too. Gone.

Seigl had to concede, he did rather resemble a partly deflated balloon. During the wonderful manic interlude of nearly three weeks he'd lost over twenty pounds. His face was thinner, and wiser. But his skin was sallow and loose at his waist and torso, like elephant skin he thought it, repulsive. He would hardly have wished any woman to embrace him. When he'd had to strip for Friedman's examination he'd felt ashamed and wanted to cover himself with his arms.

"It was all an illusion, then? A delusion?"

Friedman, examining Seigl's heart, declined to reply.

Seigl hadn't yet looked through the hundreds of pages he'd written in his manic zeal. Poetry, play, novel . . . Hadn't dared look.

Friedman told him that there was sometimes a "considerable strain" on the heart during such bouts of hyperactivity and sleeplessness, and that he was referring Seigl to a cardiologist for a stress test. Seigl stood taciturn, detaching himself from the scene. Damned if he would tell Friedman that his rapidly beating heart had kept him awake sometimes even after the symptoms of euphoria and mania had passed. He didn't want to complicate matters. He didn't want to seem always to be complaining.

"I've never been a hypochondriac, Doctor. So this is hard for me."

What sort of a boast was that? Ridiculous.

Friedman said tactfully that such things were hard for everyone.

Friedman said that he, Seigl, was not a hypochondriac. More likely he was the reverse: a man unable to comprehend that he was ill.

Seigl laughed. The need to be witty was overwhelming as the need to sneeze.

"The very paradigm of our civilization, Doctor! I see."

Friedman wrote out a new prescription for Seigl. When the men shook hands as Seigl prepared to leave, Seigl had to resist the impulse to squeeze the neurologist's hand tightly. He said, deeply moved, "Thank you for taking me back as a patient, Doctor. Evidently I was"—searching for the precise word, needing to have the last word—"in the grip of hubris. Denial."

◎

AFTERWARD SEIGL WOULD think, He knew I'd be back all along.

THERE WAS HIS assistant Alma Busch waiting for him in the outer office. Like a gaudy brightly hued butterfly amid ordinary moths. Seigl was both bemused and annoyed by the way others looked at her. Alma was gripping a magazine titled *Allure*—ridiculous title!—close to her face, creasing her forehead with the effort of concentration. The glamour-face on the magazine cover mimicked and mocked her own.

For this visit to the neurologist's Alma was wearing a grape-colored jacket and trousers in an aggressively shiny synthetic material meant to approximate leather. Her boots were simulated cowhide, brassy hoop earrings swung at her ears. Her ash-blond hair was stiffened by static electricity and cascaded like a mane onto her shoulders. Her full, round face was eerily white and the blemish on her cheek was prominent. And her mouth that cheap luscious red. In his distraught mood Seigl stared at her—his assistant!—as if he'd never seen her before. Sometimes, Alma annoyed the hell out of him. She was absurdly dressed for the occasion, and, moreover, chewing a large wad of gum. Gum! Across her shiny grape-colored knees was Seigl's ivory-handled cane, like a cheerleader's baton.

Seigl had declined to use the cane, limping into Friedman's office. It had been humbling enough to his pride simply to return.

Alma's eyelids fluttered, guiltily she tossed aside *Allure*.

"Mr. S-Seigl? It's time to—leave?"

Seigl grunted impatiently, heading for the door. Alma snatched up their coats and hurried in his wake.

In the elevator Seigl said stonily, not looking at her, "Alma. That gum. It's repulsive."

Alma flinched as if Seigl had struck her. She mumbled she was sorry. Trying to be unobtrusive, with childlike haste she detached the gum from her mouth and wrapped it into a tissue.

When the elevator door opened, Seigl took the cane from Alma, and stalked off.

SEIGL DROVE. For as long as it was humanly possible Seigl intended to drive his car. But he wanted his assistant beside him, just in case.

They stopped at Seigl's drugstore in Carmel Heights to fill the prescription. Waiting for it, leaning on his cane, Seigl examined wheelchairs, firing questions at a salesclerk. These were repulsive objects, too, but only if you were in a state of denial. Otherwise they were wonderfully practical, the power-driven chairs were brilliant inventions. The salesclerk inquired tactfully: to rent or to purchase?

Seigl said, "Neither. Just now."

2

THERE WAS NO HOUR, no singular moment when she thought *I will kill him.*

Though for months the fiery whispery words *Hate hate him hate the Jew* consoled her and perhaps thwarted the more desperate *I love him: why doesn't he love me? The bastard!* For the Tattooed Girl was the first to concede her weakness for adoring any man who refrained from kicking her in the gut, as she adored any man who did kick her in the gut, out of a craven need to adore any man.

But not the Jew. Him, I hate!

So the thought that she might easily kill her employer who trusted her didn't come to the Tattooed Girl fully formed. Few thoughts came to her fully formed. Alma's thinking followed acts performed by her body. She surprised herself by uttering things she had not known she knew. Often she thought *I'm smarter than I think I am!* Often, her hands surprised her.

She was watching her hands now. Stubby child's hands. Angry hands, clumsy. Her mother had scolded her for being clumsy-on-purpose. Alma saw her hands slyly wrapping the dish towel around the water glass and she saw her hands smash the glass, safely wrapped in the towel, against the sink. The sound of the breakage was muffled, no one could have heard. Even in the dining room beyond the swinging doors where her employer, reading and taking notes, sighing and muttering to himself, sat at the dining room table absentmindedly awaiting dinner.

Alma laughed aloud, nervously. What was this?

Most of the glass fragments were too large for her purpose but a few were small enough, needle-sized, and these Alma further crushed into tiny fragments inside the towel. She didn't want splinters too large. Even the size of peppercorns was too large. The fragments, approximately half a teaspoonful, she brushed into the steaming seafood casserole from The Food Shop which she'd heated in the oven at 375° F as directed. With a spoon she carefully stirred the fine-broken glass into a corner of the casserole thinking *He will never know. No one will know.* It was a Tuesday evening in early March. Several days after Seigl's thirty-ninth birthday. The humiliation, for the Tattooed Girl, of that birthday party. But even at the time, in the depth of her misery, here in this same kitchen the Tattooed Girl had not thought *I will revenge myself for this: I will kill the man who has insulted me.*

Seafood casserole! One of Seigl's favorite meals. He had Alma order it from The Food Shop at least once a week. The casserole was so expensive, like everything else at The Food Shop, Alma had thought at first the price must be a joke. But Seigl, who wished to think of himself as frugal, plain-living as a monk, took not the slightest notice of the prices of things. *Because he's rich, see? Rich Jew.*

Giant shrimps, crabmeat, slices of lobster in a heavy cream sauce, rice . . . Alma's mouth watered though she disliked seafood and had already eaten her supper, and would be eating again later, through the remainder of the evening in fact, leftovers and jelly toast before bed. Through most days the Tattoed Girl ate: browsing, you could call it. For the Tattooed Girl was always hungry.

"Mr. S-Seigl?"

In the dining room her eccentric employer was hunched over a book as usual, a book with the boring word *history* in its title. He'd dragged a desk lamp into the dining room and had placed it on the table, Alma had to be careful of tripping over the damned cord. Seigl's hair was straggling over the collar of his crookedly buttoned white shirt and his jaws sprouted whiskers like quills. His new glasses slid down his nose. He had a new, annoying habit of pulling at his lips as he read. Since that night he had wakened Alma to come help him into the house, for he could barely totter on his legs, he'd been subdued, moody. He had had no choice but to ask her to accompany him to the doctor: now, Alma knew he was seeing a "neurologist." She understood that Seigl was embarrassed and ashamed of what had happened to him and that he resented her for having been a witness. Still, he'd needed her. Not just one of his legs had gone numb that night, but he'd been pretty drunk. Wherever he'd been, he'd been drinking whiskey. Damned lucky he hadn't had an accident driving his car or been arrested for drunk driving.

Alma, thank you. That was all the Jew could bring himself to utter, afterward.

With steady hands Alma brought Seigl's dinner to him, waiting patiently for him to glance up and notice her, move his papers and books aside so that she could set the hot plate down. It was burning her fingers! Damn but he was lost as usual in his stupid book, always the man was lost in a book. It was 8:30 P.M. and the meal had already been delayed. (Except: with a pang of dismay Alma saw that she had forgotten to set a place for Seigl. No place mat, no silverware and napkins.) Seigl glanced up at last, frowning. "So soon? Well. Set it down." When Alma hesitated he said impatiently, "Anywhere will do, Alma. Thank you."

It was one of the Jew's cranky days. After the birthday he'd been hungover and morose and when the telephone rang and it was his woman friend Blumenthal he had not wanted to speak with her. He had forbidden Alma to ask about his health in any way as if she gave a damn how he was feeling, anyway she could tell by the look in his face. His eyes were stark now in their sockets with a new, sobering vision. His cheeks were lean, with vertical lines. There was a crease between his eyebrows that looked like it had been made with a knife. *Now you know,* Alma thought, satisfied. It was the knowledge she'd seen in her grandfather's face, the furious old man had had no choice but to accept. *God has laid His hand on you. You are fucked.*

Alma hesitated, holding the plate. Her hands had begun to tremble. Seigl made an impatient gesture to take the plate from her and Alma stepped back, stammering, "Oh, I n-need to get the—" meaning the place setting, but the words wouldn't come out, and somehow the heavy plate slipped from her fingers, fell onto the table and splattered scalding-hot casserole onto Seigl's papers, books, hands. Seigl cried, "God damn! God damn fucking clumsy! What the fuck are you doing, you idiot!"

Hiding her face in her hands, the Tattooed Girl fled.

3

B UT NOW THE thrilling words *I will kill him. The Jew. No-body will know. Who will know?* had been unleashed. Like tied-up dogs in a yard. Breaking their ropes. Or breaking their frayed old collars. Running, yelping. Run, run! *I will. I will kill him. Anytime I want to. Who's to stop me?*

The Tattooed Girl moving in a dream through the long hours of the day and into the night.

The Tattooed Girl in a bliss of revenge. For wasn't the Jew of that family of rich banker-Jews who'd shut down the mines of the Akron Valley? Wind Ridge. Bobtown. McCracken. Cheet. *You have no right. You buy and sell souls. You are the Anti-Christ. I am your punishment. I bring not peace but a sword.*

If Delray Busch could know, he would forgive her.

Daddy would forgive her, his baby-girl Alma. He would pull her onto his lap and tickle her with his whiskery kisses. He would blow in her ears and make her shriek. He would toss her toward the ceiling and catch her in his strong, hard arms.

"Dad-*dy*. Dad-*dy*. *No.*"

Terrified of not being caught by him. Terrified of falling to the floorboards covered in a thin chenille rug.

(For Daddy had dropped her, once. Or more than once. For a long time she'd believed it was her baby brother Hardy he'd dropped, now she wasn't so certain. She did remember the shrieking, though. She remembered Daddy's voice raised in grief and anger.)

DANCING! SO HAPPY!

Her lover loved her again. Love love loved her again.

She was staying the weekend with him. They'd gone to a party across the river. A heavy metal scene. Christ she was hot. Dancing like on a hot tin roof. Dancing like she didn't give a damn if her heart burst. Barefoot and shrieking eyes shut tight flailing her wild hair forward and back, forward and back like a whip. The gearing up noise of heavy metal that's a shot to the heart. Christ she loved it. She was just a kid fourteen years old loving it. That down-dirty deafening bass that's like a diesel rig climbing a long slow grade. Christ you never want it to stop: never.

Holding the guys' attention she was drawing Dmitri's attention, too. Dmitri's wandering eyes. Dmitri's sly smile. The Tattooed Girl was burning hot waving her arms as she danced like a wounded pheasant in the underbrush.

"I'm gonna! I'm gonna do it! Kill the Jew! One of these days! He provokes me, I'm gonna!"

The guys laughed egging her on.

Guys who didn't know the Tattooed Girl, didn't know the situation of her employment, had to wonder what she was talking about. Had to ask.

"Gonna! Gonna! Gon-na! Think I won't? Hey listen: nobody'd know. Anything can happen to a cripple."

She was panting, breathless. A strand of hair fell across her mouth. She spat it out, almost gagging.

There stood her lover smiling at her as you'd smile at a small show-off child. "Alma babe, you're far-out. You're fantastic. But you're just kidding, right?"

No! The Tattooed Girl was not fucking kidding.

"Why'd you want to kill Seigl? Or anybody? You'd get caught. You'd get into serious trouble."

The Tattooed Girl shook her head vehemently.

"Don't give a fuck. I'm gonna. He provokes me, the dirty Jew I'm gonna."

Dmitri was staring at her in a way she liked. For once seeing her. Fucking seeing *her*.

"Well I'm not kidding. I'm gonna kill him. One of these days. For the hell of it I'm gonna." The Tattooed Girl was laughing, out of breath like she'd been running for miles. Her silver lamé tube top was soaked through and slipping halfway down her breasts. What her mascara looked like, she didn't want to know. She was waiting to dance again, waiting to regain the beat. Dmitri wasn't a dancer. Dmitri liked to watch, though. He stroked her hair and took her by the nape of the neck. Christ she loved this. Shut her eyes and melted against him. A big silky sexy pussycat melting against him. Loving up his groin.

Dmitri gripped her hands on his buttocks. He didn't like her to feel him up with anybody looking on. In a lowered voice he said, "I'm not telling you to kill the Jew or anybody. I'm not. I'm telling you not to, babe. But if you do better wait for the Jew to name you in his will, leave some money to you, see? Make you his beneficiary. That's the smart move."

The Tattooed Girl kissed him full on the lips. The Tattooed Girl ground her groin against his, writhing like a snake. The heavy rock music began again, pulling her away. She saw his staring eyes on her, though.

Fucking seeing *her*: Alma Busch.

NOW THAT SHE'D hardened her heart against Joshua Seigl, reasons came to her for what she would do. Like a court trial it was. The verdict was handed down: GUILTY. Now you needed to see why it was just.

And the death sentence was just.

"Not just he's a Jew. There's good Jews and bad Jews. But . . ."

Seigl was moody a lot. Rude! On his good days he was respectful to her as he'd been in the beginning and often he gave her extra money and spoke of sending her to the local college but on the other days when his legs gave out or he couldn't concentrate on his work he sulked and hid away like a sick dog then called for her and expressed impatience she didn't get to him in ten seconds and he bossed her around as bad as her daddy ever bossed her mother and she heard that edge of exasperation in his Jew-voice familiar to the Tattooed Girl from other relationships with other sons of bitches and the essential message was *Look, he doesn't love you. Doesn't care a fuck about you.*

(And she'd thought maybe, sort of, months ago . . . Poor stupid Alma to think her rich Jew-boss might fall in love with her and marry her. Christ!)

(No wonder Dmitri laughed at her. Saying her brains were mostly in her cunt.)

Hate him. Hate him to death. The way he'd looked at her in disgust in the doctor's waiting room and the others had seen. The nurse at the receptionist's counter had seen. Saying her gum was *repulsive* which was his way of saying Alma Busch was *repulsive*. That was a word she associated with snakes: *repulsive*. Then, how disgusted he'd been with her for spilling his fucking seafood casserole dinner. When it wasn't even Alma's fault, it was his fault! Because the plate had burnt her fingers because he hadn't shoved his fucking things aside in time, how was that her fault? She'd run away to hide. She knew he'd been unjust and she knew that he knew, too. In his shrewd Jew-heart the man knew all things. But when about forty minutes later she cautiously returned to clean up the mess he was gone. Took his cane—she'd checked, yes it was gone—and left the house. Left the house at nine o'clock without telling her where the fuck he was going, to punish her, she knew. (Staying with that woman professor. She guessed. Blumenthal was the name, a typical Jew name.) (And what if Seigl decided to marry this woman? He was anxious and excitable and likely to do crazy things. What would become of Alma? She could guess: kicked out on her ass. For all the Jews cared, she could turn tricks with the cokehead hookers on Union Street.) Still, it was a relief, Alma had to admit. He hadn't eaten the ground glass.

Alma cleaned up the mess on the table as best she could. At the kitchen table she devoured, with a table spoon, more than half of what remained of the casserole. So hungry!

Did she swallow a few grains of ground glass? Maybe. Most of it had been in Seigl's serving. But she figured a little ground glass wouldn't hurt going down. People swallow dirt, after all. It's said a person eats seven pecks of dirt a year, right? Or maybe it's seven spiders. Since spiders crawl around at night and people sleep with their mouths open. So, seven spiders or seven pecks of dirt, none of it kills you. And a little ground glass, if that's what Alma swallowed, eating rapidly and ravenously as she was, it wouldn't kill Alma, either.

THE WORST INSULT had been the night of Seigl's birthday party.

At the start Seigl was inviting only ten or twelve guests, then the number rose to twenty, then to twenty-six, and finally to thirty-five. Thirty-five people for dinner! A catering service called Les Amis was engaged. Tables and chairs had to be rented. Most of the arrangements were being done by Seigl's woman friend Blumenthal, he told Alma, but Alma had to help set up the house for the party and would help the caterers. On the day of his birthday, Seigl typically barricaded himself away in his study, letting Alma deal with the ringing telephone, the flower and wine deliveries. Alma became increasingly excited, apprehensive. She had never had so much responsibility. For instance, several cases of wine were delivered in mid-afternoon. When Alma saw the size of the bill, she nearly fainted. "This isn't right. This is a mistake." The delivery man insisted it was no mistake. Alma hurried to Seigl who refused to leave his desk and check out the wine in the kitchen. "But Mr. S-Seigl, what if it isn't all there?" Alma fretted. "What if there's some wrong bottles mixed in?" Alma knew from Dmitri Meatte how particular some men were about their wine. But Seigl just shrugged. "Alma, I can't be bothered with trivia. I must work."

Work! On his birthday.

Sondra Blumenthal arrived early to help "coordinate" as she called it. Alma opened the door to the woman, behaving very coolly and politely. They had spoken a number of times on the phone. Now Alma saw that Sondra Blumenthal wasn't young and wasn't very attractive. She had an angular bony face, a long nose, very plain eyes you'd swear were lashless. When she smiled, her gums showed. She was wearing a black dress like something you'd wear to a funeral and her hair was nothing special. But there was a bossy school-teacher way about her Alma knew she must not challenge, for the woman would complain of her to Seigl. *This bitch has your number*.

As soon as she stepped into the foyer, Blumenthal asked Alma, "How is Mr. Seigl today? Is he well?"

Alma stiffened. Such a question, from a stranger. Alma turned away without answering.

In her room downstairs, Alma dressed for the party, too. She brushed her hair until sparks flew. She tamped it down with barrettes so it wasn't so flyaway. She made up her face carefully, powdering over the tattoo. (You could still see it, of course. But it looked less like dried blood and more like just a raised blemish in the skin.) Alma had a black dress with a rhinestone belt and a scoop-necked black lace bodice she'd bought at a post-holiday sale at Penney's she thought would be OK for her, since she'd be wearing a white apron over it. In the mirror, she looked a little anxious but sexy as hell. The bodice fit her bust tightly. She wished her lover could see her, he'd be jealous.

When the caterers arrived, Alma was made to feel unwanted in her own kitchen. "Out of the way, miss. Excuse us." And, "Can you stand aside, miss? We're busy." There were three of them, in white jackets and trousers; the eldest called herself Madame Zee and appeared to be the boss. Alma had never seen anything like the caterers' brisk, military way of working. She was astonished by the amount of food they'd brought. Madame Zee looked through Alma rather than at her and gave her orders without adding "please." Still, Alma was eager to do well. She wanted Madame Zee to think highly of her. But when Alma tried to carry one of the appetizer trays out to the guests, Madame Zee said sharply, "No." Through the interminable, exhausting evening—nearly five hours!—Alma was never allowed to serve food or wine, only to collect dirtied plates and glasses. She was put to work, in her black lace and rhinestone dress, mostly scraping garbage and rinsing plates to stack in the dishwasher. Wineglasses, she had to dry by hand.

Returning to the kitchen with the first of the plates, in a haze of self-consciousness, Alma was stunned when Madame Zee hissed at her, "Miss, we don't stack." Alma blinked in confusion. What? Madame Zee repeated, "We don't *stack*." She grabbed the several plates which Alma had stacked together, and dropped them on the kitchen counter. The assistants cleared the tables by carrying plates singly, not stacking them, so Alma guessed that was what she'd been supposed to do, but how did you know? Why did it matter? Her eyes filled with tears of shame and rage. Strands of hair began to loosen and fall into her face. She was sweating beneath her arms. By the time coffee was being served and Seigl's three-tiered chocolate birthday cake was brought into the room, with its thirty-nine festive candles burning, and his friends loudly singing "Happy Birthday," Alma was sulking.

She waited for Seigl to call for her, to ask, "Where is Alma? My assistant Alma?" But he never did.

Of that humiliating evening Alma would keenly recall peering through the doorway into the dining room as Madame Zee and her tightassed assistants brushed past her. There was Seigl at the head of the table which had been transformed, flowers, candles, gleaming glassware and silverware, a white linen tablecloth; there was the Blumenthal woman, baring her gums like a barracuda, seated to his right. Seigl was wearing a dark suit that looked expensive, that Alma had never seen before, and a patterned necktie, and his face was clean-shaven and glowing, he was so *happy*. You would not guess that this was a man anxious about his health. You would not guess that this was a man who moaned and bitched to himself how he was a failure. Nor would you guess that Seigl was thirty-nine, and not twenty-nine. Alma stared. There was that dark Jewish look, Alma supposed that was how you'd describe it, a kind of Arab look, sexy, but also shrewd, smart, the heavy dark eyebrows and striking eyes, the red fleshy mouth. Alma felt the attraction powerfully.

Alma was dismayed, her employer had so many friends. And they were women as well as men, some of them older, a few younger. Some were very attractive individuals but others were plain and dumpy and some were homely. Why'd anyone like them, much? Who were they? Now some of them were standing, one by one, raising their glasses, making toasts to Seigl, like people on TV. You would swear they had prepared words. Must be reading their words! For how could they make up such words, so fluently, as Seigl did, too? All this mystified Alma. She hated it, she was made to feel so stupid. Her very tongue was fat and sluggish in her mouth. She supposed that Seigl's guests were people like him, writers, professors, maybe lawyers, well-to-do neighbors. But there were younger people who looked like college students. Why did they like one another so much, and why did Seigl like them? All that evening Alma had been hearing them talking and laughing together, it was like they spoke a language foreign to her, though their words were meant to be English, like hers. She was sick with jealousy. She could not grasp this mystery. The ugly tattoo on her cheek pulsed with chagrin. She picked at it with her nails, smearing the powder, not caring if she drew blood.

Why did people care for one another, where there was no sex connection? That was the mystery. Except that she was crazy for Dmitri Meatte, Alma feared and disliked him, and could never be a friend to him. If he ceased utterly to want her, she would wish him dead.

"Out of the way, miss."

"You're blocking the way, miss."

Alma shoved blindly at someone's arm. "Fuck you."

She stalked out of the kitchen and ran down the back stairs to her room.

GUESTS BEGAN LEAVING around midnight. The caterer's van departed around 2 A.M. By this time the Tattooed Girl was sleeping a dull stuporous sleep beneath layers of bedclothes, knees drawn up to her breasts and breasts sprawling loose inside her flannel nightie. If that woman slept in Joshua Seigl's bedroom that night, the Jewess with the barracuda gums, the Tattooed Girl was spared knowing.

4

Driven by thirst, I eyed a fine icicle outside the window, within hand's reach. I opened the window and broke off the icicle but at once a large, heavy guard prowling outside brutally snatched it away from me. *"Warum?"* I asked him in my poor German. *"Hier ist kein warum"* (there is no why here), he replied, pushing me inside with a shove.

This passage from Primo Levi's *Survival at Auschwitz* had long haunted Seigl. *Hier ist kein warum.* A profound insight though spoken by a brute. Yet we must ask *Warum?*

"So long as we are human, we must ask."

5

AND ANOTHER GERMAN QUOTATION Seigl liked:
Der Herr Gott ist raffiniert aber boshaft ist Er nicht.
Was it true? "God is subtle but not malicious."

This was a quotation beloved of Albert Einstein. Seigl was struck by it though hardly believing in God, still less in Einstein's austere rationalist God. He supposed that the remark was purely wishful thinking. You would wish that Der Herr Gott wasn't malicious, therefore you flatter Him by claiming He is not.

Saying one thing, meaning its reverse. It was a season of such strategems.

"OF COURSE I love you, Sondra. It's only just . . . At this uncertain time in my life . . ."

They were wiping tears from their eyes in the bright cold wind on Seigl's terrace overlooking the river. In the hazy distance, like an Impressionist painting, blue-gray Lake Ontario. It was mid-March, you wanted badly to believe that spring was near. Snow remained, but each day the sun rose higher in the sky, and waned a little later.

A season of hope. Seigl had hope! God damn, yes.

"... I don't want to hurt you. Or Ethan. I've been ... thinking about that, about you, and wondering ..."

Here was why Seigl was hopeful: he wasn't in a wheelchair (yet) and his new medication seemed to be helping (to a degree) and he was working again after a spell of despair.

He was hopeful that he could keep Sondra Blumenthal as a friend. A dear friend. Even as a lover ...

Sondra said, with her usual enthusiasm, as if she'd never before seen this view from Seigl's terrace, "It's mesmerizing here. You could watch the river for hours. If I lived here ..."

Seigl felt an impulse to say: Come live with me, then! You and Ethan.

The impulse passed. The moment was passing. Shortly now Sondra would say she had to leave to pick up Ethan from school and take him to his music lesson.

Piano? Violin. Seigl kept forgetting.

In the eye-smarting wind Seigl was holding his friend's gloveless hand. They stood near the railing without leaning against it since Seigl wasn't certain the damned thing was safe. He would have it repaired as soon as the weather turned warmer. And other repairs the old house needed. He'd have his assistant look into them. This past winter he'd let many things slide, he'd been distracted and *not himself* as the expression has it.

If not myself then who am I?

The lies we tell. Even to ourselves.

As lovers he and Sondra Blumenthal were tender with each other. They were friends who'd become lovers and were uncertain of their deepest allegiance: to this new, sometimes awkward tenderness, or to their older companionableness? And then there was sex: always stark, tyrannical. To think of an old friend in sexual terms is a radical act of the imagination.

Sondra wanted him to marry her, Seigl knew. She was a woman of too much pride and natural dignity to acknowledge anything so conventional, so mundane. And she was no longer young: nearly Seigl's age. He couldn't blame her. He did not blame her. He wished . . . *To be married. Not to marry.* He would have liked to have been married to Sondra from a time when they'd both been young, in their early twenties, and so by now they'd have had the experience of growing up together. Become adults together. Wry, droll, wounded and wise adults. And Sondra's son, Ethan, for whom Seigl felt a complex sort of emotion: Seigl would have liked to be the boy's father in more than just by name, adoption.

Most of their friends were long married and settled in their lives. Even the divorced had remarried, and were settled in their new marriages. Their children were beyond childhood. Seigl would have wished this, or told himself so. He saw himself, in this matter of marrying at thirty-nine, as a man running, limping-running, beside a train as it pulls out of the station. Will he catch the train? Will he miss it? Comic suspense as he grabs at the rail of the caboose and tries to swing himself up onto the steps . . .

Seigl played chess frequently with Ethan Blumenthal. He was touched by the boy's earnestness and impressed with his intelligence. So like himself at that age—eager to learn the games of adults. As if chess were a way *in*. Seigl would have been astounded to be told that, thirty years later, he was still looking for that way *in*.

Seigl commended Ethan when he played well. But Seigl wouldn't allow Ethan to win, not even a single game, because he knew the boy would understand he'd let him win, and the winning would have no meaning. "I guess I'm pretty stupid," Ethan said frequently, "—I guess you think I'm pretty stupid, Mr. Seigl." "Not at all," Seigl said, warmly. "I think you're damned smart. Call me 'Josh.'" He saw Ethan blink away tears. He saw Ethan's delicate mouth harden, in an expression of hurt, disappointment. He heard the boy's quickened breathing. And another time Ethan would say, wiping his nose with an angry gesture of his hand, "I really am stupid!" as if they'd been arguing this issue, as if this, and not the game, were somehow the point of the game; and Seigl knew he must repeat no, no Ethan wasn't stupid, he shouldn't be discouraged because . . . Seigl liked it that the games were between Ethan and himself, and Sondra kept her distance, but he didn't like it that chess was beginning to mean too much to the eleven-year-old. Uneasily Seigl thought *He's telling himself if he plays chess well, this man who has barged into his life will marry his mother and become his father.*

The logic of fairy tales. Yet Seigl understood: his sense of his own father was blurred, uncertain. Sometimes he believed that everything he'd ever written, every effort of his imagination, had been an attempt to pay homage to Karl Seigl, who had eluded him.

Ethan never spoke of his father to Seigl, even when the subject might have come up naturally. Sondra had said ambiguously that the boy's relationship with this absent father "wasn't ideal."

Of Ethan, Sondra said to Seigl in a light tone, though her meaning was unmistakable, "Don't make promises you can't keep, Joshua. Promise?"

Seigl promised.

Sondra said now, glancing at her watch, "It's late. I must leave."

They stepped from the windy terrace back inside the house. Seigl's eyes smarted from the strong bright light. Sometimes, the vividness and vibrancy of the outer world, including too the world of other people, assaulted his brain like pelting needles.

He told himself: It's been a good day. You're on your feet.

It was Seigl's study they were stepping into, a large room with windows on three sides, floor-to-ceiling bookshelves and tables upon which papers and manuscripts had been neatly placed. This room, Sondra had often seen in its earlier, pre-Alma state of disarray.

Sondra said, "She has made a difference in your life, Joshua. This 'Alma.' At least visibly."

Seigl said tersely, "She's invaluable."

He would say no more. He understood that Sondra disliked and disapproved of Alma Busch, as other friends of his did. But he didn't discuss the subject.

Seigl walked Sondra to the front door. He was grateful to be able to walk, capably, with his cane. If his right leg ached and tingled, if there was a curious shimmering of his vision intensified by the several minutes outside on the terrace, Sondra needn't know. She was in the habit of exclaiming how well he was looking. Especially when they were intimate, lying together in a darkened room, she would have liked to know every fact about her lover's yet-unnamed nerve disorder. She would have liked to speak with him on the phone several times a day, to be informed of every nuance of every symptom of his, the fever chart of his emotions through the length of a day and how well, or ill, he slept each night, but Seigl was hardly one to share such confidences. Never!

Often Sondra said he was very brave. Seigl's droll response was, he'd rather not have to be.

Almost shyly she said now, lifting her eyes to his, "I'll see you tomorrow evening, then? The usual time?"

"If you still want me."

"Oh, Joshua. What a thing to say."

She leaned quickly to him, to kiss him. She didn't want him to see the alarm in her face. Her kisses were like exclamations. Seigl gripped her shoulders and kissed her more forcibly.

Seigl watched Sondra descend the nineteen stone steps to the sidewalk, turning to wave back at him, smiling. Sondra Blumenthal was an attractive woman past the bloom of heedless youth and Seigl loved her, his heart was deeply moved by her. Again he felt the impulse to call her back . . .

He shut the door. Somewhere upstairs in his house was the sound of a vacuum cleaner.

6

I NVALUABLE."

He wasn't sure that this was so. The irony of the remark pleased him, though.

On a wall of his study where he'd affixed postcards from friends there was a reproduction of a Henry Moore sculpture: a voluptuous sprawling female figure with an egg-sized featureless head. Long before Alma Busch had entered his life he would gaze at this, revulsed, yet fascinated. *I am I* such figures seem to declare.

He stood listening: Alma was thumping about upstairs. Like a girls' gym class she sounded, graceless, heavy-footed, yet earnest. Even Alma's blunders were well intentioned. Always the girl meant well. To let her go would be impossible.

Alma kept Seigl's house in order. There was no need for a cleaning woman to come once a week. Simple repetitive household tasks that would have been maddening to Seigl seemed to be consoling to her. Sometimes he would swear she was blind, making her way through the rooms of his house by touch and smell. Her face was blank as an aboriginal mask. Her eyes were narrowed to slits. She held objects as if needing to grasp, to grope, before knowing what an object was. Often he caught a glimpse of her, through a doorway, frowning, her lips moving as if she were talking to herself, urgently. At such times she was oblivious of Seigl as if he had no existence. Almost, he was made to wonder if he'd drifted into a stranger's dream: if Alma Busch suddenly wakened, he would vanish.

Vacuuming was one of Alma's favorite household chores. Furniture and floor polishing, sink scrubbing with Brillo pads or brushes. She liked to "run" the laundry as she called it. She'd taken over most of the ironing, that Seigl had always sent out. "See, Mr. Seigl, it's a lot cheaper. And I'm good at it." She was never so happy as when she charged about the house with a roll of paper towels and Windex in hand. In Seigl's study she was less confident, never taking the initiative but waiting to be instructed what to do. In the kitchen she was even less assured, and seemed always to be breaking things, or stymied by their operation. She'd never learned to cook, she claimed. Or, she was "no good" at cooking. In that distant world from which she'd come, Seigl guessed, men had been served by women, men had harshly judged the food prepared for them by women, and Alma had grown up with such knowledge. She behaved as if every meal prepared for her employer was a sacred ritual at which, talentless as she was, she must fail. Most of Seigl's dinners continued to be delivered by one or another of the food shops in the vicinity, though Alma was now the one to order them.

"Alma, come sit with me. Have your dinner with me tonight."

In his euphoric mood Seigl had been feeling magnanimous, yes and he'd been feeling lonely, so he'd invited his assistant to join him, and the way Alma had gaped blinking at him, you'd think he'd uttered something obscene. She'd backed off stammering she could not, there was "too much to do" in the kitchen.

He guessed she had a boyfriend. And she had difficulties with the boyfriend. For sometimes she was avid for her evenings and days off, and stayed away for an entire weekend, Friday night, Saturday night, Sunday night, but other times more recently she said with a sullen shrug she'd be staying in.

She went to church sometimes. Seigl was touched: Alma Busch believed in God!

Yet this was typical of her class, her type. An irony of history. *Those in whom God does not believe, believe in God.*

Seigl had never questioned her about her beliefs, though he wanted to. Nor had he dared to ask her about the strangely shaped mark on her cheek. The smudged-looking marks on the backs of her hands, like ragged gloves. Birthmarks, probably. He was sure that Jet must be wrong. (Jet was wrong about everything. That was Jet!) More than once it had crossed Seigl's mind, gazing at his assistant as a lepidopterist might gaze at an exotic butterfly, that he might offer Alma the possibility of cosmetic surgery to have the marks removed or at least lightened. *Your beauty shouldn't be defaced, Alma.*

But how could he find the words, Christ! he could not.

BEFORE SONDRA BLUMENTHAL had left, Seigl gave her a folder of new Virgil translations. He was both eager and anxious to hear her response. He'd been working so long in the dark. He hadn't told Sondra that somehow in his "manic" state he had lost or destroyed a portion of the *Aeneid* manuscript as, evidently, he'd lost or destroyed pages of his novel and his play.

Seigl tried to remember: had he been disgusted with what he'd reread, or had he simply, accidentally, lost it?

At first, he couldn't believe the missing pages were missing. He looked repeatedly through the same mess of papers, with the gape-mouthed compulsion of a zombie. "No. No. No. No. *No.*" At last he'd enlisted his assistant in the desperate search. Alma had been diligent, going through drawers and files in his study where, obvi-ously, the lost papers could not be, unless Seigl had hidden them away in a fit of total madness. On her hands and knees she'd peered into the backs of closets. She'd gone through every wastebasket in the house and braved the cold of the day to retrieve the contents of the trash cans she'd set out at the curb, in search of Joshua Seigl's scribbled pages. As if they were pure gold, and not very likely dross! Even after Seigl had given up, Alma doggedly continued. "I feel so bad, Mr. S-Seigl, that time I . . ." Alma was trying to speak of the farcical episode in the dining room when Seigl had grabbed for a plate of hot food and Alma had dropped it onto his things. Seigl had screamed at her, terrible wounding words he couldn't believe that he of all people had uttered. (He hadn't apologized. Couldn't bring himself to relive any of that ludicrous scene.) The defaced pages, Alma had wiped clean of the gluey mess and laid out neatly to dry on the dining room table, and these Seigl had been able to read, so none of these had been lost. But other pages, older material, seemed to be gone, and Seigl knew he had only himself to blame.

Christ: he'd been drinking, too. Not just he'd been in a manic state, which meant a rapid heartbeat and soaring blood pressure, but he'd been drinking, too. Wine, beer, whiskey. Whiskey! Seigl wasn't a man for hard liquor. And cruising Union Street, picking up hookers . . . He must have been deranged.

Hey honey? You lookin for a date?

Hey sugahhh!

They'd laughed at him. Pouring sweat, his jacket unbuttoned. Looking and sounding like a professor. In some weird needy state beyond words.

In their streetwise wisdom the hookers had made him use condoms.

Seigl shuddered to think: he might be HIV-positive now. And he might have infected Sondra. She'd known nothing of her lover's frantic after-hours life, of course. She'd believed he loved her, she'd trusted him . . .

Seigl tasted panic just to think of this. He couldn't allow himself to think of it.

Madness. Mania. But it was finished now. He would be stone cold sober and sane for the remainder of his life.

He hadn't been able to apologize to Alma, he simply couldn't. He tried not to lose his temper with her, for he needed her so badly. Yet his moods flared up like flash fires, and quickly subsided. *I hope to Christ I don't remind her of someone. Why she looks at me cringing like a kicked dog.*

It was true, as Sondra said, that Seigl's assistant had made a difference in his life. She'd helped him organize years of accumulated papers, books, galleys, drafts of manuscripts. Seigl had come upon near-completed essays amid the chaos with such titles as "Visions of the Apocalypse in Classic and Contemporary Art" and "Bioethics and Tragedy," which he'd revised and updated and placed with prestigious journals he hadn't sent work to in years. In Alma's presence he was never obliged to feel embarrassment or self-consciousness for she rarely glanced closely at anything that passed through her hands, unless Seigl had instructed her to do so; it intrigued him to witness an individual for whom print had little attraction or charm, which was wholly unlike Seigl or anyone close to him. Though words sometimes puzzled Alma, she never looked up any word in any dictionary; a word was like a pebble to be turned briefly in the hand, and tossed away, with no expectation that it would be encountered again. Early in her employ in his house Seigl had noticed her craning her neck to peer at a row of books on a shelf, books in several languages with *Joshua Seigl* stamped vertically on the spines, yet she'd showed little further curiosity.

He'd warned her not to ask about his health, of course. Yet it rather hurt him, she made no inquiries at all. After the visit to Friedman's office, for instance. Did she even know what a neurologist was? In her tactful mumble she might say, "Mr. Seigl, don't forget your pills," for Seigl had a habit of placing pills that had to be ingested with food in strategic locations on the dining room table, and then forgetting them, or she might murmur, "*I* got your cane, Mr. Seigl," if Seigl seemed to be forgetting it. But nothing further passed between them on the subject.

The vacuuming upstairs had ceased temporarily. Seigl called up the stairs, "Alma? When you have a minute, I'd like to speak with you."

Within seconds he heard Alma's footsteps. She walked quickly, heavy on her heels.

Alma came downstairs, breathless. She'd tied her ashy hair into a kerchief and was wearing a soiled apron over her work clothes. She was beautiful and faintly absurd and touching as a kewpie doll. Seigl resisted the impulse to laugh in delight at her.

He said, "My friend has gone. But I'll be having dinner with her tomorrow evening. So you won't need to prepare anything."

Alma nodded stiffly. There was a faint sullen cast to her mouth when the subject of Sondra Blumenthal came up, however casually.

"Everything looks fine here. Where you've vacuumed."

This was the kind of praise Alma liked. She smiled and mumbled thanks.

Walking with his cane, Seigl led Alma toward the rear of the house, through the long living room. She followed unquestioningly. Seigl would have the idea afterward that she'd known what he was going to say. These words he'd been rehearsing for several days.

"Whatever the condition I have, whether it's a singular disease or a congeries of symptoms, the doctor has said it seems to be 'progressing.' We don't need to go into details." Seigl opened a door to the back hall, that connected with the kitchen and the pantry and the back stairs. "But, just as a precaution, I'm thinking of having a wheelchair ramp built, at the back of the house."

Seigl avoided looking at Alma. The last thing he wanted to see in her face was pity.

She didn't speak. Seigl continued, "I'd like you to make the initial arrangements, please. You can look in the Yellow Pages under 'con-struction.' Get two or three estimates. Don't trouble me with any of it until you have some figures. Then, we'll see what comes next." Seigl paused, feeling very tired suddenly.

Alma murmured, "Yes, Mr. Seigl. I will do that."

She would say nothing further. She would make no inquiries.

She seemed not surprised. Not in the slightest.

7

For I have eaten ashes like bread and mingled my drink with weeping.
In the late winter and spring of the year the Tattooed Girl took heart, at last she would be revenged against her enemies.

Those that scorn us are our enemies. Those who love us not.

The Tattooed Girl rejoiced in her wickedness. She would tell her lover *See? I told you. You didn't believe me.*

After the Jew's death. That death would come soon. The Tattooed Girl could sniff it, in the wind.

8

FROM A HIGH window she'd seen them, the Jew and his Jewess lover.

On the terrace above the river. Standing close together. Seigl was taller than Blumenthal by several inches. His hand moved upon the woman's shoulders, casually and with affection. You could see. They talked all the time. They had so much to say to each other! Even when the Tattooed Girl tried to overhear, she could not.

Never would she forgive the Blumenthal woman: speaking to her so bossily on the phone. Calling so many times. Always the subject was *Mr. Seigl's birthday party,* or *The party.* Always an edge to the woman's voice giving instructions like a schoolteacher. This, that. This, that. Alma this, Alma that. While she, Alma, must call the other woman "Mrs. Blumenthal" for they were not equals. The Tattooed Girl was not an equal of any of them and always she was made to know this.

And at the birthday party when everybody was so happy, the Tattooed Girl was put in her place like a kicked dog.

Never would she forget that insult. Like a dull hurting back molar, its roots deep in her jaw.

Even when her employer noticed her to praise her it was praise of a dog or a retarded child.

Nice vacuuming, Alma! Floors are so clean.

Thank you, Al-ma.

When no one observed she went outside onto the terrace. A harsh wet smell of the river below. The wind whipped her hair, her eyes smarted with tears. There was a fine crusting of snow where the sun hadn't reached between certain of the flagstones and against a wall. A deck chair had been overturned in the wind and so she set it right. Her employer praised her for such neatness not seeing the rage in it.

The Jew and his Jewess. The Tattooed Girl had no wish to imagine them in bed together. Fucking! What a laugh. Her lips drew back in a smile of derision. She was so much better-looking and younger than the Blumenthal woman, but she was not a Jew.

She drew back from the edge of the terrace for the view down to the river below made her dizzy. Like traveling in a car at too fast a speed. A sick excited sensation in the pit of the stomach. *You could throw yourself over. They would be sorry then!*

The Tattooed Girl saw her stubby fingers grip the iron railing and gave it a hard shake. She stooped to examine where the railing was secured to a brick wall. Smiling angrily she shook, shook, shook the railing until it loosened. Bits of mortar fell from the wall. Rust from the railing came off on her fingers.

Next time they came out here, if they leaned against the railing.

What they deserve. Fuckers have everything.

She would loosen other railings, too. Those beside the nineteen stone steps leading to the street, and those at the rear of the house. She would loosen steps with a hammer. Who would know? (For she worked in darkness.) The Jew himself would not know. Only when the Tattooed Girl stood over him gloating would he know, too late.

IN CHURCH SHE HID her face and prayed and laughed inside her hands. Hymns were sung loudly but the Tattooed Girl did not sing for her voice was nasal and flat. Jesus who had disdained her for years was contemplating her anew. She was cruelly treated in the midst of riches. If thine eye offend thee pluck it out. If the Tattooed Girl was wicked, her enemies had made her so.

For no one loved her: there was no one to whom the Tattooed Girl was beloved.

"ALMA? I WONDER if you could help me . . ."

Yes, Mr. Seigl.

"Some pages seem to be lost. This writing I've been doing in the dining room. I've looked everywhere, I can't understand how these pages could be lost . . ."

Desperate he was sounding. Pathetic. Why didn't he summon the Blumenthal woman, needing help?

Alma murmured Yes, she would look.

In her heart laughing at the grown man so stricken by the loss of his precious *pages*! Like he'd shit his pants when he couldn't find them. *Graven images. Those that boast themselves of idols.*

It was the Tattooed Girl who had stolen away the pages. Torn them into shreds. Poetry some of it was. And all of it bullshit. Who gave a fuck for what the Jew was scribbling hour after hour, sweating like a pig in a fever? Printed pages in books, who gives a damn for them? If the books added up to anything there would not be so many of them but only a few. The Tattooed Girl had come to think since becoming Joshua Seigl's assistant that those who practiced such bullshit knew what its true meaning was. Yet the hypocrites prevailed.

Strange that a man could be so wounded, in the loss of a dozen sheets of paper. How much more deeply might the man be wounded, a knife in the heart!

Never would the Tattooed Girl use a knife. The Tattooed Girl was too cunning.

SHE HELPED WITH the wheelchair. It was to be taken in the car.

"Just in case" it was needed.

For Seigl was to stay for three nights at a university. A driver came for him in a limousine. His assistant would not be accompanying him. She stood on the sidewalk hugging herself tightly, her hair whipping in the wind as the elegant long black car drew away from the curb.

If you loved me I would love you. I would adore you. I would die for you.

THINGS THE TATTOOED GIRL did in the spring of that year, impulsively. Never thinking that such actions by one so powerless could have any consequences.

Several times, she mingled his pills. With a nail file shaving away at large white pills to make them of the size of smaller white pills with which they might be easily confused. (In her employer's medicine cabinet were five prescription medicines now. Five! Two were from the neurologist and two were from a cardiologist and one was from yet a third doctor.) Some of these pills Seigl took in private and some he swallowed down absentmindedly at his meals. The Tattooed Girl felt both a thrill of elation and alarm and lowered her burning eyes from his face that he should not perceive the wickedness in her heart.

No matter the pills he took, in whatever combinations, Seigl continued to have "good days" and "bad days" as before. This was the pattern of the disease. On the good days he could walk unassisted and on the bad days, he could not. On the best of the good days he was almost as he'd been when healthy. (Except he must not tire himself out!) On the worst of the bad days he remained in bed, unable to walk and complaining of double vision, in his room that was now downstairs at the rear of the house, which had been made over into his bedroom. Almost, Alma felt sorry for him at such times. . . . For on the telephone he talked with a desperate energy making plans for the future and when he hung up the phone, he was stricken with tiredness.

The wheelchair that had been rented had now been purchased and was kept in a corner of Seigl's new bedroom. A ramp was being built at the rear of the house, where it would not be visible from the sidewalk.

Other pages of her employer's the Tattooed Girl stole away out of meanness. Not daring to take new work, for he might suspect her, but pages from older manuscripts in his study. Books on several occasions including one of the books presented to him at his birthday party she stole away in her shoulder bag. Amid so many books, how could one matter? And a fancy silver fountain pen that had been a gift to Seigl, and a wavy-green-glass paperweight he had said was "Venetian glass"—whatever that was—and small jars and carved figures. These she made gifts of to Dmitri Meatte who thought them of little worth.

Get the Jew to marry you, babe. That's the way to go.

Dmitri was laughing at her, she knew. But one day he would cease laughing.

IN THE SPRING friends came to visit her employer more often, for he left the house less frequently. Some of these visitors were from New York City and one was from London. But most were local, familiar faces to Alma, who smiled when they greeted her and called her "Alma" as if she was in their hire, too, like a common hooker. She hid her resentment of them even as she spat into the drinks she was obliged to fetch for them or the Peking tea she was obliged to brew in a squat heavy teapot. Often the visitors brought books to Seigl and some of these books were their own, inscribed by them, with their photographs on the back covers, better-looking and younger than in life. There were women of Blumenthal's age and younger and some of these better-looking than that bitch, and by their manner with Seigl the Tattooed Girl could see that they liked him. Despite his uncertain health they liked him a lot. (Were any of these lovers of Seigl's? The Tattooed Girl had reason to think they were, or had been.) Several of the chess players came to the house on evenings Alma particularly disliked, for she believed these men recognized her: they had seen her at The Café, in her former life. One day Alma was panicked seeing a fattish bald-headed man ascend the stone steps and ring the doorbell and this man she believed to be one of the crude tricks Dmitri had forced upon her in the motel by the river but this visitor turned out to be somebody different. Maybe!

One of the chess players was named "John"—an elderly white-haired gentleman with palsied hands. When Alma opened the door to him his amazing blue eyes lit upon her smiling and he spoke so warmly to her, with such kindness, Alma bit her lip to keep from crying. " 'Alma.' A beautiful name for a beautiful girl."

Yet later, when the visitors were gone, the Jew in his abruptly sour mood ruined Alma's happy mood by speaking sharply to her. He had overheard her answering the phone in the hall. "If you'd learn to clear your throat before you lift the receiver, Alma. Not after. So you don't sound as if your head is stuffed with glue." Alma limped away hurt. Seigl had scolded her for this very failing in the past. In her heart cursing *I hate you! I will kill you.*

In A closet off the kitchen were aerosol containers of insecticide, years old. But the nasty smell of the liquid was so strong, even a few drops in Seigl's food would be detected. There were pellets of rodent, roach, and ant poison she sniffed at . . . But if Seigl died of actual poison, it might be detected. If it was detected, Alma Busch would be arrested. They would check her record in Akron County, PA. They would learn of warrants outstanding in Pittsburgh from which she had fled.

The following evening Seigl had invited two friends who were New York editors to have dinner with him. It was not to be a formal dinner he instructed Alma but she was to order beef bour-guignonne—"beef burgone" as Alma carefully pronounced it over the phone—from Les Amis. Also wild rice, "mixed baby greens," and a fruit tart dessert. As Alma worked in the kitchen her thoughts were beating like the wings of panicked birds. There was a dull heavy ache in the pit of her belly, her period had begun which always she hated, since the age of twelve. A curse it was, men could laugh at and scorn. She watched her hands helplessly. What could she do, she must do something! Bitterly she hated her employer for she could hear him talking and laughing with his visitors. Bitterly she hated him for he insulted her daily, hourly. There came a hot seeping in her loins like a rebuke. Always at the start the menstrual blood was slug-gish and thick and black, repulsive to see and to smell. Alma could not bear to think of her brothers' teasing. Her mother had slapped them, furious with them. But her father had been furious with the three of them making no distinction, if he could catch them. *I am filth and abomination, God save me from myself.* In a sudden trance of con-centration the Tattooed Girl worked her fingers into the crotch of her tight-fitting panties and inside the crevice between her legs where the tampon already soaked with blood was jammed. The fin-gers came away slick with blood, she wiped onto pieces of tender-cooked beef and stirred the beef into the wine-rich sauce. Again, and another time, she thrust her fingers into her body that was knot-ted with pain and brought them out in this way, in triumph, in her trance of concentration.

Red meat is blood-meat, beef is soaked in blood. The Tattooed Girl smiled to herself thinking, who would know?

◎

"IT'S JUST WHAT happens. What God lets happen."

On Easter Sunday, the Tattooed Girl sat alone in a rear pew at the Lutheran church. If she had become a familiar sight to some eyes in the congregation she failed to respond when greeted. Often she hid her face, whispering to God and to Jesus Christ for strength. The world was a place demanding strength. Little was respected except strength. Beside her sat a heavyset middle-aged man who coughed and snuffled and blew his nose noisily through the service distracting the Tattooed Girl from the triumphant words of Jesus as the minister proclaimed them *I am the resurrection and the life: he who looks upon me shall be saved* so that by the time the final joyous hymn soared the Tattooed Girl was sick with disappointment.

Oh, fuck it. Laugh.

Laugh-laugh. You're the babe for laughing.

She saw her mittened hands gathering wadded tissues. Left behind in the pew. Thick with mucus they were, disgusting. Teeming with germs. Bacteria? These she brought back to the house and these she would steep with the strong dark tea her employer drank through the day.

"Just what happens. What God lets happen."

The Tattooed Girl smiled thinking of Jehane de Brigue. What God had let happen to His "healer."

9

Maybe someday it will be cheering to remember even these things.

This line of Virgil he'd long contemplated. For was it an expression of the most profound pessimism, or, perversely, optimism?

Seigl was an optimist! He'd made that discovery when Friedman told him at last the medical term—the "name"—of his illness. For he'd said to Friedman, with a shaky smile, but definitely a smile, "In all knowledge there is comfort. Thank you, Doctor."

IT WAS A coincidence merely. Coincidence without significance.

The day of the diagnosis, Seigl received a small package in the mail postmarked New York City. His assistant opened it as she opened all his mail and brought it to him, mystified: a first edition copy of *The Shadows* that had been badly waterstained, torn and gouged-at as if with a knife. The jacket cover, a twilight rural scene two-thirds darkened earth and one-third pale sky, had been scrawled over in red crayon—or was it lipstick?

JEW HATER JEW

"Jesus! Who sent this, Alma? Is there a return address?"

There was none. The book had been sent via media mail, at an ordinary rate.

Sickened, Seigl placed the book on an edge of his desk atop his dictionary. He couldn't bring himself to examine the desecrated book further. Yet he couldn't bring himself to simply discard the book as if it had no meaning. That day Seigl was working in his study and was on the phone intermittently and as he spoke in a seemingly normal voice his gaze drifted onto the angry bloody words

JEW HATER JEW

like a shout that kept reverberating in his ear. A Zen koan of a curse he thought it. He had no doubt there were further curses inside but didn't want to look.

Later, in another room of the house, Seigl glanced up to see his assistant standing uncertainly in the doorway. "Alma? What is it?" Wordlessly she brought to him, to show him, the mutilated book opened to the title page, where in Seigl's tight, terse hand he'd inscribed

to Jet, beloved sister
with love & much hope
Josh
18 June 1990

10

Optimist: this was Seigl's new sense of himself. Now the long winter was ending. Now he strolled or sat outside, in a heavy sweater, in the sunshine. Sometimes he even worked on his terrace, for brief periods until he became too cold.

On good days he was damned grateful for his health and on bad days, well—he could always be grateful he wasn't worse.

He was beginning a new course of medication. A physical therapist came to the house twice a week leaving his muscles aching but his spirit rejuvenated. He was elated by invitations that, a half-year ago, would have depressed him: he'd accepted an invitation to give a two-part Tanner Lecture at Princeton on "any subject" of his interest. He'd agreed to lecture at Cornell, the New School, and Berkeley. (Berkeley! Thousands of miles away, yet Seigl had no doubt he would do it, wheelchair or not.) Two recent essays of his in the *New York Review of Books* had been very well received and had brought calls from editors inviting him to write for them. Though his play *Why/Warum?* was hardly more than a jumble of surreal scenes, he had shown it to a director friend at the Public Theater who was eager to workshop it in the fall. He'd abandoned his novel-fragment *Redemption,* quite the strangest thing he'd ever attempted, a bizarre future-set parable Seigl scarcely recognized as his own writing, but he had been stimulated by the experience of writing fiction again, working so intensely inside his imagination, and was thinking he might try again, in a more realistic setting.

And there was his ongoing Virgil translation. Sondra Blumenthal had praised it. Months of deeply engrossing work lay ahead.

And he was seeing friends more frequently. He was playing chess, and he was having people to dinner at the house at least once a week, as he'd never done before the onset of his illness.

Optimist!

He regaled his friends with his newly acquired born-again attitude. "I can't remember now what the hell I used to be so anxious about. Most of the years of my adult life. Was I crazy?"

11

S HE HATES ME. That is her mission now."

The savage assault from Jet had shocked Seigl, yet allowed him the luxury of knowing, rare in his life, that someone hated him. No doubt his sister was deranged, yet her hatred must seem to her pure, even righteous.

JEW HATER JEW. What did it mean?

From the deranged sister's perspective it meant that he, Joshua, was a hater of Jews, because, from the deranged sister's perspective, he had failed to "live up to the promise" of *The Shadows*. Yet it meant, too, obviously, that Jet was the Jew who "hated" her brother who was insufficiently Jewish, in her eyes.

Since the farcical scene in Seigl's study in December, and Jet's abrupt departure from Carmel Heights, Seigl had considered trying to contact her, but not very seriously. When he thought of her, it was relief he felt, mainly: not shame, not guilt, still less a sense of brotherly responsibility for her. He had no sentimental familial yearnings. She was right to perceive in him a certain icyheartedness. And she was right to have perceived that, by his stubbornness in keeping his assistant, exactly the assistant he'd wanted, Seigl was choosing Alma Busch over Jet Steadman-Seigl.

"As if there could be any choice." Seigl laughed.

I 2

I N THIS NEW SEASON there was Alma Busch more and
more on Seigl's restless mind. This girl-assistant who was becoming by slow degrees Seigl's *girl-attendant.*

No stranger to trouble myself I am learning to care for the unhappy. Like
Virgil's Dido she seemed to him, had seemed to him from the start,
not in eloquence for she had none, but in her manner and her physical being.

Her touch.

"ALMA? THAT MARK on your cheek . . ."

At once Alma's hand flew to hide it. Her moist eyes narrowed in
surprise and chagrin.

Seigl spoke gently, kindly. "I've wondered—is it a birthmark?
Or . . ." His voice trailed off in embarrassment. And he'd meant
only well.

There was a painful pause. As when a professor asks a difficult
question and no one volunteers to speak. Your impulse is to answer
the question yourself, or to deflect it with more words. With experi-

ence, you learn to wait. You force yourself to be silent to give another time to speak.

Finally Alma said, almost inaudibly, not meeting Seigl's eye, ". . . birthmark."

So he'd been right. Jet had been wrong, thinking it was a tattoo.

"It isn't unattractive, Alma. Not at all."

Alma laughed harshly. Her eyes were without mirth, and her face had hardened. From the sullen cast of her mouth Seigl guessed that she didn't find the birthmark at all attractive. He'd blundered by bringing up the subject, no doubt. But he persisted:

"Have you ever thought of having it removed?"

Alma was backing away now, eager to escape. Seigl was sympathetic with her, but disappointed. And annoyed. What prevented them from speaking of the birthmark objectively? It was the first thing you noticed when you saw Alma Busch. It leapt out at you, though it was a faded rosy-brown, as vividly as her unnaturally red lips. Seigl had been seeing it for more than five months. He did find it attractive, as he found Alma attractive. And yet.

Your beauty, Alma. Shouldn't be defaced.

Alma answered Seigl's impetuous question by shaking her head in a way that might mean yes, or no, as she fled the room.

Seigl should have called after her, "Alma! I'm sorry," but he did not.

For hours afterward he smarted from the encounter. Alma's childish behavior. Yet she was a grown woman, probably older than he'd originally thought, hardly a child, and this was a subject they might discuss rationally. Seigl didn't consider for a moment that the birthmark was none of his business for his assistant had become his business, he felt a moral obligation to help provide for her if something happened to him.

"ALMA? WHICH CHURCH is yours, which do you go to?"

Alma frowned. Was this a trick question of Mr. Seigl's?

"Different ones. It depends."

"Which was your church when you were growing up—in Pennsylvania, was it?"

"Different ones."

"You do believe in God?"

Not ceasing her work Alma laughed, mildly embarrassed, and said yes she guessed so. "Sure."

Seigl waited for her to say more. But what was there for his literal-minded assistant from somewhere in western Pennsylvania to say?

He could hear himself sounding pedantic, dogged. But he didn't want to alter his tone. His question was serious: he'd been wanting badly for months to ask his assistant these questions. "Is your God a 'person,' Alma, with characteristics like a human being?—for instance, an elderly man? A patriarch?"

Alma frowned, narrowing her eyes as if to envision God. Her expression was respectfully blank.

"Or is your God more of a principle, Alma? An ideal?"

Alma mumbled she guessed so. "Yes."

"Do you pray often to this God?"

Alma shrugged. How often was "often"? She shook her head ambiguously.

"When you pray, does God ever answer you? I mean—does God ever seem to speak to *you*?"

At this, Alma laughed. A snorting derisive laugh. But immediately her expression went grave again, respectful. She murmured she guessed not. "Not too often."

The exchange would have ended here, except: there was a new edge to Alma Busch, since Seigl's query about the mark on her cheek. He had been thinking afterward that the backs of Alma's hands and other parts of her body were similarly blemished, and it might have been tactless of him to speak of having just the mark on her cheek removed. Was Alma angry at him? It was difficult to imagine Alma angry at anyone; she'd hardly defended herself against Jet, and had never uttered a word of complaint about Seigl's sister after-ward. But the other day he'd overheard her clearing her throat before she answered the phone to say with unexpected precision and dig-nity, "Hello. Mr. Seigl's residence." That morning he'd overheard her speaking with Andre, the young Jamaican physical therapist who came to the house twice a week, the two of them talking together for some time, even laughing together, and this seemed new to Seigl, too, and startling. He supposed that Alma might be interested in physical therapy as a career and had questions to ask about training. With a pang of loss he thought, she won't be my assistant forever.

Now Alma said suddenly, "Why are you asking me these things, Mr. Seigl?"

"Why? Because I'm curious."

"But why?"

There was a startling opposition here. Though Alma's voice was low, scratchy, not aggressive. It was the first time she'd directly ques-tioned him in their months of daily contact. Seigl said, smiling, "Why? Because your answer is of interest to me, Alma. Your thoughts on the subject of God."

Alma frowned and drew her elbows close against her rib cage in that odd, awkward nervous mannerism, as if she were holding her-self tight, to the point of pain. She said, "But why does it matter what I think? Somebody like me."

"Your ideas are perfectly valid. Your thoughts on the subject of—"

"All the books in the house here, people's thoughts, what's the point of *more*?"

"But you are you, Alma. You are unique. That's why I'm inter-ested in your thoughts."

Under Seigl's scrutiny, Alma began to mumble and lose her way. She said, vaguely, "If smart people know, and say what they know, why are there . . . I mean, there wouldn't be so many books, would there?"

Seigl laughed heartily. He liked this insight, though he had no idea how to respond to it. Like a shy backward student Alma Busch had suddenly surprised her teacher. And like a practiced teacher, Seigl deftly shifted the subject.

" 'Of the making of books there is no end.' The human mind is forever questing, Alma!"

It was one of Seigl's cardiology examination days. While panting on the diabolical treadmill, he'd given evidence, finely recorded, of having what the cardiologist called, and what no other examining doctor had ever discerned, a "leaky" heart valve. Now, he was on a powerful beta-blocker medication, and had to be periodically re-examined. And in the cardiologist's office he found himself replaying the exchange between him and Alma, wondering if he'd said the right thing. As an intellectual, as one who has frequently taught, he could not bear to be in the wrong, and to be perceived by another as in the wrong; yet he couldn't see how he might have spoken more eloquently or more convincingly, under the circumstances. He was left intrigued, yet disturbed. For it seemed to him now that Alma Busch had become silent not because she had nothing further to say on the subject but because she had considerably more.

Why does it matter what I think? What you think? About God, or anything? It's all just words.

"SOME PEOPLE SAY this never happened."

"What never happened?"

"This."

Gravely Alma pointed to the word *Holocaust.*

Seigl was shocked. "Alma, what do you mean? The Holocaust 'never happened'?"

Alma laughed uncertainly. "Some people—I heard—they don't think—whatever it was—happened."

Seigl was preparing the keynote address for a symposium titled "Revisionist and Postmodernist 'Histories' of the Late Twentieth Century" at Cornell the following week, in mid-April. He would be speaking primarily on the phenomenon of Holocaust "denial" as it first emerged immediately following the end of World War II, in Europe, and as it developed through subsequent decades in Europe and the United States. Seigl had numerous, perhaps too many books on the subject in his library and had purchased more via the Internet; his desk and an adjacent table in his study were piled with them. It was a subject he'd written about before, and had a particular interest in since his father had many times told him that his grandfather had predicted there would come a day when "no one living" would believe what had been done to the Jews of Europe, in a calculated genocidal political action. Because "no one living" would wish to believe such evil had ever been perpetrated.

Seigl had not doubted that his father spoke sincerely. Yet, he'd had to wonder how his grandfather Moses Seigl had been able to predict the future to a young child, in 1939; for the last Karl Seigl had seen of his father was at that time. Seigl had come to suppose that it was another person, probably an older man who'd survived one of the camps whom Karl Seigl had encountered in New York City. He had never questioned his father, of course.

This was not one of Seigl's bad days by any stretch of the imagination. Yet his eyesight was annoyingly blurred even with his glasses and so he was block-printing his lecture on long sheets of paper which Alma diligently photocopied on the machine in his study, and would take to the village to have a professional typist transcribe it onto a hard disk. Seigl would not have thought that his assistant had any interest in what he was writing, but her manner seemed earnest.

"Of course the Holocaust 'happened,' Alma. Not in one place but in numerous places in Europe. 'Holocaust' is a term to indicate the systematic genocide of more than six million Jews and the deaths of more than five million Gentiles in Europe by the Nazis. Treblinka, Ponar, Belzec, Chelmo, Birkenau, Auschwitz, Bergen-Belsen, Buchenwald, Theresienstadt, Dachau: these were death camps, labor camps. These were places, Alma. As real as these walls that enclose us here." Seigl tried to speak evenly, not wanting to become emotional. He had had practice in public forums with Holocaust deniers and had learned to steel himself against their hostile, jeering, yet formulaic questions; but he would not have expected his assistant Alma Busch to be one of these. It shook him to think her skepticism might be somehow natural, instinctive. *No one wishes to believe such evil has ever been perpetrated.*

Of course, the Holocaust deniers knew perfectly well that the Holocaust had occurred. And they wished to revivify it, through their attacks against Jews.

Alma was hugging herself nervously. She looked like a schoolgirl who has dared to contradict her teacher. Stubbornly she repeated, "Well. Some people say . . ."

"Who, Alma? Who are these authorities?"

Alma stood wordless.

"The Holocaust is as documented as the Civil War, Alma. Do you doubt that the Civil War occurred?"

Alma shrugged. She shook her head, no.

"But how do you know? You didn't observe it, did you?"

Again, though rather sullenly, Alma shook her head.

"In fact there is more evidence for the Holocaust than for the American Civil War, since there are eyewitness survivors still living."

"They could be lying. People say."

"Why?"

Alma squeezed her torso tightly, shaking her head. Her ordinarily childlike docile face had taken on a hard, blank-doll glaze.

"Why, Alma? Why would anyone 'lie' about such atrocities? Why would thousands of men and women tattoo numbers on their wrists, in exactly the same way, and with their numbers, in the hundreds of thousands, precisely chronologically calibrated?"

Alma cried, "I don't know. How would I know!"

It was the first time she had ever spoken so, to Seigl. He stared at her in amazement. She said, as if relenting, "I mean, I don't know, Mr. Seigl. That's why I was asking." She'd gripped her left wrist with the fingers of her right hand and was agitatedly rubbing it.

Seigl was aroused, excited. He felt in Alma Busch a blind groping implacable will stronger than his own will. Her eyes seemed to him literally blind, the eyes of an undersea creature, nourished by darkness. "Alma. Here are survivors." He opened one of the larger books of photographs. These had been taken by the photographer Margaret Bourke-White at the time of the Allied liberation of Buchenwald in spring 1945. "Human skeletons. Yet they manage to stand. Their eyes are blank, their brains have been damaged by malnutrition." Seigl turned the page as Alma stared. "These are the dead, Alma. Stacked like firewood to be burnt. You see those people walking along the road? They lived in the vicinity. There was a town close by. They could smell human beings being burnt, cremated. They seemed scarcely to care. They were 'Christians.' " Alma recoiled, a hand over her eyes.

She left the room. She would say nothing about what Seigl had shown her, that day. But next morning, bringing Seigl a pot of tea, she said in a reedy, ringing voice, "They could be faked, Mr. S-Seigl! Photographs. Like in movies."

Seigl regarded her coldly.

"All right, Alma. You can leave now."

"Well, they could. A movie is faked, it's *pictures*."

Alma hurried from the room. Seigl felt the floorboards vibrate beneath her clumsy feet. He vowed he would never speak to his assistant again about this subject, it so upset him. And the girl was only just ignorant after all, as Jet had identified her: an Aryan peasant.

"MR. SEIGL?"

"Yes, Alma."

"I guess . . . You lived this?"

Seigl glanced up, and was stunned to see Alma holding a copy of
The Shadows against her chest. Incredibly, it appeared to be the battered copy that Jet had sent, minus its cover which Alma had removed, perhaps, out of tact.

"Alma! You've read my novel?"

Alma was blinking rapidly, as if thinking what to say. Seigl supposed she'd read the beginning, at least. Maybe she'd skimmed the
rest. Maybe, a slow reader, she was still making her way through the
one hundred eighty compactly written pages. *The Shadows* was a novel
in genre only: it contained few dramatic scenes, virtually no dialogue,
its lengthy, Proustian paragraphs frequently ran for pages. Seigl had
imagined it as the verbal approximation of memory, experienced in
an undersea, undulating zone of sublunary consciousness. Alma
said, choosing her words with care, "I started it. Last night."

Seigl smiled foolishly. His heart kicked! His leaky-valved heart.
Never would he have expected Alma Busch of all people to be
standing before him, clutching a copy of *The Shadows* against her
young shapely body.

Alma said awkwardly, "It's sad. It made me cry. I was thinking . . .
how my own family would be. If it was us."

Seigl said, "Well." He too was overcome with awkwardness. For
years he hadn't been able to bear speaking of *The Shadows* with any
reader; he'd come to fear and loathe praise, and questions about the
novel's relationship to his father's family roused him to anger. He
had never been criticized to his face, and wondered if he might pre-
fer that. Even the few qualified reviews the novel had received were
respectful, complaining of the young novelist's expectations that a
reader might wish to work quite so hard to read his novel.

Alma said, shyly, " 'Jacob' is meant to be you, I guess, Mr. Seigl?"

Jacob Seigl was the novel's first, eighteen-year-old speaker. He'd
been born in 1921 in Munich. Did Alma truly believe that he, Joshua
Seigl, was over eighty years old? "No, Alma. Not exactly."

Alma protested, "He talks like you. He sounds like you."

"No, Alma. Jacob doesn't sound in the least like me. The novel's language has been composed to make you think so, as if the speaker were addressing you intimately; as if, almost, the speaker is *you,* having these experiences long before you were born."

Alma smiled, confused. "But Jacob looks like you."

Seigl laughed. "Have you ever seen Jacob Seigl, Alma?"

"But—Aharon and Erika, they were your parents?"

Alma was looking so anxious, Seigl was reluctant to correct her.

"Alma, dear, no. Aharon and Erika are wholly fictitious characters. They were based upon my father's parents, or, rather, my father's memories of his parents as he described them to me, but I never knew those people: they died a quarter-century before I was born. Everything in *The Shadows* is invented except the landscape and certain dates in the history of Germany and the War."

" 'Invented.' " Alma looked as if suddenly there were a bad taste in her mouth.

Seigl said, "*The Shadows* is a novel, Alma. I'm sure you've read many novels? Even when a novel is 'real,' its subject is its own language. Like music."

Alma was shaking her head, frowning. Seigl could see that the subject had become disagreeable to her. *She feels she has been tricked. Poor Alma!* He wanted to apologize to her.

Alma said, "What happened to somebody else, you have a right to pretend it was you?"

"Of course I have a 'right,' Alma. And so do you."

"To lie about who I am? My name? What happened to me?"

"Not to lie. I meant, to invent: if you were writing fiction."

"Why is that different? *This* isn't different." Alma held the battered copy of Seigl's novel, now rather disdainfully. Its sorry state, water-stained and stabbed-at, seemed a sudden manifestation, as in a fantasy film, of its spiritual worth.

Seigl felt the absurdity of the situation. He hardly needed to defend the human imagination! And to an uneducated slow-witted girl who could barely place one word in front of another. Yet he heard himself saying, protesting, "Alma, you have the wrong idea. Just because a novel is formally invented hardly means that it isn't about something very real in the human spirit. You read the Bible, don't you? Your ministers preach from the Bible, don't they? The Bible is hardly 'real.' "

Stony-eyed Alma stood blinking at him. The horror struck Seigl, she believed the Bible was *real*?

"Alma, I think of myself as writing stories for others. In place of others who are dead, or mute. Who can't speak for themselves."

"But you don't *know*. You write like you know and *you don't know*."

"I know what I've been told, and what I can imagine. I know what I, myself, have felt."

Alma said, disgusted, "You're stealing from them. Some people you didn't even know. And other prisoners in 'D-Dash—' "

" 'Dachau.' "

"—in that place, you're pretending you were there with them."

Somehow, this seemed to Alma the most repulsive act of all.

"You made 'Dash-aw' up, too, didn't you! You made it all up! You pretended you were there, and you weren't. It's all *lies*."

Alma placed the mutilated book on the edge of a table some feet from Seigl, as if not wanting to come any nearer to him. Her hands with their cobwebbed backs were trembling. Seigl observed in silence. He had not a word more to say on this sorry subject.

She hates me now. I broke her heart.

13

HIM? MEATTE'S GONE."

The Tattooed Girl stood transfixed. Gone?

She had not seen her lover in three weeks. She had waited for him to call, and he had not. Until finally she called the number he'd given her, telling her never to call unless it was an emergency, but this number was disconnected. And calling information she was told *There is no listing of that party in this directory.*

In these three weeks it was spring. It had become spring. The sun-warmed air gnawed at her, roused her to a terrible yearning between the legs, she could not bear.

Sick at heart and hating him. And the last they'd been together, he'd told her he was crazy about her.

Finally she went to the place he lived, he'd taken her to many times, but he'd forbidden her ever to approach except by his invitation, but there were others living there now, who claimed not to know him. The Tattooed Girl wanted to scream at them knowing they were lying.

Now the Tattooed Girl was desperate, she had no choice daring to go to The Café where he had forbidden her ever to enter warning he would strangle her with his bare hands if she did so. If she even showed her face in the front window. She was terrified of entering the restaurant she had not entered since that first night he'd been kind to her so long ago though guessing he would not be there, and he was not. And when she asked for Dmitri Meatte she saw the pity and scorn in the men's eyes.

They were laughing at her she could see. The other young waiter, and the other one. The cashier. In the kitchen the cook and the busboys were laughing, laughing. A boy with a rash-reddened wedge face and a slimy lower lip leaned so close to Alma, she could smell his sour breath. Saying, "Want me to take you to Meatte, sweetheart? I can."

"Just t-tell me where he is."

"See, sweetie, Meatte told me: 'When my girl comes looking for me bring her to where I am. Don't tell her 'cause she'd get lost. She ain't so bright, she'd get lost.' That's exactly what Meatte said, ain't it, Bo-Bo?"

Bo-Bo shrugged irritably.

The rash-reddened boy was laughing like a deranged parrot.

"Here's a girl wants her Meatte! Wants her Meatte-Meatte!"

The kitchen smells assailed her. Hot grease. She couldn't breathe. One of the busboys nudged at her breast, grinning. The Tattooed Girl was panicked suddenly thinking they would gang up on her. Even the cook her daddy's age. Blindly she pushed past them, careened against a counter searching for something sharp or something hot. Her fingers snatched at a deep-frier as the cook cursed her seizing her by the back of the neck and walking her swiftly to the rear door, shoved her out into the alley against the trash cans.

"Keep your fat ass out of here, bitch."

Ever afterward, the Tattooed Girl would hear those hyena howls of laughter.

14

He has seen into my soul. Now he knows.

Yet it was strange: he hadn't asked her to leave. Yet.

After she'd mouthed off like that, another employer would have fired her at once. Kicked her out. Alma Busch's fat ass, unwanted. What she deserved.

But, *Seigl!* You could not figure a Jew.

"Alma."

She was standing hesitantly in a doorway. She could not recall why. Where she was going. In her mind she was pushing away the men's grabbing hands. She was snatching at the deep-frier filled with hot grease and sliced potatoes on top of the stove. She might have overturned this onto those who mocked her, and onto herself. Her disfigured hands, her ruined face. In her memory the man who'd been her lover was with the others laughing at her. *Fat ass. Bitch. Out of here.* It was a deserved punishment though she could not remember why.

"Alma, is something wrong?"

The Tattooed Girl turned a vague blank dead-doll face toward this voice.

Seigl. Her employer. The Jew, who'd been so kind to her.

Between them now there was an air of caution, unease. Alma had at once accepted it, that she would be asked to leave, yet two, and now three days had passed, and Seigl had not asked her to leave, though there was a stiffness to him now, a wariness in the man's eyes. Always, since coming to work for Seigl, in this house, she had believed that no words Alma Busch might utter could have the slightest significance and so it surprised her, that Seigl had spoken to her as he had. She had seen the shock and hurt in his face, was this caused by *her*?

Wanting to say, But I'm nobody. I'm nothing.

Wanting to say, Just kick me out. I deserve it.

Her employer was so polite! It could not be real, could it? She was hating him less, maybe. He was taking that from her, the thrill of her hatred.

Though he was still *the Jew* to her—the rich, smug Jew living in this house. That, she would not forget.

Now he was asking, was something wrong. Because she had been behaving so strangely these past few days. Staring and seeing nothing, biting at her thumbnail until it bled.

Mutely Alma shook her head.

"Since the other day, our discussion . . ." Seigl spoke like one who knows beforehand what he will say. Alma who seemed never to know what she would say was grateful for this. The Jew speaking in his Jew manner, like a professor. He would not be emotional now, and he would not surprise her. Alma recalled how she had taken comfort of a kind in school hearing a teacher's voice, the words prepared and uttered for years, washing over her, lulling, impersonal. She did not want the personal, she did not want to be Alma, and to be hurt, and to bleed, in this place. "You said you had heard that the Holocaust never 'happened'? I've been wondering who told you that, Alma. Because obviously somebody told you. It can't have been a supposition you've made for yourself."

Alma was biting at her thumbnail. Seigl waited patiently for her to speak.

"Maybe in school . . . ?"

"In school? One of your teachers? I doubt that."

Alma tried to remember: there had been a film, maybe. A film about the Holocaust, and Jews. She hadn't seen it, hadn't been in school all that week. Eighth grade, or ninth. Somebody said it was a Jewish holiday, some kind of holiday: Holocaust?

Alma's mouth was going sullen. The kind of mouth you got slapped for back home.

"OK. I don't know."

"Was it someone in your family, Alma?"

"Someone—what?"

"Telling you the Holocaust was a fraud."

" 'Fraud'? I don't know."

"You said, the pictures could be faked. The photographs I showed you. They were originally published in *Life* magazine. Why would *Life* magazine have published fraudulent photographs? It was hardly a Jewish publication."

Alma shrugged. Why? She had no idea.

"Was it someone at your church? In Pennsylvania?"

Alma gave an impression of thinking. She shook her head slowly.

"It would not have been someone more recently, in Carmel Heights?"

Again, Alma shook her head. No?

Seigl sighed. He was close to being pissed with her, she knew.

The Tattooed Girl, her blind implacable will. *You made it all up. It's all lies.*

"Alma, I don't mean to interrogate you. But it's disturbing to me that you, of all people, so good-hearted a person, so naturally generous, should have stereotyped ideas about Jews. Because obviously these ideas are not your own, they've been imposed upon you by your elders."

Alma smiled guardedly. Yes?

Seigl stroked at his chin. He'd begun to let his beard grow back but it was a shorter, trimmer beard now. His clothes were less disheveled though they fit him loosely, he'd been losing weight for months. Some days, you could see that this was a sick man: that haunted look in his eyes. Other days, you could not. When Seigl was looking ill Alma felt a pang of concern, that he really was sick, something would really happen to him . . .

"Do you personally believe, Alma, that Jews are somehow different from you and your family? Jews are—what? Exotic? Treacherous? Dangerous? Not to be trusted? Likely to swindle you? A separate and distinct race of human being?" Seigl smiled. He might have been speaking to a small recalcitrant child. "Surely you aren't one of those who think that Jews have horns, are you?"

Alma frowned. What kind of horns?

"Horns like this." Seigl made horns with his fingers, protruding from his forehead. The gesture was meant to make Alma smile, and so Alma did.

With a clumsy sort of levity Alma said, hugging her rib cage, "Well. Not *you*." She laughed, more shrilly than she wished. "I guess."

"Maybe I've had my horns removed, eh? They do that with goats. Saw 'em off."

Alma said carefully, "A Jewish person is no different from—any other person. Except in history, I mean." Alma frowned, not sure what the hell she meant. She resented it, Seigl watching her so closely all the time. "In a way of thinking."

"Which way of thinking, Alma?"

"A Jewish way . . . I guess."

"Which is?"

Alma's eyes evaded his. Those Jew-eyes! This was why she hated him.

" 'The Chosen People.' That's what you—that's what they call themselves. Jewish persons."

Seigl laughed. "They do? Have you heard this, personally?"

Alma smiled. No.

"Do you think I'm Jewish, Alma?"

Alma frowned. What was the answer to this?

"But I'm not, Alma. I'm not Jewish."

Alma's eyes lifted to his, shocked.

"You seem surprised. In fact, I'm not Jewish: my mother was a Gentile. That Presbyterian church I've let you out at, it's the very church I was baptized in. A long time ago."

Alma stared at him. "You're kidding, I guess . . . ?"

"Kidding? Why?"

"You are Jewish. 'Seigl.' "

"My father was Jewish. Not my mother. I can't be Jewish then by birth. And I'm not Jewish by conversion. I have no religion, Alma. Not the kind you check on forms."

Alma continued to stare at him. The Jew: what was he saying?

"Of course, the Nazis would have classified me as Jewish. I'd have had to wear a yellow star. Maybe that's the kind of 'Jewish' you're thinking of? A Nazi-Jew?" Seigl was trying to speak as if bemused, but Alma knew better.

There was a roaring in her ears like distant waves. Alma stood as if dazed. Not a Jew! Not a Jew!

"Are you disappointed, Alma? Why?"

She went away from him. She would have a vague memory of him calling after her. The mark on her cheek pulsed like an infection.

Not a Jew! And she had hated him so long.

◙

IN HER ROOM the Tattooed Girl shut her hands into fists and beat beat against her thighs. She saw her pale glaring face in the mirror brainless as a moon.

What had Seigl said: his mother was a Gentile? Not a Jew? *He* was not a Jew? To be Jewish, you had to have a Jewish mother? Was this so? Then why didn't such a person as Joshua Seigl change his name? Why would he wish to be mistaken for a Jew, except to deceive?

She wondered what Dmitri Meatte would say to this. She would have liked to spit it into his face: Seigl is not a Jew.

She was too upset to return upstairs. She thought, A man who plays at being a Jew is worse than any Jew.

"Because he declares himself a 'Jew'—and he lies in this."

This seemed right to her. She was exhausted. She sank into a deep stuporous sleep from which she wanted never to wake.

1 5

H E WAS AN optimist!
    He didn't believe in sin. Still less in original sin. He believed in personal failings.

HE WAS AN optimist.

"An optimist is one who has no choice."

IN EARLY MAY he called his closest friends to tell them he'd decided to undergo a radical chemotherapy treatment his neurologist had suggested to "halt the progress" of his deteriorating condition. It involved a week's hospitalization, IV fluids would drip continuously into his veins. He was likely to suffer mania, depression. It would be a rough siege. After he was discharged he would have more chemotherapy, probably.

He heard Sondra Blumenthal draw in her breath.

"Oh, Joshua. Is this safe?"

" 'Safe'? Is life 'safe'?"

"Don't make jokes, Joshua. *Is* it safe?"

Seigl gave an impression of pondering the question.

"Friedman says yes. To a degree."

"What are the possible side effects?"

Seigl laughed irritably. You had to hand it to the woman: going for the jugular.

"AN OPTIMIST IS one who lives in the moment, but plans for the future. As if he won't be there."

Seigl made an appointment to see the family lawyer, Crossman.

This visit he'd been postponing for a decade.

Time to draw up a will.

He said, "I want not to be distracted by the 'future.' I want to be responsible, as I guess I haven't always been."

Seigl meant, and Crossman knew that he meant, Seigl's lifelong indifference to finances, family investments, property. The estate his father and his father-in-law had amassed that had been left to a small circle of heirs.

Seigl saw Crossman's agile eyes drop toward his, Seigl's, knees, legs. And lift again to Seigl's face.

The lawyer said, carefully, "I'd been wondering when I might hear from you, Joshua."

The Karl Seigl Memorial Foundation. Seigl signed documents, and by the time he left Crossman's office he was poorer by twelve million dollars.

THERE HAD RETURNED to Seigl's life, at about the time that Seigl was being made to consider his mortality in more than theoretical/poetic terms, the young scholar whose surname was Essler.

We might be related. Very distantly. Cousins?

They met again at a religious studies conference at Columbia University in April. At the conclusion of a panel discussion in which Seigl had been a dominant voice, Essler approached him awkwardly. "You probably don't remember me, Dr. Seigl, but—" Seigl interrupted, "Certainly I remember you. 'Jeremy Essler.' You're writing a dissertation at the University of Rochester on Holocaust literature. In fact, I've been thinking of you."

Seigl invited Essler to join him and several others for dinner. Next morning they met for breakfast and talked for hours. By the time they shook hands in parting, Seigl had asked Essler if he might consider, sometime in the future, acting as Seigl's literary executor.

Quickly Seigl said, "It wouldn't be pro bono. You'd be paid a salary out of a foundation I'm establishing."

"Dr. Seigl, I'd be deeply honored. Thank you!"

The young man spoke so eagerly, Seigl felt a pang of dismay.

"Probably it won't happen for a long time. Decades."

Essler smiled. Since Seigl had seen him the previous fall he'd grown a beard, sand-colored, trimmed short, that made him appear older, and on the third finger of his left hand was a gold wedding band which he was turning compulsively.

"I'm not impatient, Dr. Seigl. I can wait."

INVITATIONS FROM EUROPE: the Swedish Book Fair in September, the Frankfurt Book Fair in October, and in November a symposium in Rome on a fashionably esoteric topic, "The (Re)Discovery of the Body: Ancient and Modern Visions." Seigl had no new book, but there were new translations of older books of his being published abroad. It was as if his posthumous life was well under way, without his knowledge.

His immediate impulse was to decline the invitations. He'd been declining similar invitations for years. Then it occurred to him: if the chemotherapy worked, he might be fully restored to his health. (Not that Seigl could recall what "his" health had ever been. It seemed touchingly distant to him now as his childhood.) If he was fully restored to his health, he must accept! Ever new adventures awaited Joshua Seigl, intellectual, romantic, erotic.

He would visit Munich, where out of a dread of vertigo, the vertigo of history, he had never gone. And maybe Dachau, too.

"My origin."

It was an obscene riddle. If Karl Seigl hadn't been sent away by his desperate parents in 1939, to be taken in by relatives in New York City, how could Joshua Seigl have come into existence, twenty-five years later?

AND ALMA BUSCH was a riddle. Lingering now in the doorway of Seigl's study after she'd brought him his mail.

"Alma, yes?"

Since their last exchange the previous week the mood between them was subdued, muted. How many times Seigl had heard that nasal reedy astounded voice *You are Jewish*. Alma had a way of seeming to fade out of a room when Seigl glanced up, as if her fleshy body were an apparition. He spoke to her only when required, though always kindly. He'd been furious with her and had disliked her and he was telling himself he felt sorry for her, never would he speak ironically to her again, or with emotion quavering in his voice.

She said, faltering, "What—is going to happen?"

"When, Alma? To whom?"

He supposed she had overheard him speaking on the phone. But he would make her explain.

"You're going to the—hospital? For ch-chemotherapy?"

"Yes. But not for cancer. This is something different."

Alma regarded him with such forlorn, frightened eyes, Seigl was touched.

He told her of his plans. A week in the medical school hospital. A "new, radical" treatment for his condition. When he was discharged, if he needed home care, he would hire a nurse, of course. "I wouldn't expect you to do that kind of work, Alma. You aren't trained, and it isn't the kind of work you've agreed to."

"But I work for you. I would be here."

Alma was holding her arms tight against her torso, flattening her breasts between them in a way that must have been painful. Seigl wanted to seize her wrists and yank her arms apart. Her beautiful body, so deformed! He looked away from her, speaking rapidly, as if impersonally. "In fact, I've been thinking you could take some time off, too. You've been here in this house, as my assistant, without a break for months. You don't even take weekends off any longer. I haven't wanted to ask why."

Alma, staring at him intensely, said nothing.

Seigl was wondering: did he want to send Alma away? Was that the point of this conversation?

"You could take a vacation. Visit your family . . ."

Alma protested, "I'm working for you, Mr. Seigl! I should be helping you. When you're in the hospital . . ."

"But this is an opportunity for you to take a break. You must miss your family."

Alma gave a bitter bemused little cry. As if she knew quite well that her employer was tormenting her.

"See, Mr. Seigl, I don't have any 'family' anymore. I'm working for *you*."

Seigl thought guiltily, But I'm not your family.

In the early evening, Seigl entered the kitchen where Alma was preparing his dinner. Rarely did Seigl enter the kitchen when Alma was in it, his presence so distracted her. She would cease whatever she was doing and stand at attention waiting for him to speak. If he was simply going to the cupboard, or to the refrigerator, she would wait in silence until he turned to leave. Now she nearly dropped a heavy casserole dish she was bringing to place in the oven. He heard her draw in her breath. He said, "Alma, I've been thinking: while I'm away, why don't you start a course of some kind? There's an excellent night school at Mount Carmel College, for adults. There are other schools in the city. I'll pay your tuition, of course." Seigl spoke warmly now, in his rapid, impersonal voice. He might have been speaking to a stranger. "You could learn to type on a computer. You could enroll in a degree program: in a business school. There's an education school at the University of Rochester. You said you had a high school diploma, why not continue your education?"

Alma's eerily colorless silvery eyes were fixed upon Seigl's chest. Yet she seemed scarcely to be seeing him.

As if taking a course is the answer to the riddle of Alma Busch's life. Seigl felt ashamed of himself, without knowing exactly why.

16

SEIGL WOULD HAVE no visitors at the hospital, except his assistant, who was to bring him mail, newspapers, books and things he needed from home. But Alma arrived early and remained through the day.

"Alma, you don't have to stay here. You can leave."

He'd told himself on the eve of checking into the hospital that he wasn't frightened. He was an optimist now, and an optimist is never frightened. "I've been feeling very American lately," he told his friends. "My old, European soul is being sloughed off." He was being fanciful, yet perhaps there was truth in what he said. He'd told himself too that he was looking forward to this week of privacy. Rather like being imprisoned, in a cell the size of a bed. Hooked up to a magical potion dripping into his veins. This would be an intellectual and spiritual retreat. He was sure it would be "good for him" in ways other than merely physical.

At first, Seigl was able to work. To a degree. He wanted to concentrate on the *Aeneid*. He was fierce and stubborn in his dedication to the massive poem even as, he was beginning to sense, his motive for having begun translating it was waning. Virgilian melancholy and subordination to destiny had less appeal to him now, he didn't know why. His soul had been altered by the alterations in his body. His soul was a shadow, a reflection of his body. Was that it?

He vowed he wouldn't give up. Always, he loved the poetry.

Except: the precision required in translating Virgil wore him out far more rapidly than it usually did. Especially, reworking the numerous passages he'd lost exhausted him, for he was trying to remember what he'd originally written. It sickened him anew, having lost so many hours of work. "What I deserve, I suppose. For being so careless."

Alma, seated at his bedside, glanced over at him. Had Seigl spoken aloud?

It was beginning to be difficult to tell. What were his thoughts merely, and what were his spoken words. He was certain he'd told the young blond woman who was his assistant to go home, she needn't remain with him, but he couldn't be absolutely certain if he'd spoken these words aloud. He wasn't certain of her name: " 'Alma'?" Suddenly the drug dripping like acid into the bruised vein at the crook of Seigl's left arm was having a bizarre effect upon his mind. Like a funhouse mirror. Like a flight of crooked zigzagging steps. You start confidently to climb, and find yourself . . . Where?

Seigl was writing by hand, block-printing laboriously. He asked Alma to bring him his laptop, he'd never much used at home disliking its small screen, but now the screen was impossible, the tiny letters swimming like ants in his vision. He saw that the absurdly lightweight mechanism contained an X ray of his brain: that was what the screen showed! He shoved it from him, frightened. "Mr. Seigl? Is something wrong?" The corrosive liquid dripping into his vein was circulating to his heart. He moaned in fear.

Alma hurried to get a nurse.

Later, he heard women's voices from somewhere close by. One of them repeated his name *Mr. Seigl—Mr. Seigl—Mr. Seigl*—in a way fascinating and mysterious.

She loves me he thought. *She will protect me.*

Another day? He was ravenously hungry. His hand shook lifting a spoon. Flowers were delivered: a half-dozen long-stemmed waxy-white roses. Seigl squinted at the card, couldn't make out the name. There was some joke (his?) that the President of the United States had sent these flowers. Squinting at Virgil's Latin lines now made the translator sick.

Alma read off names. Names on cards? These were friends Seigl could dimly recall. Out of pride he'd forbidden any of them to come to the hospital to see him. Wouldn't advise it, the neurologist had warned.

Liquid meals. Bouillon, skim milk. Jell-O. How delicious Jell-O was! Seigl had devalued this astonishing invention. He wondered if strawberry Jell-O was an American invention.

"This. We'll have this. All the time when I get out."

Alma, quietly opening mail, glanced over at him. Possibly he'd spoken aloud, but what had he said?

Now he was fully awake. Tottering into the bathroom with the IV gurney attached to his arm was an excellent way of being wakened fully. Returning, and climbing onto the bed. These hospital beds were marvels of machinery. Cranking up, cranking down. Seigl was all-business now going through a copyedited manuscript. When he was finished with each page, Alma took it from him. She would fax these pages to the editor in London. His assistant was learning to decipher editors' scrawls, and would read queries to Seigl. This way, he could work with his eyes shut.

And there were phone messages, numerous messages Seigl was determined to answer.

Dialing numbers from his hospital bed. Except Alma was better able to dial these numbers for him. When Seigl spoke, he made an effort to speak clearly, forcibly. He wanted no pity from anyone. He wanted no tales told of him. *A degenerative disease. Wasting disease. Poor Joshua must be desperate.* In mid-sentence he began to forget to whom he was speaking. Fascinated, he could see himself forgetting: it was like watching a short thread being drawn through a needle's eye.

The receiver began to slip from his drowsy fingers. The young blond woman with the birthmark on her face took it from him. "Mr. Seigl has to hang up now. He will call you back another time."

Seigl began to weep. For he knew it would never be *another time*.

THEY WERE WAKING him. More blood to be drawn? His parched mouth gasped like the mouth of a giant pike caught by a hook through its upper lip. Friedman had come to examine him, and went away again before Seigl could joke with him. Seigl sulked, misunderstood. He was ravenously hungry but a few swallows, and he began to gag. Still, sunshine flooded through the window like a shower of gold. He stared, deeply moved. *This has been arranged for me. I am a privileged patient.*

Somehow, without his knowing it, the lye solution was dripping now into Seigl's right elbow, into another bruised but durable vein. Seigl was eager to believe this meant he had passed the midway point.

Seigl no longer tried to work. No longer the pretense of work.

It was laughable: the absurdity of "work."

Squinting his eyes to read even the newspaper made him nauseated. The most he could manage were the comic strips. (But Alma had to read the dialogue in the little balloons for him.) If he picked up a pen, and tried to write, his fingers balked. Swollen from cortisone they were, unmanageable.

He wanted only to be touched. Sponge-bathed very gently.

Alma took over this task. Alma was awkward but determined.

He winced, his skin hurt! As if the outermost layer had been peeled away.

Alma said she was sorry.

Seigl hadn't strength to ask for what. Why?

Alma said she was sorry, the things she'd said.

The room was darkened, it might have been night. Seigl slept. There was some controversy, his friends were heatedly discussing it, whether in fact Seigl had died. Yet at the floor of the sea he was drifting with the current, and was fully conscious of being alive. It was silent, so far beneath the surface of the water. Shadowy shapes glided near, soundless. Their blade faces and open, staring, lidless eyes.

In this place he was creating a magic code. Words and numerals. The laptop he'd detested was restored to him, now its screen was luminous and magnified and he commanded it. Here, at the bottom of the sea, Seigl was granted the power to deflect the course of Time. He could control Time before his birth by a special key on the laptop. You depressed "code" and then this key, at the upper-right of the keyboard. In this way Seigl was empowered to repeal the Nuremberg Laws of 1935! This was the secret. To deflect the course of the War, and of the Holocaust, it was necessary only to repeal the Nuremberg Laws. Seigl understood, he hadn't the power single-handedly to deflect the course of Time altogether. But the Nuremberg Laws, yes!

That was why he was so happy, waking. Alma stared at him in surprise.

She'd brought his CD player. Since he hated TV. During his waking hours they would listen to music. This too was something he could do with his eyes shut. He'd requested Mozart, piano sonatas. Bach, cello sonatas. Chopin's *Preludes*. Piano pieces by Ravel, Debussy, Bartók. Cello, not piano, sonatas of Beethoven. The great piano sonatas of Beethoven were too exhausting for Seigl to listen to, in his weakened state.

Alma was sitting with her head back against the wall, arms folded beneath her breasts. Like the nurses she was wearing white. Like the nurses she was wearing her hair close to her head, brushed back from her forehead. Seigl could see: her forehead was creased with near-invisible lines. Seigl wanted to take hold of her hands and com-fort her. *Of course, I love you. I will never send you away.*

He was so happy! Such visions were granted him.

Yet: the siege continued. He tried to explain to the doctor that he was cured now, he could go home now, but the siege continued. The terrible dripping into his veins continued.

Like a waning moon her face shifted out of focus. Seigl tried to draw her attention to him but could not. His limbs were heavy as lead, paralyzed. The room began to darken. The piano music faded. A terrible depression swept over him like surf. In fact he was lying exhausted on a debris-littered shore, and dirty water broke over his body like surf. In this ridiculous open-backed nightgown he lay, naked beneath. He was humiliated, beaten. He was sick with terror that he would drown. *I will never leave here. This is my tomb.* He had lost all strength. He was too weak to deflect the passage of the present moment, let alone the course of history.

Sensing his weakness, smelling blood like predators, the souls of the dead hovered near. In Homer's Hades *Up out of Erebus they came flocking. Thousands swarming from every side. Shambling, shiftless dead.* Al-ways he'd been troubled by these lines in Homer, that the dead were shambling, shiftless. They had lost their dignity, they were no longer fully conscious. It was horrible to think that among them were Seigl's elders. His parents, grandparents. His ancestors. It was his duty as their son to nourish them with blood, otherwise they were too feeble to speak. And yet—he had only his own blood, he could not survive without it. Alone of this company only Joshua Seigl was alive. Like bleating sheep they called his name, groping blindly for him. He had to escape them. They smelled him, groped and clawed for him. *Joshua! Joshua!* But here was his salvation, they could not see.

Seigl woke, sweating and agitated. He'd cried out in his sleep.

But he'd escaped Hades, he was alive.

Alma emerged from the bathroom, unsteady on her feet. Her face was drawn with exhaustion, he'd never seen her looking like this. He began to speak rapidly, pleading: "Alma! You were right—I lied. I couldn't tell the truth. They tried to buy their way out—to deny that they were Jews. I lied for them! They argued that they were Christians, they'd married into Protestant families and they'd converted. They begged, they pleaded, they tried to negotiate with the Reich, they made payments to Nazi officials to allow them to emigrate, the Nazis took their money—of course!—but it made no difference, their property was 'Aryanized,' they were herded into the camps like the poorest of the Jews, the Jews they scorned, that's why I call them 'the shadows'—they were never real. Alma, you were right, I'm so ashamed." Seigl's voice was shrill and desperate. There was no sensation in his legs, he'd become a torso to be stacked like firewood. "They—they sent me away. I was saved. I was the only one. I couldn't betray them, I had to lie for them! I'm so—"

He was delirious, raving. Alma grabbed his hands where he was trying to yank out the IV needle. "Stop it! It was a long time ago, it wasn't you. All that is crazy. What you need is to get *well*. None of that matters, see?"

She was strong, stronger than Seigl in his flailing, weakened state. He had no choice but to give in.

17

M Y HEART IS filled with HOPE
This is REBIRTH
My REDEMPTION

Every cell in my body will be cleansed & made new. I believe this.
She has saved my life.

Yet: of all the words known to me, there are none. Her touch.

18

LIKE A DEEP-SEA predator scenting blood he came. He was sitting at the foot of the nineteen stone steps, smoking, when Alma's taxi pulled up. She saw he'd been there some time, the sidewalk at his feet was littered with butts.

"Hey babe."

His shaved head was smaller and meaner than she remembered. Only a thin stubbled layer of hair remained like lichen over stone. And his jaws were stubbled, hinge-like. When he smiled, the lower part of his face seemed to be detaching itself from the rest.

The Tattooed Girl's lover. Coming to reclaim her.

It was the eve of Seigl's discharge from the hospital. Each night, Alma had stayed until the nurses asked her to leave, when visitors' hours were over at 11 P.M.

"Babe? I want to see you."

She told him no.

"Let's go inside. We have things to talk about."

She told him *no*.

He stared at her disbelieving. Was this the Tattooed Girl? He was still smiling his hinge-like smile. His predator eyes keen and alert upon her.

"What d'you mean, babe: 'no'? What the fuck is 'no'?"

The Tattooed Girl was wearing white, like the nurses at the hospital whom she so much admired. White rayon trousers, a white rayon shirt and white cotton sweater buttoned partway over her bust. Thin white socks like a little girl's socks, and sandals with crepe soles. Her hair had been brushed back from her face and tied with a scarf whose ends fell on either side of her head. Her mouth was pale, of the hue of lard, without lipstick. She'd lost perhaps ten pounds and was thinner in the face and breasts. She was standing with her legs apart and slightly bent, and her hands, stubby-fingered, were visibly trembling.

Her shaved-headed lover said, with a fond, sneering laugh, "Look, babe. You came looking for me. So here I am."

He told her he was bartending now, in the city. It was work he liked but only part-time. He'd had enough of fucking waiting tables, he said. He cursed the manager at The Café. Cocksucker sonofabitch. Asshole better not get in his way. As he talked, the Tattooed Girl understood that he needed money. This was the tone, these were the facial grimaces, that signaled a man in need of money. When he appoached her, she could smell that need. A cheap metallic smell it was like copper pennies held tightly in the hand.

When he touched her, she threw off his hand.

No, she said.

"What the fuck do you mean, 'no'?"

He was becoming seriously pissed at her: couldn't she see?

Still she told him to go away. He couldn't come in the house, she said.

(Alma had left the house lighted. She always did, leaving for the hospital in the early morning so that, when she returned, alone, more than twelve hours later, it would seem to her that Seigl was already there, inside.)

Mr. Seigl was there, she said. She was not allowed to have visitors.

Bullshit, Dmitri Meatte said. "You told me you have a room. Take me there." He peered at her suspiciously. His hinge-smile had ceased. "Unless you're sleeping with the Jew, huh? That's it?"

She told him again to go away. She didn't want to see him.

"Are you crazy, Alma? You know you want to see me." He came closer. The metallic smell was stronger. "You know you want it."

Alma shook her head no. Like a stubborn child, frightened, yet standing her ground.

He told her she'd be fucking sorry.

He told her he needed money.

He told her he'd be calling on Seigl, and telling him an earful, if she didn't give him what he wanted. And fast.

Panicked she shoved him in the chest. He called her cunt, and grabbed her hair. He would have struck her in the face except she kicked him in the groin, reacting purely out of instinct, blind and desperate. He gave a high-pitched bat cry. His face crinkled like an infant's. As he backed away doubled over, groaning and gasping for air, and cradling his genitals in both his hands as one might cradle precious eggs already broken, she warned that she would kill him if he came there again.

The Tattoed Girl fighting for her life.

19

ON THE FIRST day home from the hospital, Seigl slept.

On the second day home from the hospital, Seigl began to recover his appetite, and ate.

On the third day home from the hospital, Seigl gave his assistant Alma Busch a gift to thank her for her "vigil at my side." It was a necklace that had belonged to his mother.

This necklace was the most beautiful thing Alma had ever seen.

It consisted of three strands of jade-colored oval beads of opaque glass that looked sculpted. The strands were of varying lengths, falling midway to her waist. Lowering the strands over her bowed head, gently untangling the beads, Alma's fingers shook. In a nearby mirror Alma's stunned face was made beautiful by its proximity to the necklace and for some seconds she stared at her reflection without recognition.

She would not utter the words *Thank you*. She would not trust her voice.

There was her employer's smiling face in the mirror behind her. He was telling her the necklace was Venetian.

" 'Venetian'—what's that?"

"From Venice. Italy. We'll go there next fall, on our way to Rome."

20

I'VE GOT TO get out, Alma. Can't breathe."

On the morning of May 19, five days after he'd been discharged from the hospital, and improving rapidly each day, Seigl became restless and insisted upon hiking in Mount Carmel Cemetery, where he hadn't been in months.

Alma would think his remark about needing to get out a strange one. For each day since his discharge from the hospital Seigl had been outside, if only on the terrace overlooking the river, sitting in the sun, a book on his lap, gazing into the distance. More recently he'd been walking in the neighborhood. In the hospital he'd lost fifteen pounds but the treatment had been successful, Seigl's doctor said.

Seigl agreed. "I feel like a new man. Every cell in my body has been cleansed."

When Alma hesitated, not knowing if Seigl wanted her to come with him, Seigl said, eagerly, "Come with me, Alma! We've been stuck inside too long."

Alma asked, Should she bring the cane?

Seigl said, laughing, Fuck the cane.

It was a warm, thinly overcast day. The wind from Lake Ontario smelled of imminent rain. Yet the sun was reflected, whitely, strangely, from myriad surfaces, as if the lush green of May was mostly moisture, and ephemeral. Alma would remember that Seigl seemed determined to get to the cemetery, and, at the cemetery, he was determined to climb the hill.

"The last time I climbed Mount Carmel, I was an ignorant man. This time—I'll see things differently."

Seigl spoke excitedly. Alma saw that his skin, sallow for so long, was flushed, ruddy. He wasn't wearing his glasses, his eyes were clear and alert. In the hospital, intermittently, he'd been raving, delirious. The nurses had told Alma not to be alarmed, it was a temporary effect caused by the powerful steroids. But Alma heard that edge of excitement and elation in his voice, and it made her uneasy.

(She'd disobeyed him and brought along the cane. Hoping that, if Seigl noticed it, he wouldn't be angry, or hurt.)

That morning, Seigl had wakened and come downstairs by 7 A.M. He'd worked outside on the terrace, he'd made several telephone calls. He would be having dinner with Sondra Blumenthal that evening, and would arrive at her house by 6 P.M. to play chess with her son, Ethan.

Alma had never met the child Ethan. She'd heard "Ethan" spoken of occasionally. Calmly she thought *I don't hate any of them. No longer.*

She thought *I am the one he loves.*

For this truth was clear to her: and did not require saying.

Any more than it requires saying that there is God, and God is God.

BY THE TIME they reached the cemetery they'd been walking uphill steadily. Alma was beginning to perspire beneath her arms and at the nape of her neck beneath her heavy hair. Seigl was walking so quickly, Alma could barely keep up with him.

Inside the gates, Seigl declined to take the zigzagging gravel drive to the top of the hill, and insisted upon climbing a flight of stone steps built into the hill. Alma saw how high, and how steep, these steps were, and began to protest, but Seigl said, frowning, "Alma. You're my assistant, not my caretaker."

Alma wondered: could she climb those steps herself? There were many more than nineteen. And some were partly crumbled, covered in moss. There was a rusted iron railing on one side of the steps that looked useless.

Alma said, faltering, "Mr. Seigl, I—I don't think—"

" 'Joshua,' Alma. I've asked you."

" 'Joshua.' I don't think—"

"You are not my assistant to 'think,' Alma. You're my assistant to 'do.' "

Uttered in Seigl's lightly chiding teasing voice, this was not exactly a reprimand.

"*This* we can leave in the grass!"

Seigl took the cane from her and flung it aside. Days later it would be discovered amid the grave markers of strangers and brought to the cemetery groundskeeper.

Alma smiled, frightened.

Nearby was the groundskeeper in fact, noisily revving up the motor of a tractor mower. Alma looked to the man as if in appeal: middle-aged, with a fringe of gray-grizzled hair, a hefty torso and coarse dark skin like tree bark. Rudely he stared at Alma for a long moment before seeing who the man was with her, calling then, "Good morning, Dr. Seigl!"

Seigl called back, waving, "Good morning, Luigi."

Alma thought, He will tell him not to climb those steps, they're dangerous.

Seigl began the climb energetically. Why he was so eager to get to the top, Alma could not guess. He was wearing baggy khaki shorts, a white T-shirt that fitted his body loosely, a soiled baseball cap. And on his feet his old, smelly, waterstained running shoes. Alma, behind and below Seigl, craned her neck to watch him. Only midway in the climb did he pause for breath. She saw him gripping the railing, which held. Alma had become short of breath almost immediately, rivulets of sweat running down her face. If her employer turned to glance at her, he'd laugh at her discomfort, he'd tease her, but he seemed to have forgotten her, beginning his climb again. By the time he reached the top he, too, had slowed his pace.

The sun, thinly veiled by cloud, shone opaquely on all sides.

The mower had started. A deafening roar.

At the top of the hill, Seigl turned aside as if stricken by a new thought. Alma, craning her neck, called out, "Mr. Seigl—?" She hurriedly climbed the rest of the way. One of the steps was loose, her foot nearly slipped. There was a smell of lush, damp grass on all sides. Something was wrong here, something was jeering and mocking. When Alma reached the top of the steps there was Seigl hunched over, pressing the palm of his hand against his chest. She tried to take hold of his arm but he pushed her away without seeing her. His face was contorted, almost unrecognizable. She cried his name, she asked what was wrong, she was overcome with panic trying to hold him but he pushed away from her, stumbling, livid with pain. As Alma stared in horror she saw him lose his balance and fall backward down the steps, heavily, like a dead weight, onto the hilly ground thirty feet below where he lay broken and still as if already dead.

I screamed, no one heard me, I climbed back down the steps to be with him. I don't remember after that. There was a loud roaring noise. In the ambulance he was still alive, he was looking at me. He put out his hand to me, he called me Alma . . .

IV

The Shadows

I

I T WAS A TIME of deep plunging sleep and when she woke each time he was still dead.

2

"CREMATE.' 'CREMATORIUM' . . ."

Her lips moved, she must have spoken aloud.

They hadn't wanted her with them. It was a private ceremony as they said.

His family, his close friends. Only his very close friends were invited.

They had not wanted Alma Busch who'd been Joshua's assistant. Alma Busch The Tattooed Girl!

Yet finally she was allowed. She had had to beg. But she was used to begging, she was good at begging. Her doggy eyes, bloodshot from crying. Someone took pity on her, among the Steadman relatives.

And so she was shunned by his people, but allowed. At the rear of the chapel where no one need see her.

(A strange chapel it was: no cross. Only just a platform bearing the coffin. Maroon velvet drapery as in a theater. Where was the furnace? Her nostrils widened, sniffing.)

"He should be buried. In a real grave. In a cemetery. So that . . ."

She wiped at her nose. Was she whispering aloud? It was none of their business what she was saying, they had no right to judge.

Yes! She would sit alone yet obtrusive as a bad smell at the rear of the windowless chapel. She wore a shiny black dress with a black shawl, or was it a curtain, ugly and graceless, wrapped around her, their eyes raked upon her in grief and repugnance she was allowed to see. *Know that you are not wanted. Know that you are despised.*

In her grief and confusion nonetheless she saw: the sister was not present.

His sister who'd struck her. His sister who had sent the mutilated book. His sister who had peered into the Tattooed Girl's heart.

She shrank from their eyes, though they were no more than shadows. She would ignore them as they ignored her. His relatives she'd never met and would not meet, and his "close friends" whom she'd seen at the house numerous times and served bringing drinks, food, taking away their dirtied plates and glasses, *oh thank you, Alma,* they would murmur scarcely seeing her and now they would ignore her for her way of grief was vulgar. Among them the woman who'd loved him and who despised Alma Busch and would spread lies about her in grief and fury at his death.

Alma was sobbing openly. Sitting stiff in dignity as you'd sit in pain. Her arms were folded around her rib cage, tight. Gripping herself tight to keep from exploding. To keep from breaking. Her ash-blond hair was greasy, uncombed. It had been jaggedly cut to an unbecoming length just at her shoulders. Her face was sickly white, without makeup, soft as a runny pudding. No longer a girl's face but swollen and shiny as if roughly polished. The tattoo on her cheek was a lurid smudge you wanted to wipe off with a tissue.

Recorded piano music was playing. One of those pieces he had asked her to bring to him at the hospital. Mozart, Schubert . . .

The sound of it pierced her heart. It would drive her from the chapel.

Before the coffin was borne away. Someone rose to speak but already at the rear of the chapel the Tattooed Girl was pushing out of the pew, stumbling out of the chapel. Before the coffin was carried away to the furnace and nightmare flames.

3

STILL SHE HAD the key to the house. For still she was
Joshua Seigl's assistant. She would be Joshua Seigl's assistant for the remainder of her life.

The family wanted her gone. But he'd left instructions protecting her. He hadn't expected to die yet he'd left detailed instructions protecting Alma Busch after his death.

She held the key to the house, his house, in her perspiring shaky fingers. Always she would keep this key close by her, in a pocket, beneath her pillow at night, or literally in her hand. For if she lost the key to Joshua Seigl's house she would lose everything.

Got to get out, Alma. Can't breathe!

Come with me, Alma.

She fell onto her bed fully clothed. Even her shoes. Shiny black patent leather shoes for mourning. A crease in the bedspread would leave a sharp serrated crease in her face. She was neither drunk nor drugged but her sleep was stuporous and when she wakened eleven hours later it was to the knowledge that Joshua Seigl was still dead.

◙

"HE HAS MADE you a beneficiary of his estate."

A stone head with eyeglass-eyes regarded her with cool civility.

"Crossman" was the name. It was like trying to cup water in her hands, Alma kept forgetting.

She'd swallowed three tablets prescribed for J. Seigl. Muscle relaxant. Pain control. May cause drowsiness. Do not combine with alcohol. Do not operate large machinery. The drug had a coarse-chalky-milky effect upon her brain that would have made her uneasy in other circumstances. In Crossman's office it was a comfort.

For "Crossman" was a lawyer. Alma understood that he had power over her, power delegated to him by Joshua Seigl, and so she smiled at him with clumsy coquetry. She knew no other way to confront a man of such severity wearing a suit, a white shirt, a necktie.

Reading to Alma Busch from documents spread out on his desk. Peering through his eyeglasses at her as you'd peer at an insect through a a magnifying lens. ". . . concerned for your welfare, it seems. He has made you a beneficiary of his estate. Specifically, he has left a certain sum of money in trust for you, out of which you will receive a monthly stipend for the remainder of your natural life, at which time the trust will revert . . . Over and above this monthly stipend, the estate will pay for your tuition, room, and board at any fully accredited institution of higher learning including secretarial school and nursing school . . . It is stipulated in Mr. Seigl's will that you, Alma Busch, be retained as an assistant to his literary executor if you and the literary executor agree to this arrangement, and that you continue to reside in the house at eight Greaves Place if you so wish for a period of not more than five years at which time the property will revert to the estate . . . Do you have any questions, Miss Busch?"

Alma frowned, wiping at her nose.

". . . questions, Miss Busch? You must have questions."

Alma tried to think. The chalky-milky seepage in her brain was making it difficult to think. She'd forgotten the man's name but knew that what he'd told her was important. "... I should k-keep doing the things? I'm Mr. Seigl's assistant?"

"Yes. If you wish. For a while, at least."

"Like, answer the phone? Bring in the mail, open it ... some of it, I can answer. Mr. Seigl taught me how. And there's typing ... filing. I should keep doing the things?" Alma was anxious suddenly that she'd misunderstood.

The man, the lawyer, stared at her with undisguised contempt. Like static it was, confusing her. For his voice was so polite.

"Yes. Until such time as you meet with Mr. Seigl's literary executor. His name is—"

Alma interrupted, laughing nervously. "I should k-keep doing the things, like he taught me? And I can live in the house like before?"

"Yes, Miss Busch." The voice was even, only the set of the jaws suggested contempt. "You may continue to 'do the things.' Until such time as you meet with Jeremy Essler who will know more precisely, more professionally, what's to be done with Joshua Seigl's estate."

Alma smiled. She hadn't heard most of this.

It was enough to know, Seigl needed her. Even after his death he needed her, and he could trust her.

Alma stood, uncertainly. Was it time to leave?

The static in the air was so loud, she would think afterward that the lawyer had in fact told her to leave. Abruptly she turned and walked out of the office still smiling as the man stared after her in astonishment. He would say afterward to Seigl's relatives and to others how "Alma" had come into his office coked to the gills: he knew the symptoms. Stumbling out of his office, and those wild fish-colored eyes. Smiling!

Like Alma Busch had won the lottery.

4

I'M WORRIED NOW, there isn't God. And there isn't . . ."

She was talking to herself. Prowling the locked, brightly lit house. Sometimes, in fear of her former lover breaking in, she carried a steak knife from the kitchen with her; this knife, she made certain she kept on her bedside table when she went to bed at night, and the door to her room locked.

"There isn't God, maybe. And now there isn't . . . him."

She meant to say "Mr. Seigl" but he'd asked her to call him "Joshua." Neither name could she utter.

Seigl had not believed in God. What he'd believed in, Alma would believe in, too; but she could not remember what it was. Books?

She had straightened all the shelves of books. The spines were even now, there was a pleasure in seeing such orderliness. His study was immaculate. He would laugh in amazement to see. *Alma! What have you done?* The manuscripts he'd been working on at the time of his death were neatly stacked on a table in his study. Correspondence was opened, letters smoothed out awaiting someone to read them.

When the phone rang, Alma cleared her throat before lifting the receiver and saying, "Hello. This is Mr. Seigl's residence. But . . ."

The man who was Joshua Seigl's "literary executor" had called several times. Alma listened politely as "Jeremy Essler" spoke but when he suggested coming over, when would be a good time for him to come over to the house, Alma stammered and made excuses. She was "too busy with things" right now. There was "too much" happening.

After a few days she ceased answering the phone. Messages went onto the answering service, that would have to be enough.

A lawyer for the Steadman family called several times. Insisting that his clients be allowed to "make an inventory" of the household. A court injunction was imminent forbidding Alma Busch from "removing any property" from the household. Alma scarcely listened to these messages, deleting them as the stranger's self-important voice droned.

"I don't want anything. There's nothing I want."

On the dining room table she'd placed his books. Beginning with *The Shadows.* She'd been trying to read the books but lines of print swam in her vision, she felt nauseated. Was this all that remained of Joshua Seigl, these . . . books? She turned them in her hand. Paper, print. It was nothing, was it?

Trying to remember why she'd hated him so.

(Because he was a Jew? What did that mean?)

It made no sense. She could not remember. In her pocket was the key to the house, she touched it repeatedly, held it in her hand.

" 'He has made you a beneficiary.' "

She knew the word: beneficiary.

" 'Because he loved you. He loved you best. He still loves you. See, that's why? Alma.' "

5

"MISS BUSCH. Tell us again what happened in Mount Carmel Cemetery on May 19, approximately eleven A.M."

Oh Christ why she was making such a bad impression on the police detectives, she was thinking of how she'd been arrested in Pittsburgh, more than once she'd been taken into custody by street cops and one time with a girl who'd slashed at them with a razor out of her boot and so the Tattooed Girl had been roughly handled, she was beginning to tremble thinking of this, how they'd cuffed her wrists behind her back and so tightly she'd cried in pain and in disgust with her crying they'd jerked her arms up behind her back practically to her shoulders until she fainted with the pain and urine leaked out of her soaking her clothes. And, oh God she was thinking of the bench warrants for her arrest in Akron County and in Pittsburgh, for passing bad checks, for soliciting, she'd slipped out of town with a man who'd claimed to be crazy for her and would drive her across the country to San Diego where he had a condominium on the ocean, he promised!

"Miss Busch? Again, tell us what happened. You climbed the

steps in the cemetery behind Mr. Seigl or you were waiting at the top of the steps for Mr. Seigl, which was it? The groundskeeper has said, when he looked up . . ."

Alma smiled nervously. She'd told them, or tried to tell them, but her tongue was too big for her mouth. She was rocking forward and back in the hard vinyl seat hugging herself tight. See, she was waiting for them to say the gloating words *You are under arrest.* Both the men would rise then, and move upon her, and one of them would have the handcuffs. Their eyes on her ardent, eager. For arresting and handcuffing is better than sex for a cop, any-age cop. No words happier than *You are under arrest.* Alma was listening so hard for these words, almost she believed she'd heard them.

"Miss Busch? Do you understand the question?"

Alma wiped at her mouth. "What? Say it again . . ."

Miss Busch. Alma Busch. The name meant nothing to her. Pronounced by strangers like the name of a disease.

". . . Joshua Seigl's assistant? For how long? Since when?"

On her fingers she counted the months. The first time, she counted six months; the second, seven. Coldly the detectives regarded her as she shifted her weight in the vinyl chair feeling the lower part of her face shift too, her mouth smiling in a desperate plea. "I guess—seven months? Since last November."

At a distance she heard her own plaintive voice. A guilty voice. She was describing how she'd told Mr. Seigl not to climb the steps because they were so steep, she'd followed behind him, and at the top he had . . . Pausing then in horror recalling how he'd pushed away her hand, his face contorted in pain, and when she'd tried to hold him . . .

There was a long pause. The interview was being taped. But both men were taking notes, too. In her pocket was the key to Mr. Seigl's house. If she lost it, she would lose everything.

"Miss Busch . . ."

Was she supposed to answer? Like in school, raise her hand and say, That's me?

". . . we've been told by several parties who have come forward since the 'accident' that you boasted of planning to kill your employer Mr. Seigl. Did you?"

The Tattooed Girl sat stunned.

The detective repeated, "Miss Busch? Did you boast of . . . ?"

A long time passed. Then, with clumsy coquetry, the Tattooed Girl managed to say, "W-why'd I do *that*?"

"Because, as our informants say, Mr. Seigl was a Jew."

"He—he wasn't a Jew."

"Miss Busch, did you say these things? Before witnesses?"

Her former lover had betrayed her. Some of the other guys. His friends. Maybe someone had been arrested, he'd informed on her to make a deal. The Tattooed Girl was having trouble thinking as she was having trouble breathing through her fishy-gaping mouth. Thinking was like passing clumsy-sized stones from one hand to the other trying not to drop any . . .

The name *Busch* was being enunciated. *Busch Busch Alma Busch.* The cassette in the tape recorder turned. There were more than two shadow-figures in the room, she saw now that there were others. All were watching her closely, ardently.

". . . say these things? 'Planning to kill' your employer? And steal from him? Or 'get him to marry you, leave you money' . . . ?"

The Tattooed Girl hid her face in her hands.

In a loud laughing voice crying, "Why'd I do *that*! I wouldn't do *that*! I . . ."

I loved him. I would die for him.

That he was a Jew, I loved him.

Hunched in the hard vinyl chair that made her ass sweat, like a cringing dog waiting for the words to be uttered *You are under arrest.* Now they would cuff her wrists behind her back and lead her out, to be locked up in a holding pen. But when she looked up cautiously she saw that they were only just watching her.

They released her! They did not arrest her.

They told her that the "investigation" would continue. She was warned not to leave Carmel Heights.

Giddy with relief the Tattooed Girl laughed. "Where'd I go, if I left? There's no place."

6

S HE STOOD BESIDE the ringing phone. She watched her
hand hesitate, then reach out to lift the receiver.

"... Mr. Seigl's residence."

She'd forgotten to clear her throat. Her head was filled with mucus. Her voice came out flat, nasal. She sensed the party at the other
end of the line recoiling in disdain.

A voice identified itself as "Crossman." Alma needed a moment
to think who Crossman was.

Not one of the detectives. The lawyer.

He has made you a beneficiary.

Strange that Crossman who'd stared at her in such dislike was
calling her now to offer advice. Telling her that, for her own good,
she should seriously consider "retaining legal counsel."

Alma said nothing. She was breathing through her mouth, wetly.

Crossman told her that Carmel Heights police were investigating
Joshua Seigl's death. Though the medical examiner had ruled that
he'd died of a heart attack, still Seigl's relatives were accusing Alma
Busch of "having a hand" in his death.

There was talk of an "eyewitness" in the cemetery who'd seen them "struggle" at the top of the steps. There were said to be other witnesses, informants. Did Alma know anything about these?

Alma mumbled a vague reply. She stood barefoot in a part-buttoned white cotton shirt of Seigl's, no bra beneath. White cotton panties thin from numerous washings. Even as she stood pressing the receiver against her ear she was forgetting who'd called.

It was a man's voice. A deep-chested voice. Warning her she should not speak to the police without a lawyer present. "For your own good, Miss Busch."

The voice went on to ask if she had paper handy, a pen? To take down the name and telephone number of a good defense lawyer.

A yawn overtook Alma with the sudden violence of a sneeze. "Sure."

She had no paper, and she had no pen. While the voice continued to speak, she hung up the phone.

7

MR. S-SEIGL—?"

She was in the kitchen, she'd swear she had heard his voice. As if he'd just let himself in the front door and in another moment she would hear his heavy footsteps in the hall.

She smiled. He has a way of talking to himself, you were confused not knowing if he was talking to *you*.

"Mr. S-Seigl? I guess . . ."

She forced herself to wait, to hear his reply. Even though she knew he wasn't there.

Glancing at the clock: ten-twenty. Night. But how had it gotten to be night, so quickly? The date was May 27, she knew because it was a Monday and the beginning of a new week and there was the calendar on the wall beside the refrigerator.

Alma was standing vigilant. Rarely did she sit down to eat, since it had happened. *It* was Alma's word. Not *his death* but only just *it*. For she could not have acknowledged *his death, and the end of my life*. She had not the words for this, nor would she have wished to perceive herself as *pessimistic*.

In one of the interviews she'd read, Joshua Seigl was quoted as saying *I am neither a pessimist nor an optimist but a realist.*

"That's right. 'I am a realist.'"

She was being asked questions now, in this unexpected phase of her life. She was being interviewed. Seigl had been the first, asking her about God, going-to-church.

Alma found herself crouched in front of the refrigerator, eating. She'd believed she was not hungry, the mere thought of food would make her gag, yet once she began eating she ate hungrily, stuffing her mouth.

Before *it,* she'd been plenty hungry. After *it,* she'd had a lot of stomach trouble. She ate, too quickly. And then her guts hurt. Damn it was like snakes writhing in her intestines. Some nights, she was on the toilet a half-dozen times.

"Serves you right. Eating like a pig."

(Who'd said that? Not Seigl. Not ever Seigl. Her mother, maybe. Or Dmitri.)

Strange it was to Alma, and repulsive. That the life of her body should continue more or less as before. The way, after her grandmother died, a long time ago, there was a morning-after the funeral, and then two-days-after, finally a week-after, and a month. And pretty soon people were forgetting including Alma.

It was disgusting, how she had to eat. And her bladder and bowels became bloated and had to be relieved, like an animal she relieved herself. She slept, she ate. The cycle persisted. Never would it cease until she herself ceased.

Got to get out, Alma. Can't breathe.

It had not been true, that Seigl had spoken her name in the ambulance. She would say this, she would swear this to his relatives, but it was not true. He had been unconscious, strapped onto a stretcher. An attendant had held an oxygen mask to his face. None of it had anything to do with Alma Busch, and would not. Seigl's skin had gone gray. His soul, if that was what it was, that looked at you out of his eyes, had vanished. It was turned inward, it was becoming smaller and smaller like a flame about to go out. Alma knew, Alma understood that he would die. He would die, she could not keep him with her. Yet she prayed *God don't let him die, God I love him don't let him die You won't will You? Won't let him die?* rocking forward and back on the seat like an animal in pain. It was then, or it might have been a little later, a young Asian-girl attendant was trying to stop Alma from clawing at her forearms, frantically at her arms and the skin around her mouth. Drawing blood from the roughened ugly skin (the "birthmark"!) on her right cheek.

In the emergency room he was gone from her. In a curtained cubicle she was kept captive. Never would she see him again. Hands restrained her. The Asian girl was wiping away blood, applying disinfectant to Alma's wounds. Ridiculous superficial scratches they were, laughable. Like her pleading *God don't let him die. God I will be good all the rest of my life I will never ask another thing of you God—*

As if God was listening, what a joke.

Listening to Alma Busch, what a joke.

Nights when Alma couldn't sleep in this house which was nearly every night she prowled the rooms upstairs and down. In her soiled nightgown, barefoot. It was crucial to keep the house brightly lit. All the rooms, three floors. Why, Alma was trying to think.

"So, if he sees it . . . He will smile and think somebody is home."

Tonight she was wearing the Venetian glass necklace, too. Carefully she'd lowered the strands of beautifully sculpted jade-green glass over her head, carefully she'd untangled the beads. No one had ever given her such a gift. No one had ever valued her as Seigl had. She knew, if Seigl saw the necklace around her neck, he would smile.

We'll go to Venice, Alma. On our way to Rome.

She would surprise him, too, by enrolling in a course. The lawyer, what was his name, who'd stared at her in such contempt yet had called her, yes he'd called her on the phone to . . . warn her? He had seemed to like her, then. He'd been the one to speak the word *benefi-*

ciary. It was a new word, a very special word, and it applied to her, Alma Busch. It did not apply to anyone else, no one in her family and not to Dmitri Meatte that bastard. It applied to Alma Busch and it meant that *the estate will pay for your tuition, room and board at...* *secretarial school, nursing school...* There was a nursing school in Rochester. She would go there.

Seigl would like that, she'd become a nurse. She could imagine him smiling. *Well, Alma! Very good.*

Almost, she could hear his voice now. She could hear him in the front hall. A subtle vibration of the floorboards, his footsteps approaching her.

She smiled. Hastily she set aside whatever she'd been eating (a heel of stale French bread sloppily smeared with raspberry jam, the kind of jam where the damn seeds get stuck between your teeth) on a counter, and she left the kitchen, forcing herself to remain calm, she was making her way barefoot through the brightly lighted yet so strangely empty dining room, and the hall, and she would have entered Seigl's brightly lighted study which was his special place, and had become her special place, except a shadow-figure of about Alma's height moved swiftly at her. So fast!

Before Alma could draw breath to scream, the knife blade was flashing.

"You! You killed him! My brother."

Astonished, Alma tried to ward off the blows with her hands, her forearms. She had an impression, rushed and blurred as if undersea, of a woman's grim cosmetic face, mask-like, the lipsticked lips drawn back from the very white teeth. Still the knife stabbed, sank into the flesh of her left shoulder, and into the upper left side of her chest, and into the side of her neck, as now short bleating cries issued from her, cries of surprise, shock, bewilderment more than terror or even pain, for it seemed she felt no pain exactly, these were quicksilver flashing blows like lightning, even the sudden spurting of blood was painless, or nearly. Alma was backing away, stumbling, crying *No! no don't hurt me!* though lacking the breath to articulate the words as she would lack the strength to ward off her maddened assailant. They were in the front hall. They were staggering toward the living room. Still the knife flashed, rose and fell unerringly, thirty-two stab wounds in all, deep bleeding wounds in Alma's upper back as she fell, at the nape of her unprotected neck and the back of her head as she tried desperately to crawl away, whimpering, sobbing, but there was the woman close behind her, straddling her, panting, cursing elated, "You killed my brother!" until finally Alma Bush fell to the carpet and lay writhing, moaning, still trying to ward off the knife's blows but more feebly now, bleeding from dozens of wounds and her right thumb nearly severed, bleeding from gashes in her breasts, in her belly, cruel fierce blows between her thighs, and Jet struck the final blows as you'd strike with a hammer gripping her fist tight around the handle of the knife, an eight-inch stainless steel German blade she'd purchased that afternoon for this purpose in an Army-Navy outlet store in Rochester, and as Alma shuddered bleeding to death Jet stooped to remove the necklace, her mother's beautiful Venetian necklace . . .

"And a thief. You're a thief, too. Murderer!"

Seeing that the necklace was slick with blood Jet let the knife fall onto the bleeding body. She rose shakily to her feet and stumbled away reasoning it must have been the necklace she'd come for, somehow in a dream perhaps she had known it was stolen. Gently she would wash it in warm soapy water in an upstairs bathroom sink.

Seeing then in the mirror, in surprise: blood in her hair? And on her white silk blouse, and on her belted, beige linen trousers? She removed the soiled clothing hastily and tossed it into a heap. She had no choice but to take another bath, her second of the day. Running water noisily into a tub. She was lavish with bath salts, always Jet was notorious for her lengthy fragrant baths. Last time she'd stayed in this old house she'd bathed in this tub and used these lavender-scented bath salts missing her Jacuzzi back in Palm Beach. Still she would bathe luxuriantly in the hot steamy restful water and afterward she would sleep. She was so tired! Her eyelids kept closing. Thousands of miles she'd traveled to complete this task and how many years—all of her life?

She would sleep. But before she slept she had to return downstairs. She knew there was something she'd left undone . . . She was barefoot, naked inside a quilted white satin robe. She'd washed her hair but had neglected to comb it out. More important for her to return downstairs. In the living room she righted an overturned cane-backed chair. She saw a trail of blood on the thick-piled Chinese carpet but chose not to follow it. She set up the chessboard on its little cherry wood table near the fireplace. Their grandfather's exquisite carved ivory chess pieces. She and Joshua had played chess as children, it was one of the bonds between them. Later, she would sleep. There was time for that. She called Aunt Trina and told the confused-sounding old woman that she wouldn't be returning to the house that night, she was staying elsewhere. She called her friend Daryl Meyer who'd been a lover a long time ago and told him her plans had been changed for the next evening, unavoidably. She called Crossman at home and told the lawyer he should come over to Joshua's house.

Crossman, surprised to hear from Jet, asked why?

Jet said he'd know when he arrived.

Crossman began to ask another question in his bossy-lawyer way and Jet interrupted, "It's over. There's justice now."

P.S.

Ideas,
interviews
& features ...

About the author

About the book

Read on

Profile of Joyce Carol Oates

By Eithne Farry

ON THE WALL above Joyce Carol Oates's desk is a 1957 quote from the film director Alfred Hitchcock. It says: 'It's only a movie, let's not go too deeply into these things.' These simple words of advice were given to Kim Novak when she was feeling agitated and despondent on the set of *Vertigo*. 'I thought it was good advice,' says Joyce Carol Oates. 'Writers can get too intense and too emotionally involved with their work. Sometimes I tend to get a little anxious and nervous about my writing, and I can make myself unhappy, so I look up at that quote and think, it's only a book, don't worry, it's not your life.'

But writing is an intrinsic part of Joyce Carol Oates's life, the biographical details overshadowed by her literary output. To date, Oates has thirty-nine novels, nineteen collections of short stories, and numerous plays and non-fiction works (including monographs on boxing and the American artist George Bellows) to her name – as well as those of her pseudonyms Rosamond Smith and Lauren Kelly. By the time this interview appears that number, in all likelihood, will have increased. 'I like writing, and I'm always working on something; if it's not a novel, then it'll be a short story, or an essay, or a book review.'

From an early age Oates was fascinated by words; she began writing when she was very young. 'Even before I could write I was emulating adult handwriting. So I began writing, in a sense, before I was able to write.' Her first stories were about cats and horses. 'I love animals. I'm very close to animals.' Born on Bloomsday – 16 June 1938 – she grew up on a small farm in Lockport, New York, and studied at the same one-room school her mother attended. Her grandparents had a hard life: Joyce's father and his mother moved frequently 'from one low-priced rental to another'; Joyce's mother was handed over to the care of an aunt when her father died suddenly and left the family impoverished. 'Is die too circumspect a term?' asks Joyce. 'In fact, my maternal grandfather was killed in a tavern brawl.'

Oates is the eldest of three and her childhood territory was mapped out in books. She was a voracious reader; by the time she was in her teens she was devouring Henry David Thoreau, Hemingway, Emily Bronte, Faulkner – and she can track the influence of these major writers in her own work. She explains: 'I think we are most influenced when we are adolescents. Whoever you read when you're fifteen, sixteen, seventeen, eighteen are probably the strongest influences of your whole life.' She adds, 'I think it's true for all artists: as an adolescent you don't have much background, you don't know much. I can imagine a young artist who's, say, thirteen years old and seeing Cézanne for the first time being very, very overwhelmed. But it's ▶

Profile *(continued)*

◀ not going to have the same impact when you're forty.'

Oates majored in English at Syracuse University (to which she won a scholarship) and won the *Mademoiselle* 'college short story' competition in 1959, when she was just nineteen (Sylvia Plath received this coveted award in 1951). She gained her master's degree from the University of Wisconsin in just a year, and had already embarked on her prolific writing career at this point, at times publishing two or three books in the space of twelve months. In 1962 she and her husband Raymond Smith moved to Detroit and stayed there until 1968, witnessing at first hand the civil unrest that overtook many American cities. She was 'shaken' by the experience, and 'brooded upon it'. She is now a professor at Princeton, but the violence and unease of the Detroit years still make their unnerving way into her fiction some thirty-six years later.

The sheer amount of Oates's output can be bewildering. Her biographer Greg Johnson recalls his first visit to the Oates archive at Syracuse University, when he was beginning research for *The Invisible Woman*, his book on Oates. 'My overwhelming impression was of the sheer amount of labour represented by these manuscripts ... the novel manuscripts in particular were astonishing in their complexity.' Oates explains, 'I like writing. I'm not a person who thinks in terms of her career. I think in terms of the work I'm doing.' She adds, 'I don't think I'm incredibly disciplined. I write in the mornings, I sometimes write through the

❛ I'm not a person who thinks in terms of her career. I think in terms of the work I'm doing ❜

afternoon, even the evening, but not every day. It's not a schedule that's rigid.'

Her earlier fiction was written in 'one headlong plunge', a rush of words across the page. Then she would 'systematically rewrite the entire manuscript, first word to last … and this was the triumph of Art … control imposed upon passion'. Oates still writes every manuscript in longhand first, and then continues her work on a typewriter, editing each book as many as five times before she is happy. 'I don't have a computer. And I won't let things go until I'm happy.' She doesn't have hobbies, but likes to run, hike and cycle in the summer, before heading back to the study to get back to her writing. 'I'm just trying to do the best work I can. Most writers are trying to do the best they can. You hope someone responds to the work, but then you move on to a new project.' It's a pragmatic attitude to a prolific career. 'People can get depressed and suicidal and upset with their work, but I look at that Hitchcock quote on my wall and remind myself it's only a book, don't worry, it's not your life. It's a good cautionary tale.' ∎

> 'Oates still writes every manuscript in longhand first, and then continues her work on a typewriter, editing each book as many as five times'

Life at a Glance

Joyce Carol Oates

BORN

16 June 1938, Lockport, New York

EDUCATED

BA from Syracuse University; MA from the University of Wisconsin

CAREER

Lecturer at the University of Detroit, 1962–8; Lecturer at the University of Windsor, 1968–78; Distinguished Professor of Humanities at Princeton University, 1978 to the present day.

SELECTED BACKLIST

Most recent novels

I'll Take You There *(2002)*, **Middle Age: A Romance** *(2001)*, **Blonde** *(2000)*, **Broke Heart Blues** *(1999)*, **My Heart Laid Bare** *(1998)*, **Man Crazy** *(1997)*, **We Were the Mulvaneys** *(1996)*, **Zombie** *(1995)*, **What I Lived For** *(1994)*, **Foxfire: Confessions of a Girl Gang** *(1993)*, **Black Water** *(1992)*, **Because It is Bitter, and Because It is My Heart** *(1990)*

Most recent short story collections

Faithless: Tales of Transgression *(2001)*, **The Collector of Hearts: New Tales of the Grotesque** *(1998)*, **Will You Always Love Me?** *(1996)*, **Haunted: Tales of the Grotesque** *(1994)*, **Where Are You Going, Where Have You Been?: Selected Early Stories** *(1993)*

'Rosamond Smith' novels

The Barrens *(2001)*, Starr Bright Will Be
With You Soon *(1999)*, Double Delight
(1997), You Can't Catch Me *(1995)*, Snake
Eyes *(1992)*, Nemesis *(1990)*, Soul/Mate
(1989), Lives of the Twins (1987)

Novellas

Rape: A Love Story *(2004)*, Beasts *(2002)*,
First Love: A Gothic Tale *(1996)*, The Rise of
Life on Earth *(1991)*, I Lock My Door Upon
Myself *(1980)*, The Triumph of the Spider
Monkey *(1976)*

A Critical Eye

AS WITH ALL of Joyce Carol Oates's many novels, critics found much to praise in *The Tattooed Girl* – from her impressive handling of her character and theme, to the cracking pace of the plot. Many were awed by Oates's productivity, and commented accordingly.

Meaghan Delahunt wrote in **Scotland on Sunday**: 'The Oates œuvre is daunting – it would make most critics and writers sleep easily to think that Oates turns out dross, but the fact is her work is of a consistently high standard. The latest is no exception – engaging ... and strikingly well written.'

Toby Litt, a self-confessed Joyce Carol Oates 'virgin', admitted in the **Guardian** that 'there's a danger of the first-time reader feeling overwhelmed by the sweeping flood of her productivity'. But he added: 'the reason for starting to read Oates, however, is just where you would hope: the storytelling, which is extraordinary'. He particularly admires the way the conflict between Alma and Seigl mirrors the 'larger cultural ones of Christianity and anti-Semitism, Holocaust history and Holocaust denial ... all of which adds up to a completely gripping tale told in an almost maniacally propulsive style.'

David Robson of the **Sunday Telegraph** agreed, saying that 'their love–hate relationship is anatomised with all the quirky skill one has come to expect from Joyce Carol Oates. There are times when you think that the protagonists are going to end up marrying, other times when you think one is about to murder the other. This gives the narrative a rather gothic flavour ... Oates is a master of many moods and finds space in her fast-moving narrative for moments of real tenderness.'

Viv Groskop was also won over by Alma and Seigl's relationship, remarking in the **Sunday Express** that 'while the subplot that traces Alma's thoughts about Seigl's Jewishness and his book on the Holocaust is thought provoking, it's the warmth of their strange relationship which is endearing. Most readers will remember this novel for what it has to say about love rather than what it has to say about prejudice in modern America.'

Justine McCarthy observed in the **Irish Independent** that 'every gesture, every character, every word has a purpose. The themes are enormous – identity, prejudice, power, pre-destiny. The prose is clear ... the suspense builds. The parable is acute and thought-provoking, delivering new perspectives to age-old ponderables.'

But for the **Observer**'s Anita Sethi it was Oates's poetic depiction of pain that was truly remarkable. '*The Tattooed Girl* is as startlingly sharp as it is tender, cutting through taboos of physical and sexual abuse so that the pain of the inarticulate is given a voice so real it prickles the blood. The novel is soaked in the menacing atmosphere of a feverish nightmare, a hell on earth, in which the beating, porous heart is a time bomb.' ■

Behind the Scenes of
The Tattooed Girl
By Eithne Farry

'EACH NOVEL IS like an adventure,' muses Joyce Carol Oates. 'Yes, I think that's a good way of looking at it.' In a writing career spanning some forty years – and thirty-nine novels – Joyce Carol Oates has definitely relished literary derring-do. Her novels, from *Shuddering Fall*, published in 1964, to her most recent work, have been fiercely engaged with the individual and how he or she attempts to survive in a confusing and dangerous world.

America has provided the dark backdrop for her intense personal dramas. She has tackled the plight of migrant workers in *Garden of Earthly Delights* (1967), mocked moneyed complacency in *Expensive People* (1968), and won the National Book Award for *them* (1969), a novel which explores the impact of the Detroit civil riots on a poverty-stricken brother and sister. She has written about sexual psychopaths (*Zombie*, 1995), a girl gang in 1950s upstate New York (*Foxfire*, 1993), constructed a 900-page 'radically distilled life' of Marilyn Monroe in *Blonde* (2000), and headed back to the nineteenth century for the gothic *Bellefleur* (1980). She once joked to an interviewer that her epitaph should read: 'She certainly tried,' and she has no intention of giving up yet: 'There are writers who basically write the same book, but some of us as we get older get more playful and experimental.'

Asked to describe *The Tattooed Girl*, Oates says that it has 'the structure of a thriller, a

> **Her novels have been fiercely engaged with the individual and how he or she attempts to survive in a confusing and dangerous world**

suspense novel, that was my ideal. It is of course a literary novel, but each chapter is supposed to move dramatically.' It's a genre that has great appeal for her. She has already written a series of them under the pseudonym Rosamond Smith, and is beginning a new one under the pen name Lauren Kelly. 'You move quickly, each chapter is dramatic and tight, and there's not much background or description, it focuses on the dramatic interaction between people.' It's the characters that ultimately hold most fascination for Oates, rather than the intricacies of plot. 'I'm writing about people, and my interest is in human beings. I'm not really interested in writing about concepts or abstractions. I would consider myself to be a dramatic writer rather than expository or analytical. I like to write about actual people. I was very attached to Joshua Seigl. I liked him a lot.'

It is, she says, difficult to let the characters go. 'You get to know these people intimately. You feel an emotional connection with them.' She continues, 'I know men like Seigl, exasperating and annoying, and very lovable and intelligent. The best way to be related to someone like him is as a friend. If you try to have a romance with a person like that, or try and marry a person like that, he would be impossible to live with.'

Joyce Carol Oates is often described as an American writer, one who tackles the state of the States in her work. *The Tattooed Girl* ▶

❛ I'm writing about people, and my interest is in human beings. I'm not really interested in writing about concepts or abstractions ❜

◀ is 'about identity and anti-Semitism'. 'The rise of anti-Semitism is alarming in America, and the novel is very much based on that – the hatred of people based on ignorance. The novel is inspired by what I see going on in the world after September 11, 2001.' For Oates, Alma – the girl of the title – is 'an American type'. 'She's from a background that's very poor, uneducated, very bigoted, but her tattoos are an analogue to the Holocaust victims' prison-camp tattoos, her tattoos are ugly, defacing, like someone scribbling on the wall. They are acts of vandalism on her body. They're not works of art; she didn't elect to have them. She's in a cycle of abuse, too.'

Oates frequently uses the medium of her fiction to explore what it means to be a woman in American society, but doesn't align herself with any radical agenda. 'I would be called a mainstream feminist. I'm not a radical feminist. When I began writing I used the initials JC Oates, so it wasn't clear if I were a man or a woman when I sent out my work. The stories I wrote weren't necessarily women's stories, and I wasn't writing about feminist ideas anyway, I was writing about people, characters I felt an emotional connection to.'

For all her liking of her characters, she still metes out a full quotient of violence and pain. 'Well, you know, *The Tattooed Girl* has a background of Greek tragedy – there are lots of allusions to Greek literature – and Joshua is behaving like a Greek tragic hero. He brings about his destruction through his own actions.'

Oates is still excited about the possibilities

❝ The novel is inspired by what I see going on in the world after September 11, 2001 ❞

of fiction. 'I love language. I don't think any of us can live without language. Even if we are not writing or reading, we're thinking. We're trying to live out our lives through speech. It's like a heart beating, it's the pulse beat of our lives.' She teaches Creative Writing and Literature at Princeton and is aware that the reader is 'looking for something that's exciting and original and compelling and dramatic'. 'I teach every week and I can't claim there's an epiphany or moment of revelation every time. But, for instance, we spent a whole class reading a short story by Ernest Hemingway last week. We went through it sentence by sentence, line by line, as if it were a poem. That was a great experience.' The adventure continues. ■

6 *The Tattooed Girl* has a background of Greek tragedy and Joshua is behaving like a Greek tragic hero. He brings about his destruction through his own actions 9

Have You Read?

Other titles by Joyce Carol Oates

I'll Take You There (2002)
Anellia is a student at Syracuse University,
and away from home for the first time in her
life. Headstrong, vibrant and occasionally
obsessive, she embraces new experiences
with a headlong enthusiasm for life and love.
In her quest to belong Anellia discovers the
risks and rewards of confronting the world so
passionately.

'Novelists such as John Updike, Philip Roth,
Tom Wolfe and Norman Mailer slug it out for
the title of Great American Novelist. But
maybe they're wrong. Maybe, just maybe, the
Great American Novelist is a woman.' *Herald*

Middle Age: A Romance (2001)
When Adam Berendt collapses suddenly, his
death sends shock waves thorough his home
town, the affluent hamlet of Salt-on-Hudson.
Its inhabitants are beautiful, rich and
middle-aged, and, following the demise of
Berendt, suddenly forced to confront their
own mortality and morality in this richly
comic study of middle-class mores.

'A stylish and wise chronicle of transformation and regeneration.' Jonathan Bates,
Books of the Year, *Sunday Telegraph*

'The richness and excitement of Oates' novels
lie in their hyper-real description of modern
life.' *Sunday Times*

Faithless: Tales of Transgression (2001)
In this collection of twenty-one stories Joyce
Carol Oates explores the darkest territory of

the human psyche – these stories are shot through with sexual and emotional violence. The characters consider suicide, plot murders, are the victims and perpetrators of sexual assault and stalking. *Faithless* is a startling look into the heart of contemporary America.

'Again and again [Oates] finds new language to describe the immensity of desire . . . She twists back against our assumption, seeking always the grisly pop of revelation.' *New York Times Review of Books*

Blonde (2000)

Blonde is the deeply moving exploration of the inner life of the woman who became Marilyn Monroe and a portrait of American culture hypnotized by its own myths. Poetically sensual and compulsively readable, it traces the destruction of a cultural icon, but never loses sight of the real woman behind the invention.

'*Blonde* is an epic achievement, a master-piece, a piece of art so shatteringly well-conceived and lavishly wrought that at times it does not seem like a mere book.'
 Julie Myerson, *Independent on Sunday*

'This novel deserves a wide audience. *Blonde* is what whole shelvesful of Monroe should be but are not – a fabulous reinvention of the life of a fabulous reinvention, a mirror on our collective vanities and a cracking page turner to boot.' *Evening Standard*

We Were the Mulvaneys (1996)
Selected by the Oprah Winfrey Book Club
In her twenty-sixth novel Joyce Carol Oates has written a rich, complex saga about a seemingly ideal family that is almost destroyed by the date-rape of sixteen-year-old Marianne Mulvaney. This shattering event touches off a heart-breaking journey into twenty-five years filled with shameful secrets and despair, but ends with an unforeseen miracle which emotionally reunites the troubled family. Making *We Were the Mulvaneys* her first Oprah's Book Club™ selection of 2001, Oprah Winfrey said, 'I read this book over a year ago, but this family still haunts me.'

'It is a book that will break your heart, heal it, then break it again every time you think about it.' *Los Angeles Times*

If You Loved This,
You'll Like…

The Human Stain by Philip Roth
The time is 1988 and America is aflutter following the impeachment of a president for sexual misconduct. It's also the year that 71-year-old hot shot Professor Coleman Silk will meet his downfall in the sleepy college of Athena, following his Viagra-fuelled affair with Faunie, a 34-year-old illiterate janitor with 'a laugh like a barmaid'.

In the Cut by Susanna Moore
A shivery slice of sexual obsession and sexual repression, played out like a thriller, but with scalpel-sharp observations of the meaning of language in all its nuances and ironies. The affair between academic Frannie and her lover, a married detective, is set against a homicide investigation – a young woman has been brutally killed. Proud of her 'incautious adaptability', Frannie is forced to confront the reality of violence and its aftermath.

Gordon by Edith Templeton
Walking into a pub one day in 1940s London, Louisa, a dissatisfied young woman, meets an attractive stranger. Within minutes he takes her to a park and forces himself on her on a stone bench. Excited by her submissive relationship with Richard Gordon, Louisa embarks on a haunting, humiliating affair. First published in 1966 under a pseudonym and subsequently banned in England and in Germany, this is an unsettling, eerie tale of sexual obsession.

The Average Human by Ellen Toby-Potter
The Mayborn family has cast its shadow over the small town of Loomis for generations. When June Mayborn, blessed with a preternatural sense of smell and a fondness for fire, accidentally kills an ageing cult leader, she sets in motion a chain of events that reveals a deeply buried secret. Hypnotically pitched, this is modern Gothic at its best.

The Pilot's Wife by Anita Shreve
A deft exploration of the way lies and lives are constructed. Following the death of her husband in an air crash, Kathryn's world is blown apart. When the recovered black box reveals that her husband was responsible for the accident, she is forced to question everything she thought she knew.

Wonder Boys by Michael Chabon
Grady Tripp is a hyped-up, big-bellied, ageing wunderkind of a novelist teaching creative writing at university while working on his 2,000-page *magnum opus*. Things take a turn for the skewed when his friend Terry arrives in town for a weekend of mayhem – involving a squished boa constrictor, and Marilyn Monroe's fur-lined jacket.

The Poisonwood Bible by Barbara Kingsolver
Told by the wife and daughters of Nathan Price, a fierce evangelical Baptist who takes his family and his mission to the Belgian Congo in 1959, *The Poisonwood Bible* is the story of their tragic undoing and miraculous reconstruction over the course of three decades in post-colonial Africa. Like a nineteenth-century novel, this grand sweep

of a book deals with sin and redemption, and all the muddled territory between.

Deadwood by Pete Dexter
Wild Bill Hickock is getting old, but he can still shoot a shot glass off the head of a bulldog at thirty paces. He's come to the sprawling town of Deadwood to do some gambling; dogging his footsteps are Calamity Jane and Sheriff Boone May, and the weight of his past. Fantastically realized, *Deadwood* has a raw appreciation for history, and the violence that underpins many a myth.

The Probable Future by Alice Hoffman
The Sparrow women have always been that little bit different – each has a witchy gift that changes from generation to female generation. Fusing the domestic with the dramatic, Hoffman sets about applying a little practical magic to the problem of a feckless father accused of murder.

The Namesake by Jhumpa Lahiri
Spanning three decades and as many continents, this is the involving story of Gogol Ganguli. Brought up as an Indian in suburban America, Gogol soon finds himself itching to cast off his awkward name and the inherited values of his Bengali parents. A funny and wise book about the perils of love, and leaving home.

Find Out More

Website
For a wealth of information on Oates's œuvre, log onto the Celestial Timepiece website www.usfca.edu/fac-staff/southerr/jco.html. Intended as a resource for 'fans and students and scholars of Joyce Carol Oates' work', this site has news, photos and biographical detail, as well as a comprehensive overview of Oates's work to date.

Biography
Invisible Writer by Greg Johnson. Granted privileged access to Joyce Carol Oates's letters and journals, as well as interviews with family, friends and colleagues and Oates herself, Johnson explores the relationship between the author's life and work in this definitive biography.

Visit
The Holocaust Exhibition at the Imperial War Museum, Lambeth Rd, London SE1 6HZ, England.

The Holocaust Centre, Beth Shalom, Laxton Newark, Notts, NG22 0PA, England.

BOOKSHOP

Now you can buy any of these great Harper Perennial paperbacks at 10% off recommended retail price. FREE postage and packing in the UK.

I'll Take You There
Joyce Carol Oates   0 00 714645 0   £7.99

We Were the Mulvaneys
Joyce Carol Oates   1 84115 699 X   £7.99

Middle Age: A Romance
Joyce Carol Oates   1 84115 642 6   £7.99

Blonde
Joyce Carol Oates   1 84115 372 9   £8.99

Faithless: Tales of Transgression
Joyce Carol Oates   1 84115 647 7   £7.99

Total cost _____

10% discount _____

Final total _____

To purchase by Visa/Mastercard/Switch simply call **08707 871724** or fax on **08707 871725**

To pay by cheque, send a copy of this form with a cheque made payable to 'HarperCollins Publishers' to: Mail Order Dept (Ref: B0B4), HarperCollins Publishers, Westerhill Road, Bishopbriggs, G64 2QT, making sure to include your full name, postal address and phone number.

From time to time HarperCollins may wish to use your personal data to send you details of other HarperCollins publications and offers. If you wish to receive information on other HarperCollins publications and offers please tick this box ☐

Do not send cash or currency. Prices correct at time of press. Prices and availability are subject to change without notice. Delivery overseas and to Ireland incurs a £2 per book postage and packing charge.